PRAISE FOR D[...]
AND RYAN CAR[...]

One of Crime Monthly's Top 5 Killer Thrillers of April 2022

'Powerful.'

Crime Monthly

'My book of the year so far.'

Lee Child, #1 *New York Times* bestselling author

'A heartfelt and eloquent exploration of the iniquities of racial bias.'

Guardian

'Dreda Say Mitchell has been flying the flag for crime writing for years.'

Bernardine Evaristo, bestselling author of *Girl, Woman, Other*

'A truly original voice.'

Peter James, #1 *Sunday Times* bestselling author

'A strong dose for readers interested in watching racial prejudices play out at every possible opportunity.'

Kirkus Reviews

GIRL,
MISSING

GIRL, MISSING

MISSING

DREDA SAY MITCHELL & RYAN CARTER

THOMAS & MERCER

Published by Thomas and Mercer, Seattle

www.apub.com

Amazon, the Amazon logo, and Thomas and Mercer are trademarks of Amazon. com, Inc., or its affiliates.

ISBN-13: 9781662515590
eISBN: 9781662515606

Cover design by Tom Sanderson
Cover image: © vvoe, dmitriynesvit/ Shutterstock; ©Mark Owen / ArcAngel

Printed in the United States of America

To Sharon. Our great friend who is a creative genius.

Prologue

The police officer cuffs me. I plead desperately, 'You've got this all wrong.'

I should never have come here. I should've known better.

'I know that things look bad,' I continue, trying to dig myself out of a massive hole.

Bad is the understatement of the century. It doesn't get worse than my clothes. Covered in blood. Somebody else's blood. There's blood everywhere. I look like someone who's just finished a shift in an abattoir. It's sticky against my clothes. Smeared, rich and nasty, on my hands. There's even a fine film of it in my hair. It glues the handcuffs to my wrists. Even I know how incriminating this looks. Traces of blood is how they usually catch criminals, isn't it? Except the blood covering me isn't a trace.

The other police officer, the detective, walks towards me. The street lights glint off the grey strands in his almost black hair. He averts his eyes from the blood splattered over me. That's how bad this is – even an experienced cop is horrified. Finally, his eyes draw level with mine. He looks me up and down as if he can't quite believe what he's seeing. His knowing expression tells me he doesn't believe a word that I've said.

'This isn't the first time you've been arrested,' he states. 'You know and I know that you've got a record.'

He gives me one last look, brimming with distaste, and turns to the younger officer, the one who still holds my arm after he cuffed me. 'Let's check out inside.'

The hand on my arm tightens and pushes me forward. I realise what they're doing. They can't be serious. Go back inside? Are they crazy? I'm not going back in there. The panic rises again just like before. My heart feels like it's about to burst out of my chest.

I try to stall. 'Leave me in your car.'

The detective looks back at me grimly. 'We'll all stay together until backup arrives. And, let's face it, you've done a runner before. What's the matter, embarrassed by your own handiwork?'

My face burns with shame. I shut up. There's no point begging any more. He won't listen to me. He's already made up his mind about me. What kind of person I am. Just like so many others who hate my guts around here.

The night swallows me up as the cops frogmarch me off the street and into the building. A chill runs all the way through my bones when we enter. The shadows are still thick and long, some of them dancing against the wall. The corridor yawns long and menacing ahead of me. And dark. So dark. I don't want to go back down there. I know what they'll find.

The blood on my clothes seems to stick more heavily against my skin.

The detective asks, 'Which room were you in?'

I think about lying, taking them to another room. But I know that's stupid, they'll only find it soon enough. So I tell him the truth. I'm not shocked by his look of guarded surprise.

'What have you done?' He sounds horrified. What's he going to sound like when he sees what awaits him in the room?

I don't answer. I should've kept my mouth shut from the beginning. Isn't that the golden rule of being arrested? Make no

2

comment until your lawyer arrives. So that's what I do while I'm taken to the last place I want to be back in.

We reach the room. The younger officer holds me back while the detective moves cautiously towards the closed door. He puts on those blue forensic gloves they wear. Then he reaches for the door handle. His hand lingers before turning. He pushes the door and looks into the room. Then staggers back in utter repulsion and horror. I know what he sees. And it makes my stomach heave.

It's a scene of brutal carnage inside the head teacher's office in the school.

Chapter 1

The news alert goes off on my phone in my pocket. A sensation of electricity jolts through my body. That's what always happens every time I get one of these alerts. I haven't had one for over a year now. I'm rattled. Feel like I'm on the brink of falling apart. Then again, anyone would feel like this, especially with what I've been through. I thought I'd turned the alerts off. Yesterday I'd made a decision to enjoy today and think of nothing else.

But who am I kidding?

How can I ever put it out of my mind?

They say when you're in love, the object of your love is always on your mind. And it doesn't matter what you may be doing at the time, they're still always there deep down. Perhaps you're merely doing the washing-up, shopping for groceries or watching your clothes spinning in a tumble drier, but your lover is always in your thoughts even if you're not conscious of it. It's never happened to me personally, but I believe it because I've had the same experience for the past fifteen years. But it's not a lover who's always on my mind. It's something else entirely, something that breaks my heart every hour I'm awake.

Even on a special day like today.

She's always in my thoughts.

My heart quickens with the need to find out what's on the news alert, but I can't because I'm attending one of the biggest moments of my life. It's the opening of my latest bike shop, the largest one yet – some would call it a megastore – in the shopping centre. I've worked long and hard for this moment. I force a smile to meet and greet those who have turned out to join in the celebration of my success to date. The shop floor of the business I own in the local mall is festooned with balloons, ribbons and party food to celebrate an award that will be bestowed on me today. Every year, our local council give these presentations for businesses that have contributed something to the local community. My company was singled out for its contribution to making our area of London a cleaner place and for offering employment to people with a troubled past. Troubled people like me, in other words.

The store continues to fill up with worthies and local journalists and photographers covering the store's opening. I try to forget about the news alert – *try* – when the mayor comes over to me.

'Gem, congratulations.'

'Thank you. And for the grants you and your office have so generously given. With this place we'll be able to do amazing things.'

'You deserve being voted businesswoman of the year. Your journey has been remarkable.'

My face grows hot. Sometimes I still find it hard to deal with praise because in my eyes I'm just an ordinary woman who seized an opportunity and ran with it. I'm the sole owner of five bike shops and stores called Old Gems. My business started out repairing and recommissioning old bikes, and when everyone was becoming more environmentally conscious, especially about the use of cars, sales hit the roof. Bike manufacturers started contacting me and asking for my company to become the local outlet for their new models. Soon there was so much work in the workshop that staff had to be hired.

I've always been willing to take a chance on people, perhaps because very few ever took a chance on me. Young offenders, kids who'd dropped out of school, people with health problems, all those who'd been chewed up and spat out by the world. It didn't always work. But more often than not it did.

Suddenly there's the ringing of a multitude of bike bells. Scowling with surprise, I step back from the mayor. I look over at Erin, my right hand, who gives me a far too innocent look. What's going on?

A procession of young women and teenage girls on a variety of different bikes ride into the store. My face lights up with delight. They've taken my breath away because I had no idea this was going to happen. I know each and every one of these women and girls and they are so dear to my heart.

The crowd clears a path for them to ride through the middle, creating a line going down the store.

One of the women rings her bell and then addresses the crowd. 'We come here today to salute Gem. She not only gave us confidence in riding our bikes but the bigger confidence we needed to create a great life. She doesn't come from a background of money but that didn't stop her from reaching for her dreams.'

She addresses me directly now with such pride. 'That's what you taught me, how to stand tall and reach high. I want everyone to raise a glass to the woman you call Gem Casey. But we all call her Goddess.'

I choke up with such emotion. Gem Casey, who left school with zero qualifications. When I opened my first bike shop more than a decade ago, a few girls started dropping by to check out what I was doing and selling. Once they felt safe with me they confided their stories that they didn't always feel welcome among the young lads riding out on the streets. Being the only girl could sometimes feel a bit tough. So, I started our own girl bike scene. It took off like I would never have expected. Schools started getting interested. And it gave the girls confidence to go back to those same lads who made them feel unwelcome and stake their claim.

I still have trouble believing this has all happened. To me. Gem Casey. I still live in dread that it will all be taken away from me. Just as *she* . . .

Stop.

Don't go there.

But I can't.

SHE'S always on my mind.

Always.

There's another truth lurking here. None of them knows exactly what I had to go through to get here. None of them realises that I'm the same Gem Casey whose face was all over the front pages of the newspapers fifteen years ago. What would they say if they knew what people in the place I ran from accused me of?

The news story alert goes off again. That jolt of electricity is back. I can't stall any more; I have to find out. This time, smiling, shaking hands, I deliberately move towards the exit and head outside. I take a breath and lean against a wall. I'm not sure I want to do this. It means going back at a time when my life is going sensationally forward. Then again, the alert might mean nothing at all.

Pulling out my phone I convince myself that it's probably no biggie. The story is from the area where I lived fifteen years ago, which is about a two-hour train ride outside London. The news alert concerns a school. Parents are reporting that they've been told to come and pick up their children as the school is closed for the day following an incident. Photos show police cars in the playground and a forensic team nearby . . . I can't make out what the building is that they're next to.

Speculation about what's happening is already rife across social media:

A schoolkids' fight that got out of hand.
An accident.

Then the real story breaks and I stiffen.

The remains of a body have been discovered at Princess Isabel Primary School.

They've finally found her body.

Chapter 2

'Get out of my way! I want my child!'

That's what I practically spit at the burly cop who bars my entrance into Princess Isabel Primary School. *Don't be emotional. Stay calm. Remain rational.* That's what I'd instructed myself all the way on the train from London with only my bike for company. But once the Victorian building of the school rose into view, with its huge windows and sky-high old brick walls, and roof terrace, my resolve crumbled. All I wanted was to find out if the body they've discovered in the school is beautiful, fun-loving Sara-Jane.

My daughter.

I've never moved on from the abduction of my child fifteen years ago. Hope – that's what's kept me going. But am I prepared for hearing that the bones and what's left of Sara-Jane may have been buried in a grave in that school?

'Child?' The cop glances at me, bewildered. 'What child?'

She's guarding the school gate, a place that was once so familiar to me. It's a different gate now. Back then it was the original Victorian gate made of thick, black iron with bars covering it. The old gate is long gone, replaced with a newish-looking steel one with a modern security entry system. What does remain is the inscription written in the brickwork above:

The gate was there to protect children from the evil of the outside world. It didn't protect my Sara-Jane. My heart clenches so tight I find it hard to breathe.

A commanding voice intrudes. 'I'll take this from here.'

The school gate opens wider, revealing a man in a formal suit, his trousers slightly ill-fitting at the ankle. He's losing his hair, which is a mash-up of grey and black. Do I know him? He looks familiar.

He motions me into the playground. 'You don't remember me.' After an apologetic shrug, he enlightens me. 'Detective Wallace. Although I was plain PC Wallace back then. I was one of the officers investigating your daughter's disappearance.'

'Wish I could say it's good to see you again, but it's not. All I want to find out is this: are the remains that were found Sara-Jane?'

Over his shoulder I get a glimpse of the crime scene. Several police vans are parked in the playground, people in white overalls going back and forth, who I'm assuming are forensics. Police tape surrounds a part of the school that makes my heart sink.

The chapel.

The building is a relic from the school's former religious past. Its back and side walls are nothing special. But the front wall is a sight to behold. It's made of small, irregular rose-coloured glass and pottery pieces stuck together, which the weather has smoothed over the years. Legend has it that the glass and pottery came from the once-famous, long-closed pottery and glass works. People around here take great pride in this chapel.

I hate it.

This is where all this misery started.

Nasty taste in my mouth, I quickly turn away. 'Was that where the remains were found?'

Wallace clears his throat, which I suspect is an indication he's going to become all official on me. 'This investigation is ongoing. Therefore, I'm not at liberty to give you any details of what was found—'

'It's all over the TV and radio that human remains were found,' I brutally cut in.

I get a pointed stare in response. 'You of all people should know that what the media report is not always factually true.'

He reminds me of a time I don't want to go back to. Nevertheless, I'm not finished with him. 'Remains means that whoever the victim is has been there for some time. Years? Fifteen years?'

I march past him with every intention of ducking under the crime scene tape . . . His fingers dig deep into my arm, jerking me to a jarring halt.

'Don't make a scene, Gem. You need to go now. I shouldn't have let you in. I only did so out of common courtesy, knowing your history. I'll inform you if there are any developments that are relevant to you.'

We stare hard at each other, me breathing heavily. I tug my arm free. My voice is soft and sounds so battered to my ears. 'All I want to do is finally find out the truth.'

He lets out a long sigh. 'Even if I wanted to, I'm not at liberty to give you any information.' I walk over the threshold of the school gate back into the street. He continues, making me twist back. 'I promise I will contact you. When the time is right. I hear that you've done well for yourself. That you're now a woman of means. Get back on with your life—'

Savagely, I stab a finger towards the crime scene. 'While my child might be in a grave in there? No chance.'

'Do not interfere in this investigation.'

Ignoring his warning, I head to where onlookers are gathered. The shocking news of a body found inside Princess Isabel School is probably already doing the rounds. And what will add to the distress of many, especially parents, is that this is considered the most outstanding school for young children in the area.

There's a clearer view of the school from here and that's how I see the three women who come out of the school building and start walking across the playground. Goodness me, I know two of them. Haven't seen them in fifteen long years.

No time to waste, my gaze tracking the women, I stride across the road to where they have stopped outside the school gate. The younger of the trio, the one I don't know, hangs a notice on the gate.

PLEASE NOTE THAT THE SCHOOL IS CLOSED UNTIL FURTHER NOTICE OWING TO AN INCIDENT

The cop guarding the school gives me the eye but says nothing.

The tall, elegant woman senses my presence. Brow furrowed, she stares at me, trying to place who I am. When it comes to her she sucks in an audible slice of air.

'Miss Casey. Gem Casey. Sara-Jane's mother.'

'Miss Swan.' I address her with the respect due to my daughter's former head teacher.

Clare Swan looks uncomfortable. The other woman I know is Beryl Spencer, the school's office manager. I thought she'd be long retired by now. She's much plumper now and wearing a yellow dress so bright I have to squint. Then again, she was known for her trademark eccentric clothing.

Beryl's face lifts when she recognises me. 'Well, look who it is. Gem Casey. Still riding that bike of yours?' She points at the young woman who posted the notice. 'This is Rosa, our—'

'We should get back inside.' Miss Swan cuts her short. 'Nice seeing you.'

'They've found her, haven't they?'

My words stop them both in their tracks.

Miss Swan looks at me with such sympathy. 'We don't know any more than you do. It's best if you address all your enquiries to the police.'

Then they're gone. Back into the school. Back into the building where I last saw my Sara-Jane. Then everything stops when another woman steps out into the playground. Laura Prentice. The mother of the girl who was abducted with Sara-Jane. Our gazes catch and hold. She stares at me.

The hatred she still has for me burns in her eyes.

◆ ◆ ◆

While I'm unlocking my bike I realise I have to make a choice. If they have found my daughter's remains I need to stay in the area. I know exactly where to go, but it means giving up control of my business empire for a while. For however long it takes. I'm deep in thought, considering my options, when a voice behind me comes out of nowhere.

'Great bike.'

Who the hell? I twist away from my bike. It's a woman. Early twenties. Lanky and lean. Tall with a buzz-cut that's left her with hardly any hair at all. Blue-tinted shades below heavy-shaped brows, the style young women are favouring these days. Very trendy. Whoever she is, she's packing confidence in spades. An old-style brown leather satchel is slung casually over her shoulder. And she likes lemon-scented perfume.

Narrowing my eyes, I hold back, wary of newcomers today. 'Can I help you?'

She waltzes over, her eyes more on my bike than me. There's so much admiration in her gaze that I wouldn't be surprised if she stroked it like an adored pet.

Or a beloved child.

'Have you given your bike a name? Some people do.'

Back in the day that's exactly what I would do – name all my bikes. But when Sara-Jane was taken I stopped doing it. Once you name something you start caring, start feeling love.

I'm not sure what her game is, but whatever it is, I'm not playing. Suddenly a wave of shattering tiredness hits me, so much so that I have to hang on to my bike for support. I just want to get away. So I start to mount up, but her words stop me.

'The name's Heather. Here's my card.'

HEATHER BANKS

JOURNALIST

THE ECHO

My fingertips jerk as if they've been burned. I flick it away in disgust.

Journalist. That's one treacherous rabbit hole I won't be going down. Ever again.

My contemptuous reaction doesn't faze her. 'You want to find out what happened to your daughter. I can help you. This isn't merely a human-interest story for me. We could work together to find out the truth.'

'You know nothing about my Sara-Jane—'

'Like she didn't allow that cut to her knee that she needed stitches for to stop her using her skateboard.'

My breath catches. I'm stunned. Robbed of words. Then, 'How . . . How did you know that?'

'Together we can pool our resources and find the truth about what really happened.'

What other line in bogus sympathy she has, I don't stick around to find out. I hurry on to my bike to get the hell outta here so quickly that I careen into a black van parked up on the pavement. I can just about make out someone in the driver's seat. Are they staring at me through the shaded window? Who cares, I just want out of here. I go to apologise but the van's engine revs up and it takes off at speed down the road.

I head off too. However, not quickly enough, because I hear what Heather Banks calls out behind me:

'The school was trouble from the start, wasn't it?'

Chapter 3

FIFTEEN YEARS AGO

Loud voices. Angry shouts. The protest outside Princess Isabel School was in full swing. The protestors blocked the gates. Their voices rose in anger and outrage. Chanting: 'No to large classes! No to large classes!'

Placards and banners waved furiously in the air:

OUR SCHOOL IS BEAUTIFUL JUST THE WAY IT IS.

NO TO LARGER CLASS SIZES.

AN OUTSTANDING SCHOOL MUST REMAIN OUTSTANDING.

The small group of parents and children who turned into the street froze, completely shocked by what they saw. This was the last thing they were expecting. A protest. Outside a school. Uneasy glances passed between the adults. Something was wrong. Badly wrong. This small group were families who lived on the Rosebridge Estate. Today was meant to be a very special day. It was the first day their children would be attending Princess Isabel Primary School.

The school was considered the best primary school in the area, providing a first-class education. Traditionally, its pupil population was mainly drawn from the middle class and wealthy families who lived on the south side of the school, while the children on the Rosebridge Estate had attended two other primary schools. However, the discovery of asbestos at one of them had resulted in its immediate closure. The neighbouring schools had agreed to take in the children. No one had expected Princess Isabel to open its doors to kids from the Rosebridge. The school had acted as an invisible dividing line between the north and south side of the area. The people with money and the people without. Neither side had much to do with the other. Now that was all about to change.

Gem and her eight-year-old daughter, Sara-Jane, were among the families from the Rosebridge Estate at the top of the street. Instinctively, she cushioned her only child protectively to her side. Gem had been nervous, like most parents, about her child starting all over again at a new school. Sara-Jane had been upset and tearful that all of her friends were not coming to Princess Isabel too, but her mum had reassured her that she would make new friends really quickly. Gem kept it to herself that she was jittery about her daughter fitting in. Fitting in with the rich kids at the school. Despite her misgivings, Gem was excited at the promise of new beginnings. The chance for Sara-Jane to be educated at the most sought-after school in the district was an opportunity Gem had jumped at.

Twisting her lips, Traci Waddell, one of the older mums, moved to the helm of the group in a protective manner, reinforcing her role as their leader. Those who took her small stature to think she was a pushover were soon put straight by her in-your-face attitude and voice. She was considered by many to be the unofficial matriarch of the Rosebridge.

'I thought this might happen. If they think they're going to scare us off, they've got another think coming.' Her fired-up gaze swept the group.

'They?' one of the other mums queried. 'Who are you talking about?'

'As many of you know I keep my ear to the ground, especially concerning the council. And what I heard might be waiting for us, here, today, made my blood boil.'

Traci was a thorn in the side of the council, fighting on behalf of the residents for improvements to the estate. In fact, for years she had complained that she suspected that Princess Isabel School had an admission policy that deliberately excluded children from the Rosebridge Estate. The school did have some pupils from working class homes but none of them came from the Rosebridge. When the asbestos had been discovered she had been like a dog with a bone, insisting that school places be found at Princess Isabel for some of the displaced children.

She continued railing. 'I heard that some of the snooty-posh-tosh mummies and daddies who send their kids here don't want our kids anywhere near this school. They've arranged a welcoming committee for us. Don't let them frighten you with all their talk about larger classes being a threat to their children's education. All you've got to do is keep walking behind me.'

Gem remained quiet. She kept much to herself, her slogan of life being, *'Mind your business and keep your head down.'* The only person she was close to was Traci, her next-door neighbour. Traci was forty-three compared to Gem's twenty-five, with children ranging from her eldest, a son who was about Gem's age, to her nine-year-old daughter who she had with her today. When Gem and five-year-old Sara-Jane had moved on to the estate, sensing that the young mother needed support the older Traci had taken her under her wing and in the years since had become like a big sister to her. Gem would forever be grateful to Traci for being the friend she had so desperately needed.

Whatever was going on outside the school she didn't want any trouble. Besides, she had to keep her nose clean or else . . .

Looking down at her daughter, Gem's uneasy eyes communicated, 'Are you ready?'

Sara-Jane nodded briskly back, her flash of a smile showing her braces. Her eyes were fretful behind her glasses.

Walking cautiously behind a striding Traci, the families from the Rosebridge neared the noisy protest.

Reporters from local newspapers were also present. A tall woman wearing an expensive classic black trouser suit with a turquoise scarf loosely and tastefully folded around her neck was centre stage among the reporters, one of whom was interviewing her.

'You are Laura Prentice, the head of the PTA, is that correct?'

'I am the *director* of the Parents' and Teachers' Association. Princess Isabel was the first school to set up a PTA in the area. So this school has a long tradition of being at the forefront of new things.'

'What made you organise this protest today?'

'Firstly, I did not organise this gathering.'

The shouts of the protest died down. Silence. All the parents respectfully listened to her.

'Gathering?' The reporter gave her a quizzical look. 'So you don't see this as a protest?'

'The mothers and fathers here today want their voices to be heard.' Her answer was smooth, her ability to deal with awkward questions clear. 'I have made these families, some of which have attended this school for generations, aware that this would not be my way of dealing with the situation. However, in my role I am here to support parents and the community of this school.'

'And what exactly is the situation?'

Laura Prentice paused before answering. 'This school has a reputation for excellence. Inspections have continually graded it as outstanding. The school's test results – SATs – are the highest in the area. That's due to the teachers, the families. But, above all, the children.'

'What she means,' Traci called out, her face a volcano of erupting fire, 'is that my daughter and all these other children from the Rosebridge Estate aren't good enough for this school. That they're as thick as two planks, so they're going to drag the SATs results of the school into the gutter. That's what this is really all about, not class sizes. Why else wave signs saying this school must remain outstanding?'

Reporters, sensing plenty of blood in the water, began to furiously make notes.

'No one is saying anything of that nature,' began Laura Prentice, but Traci squared up to the director of the PTA. She gestured towards the children. 'It doesn't matter what their educational achievement is, each one of these *amazing* children deserves a right to an *outstanding* education.'

A protesting parent jumped in. 'My child's teacher is likely to be spending more time keeping order in the classroom with so many extra children to teach. Including setting new boundaries for good behaviour.'

'Are you saying my kid doesn't have any manners?'

Gem didn't know which Rosebridge parent had spoken, but there was uproar. The reporters lapped it up as the noise of the protest reached a new level.

A new voice cut over the melee. 'You all want to be ashamed of yourselves.'

Silence. Everyone turned. It was Dale Prentice. Everyone knew Dale. In his fifties, with a thickset body and an intelligent mind, he usually had a nod for most. He was the local hero, the lad from a poor background who had made good. After leaving school at fifteen he had single-handedly turned a one-lorry long-distance operation into a multi-million-pound company. He might have a mansion on the outskirts of town, a villa in Italy and lead the contented life of a wealthy older man but that hadn't stopped his commitment to giving back, including pouring money into Princess Isabel School.

Laura Prentice was his former daughter-in-law and her child, his eight-year-old granddaughter Abigail, attended the school.

He levelled a grave, stern eye across both battlelines of the crowd and shook his head with irritation. 'When I was seven years old my granddad told me something. He told me he couldn't read or write. He wasn't a stupid man – in fact he was one of the quickest brains I ever knew. He never got the chance to learn because he never went to school.' He let out a dry, humourless laugh and, stabbing a finger at the gathered protestors, he challenged them, 'If my granddad as a boy had tried to come here would you have barred him too?'

Shamed into submission, the protesting parents stepped back. But just as they did that a hail of eggs came flying towards some of their parked cars, accompanied by manic laughing and jeering from one of the floors of the Rosebridge tower block that faced the school. It was a group of young lads having the time of their disorderly lives. Before they ran for it, Gem recognised two: Traci's eldest boy, twenty-four-year-old Billy-Bob and his sidekick, Jaswinder Bedi. She didn't know what the deal was with Billy-Bob, but he caused his mother no end of misery. Sometimes, through the wall, she heard the blazing rows they had at night. He was only a year younger than Gem, so as far as she was concerned he needed to stop carrying on like some teen tearaway and grow up.

With her side-eye, Gem furtively stared at Traci. Her neighbour looked mortified. Her son's behaviour had almost undone all her good work here today.

Laura Prentice arched a knowing brow at her former father-in-law. '*That* is an example of the type of behaviour we do not want in this school.'

He was bullish right back, not fazed by her at all. 'Don't you worry, I'll get that lot sorted out.'

Tension was thick between them. Dale slid his gaze to someone else – Traci. He gave her a nod and Traci seemed to relax again.

◆ ◆ ◆

Miss Swan gathered all the new parents in the main hall, her school manager, Beryl Spencer, by her side. 'I apologise for how you were met outside the school. *Your school. Our school.* Every last one of the children standing in front of me I am proud to welcome here today.'

Gem liked that, the way she talked directly to the children. To her Sara-Jane.

'Let me assure you that there will be no repeat performance of what happened here today.' Miss Swan looked every inch the headmistress now, with her stern, serious expression. 'Your child will be treated the same as any other child. You as parents will be treated the same as any other parent. If you have any problems, please do not hesitate to make an appointment to speak with me.'

Afterwards, Gem and a few parents escorted their children to the classrooms upstairs, although Sara-Jane had quietly insisted, 'I want to go on my own. I'm not a baby.'

You'll always be my baby. Still, her child was growing up, changing every day.

For a few seconds Gem watched her daughter through the glass panel in the classroom door. As a mother she found it so hard to hand her over. *Stop being silly*, she scolded herself. A school was a home from home. They would look after her precious child.

Chapter 4

CHILD KILLER

The vicious words catch me off balance as I stare at the door. I know that they're not really there. That it's a memory. A very terrifying memory from fifteen years ago. As are so many of the most painful times in my life. I manage to shake it off. I'm on the Rosebridge Estate. Staring at the front door of the flat I once lived in with Sara-Jane.

This is the place where I tried to bring up my daughter. Tried my hardest to be a good mum.

It feels funny being back because I haven't lived here since my daughter was taken. Fifteen long years.

I live in a neat three-bed house in London now. Buying this flat, which I'd once rented from the council, was one of the first things I did when my business started going from strength to strength. Purchasing it had been much easier than I thought it would be. The cash-strapped council hadn't been able resist a cash buyer. I had no intention of living here; instead I've been renting it out through a charity that helps single mums and their children get back on their feet. A temporary residence until they are permanently housed elsewhere. Lucky for me, there haven't been any tenants for the last few months which is why I can stay here now.

I've left my second-in-command, Erin, in charge of my bike shop empire. I've got a good team around me. Erin practically did all the work setting up the megastore. She's loyal and ambitious, so I know she'll keep everything ticking over. While I sort myself out, focus on my own life for a change. I've told her not to contact me unless it's really, really urgent because I need to go deep now. Back into the past, long before I had a business empire. Before I even had my first bike shop.

Knowing what happened to me here in this flat, when Sara-Jane was taken, you'd think this would be the last place I'd want to buy. Me and this estate didn't part on the best of terms, to put it mildly. The truth of why I bought my former home is very simple – owning this is my way of clinging on to my daughter's memory. So it comes as no surprise that when I step inside, I'm again catapulted back into the past. My daughter comes to me, a burning flame to light up my dark.

It's Sara-Jane. Right there in the hallway. She looks amazing, all good to go in her best clothes. Dark green hoodie, black jeans with white trim on the pocket, Superstar trainers and her all-time fav tune, Beyoncé's 'If I Were a Boy' playing in the background. And she's smiling at me. A mischievous glint in her eye behind her glasses makes her whole face glow. I'm transfixed. Can't get enough of her.

Her sweet voice speaks to me: 'Can we have cheeseburger and chips, extra ketchup for dinner?'

'You know that's weekend food.'

'Oh, please, Mummy, please.'

'Only if you get all your homework done.'

'Promise.'

'Promise. But I might be persuaded if you give Mummy the biggest hug ever.'

She runs towards me. My arms open wide . . .

I'm back in the semi-darkness of the hallway again. Back? I never left. My arms are outstretched, waiting to enfold a phantom, because Sara-Jane isn't really here. None of this is real. Leaning heavily against the front door I close my eyes. Maybe this was a mistake, coming back here. Maybe I should've let Erin book me a room at the pricey hotel on the other side of town. It feels so empty here without Sara-Jane's voice. God, the pain of losing her runs so deep. Thinking of her voice reminds me why I have to stay here. The truth about what happened to Sara-Jane is nearby.

I move around the flat, trying to reacquaint myself with my one-time home. The flat is furnished with the basics to make it easy to rent. Including the mirror that catches my reflection. I don't see my black hair, the thinness of my face, my toned and muscular body. What I see is empty. A shell. Sara-Jane's abductor didn't take only her, he took much of me as well.

I go into my old bedroom and unpack what small number of possessions I brought with me. Then I make myself go into Sara-Jane's former room. A bed, a small dressing table, built-in wardrobe, that's all that's in there. But I feel *her* presence. I turn and head into the main room and tiredness practically makes me fall into the lumpy armchair.

Around thirty minutes later there's a harsh bang on the front door. It's the noise that makes me realise that I've fallen asleep. The door goes again. Who can it be? No one knows that I'm here. My body is sore, almost creaks as I unwind my tucked-up legs and stand. I make it to the doorway and hesitate; there's a silhouette behind the glass in the front door. The darkness surprises me, which means I must've been asleep for quite some time.

'Who is it?'

'Santa Claus and her bloody elves,' comes the smart-mouth reply.

I can't help but smile. Traci. My one-time neighbour. I'm surprised she remembers me because I haven't been back here since . . . well, since. She's not alone, two of her young grandkids are with her.

Traci's in her late fifties to my forty and not hiding an inch of it. It's there proudly in her grey hair and lines around her mouth and eyes and a touch more roundness to her middle. We're in each other's arms after I open the door. I hold her tight. I have so much to thank her for. When we move apart, I feel embarrassed, ashamed. Really don't know where to look. After abruptly leaving the Rosebridge fifteen years ago, I never contacted Traci. After all the emotional support she gave me the least I could've done was write to her. Let her know that I was OK. Without this woman I'd have probably ended up in the river.

'Stop being daft.' Somehow she senses what I'm thinking. Traci's got that down-to-earth style that draws people to her. 'I don't blame you for not looking back. I'd wondered for years who was renting this place out and I have to tell you I was surprised to find out it was you.'

I don't ask how she knew it was me who had bought the flat. Or how she figured out I was back. Traci is one of these people who always knows what's happening, so no doubt word reached her when I turned up at the school earlier.

'I was sorry to hear about Roger.' He was her husband. He was much older than her. At least twenty years.

'No sorries necessary. Roger was a quiet man who didn't like fuss in this life and so didn't want it when he was laid to rest.'

Her grandchildren happily play as we catch up over a brew at the scratched kitchen table.

'I know why you're back.' She doesn't hang around. She never did. Plain speaking has always been her way.

Slowly, I place my cup down. 'What are they saying at the school? What are the police saying?'

Her kind eyes consider me over the rim of her cup before she takes a sip. 'All I know is what's doing the rounds as rumours. Bones were found. I've got a friend who works in admin at the police station. Usually she bends my ear about what's going on. Not this time. They've all been told, point blank, not to breathe a word.'

'Traci, I need to find out.'

She hugs her cup closer. 'I'll ask on the Parents' and Teachers' Association, see if anyone knows anything.'

Frowning, I ask, 'Will they help you?'

Her neck stretches up in pride. 'You betcha they'll help me. I'm on the board now.'

I can't believe what I'm hearing. Someone from the Rosebridge on the PTA of Princess Isabel School. Things have certainly changed around here.

Traci smiles. 'Laura Fancy Pants is also still a member of the PTA.'

I frown as something else occurs to me. 'But how can Laura Prentice still be on the PTA? Surely she hasn't got any children at the school. Isn't Abby her only child?'

'She's a governor of the school now, and every governor has a specific role in the school—'

'Ah, let me guess,' I interrupt. 'She's the governor attached to the PTA.'

Traci wrings her lips slightly. 'You've got that right in one. The parents on the PTA still look up to her. Even the parent who's the actual director seems to take her orders from Madam Fancy Pants.'

She shifts uncomfortably. 'Ah, she's not such a dragon really. It was Dale who got me a seat at the table.'

Dale. Of course. Abby's grandfather. He was always close to Traci. She continues, 'He made the PTA embrace the idea of families meaning not just parents. So I represent families. My grandkids go there. Granny Traci.' Her eyes suddenly light up. 'I wish I could be the director. I've wanted that role for years. The election is coming up soon.'

'So why don't you go for it?'

Traci looks crestfallen. 'I don't stand a chance.'

A lack of confidence. I see it in her face – what all of us mothers from the Rosebridge Estate felt when we entered Princess Isabel School. We entered a world where people had more money than us. Where we were told they spoke better than us. Where they got the attention of the teachers in a way we never could. And Traci had been the toughest of us, the one who was prepared to speak up when we couldn't. Now I'm a successful businesswoman people listen to me. Money talks. This leaves me feeling sour and pissed. It shouldn't matter how much money you have.

'You should do it.' I rap my knuckles against the tabletop so she knows I mean every word. 'Let the parents make their choice. I started my bike business in an archway under a railway bridge. I have five large shops, including a megastore. You've already got over the biggest hurdle, getting on the board. Now all you've got to do is put your name forward.'

Traci stands and gathers her grandchildren to her side. 'I need to go and get this lot ready for when their dad picks them up.'

She must be referring to her youngest son – no way can she be talking about Billy-Bob, her eldest. He was trouble through and through. I suspect he must be in prison. Or dead of an overdose. Poor Traci, she did her best. Us mothers do.

On the communal balcony Traci surprises me by saying, 'You've done so well for yourself. Get on with your life. Don't let the poison of the past pollute it. You should not have come back.'

You should not have come back. Is she warning me? If so, about what? Or is she worried that I'll get hurt all over again and destroy the successful life I've worked so hard to make?

Chapter 5

Something falls through the letterbox just as I drain the dregs of my final cup of tea before heading to bed. I stiffen, scowling hard. That's a bit weird, isn't it, to post something at night. Before I head off to the hallway my phone pings:

Text message: I can help you. Heather.

That young journalist. Heather Banks. How did she get my number? She must've used her contacts. In disgust I chuck my phone down. And go into the hallway. I look down near the door. And frown because it doesn't look like an envelope, so it's not a letter. It's material. Two small pieces of material. Confused, I can't quite make them out. Crouching to get a closer look I finally figure out what they are. A small pair of socks.

What nonsense is this? Why would someone shove a pair of socks through the door? They're small and pink with a red ribbon at the top and words embroidered down the side. Flipping one lengthways, I read: Princess For A Day.

A chill slithers down my spine. *It can't be.* Stunned, the blood drains away from my face.

They look like the socks that belonged to my Sara-Jane. The last time I saw her wearing them was on the day she was taken.

My mind's in a state of denial. These can't belong to my Sara-Jane. They can't. Unless . . . Feverishly, my fingers turn over the right sock, looking for proof. I find it, the hole in the heel. My worst fear is confirmed.

These belong to my missing little girl.

I choke up, fighting for air. Staggering, my back bangs into the wall, my legs go from under me and I slide down to the cold floor. Squeezing my eyes tight I hug the socks to my chest. My mind flashes back to that last day with her at the school gate. We had a teeny, tiny tiff.

'I don't want to wear these stupid socks.' Her lips compressed in a stubborn line. 'Princess For A Day! A whole day? I don't want to be a princess for a minute. No. Thank. You.'

'I thought you'd liked them.'

Her little face had screwed up. 'I was only pretending to make you happy, Mum. I want to be a boss girl, not a princess.'

'Don't give me a hard time. Please!'

I'd been against the clock that morning, needing to be at the café I worked at early to cover someone else's shift. As a single mum, I jumped on every opportunity to get extra cash.

'I know, Mum.' She looked remorseful. 'But pink is such a yuck colour. You can't skateboard in a fluffy, princess dress.'

Sara-Jane was an outdoorsy type of girl who loved climbing, jumping rope, football and anything that was active.

'Be a good girl for Mummy. And make sure you use your reading glasses.'

'I'm always a good girl,' she'd answered with a touch of sauce.

Children come in all shapes and sizes and with their own mannerisms and the one thing I loved about my daughter the most was her cheekiness. Never malicious, always about having fun.

I'd given my adored girl the usual two kisses on the tip of her nose and watched her go through the school gate. The last time I saw Sara-Jane was with a peep of her pink socks showing.

My eyes punch open with anger. Question after damning question starts to come. Who left her socks here? The vile evil monster who snatched her away from me? The thought of what he must have done to her. Might be still doing to her. I want to tear the world apart until I find him. Save my precious-precious girl.

I do what I should've done as soon as I saw her socks. I go after whoever left them. I wrench the front door open. Look over the balcony, peering deep into the darkness, but there's no one around. Maybe they're hiding downstairs, concealed in the shadows, biding their time until it's safe for them to crawl back to whatever diseased hole they came out of. I rush downstairs. Once there, I twist and turn, not sure where to go, where to look. The bastard's out there, I can feel their eyes on me. I run right and look. No one there. Rush the other way. No one there either. In a daze I stumble back to where I started and turn in a disorientating circle.

'I know you're out there.' My voice is hoarse and hurting.

I hear something like a laugh. Are they laughing at me? Then I realise it's the wind, whirling in my ears.

Someone must've seen whoever left Sara-Jane's socks. Taking two steps at a time, I bolt back up to my landing and start banging on my neighbours' doors. An older man opens the first one. I wave the socks in his face. 'Someone dropped these through my door, did you see who it was?'

He stares at me as if I've got three heads. 'What? I've been indoors all the time.'

I move on to the next door. This time it's opened by someone I recognise. One of the other mums whose child went to Princess Isabel at the same time as Sara-Jane. 'Did you see anyone on the landing, a couple of minutes ago?'

She gives me a startled look. 'Can I help you?'

What's wrong with her? Doesn't she understand English? I talk slowly, emphasising every word. 'Did you see someone walking along the balcony?'

My hard tone makes her step back, her fingers tighten protectively against the door. 'On the balcony?' The shuttered stare she gives me suggests she doesn't think I'm right in the head.

I show her the socks. 'I'm Gem Casey. I once lived here. You must remember the business with my daughter, Sara-Jane. Just now, someone dumped her socks through my door. All I want to do is find the animal who did it.'

Her sympathy is gone in a flash. Any friendliness gone in a heartbeat. Hostility is all she has now. I know why that is. It's hearing my name. Realising who I am. It reminds me that too many people on the Rosebridge Estate still hate my guts.

Screw her!

I leave and knock on door after door after door, my words rushing out louder every time. The pounding of my fist against doors becomes more frantic. There's a pounding in my head that I can't shift. My hand hurts. Things around me swirl and tip upside down. Why won't anyone help me?

I'm not falling apart. I'm not falling apart. I'm not . . .

Arms envelop me with the warm comfort of a prayer. Who's holding me? I try to shove them off. It's no use because they only tighten, accompanied by a soothing voice.

'It's all right, Gem. Everything is going to be fine.'

Traci. I look into her troubled face, her kind eyes and easy smile. She's holding me against the wall near her front door. A concerned man hovers behind her. He's years younger than her and dressed in a suit, obviously a professional man.

'Do you need help?' he asks her softly.

Traci half-turns to him. 'Leave this to me. You get yourself ready to go home.'

He stares, expression full of sympathy. Why does his face look so familiar? When he's gone, I suddenly realise I'm the centre of attention, my neighbours eyeing me like I'm a mad woman. Mortified, I slump into Traci's arms, because I realise that's exactly how I've been behaving. But I'm not crazy, am I?

With quivering passion, I declare to Traci, 'It won't get better until I know what happened to her.'

'I know! I know!' Despite her soothing tone she looks completely baffled. She guides me back into my flat. 'Why don't you tell me all about it over a strong cuppa?'

I grab her arm to make her stop. With a calmness I don't feel I show her the socks. 'These are Sara-Jane's. She hated them. Not long after you left someone posted them through the letterbox.'

'Why would someone do that?' Her creased brow tells me she doesn't get what I'm telling her.

I bit back. 'The last time I saw them on her was the day she was stolen from me. Only the monster who took her would have her socks.'

Traci's hand slaps over her mouth in dismayed horror.

I carry on, 'Whoever this scum is they're either trying to scare the crap out of me. *Or* make me stop looking for the truth about what happened to my daughter.'

'Go to the police—'

'The cops?' I scoff. 'They won't help me.'

Traci's shoulders roll back in a gesture I remember her doing so many times back in the day. It meant she was getting ready to do battle. She points at me. 'Now, you listen to me. In the morning you're to get yourself to the police station and insist they investigate who's doing this wickedness to you.' She hisses, 'Tell them, if they don't, they'll have me to deal with.'

Chapter 6

I'm a bag of nerves sitting at a table in the interview room at the local police station. Facing me is Detective Wallace. On the table between us is the pair of pink socks. Sara-Jane's socks. The socks someone kept for the past fifteen years and now want to torture me with.

'And how do you know that these socks belonged to your daughter?'

I could SCREAM. He's already asked me that question a gazillion times.

My impatience comes through me grabbing one of the socks. 'See this stitching here.' I point to a thread that should be a straight stitch but is zigzag instead. 'This was a feature of them, because I got them as a job lot down the market on a stall because they were seconds.' That's what poor mums like me had to look for, every bargain that we could get our hands on to save pennies. 'And the small hole, here, on the heel.'

Beneath hooded eyes he gives me a quizzical look. 'You just said they were a job lot. So this market stall was bound to have plenty more which it sold to other people. Which means that there are plenty of other people who have got these socks.'

'After fifteen years? They look exactly the same as the day I last saw Sara-Jane wearing them.'

At least I think this what I'm saying. I didn't sleep at all last night. Wired and tired, that's how I'm feeling. My words are a confused jumble.

Wallace has the mandatory police sympathy on his face, but the stiff set of his body tells me as loud as a foghorn that he doesn't believe a word of it.

With a lengthy sigh, Wallace picks the socks up. Shouldn't he be wearing gloves or something to try to preserve any DNA? I'd brought them here carefully wrapped in a carrier bag. He gives them a cursory examination before putting them back down.

'Look, Gem—'

'Did the police ever find any more security camera or CCTV footage?'

His eyes shutter. My hope dies. 'As the police will have explained at the time, whoever took Sara-Jane avoided all the security cameras and CCTV. Which indicates her abductor – *abductors* – knew the area well so were probably local.'

My heart sinks at the knowledge that nothing new has turned up in the investigation.

'I understand, I really do.' His sympathy feels more human this time. 'But there's absolutely no reason at all to believe these socks are your daughter's. Why on earth would someone put these through your door?' His tone changes. 'You claim this must be Sara-Jane's kidnapper. How on earth would they have known you're back on the Rosebridge Estate?'

'You saw me at the school yesterday. Lots of other people did too. Someone could've followed me back to the Rosebridge. There's an easy way to find out. Send the socks for DNA testing. That will settle it one way or the other. Or look at CCTV footage on the estate?'

He maintains his position with a slow-mo shake of his head. 'We've got a backlog of evidence that needs testing from other cases.

We can't justify testing these socks with our limited resources. Or spending hours going through security camera footage.'

My voice rises and has a strange pitch. 'You mean you don't want to.'

Wallace's chest heaves with a weary sigh. He pulls out a file and opens it. 'This is the record of a serious incident fourteen years ago . . .'

I tense up, face going hot, knowing exactly what he's about to tell me.

Fourteen Years Ago

The back of a head. That's how it all started. One minute I was walking out of the shop and the next there she was, up ahead of me.

Sara-Jane.

I didn't see her face. I only saw the back of her. Her head. Then again, I'm her mum, I wouldn't need to see her face. I know my own little girl. It was her hair that was the dead giveaway. Brown and short. My Sara-Jane never liked long hair, said it got in the way of her playing.

Oh my God, I couldn't believe what I was seeing. My daughter holding . . . Why was Sara-Jane's sweet hand holding that of another woman? Oh God, was this the monster who took her?

'Sara-Jane!' I cried out, hoarse emotion clogging my voice.

'Sara-Jane!'

I remember thinking, why isn't she turning back to me? Doesn't she remember my voice? What if her kidnapper has driven her to forget my voice? They must've given her a different name, brainwashed her into thinking she's someone else. That must be it, because my child would never forget me. Oh, my poor, precious darling girl. Mummy's coming to rescue you.

I rushed over so fast I almost tripped and ended up banging into someone else, who muttered rudely at me. I admit, I'd been drinking. OK, I'd been knocking back the hard stuff since I got up that morning. It's the only way I could get through those early days. The drink twisted reality into a hazy blur that made me feel safe. Turned my world into a place where I didn't have to think about a beast doing monstrous things to her.

After righting myself I flew over to them. I had to rescue my daughter. There was no time to lose. My hand lashed out and I grabbed Sara-Jane's arms and turned her to face me. I staggered back slightly at what she looked like. She'd changed. Was older. Where had her braces gone? Her glasses? A year of changes I'd missed. Anger boiled inside me that someone could do this to a child and her mother.

Why was her smile dying on her face? Why was she desperately trying to pull free?

'Mummy,' she screamed out.

I dragged her closer to me. 'I'm here, baby. I'm here.'

A crowd began to gather.

The child-stealer who had my Sara-Jane stared at me with shocked horror. 'What are you doing? Get your hands off my daughter.'

I shook my head, drawing Sara-Jane closer still. And growled, 'She's not your anything.' I felt the crowd around me and pleaded with them. 'Help me. Please help. This woman has abducted my child.'

The onlookers shifted with concern and indecision. They looked at me and Sara-Jane and then at the other woman, not clear what to do.

Sara-Jane yanked hard from me. I wouldn't let her go. Wouldn't. 'Mummy's here to take you home,' I said.

Tears leaked from her beautiful eyes before she started sobbing. 'You're not my mummy.'

Then the child-stealer was on me, her hand crushing my arm that held my child. MY CHILD.

We struggled. I wouldn't let Sara-Jane go. Never again. This woman, this criminal, would have to kill me first.

'Mummy! Mummy!'

Sara-Jane's screams were frantic. But I noticed that she was looking at and pleading with the other woman. That she was straining and stretching to get out of my grip. Why had she done that? Her teeth sank into the top of my arm, forcing me to release her, and I let go, stumbled back in pain. I watched my girl rush into the tight embrace of the child-napper. Kissing the top of Sara-Jane's head, the woman stared over at me, her glowing eyes a mirror of the expression I have every day. Terror that someone took her child from her.

I was taken to a police station. I didn't remember the journey. I came back to myself in the cell, my knees tucked under my chin, rocking. I felt so lost.

The doctor who examined me explained the child was called Jenny and was not my daughter. Not Sara-Jane. Then they sent a psychiatrist or psychoanalyst, a therapist, I didn't remember what the fancy title of her job was but she was someone who treated people who weren't right in the head. Probing and asking private questions, trying to make out that I was mad.

They let me go with a caution. I stopped drinking that day. Looked forward. Tucked my beautiful memories of Sara-Jane in a treasured place in a corner of my mind.

'I was having a hard time back then.' I firmly defend myself to Wallace. 'I wrote a letter which I gave to the doctor at the police station to make sure it was passed on to the mother and her daughter, begging their forgiveness for what happened.'

The pink socks on the table seem to have come alive in front me. They're telling me who they are. They say they're my daughter's. They can't tell me how they came through my letter-box, but they know who they are. With a mother's care, I pick them up and get to my feet. I wrap Sara-Jane's socks around one of my hands. It makes me feel like I'm holding her hand after all this time.

I tell Detective Wallace with all my avenging heart, 'I will never give up looking for my little girl. Never.'

Chapter 7

Something is wrong. Badly wrong. I sense the change in the atmosphere in the flat as soon as I enter. I go deathly still in the hall. My grip tightens painfully against the handlebars of my bike. The daylight wraps around me, oppressive and suffocating as a plastic bag over my head. It's hard for me to breathe. My heart . . . God . . . My heart is banging so hard against my body it feels like it's on the verge of breaking my ribs. A layer of nasty, cold sweat trickles along my hairline.

'Is anyone there?'

What a stupid question. If someone is waiting for me it's not as if they are going to alert me to their presence by answering. Then again, that's what they do in the movies, isn't it? Some half-naked young woman in a horror flick where you know that she's going be attacked and savaged and killed.

Killed.

Murdered.

Is that what someone is waiting to do to me? In the place I once tried to make a safe home with my missing daughter. Maybe I should rush out and get help from Traci next door? Yeah, but what if I'm wrong? What if there's no one here except the ghosts of the past? I'm going to look like a real idiot then.

With a twist and turn of my palm and fingers I rearrange my set of keys in my fist until a key is sticking out, a tiny makeshift dagger ready to defend me. A stab to the eye. A deep jab to the head. Thrust deep into my attacker's neck and then a solid slice along their flesh to the other side. I'm not going down without a fight.

Heart rate racking up, I move forward. Silent and cautiously with the knowhow of a burglar on the balls of my feet. My breathing is hard and hurts. And is too loud. I need to slow it down. I don't want them to hear. If they hear me . . .

I reach the threshold of the main room. My hand tightens on my makeshift blade. And . . . Jump inside. Look around. And around.

No one there.

It's just me and my heavy breathing that shatters the air. I sag with relief against the coldness of the hard wall and momentarily close my eyes. Not until that moment do I realise I'm riddled with tension from my interview with Detective Wallace. The horrible sensation of pins and needles pulsing through the soles of my feet. Am I being paranoid?

My head falls defeated to my chest. I feel broken. On the brink of being destroyed. It's when I feel like this that I question whether I'm doing the right thing looking for my kidnapped daughter. I've got enough money to have employed a private investigator to find answers, or not, and then report back to me. Why am I doing this? Why am I putting myself through the agony?

With a lengthy sigh I open my eyes and Sara-Jane's there, right in front of me.

'This is for you, Mummy.'
She hands me a card.
'For me?'

I know exactly what it is, but I keep that to myself. Seeing the anticipation and joy dancing on her little face waiting for me to open it is one of the biggest pleasures. Inside the envelope I reveal a Happy Mother's Day card. Sara-Jane has made it at school. Her big message on the front squeezes my heart. I can barely breathe.

'THE BEST MUM EVER.'

She runs into my arms and whispers in my ear. 'You are, you know. The best mum ever.'

The best mum ever. That's why it has to be ME searching for her. Her mother. The one who carried her for eight months and twenty-one days. The person who has never given up hope.

In the kitchen I go to the fridge and down some refreshing sparkling water straight from the bottle. And that's when I feel it.

The heat. The unnerving presence of another person in the room. Standing behind me.

The fear's back. *You're the best mum ever.* Using the courage from my daughter I twist around.

The bottle in my hand drops and crashes to the floor, shattering glass everywhere.

I was right all along. It's a ghost from the past. But this one is very much alive – unfortunately.

Charlie. Sara-Jane's father.

'How did you get in here?' I move back. As far away from him as possible. I don't want this dirtbag anywhere near me for fear of being infected with what I know he is.

He smiles, lazy and long. 'I've always been good with my hands.'

'So you broke in,' I snarl. 'I should call the police.'

'The cops?' He puts on a wounded lost puppy expression. 'Is that any way to greet the father of your child?'

I'd once loved Charlie with all my eager young heart. Fell hard for his looks, especially those dark eyes which were born for a girl

44

to melt in. He could run courses on how to sugar-talk a girl. Then I got pregnant at seventeen, which wasn't the best situation, but once my baby's wriggling body, so full of innocence, was placed in my arms I knew the future would be bright . . . Except for Charlie. Only with age and experience did I understand that love goes so much deeper than physical appearance. The person you love should have that extra-special something, that uniqueness that makes them shine above everyone else. It was while I was pregnant with Sara-Jane that I figured out that Charlie's special something was rotten to the core.

His leanness now borders on way too thin for his height, but he's still got that 'it factor' which captures the female eye. He's losing his hair though, which shoots delicious pleasure through me. He'd been so vain about his hair, primping and preening it this way 'n' that, insisting that when we made love I run my fingers through it. And look at him now, his crowning glory nearly gone.

I don't ask where he's living. In fact, I don't ask anything about him because I don't want to know. He's been out of my life for fifteen years and that's the way I'd prefer it to stay.

'We made an agreement years ago,' I remind him.

He rubs his fingertips along his jawline as if deep in thought. 'Well, I'd say things have changed since then.'

'What do you mean?'

'Shame about that body being found in the school.' He shakes his head with fake concern.

My heart skips a couple of beats. 'What do you know about that?'

He shrugs before folding his arms and leaning casually against the door frame. This puts me on high alert; there's nothing casual about Charlie. 'The way I hear it, you've reappeared like the Good Witch to find out if it's our daughter—'

'*My* daughter,' I savagely correct.

'*Our* daughter,' he asserts again as if I haven't spoken. 'Were the remains found in the chapel? Isn't the chapel the place where Sara-Jane and that other girl snuck out of school from?'

I storm part way to him. 'You never cared about her then, you don't care about her now. Charlie, what do you want? Really want?'

His brow arches. 'If I said I wanted to get down on bended knee and propose to you, to beg you with all my loving heart to take me as your beloved for the rest of our days, would you believe me?'

He looks so serious, like he means every last word. See, the thing about Charlie is he had such charm. He always had the right words, the right gestures, the way he moved his body to draw me back in when he'd done something wrong. I was so starving for love back then, being with a man who honey-talked me into forgiving his every abuse seemed, at the time, to be better than being with no man at all.

It was the horror of what happened the last time I shared a roof with him that woke me up. Opened my eyes wide to the fact that living with a man who treated me and my daughter like shit was not living at all. Best for me and Sara-Jane to be on our own. God, does he really think, after fifteen years, I'm on the edge of falling into his treacherous happy ever after? Again?

Moron.

I jerk and step back. As if pulled by an invisible string he moves right along with me. I keep moving back, he keeps coming forward. I feel the wall against my back. There's nowhere left for me to go. Charlie looks down on me and our eyes meet. His hand shoots out. I flinch, slamming my eyes shut, waiting. Waiting for what I know will come. Why did I put my keys away? My body trembles in horrified anticipation. His hand reaches me . . . His fingers curl in my hair. This isn't what I'd expected him to do. He leans down and smells my skin.

And whispers, 'I hear that you're living it high and happy with loads of ready cash at your fingertips.'

Swiftly, before he can stop me, I duck under his arm and rush behind him. He turns to face me. I answer him slowly, so he hears every last one of my words. 'Never. I don't owe you anything. I made it on my own.'

'That's not what a lawyer told me—'

'Screw you. And screw your lawyer. The days of you screwing me over are long gone.' He's angry, his hands flexing into fists at his side. 'If you touch a hair on my head, I'll have you before the law quicker than you can say "cheating ex-boyfriend".'

He's seething. 'You wouldn't want me to go to the papers again.'

With this threat he marches out and is gone with a slam of my door.

The papers. It makes me want to chuck up thinking about what happened in the past. *All you've got to do is give him money and he'll go away. Give it to him. You don't want the papers back in your life.* I straighten up. Give in to a bastard like him? Never. Not again.

Head hurting, I go outside on the main balcony for some fresh air. Below, I see Sara-Jane's father get into a van.

A black van.

My mind reels back . . . And back . . . That's right. I was trying to get away from Heather, that journalist. I sort of collided with a black van near the school. It shot off down the road in one almighty big hurry. Is this the same one? Was Charlie watching me? Following me?

Chapter 8

Fifteen Years Ago

'The bitch won't let me see my daughter and you're taking her side!'

The angry man's voice made Gem stop in her tracks. She knew who it was. Charlie. Sara-Jane's dad. The last person she wanted anywhere near her child's school. She was rushing, heading towards the Princess Isabel School to pick up Sara-Jane. Her heart dropped. No! No! No! The last thing she needed was Charlie creating a scene outside Sara-Jane's new school. Miss Swan, the head teacher, was still doing all she could to build bridges between the more well-to-do parents and the families of the children from the Rosebridge Estate. To calm suspicions on both sides.

And now Charlie's appearance was going to ruin all that good work. Gem had no doubt about that. Charlie's middle name was trouble. Gem hadn't seen him for two years and then recently he'd contacted her out of the blue.

Taking a fortifying breath, Gem turned the corner that led to the school gate. She shivered with horror at what she saw. A police car was pulled up on the pavement. Two officers were arguing with Charlie.

'I've got a right to pick up my daughter if I want to. She's my flesh and blood.'

One of the officers answered, 'Sir, you are making a disturbance. Outside a school.'

Clare Swan stood near the other officer, her arms folded, face taut with fury that this was happening, in public, at her high-flying school. Gem groaned when she saw the head of the PTA, Laura, brow arched, observing in the background. She was standing next to a man who Gem didn't recognise. He looked on with concern.

A short distance away, Sara-Jane was standing next to a police woman. Her head was bowed with embarrassment because she'd feel all the adults were blaming her for her father's behaviour. Gem's gut twisted with guilt and shame. How could Charlie do this to his own daughter? Pulse beating like crazy, Gem moved forward. Every eye turned to her. The other parents standing nearby, the teachers, the members of the PTA, the police. Miss Swan. Laura Prentice. The look the head teacher levelled at her said all too clearly that they were going to need to have a meeting soon. Very soon.

Gem avoided the eyes of the others and turned her own bitter gaze on Charlie as she drew closer.

She bit out, as quietly as she could. 'What the hell are you doing here? You haven't been interested in Sara-Jane for years. Clear off!'

She was the only one present who recognised how much he was relishing all the attention. Making a public fool of her. Charlie was addicted to drama the way others are hooked on drink or drugs. All he needed for his act was an audience, and he had a ready-made one at the school gate.

He spoke for her ears only. 'You give me what I want and you need never see me again.'

'I've told you I'm not giving you any money.'

Gem understood his game. If he humiliated her up in front of the school she'd be so embarrassed she'd give him the money just to make him go away.

'Come on, all you've got to do is take out a loan.'

'I did that for you two years ago. And now, like a tarnished penny, you're back. I'm tired of being made a mug by you.'

When she'd taken a loan before to make him go away she'd had to work overtime for nearly a year to pay it back. She was tired of him and stood her ground.

'Be it on your head.'

He made a big drama of stepping back. He raised his wrist to show his watch to the crowd and sighed. 'So, my little princess's mother has finally arrived. Good job *I* was here *on time* to pick her up. Who knows what might've happened to my Sara-Jane if she'd wandered on to the street.'

Clare Swan looked him up and down with indignation. 'Your daughter would have been looked after until her mother arrived.'

Charlie played to the audience. 'Looks to me like *her mother* was too busy watching daytime TV.'

Gem swallowed hard in an effort to deny him what he wanted: a full-on fight in front of the crowd.

'You're not allowed here,' Gem insisted. 'Go away. Think of Sara-Jane.'

Forlorn hope. 'Not allowed? Have you got any paperwork on you to prove that?' He turned to address the police in his fake matey manner. 'I expect you boys are familiar with this kind of behaviour. Bitter, deranged mum trying to prevent a father from being involved in his child's welfare? Yeah?'

This was too much for Gem. All her pent-up fury at this man who never gave her a penny to support his daughter burst like flood water. Despite knowing full well that her coming actions would only cement what some of the parents at the school thought of those who lived on the Rosebridge, Gem balled her hands and she lunged at him. She tried to strike him across the cheek but only caught a cop's shoulder instead.

Charlie was ecstatic. 'See that? See that? That's what I'm dealing with. You should arrest her, officers. That's assault. You think I want to leave my daughter in the care of a violent individual like her?'

The police officers tugged Gem to one side, attempted to calm her down and resolve the dispute but they were cut short.

Clare Swan walked up. She ignored Gem, directly addressing the police. 'A number of parents have expressed concerned about this individual loitering near the school, attempting to talk to his daughter through the fence. Perhaps you'd be kind enough to warn him if he does it again, he'll be arrested. Given the fact that Sara-Jane's mother' – she gifted Gem with a reassuring smile, which the young mother was eternally grateful for – 'herself seems unable to prevent these unfortunate scenes, I'll discuss this matter further with her tomorrow. In the meantime, can you do your job and tell that man to be about his business. And stay away from my school.'

The quiet teacher authority of Miss Swan had its effect and the two cops did as they were told.

Charlie agreed to leave. 'I'll go, I get it. No point in a poor dad trying to stick up for his rights in this country. We all know what the deal is.' He turned to look at Sara-Jane. 'I suppose I'm allowed to give my little girl a hug goodbye? Is that legal these days or not?'

Gem wanted so badly to stop him when he started walking in their daughter's direction, but she sensed it would not be a good look. She'd come off exactly like he said she was – stopping him from seeing his child. Charlie knelt on the ground in front of

Sara-Jane as if she were a sacred object and embraced her in his arms while whispering honeyed, fatherly things in her ears.

Sara-Jane's dour face showed whoever this was fooling, it wasn't her.

In one movement, Charlie climbed to his feet and swept his daughter up in his arms. 'Why don't you and I go for a little walk before your mother takes you back to that slum she lives in and you can tell me what you've been doing at school today.'

Charlie had lost the crowd. There were mumblings of disapproval and the cops shouted, 'Put the child down now.'

He turned to face them and began backing into the road. 'What? We're just going for a brief walk. Where's the harm in that?'

Gem was completely iced with fear. He'd threatened her that if she wasn't forthcoming with the money he would pick up Sara-Jane and head into the darkness. He'd do it as well, she knew that. Gem resigned herself to the inevitable; she was going to have find his money. Somehow, some way.

A voice in the crowd called out, 'One moment, officers. Perhaps I can have a word with this gentleman.'

It was the man standing next to Laura. Charlie put Sara-Jane down but continued to hold her hand tightly. When the man reached him, they began to speak quietly. They were soon locked in an animated and hurried conversation. They both laughed at one point. What were they talking about? No one could hear. Finally, Charlie gave his little princess a peck on the cheek and let her go. Sara-Jane ran over to her mother, who picked her up in her cold and trembling arms. And hugged her close.

The police had a word with Charlie before he strode away from the school. The crowd dispersed.

Gem watched the man who'd intervened slowly walk away.

'Do you know who that man is?' Gem questioned her daughter.

Sara-Jane turned to look. 'He's my friend Abby's dad. Her mum and dad don't live together any more.'

Ah, Gem thought, *Henry Prentice. Dale's son. Laura's ex-husband.* Scowling, she recalled the way Charlie and Henry Prentice were with each other. Their friendliness. The way they laughed. It was almost like they knew each other.

Chapter 9

My phone rings as I lift my head from observing the black van that Charlie got into, my mind wondering whether it is the same van I nearly collided with outside the school. I take the call. It's Beryl Spencer, the school's office manager.

'Are you available to come to the school?'

My heart begins thumping and thumping. My legs start shaking so badly I'm not sure how I manage to remain standing. The air turns into the thickness of a cloth rammed down my throat, making it hard for me to breathe. I know why they want me to come to the school. This is the moment I've been dreading all these years. They're going to tell me that Sara-Jane is dead.

I ride hell-for-leather through the streets, the wheels of my bike turning faster and faster as I head towards the school, Sara-Jane's socks burning a hole in my jeans' pocket. I keep taking snap-shot glances over my shoulder. I can't help it. Since Sara-Jane's socks were dumped back into my life last night and Charlie's unwanted reappearance, I have this overwhelming sensation of hot eyes watching me. Following me. Tracking my every move. I wish I could say my nerves calm down when I reach the school, but they don't. The truth is this school scares me. It always has. It's so big, with its vast windows and Victorian redbrick walls that stretch to a large roof terrace. Inside is a rabbit warren of corridors that seem to go on forever, ready to swallow you up. Endless twisty stairs.

Funny how we give over the trust of our children to places like this.

I dismount near the large 'WE ARE AN OUTSTANDING SCHOOL' banner mounted high on the fence inside the playground facing the street. Outstanding is the highest grade given to a school after an inspection. I'm not surprised that Princess Isabel remains the most sought-after primary school in the area.

Someone in the office, probably Beryl Spencer, must be watching me, because there's a buzzing sound that releases the gate, letting me in. I try my best not to look into the distance at the taped-off crime scene. At the chapel. But it's no use. It draws me. Haunts me. Is that why Miss Swan has called me to the school? To tell me that the dark, unloved ground in the chapel is the final resting place of my beautiful girl?

Inside, the school feels eerie without the natural noise of children's voices. My unease kicks in deeper. I head into the reception area where the school's latest SATs results flash with pride on a mounted TV screen.

'Hello. I'm Rosa.' It's not the office manager who greets me but the young woman I saw yesterday with Beryl and Miss Swan at the school gate. She has a strong Italian accent.

Wearing a welcoming smile, she beckons me into the admin office and shocks me when she whispers in my ear, 'Dale told me what happened to your daughter. I'm so sorry that happened to you.'

I smile uncertainly back. 'Thank you for being so thoughtful.'

'That was highly inappropriate.' The whiplash voice that interrupts us belongs to Beryl and she's giving Rosa the evil eye. 'Always – *always* – keep emotions under control. And, if necessary, offer a cup of tea.' Beryl turns her attention to me. 'I'll take you through to Miss Swan.'

We pass by her desk where there's a double photo frame. One side is a portrait photo of her husband, Teddy. The other photo is a black and white one of Beryl and her husband when they were much younger. Wasn't there a story doing the rounds about him fifteen years ago? He went missing or something? I can't remember, plus I've got more important stuff on my mind.

As we go, she sweetly whispers, 'I'm sorry too about Sara-Jane. I never really got a chance to say that when it all happened.'

Beryl was always kind to the families from the Rosebridge, like me and Sara-Jane. Batty Beryl, that's what some of the parents called her behind her back, because she was always making mistakes, like sending the wrong letter to the wrong parents, getting the term dates muddled. They also sniggered that she looked as if she had thrown on her clothes in the dark. Today she wore a kaftan that made her float about like an ageing hippie flower-child. Each to their own is my philosophy. Nevertheless, why someone as super-efficient as Miss Swan had such an incompetent, eccentric office manager none of the parents could understand.

Clare Swan, head teacher of Princess Isabel, is waiting for me in front of her desk. Despite the all-over grey hair, she still looks the same, tall and regal with a steely-eyed stare she's honed over the years in her role running this successful school.

'Miss Swan.' Even after all these years I would never address her as 'Clare'. It's a respect thing. 'Have they found her?' I just come out with it. God, I don't want this to be true, but why else would I have been summoned here?

'I'm sorry. That's not why I've asked you to come.' Bitter disappointment and relief strike me. I want to know, but don't want to know about those remains in the chapel, in case it's the worst news. 'Please, take a seat.'

There's something in her hand as she moves towards a soft seating area. I perch on the edge of the chair, my spine so ramrod straight it hurts.

She tells me, 'Fifteen years ago I meant to see you, but you had already gone.'

Does she know why I fled in the night? It still makes the bile rise in my throat to think of what happened.

'I wanted to give you this.'

She lays *this* on the table between us. Sara-Jane's school report book. Most children get a loose-leafed paper report, but at Princess Isabel they believed in keeping them in a stylish book, a year-by-year record for families and children. I pick it up and flick through and read.

English: Tries hard. Likes story writing. She needs to finish her work on time.

Maths: Shines when her work is about money.

Woodwork: The best in the class. Well done, Sara-Jane!

Then I come to all the blank pages, the pages that should have been filled up with her achievements in the following years. Blank. Empty. Like how I feel right now. A profound sense of sadness settles over me, because this book represents the promise of the life my Sara-Jane should have had.

After closing it, I look up at the other woman to thank her, this means the world to me, but I'm stopped by the expression on her face. It's awful. The veins in her neck are popping.

'This is my school and it was my responsibility to make sure all the children were safe.'

I stop her. Won't allow her to go on. 'My Sara-Jane understood right from wrong. She made that decision to leave here, for whatever reason. There was nothing you or the school could've done.' Swallowing hard, I add, 'My only wish is that it's not her remains in that grave in the chapel.'

I get to my feet. I don't want to stay here longer than I have to. It's killing me being here. Hand fiercely tight around my daughter's report book, I head for the door.

Miss Swan stops me. 'This is my last term here, I'm retiring.' Good for her. This school couldn't have had a more dedicated person running it. 'There's a leaving party organised for me. I know you may not feel it's appropriate, but I hope you can join us.'

I nod and smile, but the truth is I want to be long gone by then. Plus, some of the other parents will not want me within a mile of them. In the admin office I hustle past Beryl's inquisitive stare and reach the corridor outside. And freeze.

Walking towards me is a group of people, including Laura Prentice, Abby's mother. I notice Traci and realise this must be the end of a PTA meeting. The meetings were held in an office at the back of the chapel. Obviously, due to the body being found in there the PTA is now meeting in the school's main building.

Everyone stops and awkwardly stares. The space in the corridor suddenly feels too small.

I don't hesitate. I march over to Laura Prentice. 'I need to speak with you.'

If she thinks she's dealing with the old Gem, with her lack of confidence and need to blend in, she's sadly mistaken. Building a successful company has made me understand how to dig in and hold my ground.

Laura still has that way of looking down at me from the side of her nose. She flicks her trademark scarf she always wears more securely over her shoulder as if I'm the one she's attempting to flick away. 'I don't think there's anything for us to talk about.'

She tries to get around me, but I won't let her. 'How would you feel if those bones out there were Abby's?'

Her gaze turns molten with rage. 'Stay away from Abby. Don't go looking for her, because you will never find her.'

We both know why she hates me. Hates Sara-Jane.

Chapter 10

Fifteen Years Ago

'Sara-Jane tried to strangle one of the other children.'

The shocking statement slammed into Gem. She could not believe what Miss Swan was telling her. Gem was sitting opposite the grim head teacher in her office. There was a high-pitched buzzing in her head. Her daughter? Her good-girl Sara-Jane? Had tried to do . . . WHAT? Strangle another kid? No way! Her Sara-Jane had been brought up right.

After getting the call from the school, Gem had immediately left her part-time job serving customers in a café, her boss's threat of docking her a half-day's pay ringing in her ears. After the incident with Sara-Jane's dad outside the school, Gem was mortified by yet another serious incident.

Being in this office reminded Gem of all the times she had got into trouble at school and been marched off to the head teacher's office. For her, school had been boring. Only the children who were good at English, maths and science were praised, while those, like her, who were good with their hands and physically active, got lost. Although Gem had to concede that this office was nothing like the scary, stuffy headmaster's office at her own childhood school. Miss Swan's room was airy and bright.

The head teacher was held in high regard by parents. She was always available to talk and, when possible, showed her face at the school gate at the end of the day. Children achieving their best and the reputation of the school were her life's work. Princess Isabel had a policy of zero tolerance of violence.

Miss Swan continued. 'That is the allegation another parent has made against Sara-Jane.'

'Strangle?' Gem's stomach gave a sickening lurch. 'My daughter would never, *never*, hurt one of the other kids.'

Swiftly turning to her side, Gem addressed her daughter, who sat next to her. 'This isn't true, is it?'

Miss Swan had a policy of openness and transparency which was why Sara-Jane was also present. With consternation, Gem watched as her daughter avoided her gaze and nervously pushed up her glasses. There was a Wonder Woman plaster on one side of the glasses where Gem had repaired it, because she didn't have enough money to get it professionally fixed. They lived on a shoe-string, Gem mending bikes in their hallway on the side to bring in more cash.

'Sara-Jane! Why would you do something like that?'

'Sara-Jane does have a tendency to . . .' The head teacher chose her words very carefully. '. . . be very spirited.'

Very spirited. Gem knew what that was code for: getting into trouble. At her previous school, Sara-Jane was never naughty. However, since coming to Princess Isabel she had started to play up. Things like muttering defiantly under her breath when she didn't agree with something her mother said, not doing her homework on time. Gem didn't understand what was going on. Sara-Jane had only been at the school for six weeks.

Maybe I did make the wrong decision sending her here.

Gem tried to defend her daughter. 'She's just curious. She wants to find out about the world. But she'd never put her hands on another child.' She looked at her daughter sternly. 'I've told her that if anyone hits her she's not to hit back, she's to tell the teacher or another adult.'

Miss Swan said, 'The other child's mother wanted to go to the police—'

'What?' This was turning into a nightmare. The last thing Gem needed was dealings with the police. Again.

'But I spoke with her,' Miss Swan carried on, 'and managed to dissuade her from going down that avenue. The best way to deal with these issues is within the school. And to give you both, as mothers, the opportunity to speak with each other.'

'Of course.' Gem didn't hesitate to agree. 'Thank you, Miss Swan.'

There was a quiet knock at the door before it opened to reveal Beryl. The mismatched purple skirt, lime green blouse and white ankle boots she wore underscored why many parents called her Batty Beryl behind her back. Although Gem thought the name was nasty and unfair. Everyone should be allowed to be the person they chose to be.

'They are here,' Beryl said as if she were announcing the Queen.

Taken by complete surprise, Gem tensed. She had not expected to meet with the other mother right now. She prayed and hoped that it was another mum from the Rosebridge, not a member of the old guard. The mother entered with her child. Gem inwardly groaned. Luck was not on her side.

Of all the mothers in the world, why this one?

Laura Prentice.

Her position as the head of the PTA crowned her as the most powerful parent in the school. Laura Prentice was the type of woman who stood out in a crowd, wearing her professional facade like designer clothes. Intense gaze, tall, elegant, she could make cheap off-the-peg clothes appear high-end fashion. Such a contrast to Gem, who was turned out in a T-shirt and worn jeans.

Laura's daughter, Abigail, was very small for her age. Ribbon-tied-back long hair and a picture-perfect face with classic bow lips. But there was something about the child that put Gem on edge. The way her arms and legs moved like puppets. The way she kept her head mainly down. The emptiness in her gaze that seemed to burn right through you. Gem suppressed her shiver.

'Thank you for coming.' Miss Swan welcomed the newcomers as they sat down.

'Lift your head, darling.' Laura Prentice got straight into it, instructing her daughter in her carefully refined voice.

Gem gasped at the marks displayed around the smaller girl's neck. Red with a purple tinge. And so ugly. It looked so painful.

Gem was completely horrified at what her daughter had apparently done. 'I'm so sorry. My Sara-Jane has never done anything like this. Ever.'

Laura Prentice looked at her sharply, compressing her carefully lipsticked mouth. 'Have you read the school's discipline policy?'

Gem could only shake her head. Her anxiety deepened. She was wading into waters she was not comfortable in. Reading policies was not her thing. All that formal language turned her off. The truth was she felt out of her depth in this situation. It made her tongue-tied, grappling to find the right words. At school the parents who got listened to were those who spoke a certain way. Who knew the exact right words to say. No one listened to the Gem Caseys of this world.

They listened to people like Laura Prentice, who oozed confidence. With a shake of her shiny hair she continued. 'I produced a leaflet for all the new parents emphasising that they must read all of the school policies.' Gem swallowed like she was in a court of law. She knew how that felt. The other woman pierced her with her sharp gaze. 'Do you know how old Princess Isabel is?'

Gem was struck dumb, feeling smaller and smaller. Crossing her legs, the other woman enlightened her. 'One hundred and thirty-three years. The chapel even older. It has always, *always*, had a policy of keeping the children who come through its gates safe. This school is a place of safety. It will remain so as long as I am the director of the PTA.'

Gem felt like she was the one now being strangled. Finally she found her voice, a weak, mumbled response. 'I hate violence of all kinds. I've brought up my daughter to feel the same.'

Laura Prentice leaned forward. A scattering of tiny veins twitched and pumped blood beneath her right eye. 'My daughter is the only child I have. She is my whole world.'

Gem felt terrible because she totally understood what the other woman meant. She felt the same about her own little girl.

The older mother turned to Miss Swan. 'This is what some of the parents were worried would happen when the school suddenly increased its intake.'

Gem knew exactly what was being implied. All the children from the Rosebridge Estate were prone to violence because their homes were violent. So they came to school and started fighting. *What a load of bollocks*, Gem angrily thought. Most of the parents on the estate were ordinary people like her, who loved their children and wanted the best for them. Nevertheless, Gem couldn't deny that what her daughter had done was vicious. Terrible.

'What have you got to say?' she roughly asked her daughter.

Sara-Jane gazed at the smaller girl. 'I'm sorry, Abby. I didn't mean for it to happen.'

Abby Prentice lifted her eyes, her lips curving with a smile. The smile chilled Gem. It left her feeling like she was being dragged into a bottomless ocean. She did not know why, but it did.

Abby opened her mouth to speak, but her mother got there first, staring crossly at Sara-Jane. 'I am glad to hear it, young lady. But be assured, if this ever happens again, I won't hesitate to go to the police.'

As a gently smiling Beryl escorted them towards the admin office exit, Sara-Jane accidentally knocked over the double photo frame on Beryl's desk. It was a photo of her husband, Teddy, and another of them when they were much younger. She always kept it there. Gem had heard he'd disappeared a year ago. The most juicy rumour being that he'd run off with another woman.

'Oh, sorry,' Gem apologised, scrambling over to pick it up.

Beryl waved Gem away. 'Don't you worry about none of that. You get yourself and your little lady there home.'

She ended with a special smile for Sara-Jane. Beryl might be known as Batty Beryl by some of the parents, but she was a favourite with the kids. Despite her smile, Gem could see the aching sadness about her husband. It must be so hard for her not knowing where he was. Or maybe she did know and couldn't face the fact that he had simply left her for someone else.

When they got outside, Gem confronted her daughter. 'What were you thinking?'

Sara-Jane peered up at her, with that stubborn tilt of her chin she got from her mum. She didn't look as sorry as she should've. 'It was an accident. We were playing.'

Exasperated, Gem gazed to the heavens for strength. 'What kind of game involves leaving someone black and blue? Putting your hands around their neck . . .'

'I never did that, Mum,' Sara-Jane vigorously denied, belligerence in both her tone and face. 'It was the handle of her bag.'

Expression sober, Gem continued, 'I've always told you to make sure you play safe.' All at once she realised something. 'Where's your coat?'

Her daughter thought for a while. Then, 'I think it might be in the cloakroom or I left it in Beryl's room.'

'I'll check Beryl and Miss Swan's office and you go to the cloakroom.' Her voice hardened. 'And you're to meet me back here. I mean it.'

'OK, Mum.'

They walked off in different directions. Gem was just about to turn the corner when she heard voices. Laura and Abby Prentice.

'Do you remember what I told you?' Laura demanded of her child.

'Yes, Mummy.'

'Your name is Abby but you're really Little Laura. You have got to walk like Laura, talk like Laura, wear clothes like Laura.'

'Yes, Mummy,' the child repeated like a robot.

'Never forget that, darling.' Saccharine sweetness laced the endearment. 'You are my representative in this school among the children. I work the adults and you work the children.'

'Yes, Mummy.'

Deeply troubled, Gem rushed back the way she'd come, forgetting all about Sara-Jane's coat. She felt nauseated by what she'd heard. No wonder Abby looked so weird. Imagine a young child having the pressure of being forced to behave as an adult. As far as Gem was concerned a child should be exactly that, a child. Let them play, laugh and have fun while at the same time learn about the importance of responsibility. What disturbed Gem the most was Laura wanting Abby to be a replica of her, a mini-me.

The first and only thing Gem said to her daughter when she found her waiting with her coat was, 'Stay away from Abby Prentice.'

Chapter 11

With the harsh memory of why Laura Prentice hated my daughter buzzing in my head, I decide to storm after her down the school corridor. How dare she turn her back on me? The Gem Casey who felt inferior to her is long gone. Looking down her snob-nob nose doesn't frighten me any more.

Behind me, a warning voice stops me dead in my tracks. 'This isn't the right time. Best speak to her with a cooler head.'

I do an about turn to find a man, maybe about my age, calmly gazing at me. He's what me and my girlfriends call a looker. You know, square jaw, cheekbones, long lashes over come-to-bed eyes. I've seen his face before. Very recently. But where? Where? Of course! He was the concerned man with Traci last night on the balcony.

He strolls over to me. 'The name's William. I'm the lead learning mentor at the school. You might know me as Billy-Bob.' He sees my astonishment and laughs.

Traci's delinquent son? No bloody way! How can he have morphed into this cool, good-looking professional dude?

'Fancy a drink?'

I could do with one. 'Yeah, why not?'

When we leave the school, in the playground I glance back. Miss Swan and Beryl Spencer are standing at the window of her office, watching me go. Beryl stands in the front, Clare Swan at her back in a strange reversal of their power roles, making it appear that Beryl's the one in charge. They're so still, they barely appear alive.

◆ ◆ ◆

'You were a nightmare.' I don't hold back telling William what his behaviour had been like when I'd originally lived on the Rosebridge with Sara-Jane.

We're sitting opposite each other inside The Hangman's Retreat, the most popular pub in the area. Packed with many local faces from the Rosebridge. I try to keep mine down; I don't want any trouble.

It feels good to have a moment to take my mind off things. Only now do I realise how tense I've been, running on empty, searching for the truth.

William winces slightly. 'Nightmare? More like an X-rated horror show.'

And, boy, wasn't that the truth. Even though his mum was my close friend I made a deliberate decision back then not to poke my nose in her private business, especially about her eldest son. Then again, God knows I didn't need to, I heard enough of the trials and tribulations through our shared wall. The arguments. Smashing furniture. Traci's hoarse, gut-wrenching pleas for her boy to reform his ways. Her interactions with Billy-Bob, as most people called him back then, were some of the only times I ever heard Traci on the verge of breaking down. She was the problem-solver on the estate, the one to do battle on behalf of those who couldn't, so appearing tough and unshakeable was essential. Looking back, having to wear that armour most of the time must've been a hell of a burden.

After licking the residue of my lemonade from my lips, I ask, 'How did you manage to come good?'

He leans forward, expression serious, hand cupping his Coke. 'Most people were wrong, you know. I was never off my face on drugs. It was always the demon drink with me. Got a taste for it to help deal with life. And, I tell you this much, when it got its fangs in me I needed the strength of a hundred men to get it to let go.'

With a shake of his head, he adds, 'If it wasn't for Mum standing by me, even after all the grief I gave her, I don't know where I'd be. I've got my own place but I make sure I check on her every chance I get, especially since Dad passed away.'

I tell him something I've never told anyone else. There's something about William I find comforting. Easy to confide in.

'After I left . . . and Sara-Jane . . . Well, the only way I coped was to fall head-first into a bottle or two of hard stuff every night. Oblivion. No need to think. All my troubles gone away for a time.' I shake my head. The grief's got a hold of me again. 'I had all this emotional scarring inside me that just kept getting worse and worse. I didn't know what services I should call to help me. So self-medicating with booze was what I reached for.'

William puts his hand over mine. The consoling warmth of his skin is what I need right now. 'How did you stop drinking?' he asks.

'Most people would be telling you some kinda hallelujah moment, a lifechanging event that made them see the error of their ways,' I answer. 'Truth is, I thought I saw Sara-Jane one day. I won't bore you with the details, but I finally figured out that making a new life didn't mean giving up on my darling daughter.'

'If that's true, why did you come back? Even if you thought the body at the school was Sara-Jay's, you didn't need to physically return. You could've contacted the police any number of ways.'

Sara-Jay. He'd always called her that. If he saw her on the estate he'd call out, 'Sara-Jay.' My daughter really liked that. Liked him. She was about the only person on the Rosebridge who did.

My phone pinging interrupts my answer. I check it out. Text message:

We can find out what happened to Sara-Jane together. Heather

I nearly scream. That journalist has been driving me nuts, texting what feels like every hour on the hour. She just won't take no for an answer.

I give William and his query all my attention. 'It's the first real lead that there's been in Sara-Jane's abduction. I've never given up hope of finding her. This time, that might happen.'

'You think who they found at the school is Sara-Jay?'

The rest of the words were like stones clogging my throat. I switch the conversation. 'I heard that you went to work for Dale Prentice for a time.'

He double-blinks, as if trying to shoo away the shame from his past, and expertly switches our talk with a question that puts me off-centre. 'Have you come back to punish yourself?'

'What?' I'm flustered. 'I came back to—'

'I mean, back on the Rosebridge. Why go back to that flat with all its memories of you and Sara-Jane? You probably live in a huge house somewhere, so why not go back there every night? Or book a hotel with cosy bedsheets and towels?'

Punish myself? Is he right? Did I return to my home with Sara-Jane because the feelings of shame and guilt have drawn me back there? Or am I trying to create a second chance to protect her?

Seeing my inner turmoil, William gently adds, 'Guilt is a powerful emotion. Dangerous. The things we do in the past have the power to destroy us in the present.'

I don't get the chance to respond because a man walks into the pub and catches William's eye. He's about mine and William's age, somewhere between thirty-five and forty. They nod to each other. He's another face from the past on the Rosebridge. Who is he? It eludes me. But his appearance opens the floodgates of other customers in the pub acknowledging William's presence.

'William, you alright, mate?'

Huge smile flashing on his face he answers back, 'Richie, I'm all good. As is that lad of yours.'

'It's all down to you, William, for all the support you gave him.'

This is almost a replay of when we walked into the pub, people greeting William with affection and gratitude. It's obvious that he's hugely respected. He's moved from scum of the earth to pillar of the community. I am glad for him. And his mother.

'What the fuck is she doing here?' The nasty question comes out of nowhere, taking us both by surprise.

'Isn't she the mum of that poor kid who disappeared?'

'Came knocking on my door last night like some nutcase,' someone else chucks in, 'raving about how someone had stuffed a pair of socks belonging to that poor girl – bless her soul – through her letterbox. Pure BS if you ask me.'

'The nerve of her showing her face here again.'

I see the outrage wash over William's features. He tries to reassure me. 'They might not look it, but this is a caring community.'

'That didn't stop them from doing what they did to me.'

Suddenly he puts his palms on the table and I know what he's about to do. Rise. Rise on my behalf. Start tearing a strip off this lot for taking pot shots at me. But I don't need him to do that. I do my own rising these days. Sure, back in the day, unconfident, shy Gem Casey would've been grateful for someone to fight her battles. Not now. I don't need a knight in shining armour to save the day – although I'll admit William was polished up the way I like my men.

I stand to my full height before William can. My bold gaze sweeps the room, taking in every last one of those attempting to nail me to a cross.

Every word rings clear so this lot have got it through their thick heads. 'You can like me. Don't like me. I don't give a monkey's whether you do or not. I'm not back here to make friends. My daughter vanished fifteen years ago and now a pile of bones has turned up in that school. I'll soon know whether they're hers or not.' I want to flinch, but don't. I can't show any sign of weakness.

'You know your kids. You know their clothes. You know what they like to wear,' I carry on, pulling the socks from my bag. 'These were my Sara-Jane's. This one's got a hole in the heel. She hated them. Last night, the monster who abducted her' – abducted: that gets an audible gasp in the air. Good! I need them to understand this is real life. My life – 'dumped them, like crap, through my letterbox. Sara-Jane went to school wearing those socks. I never saw her again.'

My gaze does another sweep. 'If you have any information, you know where to find me.'

Head held high, I walk to the door. William follows me and at the threshold he does something I will forever be grateful for. 'If anyone knows who put those socks through Gem's door you come to me. None of us should be sleeping easy in our beds at night, because there's someone among us who may be a child killer.'

Chapter 12

The Girls

The girls ran as if their lives depended on it. They were in big trouble. Sara-Jane knew it. Abby knew it. If they didn't get back to school soon the odds on them being caught were high. They had broken the cardinal rule today. Never sneak out of school for longer than ten minutes. Their secret trips outside school had all started a month back when Abby had dragged Sara-Jane to the chapel and shown her a secret passageway beneath the computer desk that led out into the street near the market.

Sara-Jane didn't like it in the chapel. The angels on the stained-glass windows gave her the creeps. Especially the one with the large white wings and a face with no features. Sometimes she saw the faceless angel in her dreams.

Sara-Jane knew her mum would hit the roof if she found out she was hanging with Abby. After the strangling incident her mum had warned her to stay away from the other girl. But she didn't want to. Her friend was fun! Smart too. Because Sara-Jane was bigger and taller, most people assumed that it was her who was the troublemaker leading Abby astray. In fact it was the opposite. The smaller girl had a strong will and a mind full of mischief-making.

They sneaked out to get the broken biscuits on the stall with the kind lady who gave the biscuits to them for free. The Jammie Dodgers, that's why they were so late. Instead of the usual gingernuts she gave them, the woman had treated them to the most mouth-watering Jammie Dodgers. Biscuits with heart-shaped holes in the middle filled with a layer of yummy strawberry jam and cream. Sara-Jane was still licking the crumbs from her mouth and braces as they rushed through the street.

They couldn't run, because two primary school-aged girls sprinting in the street were bound to attract too much attention. People would notice them and start to ask questions.

Shops whizzing by, Sara-Jane held her friend's hand tight to make sure the other girl kept pace with her. Her heart banged against her chest with anxiety. If her mum found out she'd been sneaking out of school there was going to be all hell to pay. What distressed the little girl the most was the thought that she would be bringing more trouble to her mum's door. What if the police turned up again?

Sara-Jane didn't know why the police had come, but she did remember hearing her mother crying in the night. The sound had twisted Sara-Jane's heart and made her curl her legs tight to her chest.

Sara-Jane said, 'I think we might have to run.'

'No.' Abby was determined. 'We're almost there.'

'What if we get caught?' The terrifying question made Sara-Jane's heart skip a beat.

'I'll think of something.'

That's what Sara-Jane liked about Abby – she was brainy. She would think of a way to get them out of this. But Sara-Jane did foresee one problem.

'What about your mum?' Sara-Jane had never told her friend that she thought her mum, Mrs Prentice, marched around the school as if she owned it. A right bossyboots.

Abby's small fingers tightened in her palm. 'She'll believe me. Leave my mother to me.'

They swung into the street that connected to the alley. The one that led to the door that would take them back into the chapel. Now they started to run. Motor forward. The noise of the traffic on the neighbouring road sounded closer than usual. They took no notice as they ran. And ran. And . . .

Abby's terrifying scream pierced the air. The suddenness of it was like a fire alarm disturbing the quiet of the street. At first Sara-Jane didn't register what was going on. Why would Abby be screaming? her confused mind asked. It made Sara-Jane lose her footing and go crashing into the wall. She gasped with pain.

Abby screamed again.

This time it resembled the sound of an animal caught in a trap.

What was going on? What was happening?

Sara-Jane pushed off the wall and what she saw made her stumble back with gut-wrenching fear. Someone was holding Abby off the ground in a tight bear hug. They were swinging her around like she was a toy. Sara-Jane couldn't see their face because it was covered with a balaclava. They looked like a monster. Behind them were the open doors of a van. Now Sara-Jane realised why the traffic had sounded so close today; someone had driven a van down the street behind them.

Sara-Jane was frozen in shock. Her heart was beating so fast now she thought it was going to explode. What was happening?

Why was the masked person doing this to Abby? Oh God, the man was trying to drag her into the van.

Sara-Jane remembered what her mum had told her: 'There are creepy men out there who want to do harm to little girls. Anyone touches you, you scream and scream until someone comes to help you.'

And that's what Sara-Jane did, started screaming with all the breath in her body. Then she launched herself forward, still screaming like a banshee.

'Let her go! Let her go!' She lunged at the man's side, punching and kicking and scratching.

'Stop it,' he growled.

The man tried to push her off, but Sara-Jane wouldn't stop. It only propelled her to fight even harder. Scream even louder. Pounding his arms, shouting out, 'Let her go, you bastard! Let her go!'

She kicked hard and cried out as pain blasted through her foot and leg. An arm wrapped with the deadly fierceness of barbed wire around Sara-Jane's waist and lifted her high. Petrified, she gasped in shock. There were two men, not one. The arm dug deep below her ribs. Desperately, she sucked and clawed at the air, trying to get oxygen into her lungs. Trying to breathe. The man who had Abby threw her into the van.

No! No! No!

The word went around Sara-Jane's head. *I've got to protect Abby!*

But it was too late. The last thing the little girl remembered was being flung into the van. Then her world went black and changed forever.

Chapter 13

With an almighty screech that will probably wake the dead, I plunge the shockingly sharp, serrated knife into the kitchen table. The power of the blow vibrates through my arm as it goes clean through the wood. The blade juts out and quivers. This weapon is a new purchase from an army surplus store, along with combat trousers and jacket. I'm no longer the passive mother of a daughter who was lost but never found. I'm an avenger now, dressed for battle. If the cops aren't prepared to help me, I'll have to do this myself.

Evening has turned into night. I take up position on a chair by the kitchen window. And wait. Wait for the vile monster who took Sara-Jane to return. It must be them who put her socks through my door. It has to be. Who else can it be?

I might not have all the answers, but I know this much: whoever my tormentor is, they'll be back. With something else of my girl's sooner or later. I know he will. That twisted mind of his won't be able to resist. And when he comes back he'll find a bird of prey, armed with claws, waiting for him.

Me.

If that means sitting here every night until he comes back, then so be it.

I pull the knife out and twiddle the blade between my fingers to pass the time and without meaning to draw blood from my finger. It drips down to my knuckles. I'm positioned near the line of the kitchen window which gives me an eagle eye on anyone passing.

As the time ticks by something that Wallace said also ticks over in my mind: *'You only went back there last night. How on earth would the killer have known you were there?'*

He's right. Whoever left Sara-Jane's socks knows I'm back on the Rosebridge. Erin, my second-in-command at work obviously knows I'm here – for business purposes – but who else did I tell?

Traci next door.

William aka Billy-Bob, her son.

Miss Swan. I told her my whereabouts before I left her office.

Beryl. Her boss is bound to have shared this information with her.

Detective Wallace – I know, silly of me to even put him on the list.

I can't imagine any of them being involved in my girl's disappearance. Then again, one thing I've learned over the years is that curve balls come at you from the most unexpected directions. What I can't figure out is motivation. Why would any of them do this?

Then there's the people on this estate. After the furious reception I got at the pub with William a few hours ago, it will be common knowledge that I'm back. When I fled from here fifteen years ago, I left behind plenty of enemies.

The time ticks away.

Nine o'clock.

Ten.

Eleven.

There are footsteps outside. I tense. My fingers twitch around the knife. They pause outside Traci's. My breath catches. They move on. A shadow flickers across the window. Stops by the front door.

It's him. It must be.

Leaving my post, on silent feet I move to the door and hover behind it. One hand reaches for the lock, the other holds up the knife ready to pounce. Attack. My breath comes in short shallow bursts. But the footsteps move on, with a knock on a neighbour's door.

Back at my post, for the first time it occurs to me that perhaps this is a waste of time. A fool's errand to make me feel like I'm doing something. That fog of depression comes over me again. I've gone from hope to hopelessness. That's how it's always been, looking for Sara-Jane. This constant violent swinging from one extreme to the other. Slowly it's cracking me up. I can't keep doing this. Just can't.

As if mocking me, I hear the click-click of heels coming down the balcony. A darkened figure passes by the window and keeps going, the sound of their feet fading into the distance.

Right! That's it. This is crazy! I glance down at the knife in my lap, which seems to have grown even larger. What the hell am I doing? Sighing, I get up and leave the knife on the kitchen table.

Click.

Click.

Click.

The footsteps are back. Stop outside my door. I rush into the hallway. Throw open the door. A dark-clad, hooded figure is standing there with a fist raised. Hell, I've left the knife in the kitchen. I punch the side of their head with all the pent-up fury of the past fifteen years. The person topples backwards against the balcony wall. I snatch their hood off. And curse a blue streak.

It's that damn young journalist who took me by surprise at the school. Who wouldn't take no for an answer.

Heather Banks.

◆ ◆ ◆

'Did you have to hit me so hard?' She's a curious mix of sassy and terrified.

79

I grab the back of her hooded top and drag her protesting into the hallway. Slam the door shut. Switch the light on. Crouch down and begin searching through her pockets.

'Hey!' Her outraged hand tries to slap me away.

But I'm like a fly that won't go. I keep searching, my intent being to see if she's carrying anything of Sara-Jane's that she was about to put through my letterbox. The lemon perfume I noticed she wore the only other time we met is strong. Obviously, she likes it.

Purse. Notebook. Pen. Phone. Nothing else.

Shoving my face close to hers, I demand, 'Why are you here?'

She sits up and shuffles back. 'Take it easy. I know you're upset, and I get that, but you need to calm down.'

Calm down? I crowd her space even more, the citrus perfume she wears stinging my nose. 'How did you know where to find me?'

'I work in a newspaper office. All it takes is a phone call here, a phone call there along with online trawling. I checked your house, your permanent address in London, and you weren't there. This flat is registered to your name. So I put two and two together. Not hard.'

She's got one of those know-it-all voices that grates on my nerves. Then again, what else do I expect from a journalist?

For the millionth time I snap, 'You're wasting your time.'

I move back, allowing her to get to her feet. Wincing, her fingertips gingerly touch her bruised head. I pack a mean right hook.

'All I'm doing is looking for information to add to what I already know,' she insists. 'So I can find out why your daughter was kidnapped.' Turning to the front door, she continues, 'I'm sorry to have troubled you and—'

'What do you already know?' Just like she knew about Sara-Jane needing stitches after she fell off her skateboard.

'This. That. The other.' Cagey. Closed. She's keeping her cards tight to her chest. Slowly she faces me.

'Like what?' I call her bluff. If she's stringing me along I'll probably deck her with a combination left-right this time. No one, especially a member of the journalism lowlife profession, has the right to take advantage of a grieving mother.

The seriousness of her stare captures and unsettles me. 'Abby Prentice thought that she knew one of her kidnappers.'

This new information blows me away. Lifts my heart with hope. Then crashes back down to earth as the doubt sets in, as it always does. That's the problem with hope, it's got a devastating flipside – pain.

'If that's true, why haven't the cops told me?' I hear the confusion and uncertainty in my question. Leaves me with the sensation of the ground shifting beneath my feet. 'They'd never withhold that type of information from me, Sara-Jane's mum.'

'Of course they wouldn't.' There's a deliberate pause. 'But what if they never knew about it? Were never told?'

I don't understand. How couldn't the cops know about it? That makes not an iota of sense. 'They were leading the investigation. They gathered all the relevant details.'

'May we?' Heather pointedly suggests, gesturing towards the living room.

I take her instead to the kitchen. Put the hunting knife away. Sit her down at the old kitchen table. Make her a coffee – milky, no sugar – while I perch near a glass of water.

I kickstart things off again. 'Two things you need to tell me. One: how did you discover this and verify it was true? Two: why didn't the police ever know?'

'That's technically three things.'

'What?'

'Never mind.' After a sip of her coffee, she carries on, a new eagerness in her delivery. 'All I can tell you is that I have a source that was close to the investigation. You can imagine how much paperwork the investigation generated and, sometimes, things get lost. Overlooked. Filed in the wrong place.'

Heather pushes her cup to the side so she can fold her arms on the table. 'When Abby came back there was mass confusion. My source informs me that Abby told someone that one of the kidnappers was familiar. Something about him. Or maybe *her*.'

'Her?' I shoot bolt upright. The legs of my chair scrape against the floor. 'Wasn't it men? One, two, three, no one knows quite how many. There was never mention of a woman.'

'I don't know why that was never fed back to you. It's probably a man – men – however, I think we should keep our options open.'

'*We?*' My gaze narrows, digging into her.

'I'll be straight with you.' *Yeah, that'll be a first for a journalist.* 'I'm an intern at *The Echo*. Which means I don't get paid despite working my tail off day and night. What I need is a big story to make sure that when my internship is up, they keep me on. That's how I came across Sara-Jane's story. I was touched by it.'

I scoff. A journalist with emotions? Don't make me laugh.

All at once her gaze blazes, the colour of her cheeks deepening with upset. 'I mean it. Sara-Jane would be a young woman now, probably near my age. I want to know what happened to her. Why Sara-Jane has never come home.' She looks me straight in the eye, leaving me on the brink of something I don't understand. Whatever it is, it shakes me up. 'Do you want to find out who took your daughter?'

'You know I do.'

'Then let's help each other.'

Her mouth eases into a small gentle smile. It transforms her, makes her look younger. More carefree.

I lean back. 'Explain.'

Heather takes a long lug of her coffee before clarifying. 'We pool our resources. Starsky and Hutch. Cagney and Lacey. I tap into my sources and the paper's very good relationship with the police, so I'll have access to some of the details of the cold case.'

Cold case. That makes me so mad. Sad. Hurt. My daughter was never cold. Sara-Jane was fiery, always hotly in pursuit, wanting to know more about life. Her heartbeat so warm and alive beating against my body when we hugged. When I kissed her softly at bedtime.

Heather leans across. Excitement crackles in the air around her. 'Think about it, Gem. Finally knowing what happened to your beautiful daughter.'

Finally knowing. Getting justice. That's all I'm living for.

'Where do we start?'

'We need to talk with Abby Prentice. I'll pursue that end of our investigation while you get as much info as possible from the two people who know her best.' She checks her notes again. 'Her mother, Laura Prentice, who's also a governor and on the PTA at Princess Isabel School. And her grandfather, Dale Prentice.'

Chapter 14

'Did your son and Sara-Jane's father know each other?'

That's the question I confront Dale with when he walks into the lounge of his house. Last night it finally came to me what was bothering me about the terrible disturbance Charlie created outside the school fifteen years ago, calling me an unfit mum for all the world to hear. What bothered me was the body language between Henry Prentice and Charlie. The way they laughed. Then I realised. It was the behaviour of people who knew each other.

Did Abby and Sara-Jane's dads know each other?

Henry Prentice and Charlie Fraser?

And does that have any bearing on the truth about Sara-Jane?

A few minutes earlier I was standing at the gate admiring Dale's home. It's a huge property but with that isolated cottage feel to it. The house is the centrepiece of a large expanse of land, which, if I remember rightly, also contains stables with horses. There's a lovely garden out front with carefully tended plants and a closely cropped, lush lawn. It even has red and yellow roses growing up around the front door. It's the house of someone who has money but doesn't want to show off about it.

I was surprised that the person who answered the door was Rosa, the young attractive woman who works with Beryl in the school office.

Her friendly wave ushering me inside, she tells me, 'Dale is a business friend.' Brows pleating she stops, mulling over what she's said. All at once her eyes spark with light. 'Not friend. I mean associate. A business associate of my father.' Ah, she's improving her English. 'Dale found summer work for me at the school and he kindly let me stay in his house with him.'

That sounds like Dale Prentice, no doubt making sure a young person like her understands the value of real hard work. Getting your hands dirty, that's what he believes in.

She shares a bright smile with me. 'I will fetch . . . That is the right word? He is out back.'

I'm left in a drawing room. It doesn't take long for me to find the focus of this room. Photos of Dale's granddaughter, Abigail.

Abby smiling during school assembly. Abby in her riding gear sitting straight on one of the smaller horses from her granddad's stable. Abby making sand castles on a beach. In the past that child always left me with a strange sensation, a chill that I couldn't shake off. I wait for it to come over me now as I look at her. It doesn't happen. All I see in those pictures is a young girl having a great life. There's something else missing from these photos. None of them appear to have been taken after the day Abby and Sara-Jane were abducted. In this picture gallery, a red line seems to have been drawn under that day.

'Gem. I heard you were in town. It's taken you a while to come see me.' Dale greets me with that distinctive authoritative voice of his as he steps into the room.

Dale Prentice isn't letting age get in the way of being vigorous and energetic about life. How old is he now? Knocking his late sixties, early seventies. He's tanned, which suggests he's just come back from his business and house he has in Italy. Which will explain Rosa's presence and how he knows her father. He doesn't avoid my knowing gaze, but instead stares at me head-on, a reminder that he might be living the soft life but he came up the hard way.

'Did your son know my Sara-Jane's dad, Charlie Fraser?'

'Charlie Fraser? Charlie Fraser?' He looks down as he's thinking. 'No disrespect intended, but the thing I remember about him was he had a bad reputation. Wasn't good daddy material, in my opinion, for your Sara-Jane. As far as I know, he didn't cross paths with my son.' He looks at me curiously. 'Why?'

I shrug. 'Just a hunch I'm working on.'

He moves across the room to a gleaming glass drinks cabinet. 'What would you like? What's your poison?'

'Usually water.'

He turns back to me with a smile and waves us both to some comfy seats.

I confront him with another hunch, one I've had for years. 'I know what you did. I know it was you all those years ago.'

His brow lifts ever so slowly. 'Me? I've done a lot of things in my life, so which one are you referring to?'

'All those years ago I wouldn't have been able to set up my bike business if it wasn't for an anonymous benefactor who gave me a considerable start-up fund.'

He still won't look away from me. That's the kind of strength I want. He tells me, 'I didn't like the way you left all those years back. Didn't like what happened. You deserved a fresh start, and I made it my business to see that you got it.'

All kinds of emotions wash over me with the memories of being lost, isolated. That terrible sensation of feeling dead inside. 'Thank you. If it wasn't for your injection of cash, I don't know what I would have done.'

He crosses his legs in a casual way, his arm resting against the back of his seat. 'You would've gone on. That's what people like me and you from our backgrounds do. We go on. We get knocked down and we pick ourselves up.' He looks over my shoulder to one of the pictures of his granddaughter. 'She's such a lovely girl. Although, not having seen her for some time I wouldn't know how she's doing these days.'

'Why is that?'

A shadow passes across Dale's distinguished face as he stands. 'Why don't you come through and we'll have coffee.'

In the large kitchen is a woman who I assume is the house-keeper. She discreetly leaves us alone. I take a seat at the large wooden farmhouse-type table. Dale's silent while he makes our drinks. He seems much more tense.

I'm careful with what I say next. 'Has something happened between you and Abby?'

He places our mugs on the table and sits opposite me. 'I'm afraid I haven't seen much of her since the incident.' He uses the word *incident* to describe what happened. 'I fell out with her mother. She didn't want me to see Abby any more. I could've petitioned the courts, but I felt Abby had been through enough. That was pretty much the end of my relationship with my darling grandchild.'

The pain in his voice is hard to hear. Poor Dale. Everyone knew how much he adored his granddaughter.

I ask, 'Surely Abby's old enough now to decide for herself who she sees and talks to?'

He's mournful as he hugs his coffee. 'That depends on what Abby was brought up to believe about me and I doubt that was very good.'

It seems cruel to carry on this conversation, but something's not right here. 'Do you mind if I ask you how you fell out with her mother?'

Dale drinks slowly before answering, 'She blamed me for the incident.' He hurriedly adds, 'Not for the actual abduction, obviously, even Laura isn't that mad. She was convinced that when Abby came to visit me, I encouraged her to break rules and be disobedient.' He shakes his head and asks in despair, as if to no one in particular, 'Have you ever heard anything so ridiculous?'

'She blamed me as well. She thought that Sara-Jane led Abigail astray and that was my fault for being a bad mother.'

His age suddenly shows. 'Laura blamed the school for the girls sneaking out, that was on Clare Swan and Beryl Spencer. She blamed the police for not catching the kidnappers. The child psychologists for being unable to make Abby the same as she was before. I have to remember Laura was a mother who was traumatised. Can you imagine someone trying to abduct your child?' Dale swears, realising what he's said. 'I'm sorry, I didn't mean—'

'Do you think the human remains found at the school are Sara-Jane?' The words feel like jagged glass in the back of my throat.

He looks at me without catching my eye. 'Gem, I can't tell you how sorry I am about what's been found at the school. The body could be anybody. Who knows how long it's been there for? I was down on the coast the day when it all happened. I was so upset I had to catch a train home. I couldn't drive.'

There's heat in his voice now as he continues. 'Can you believe that the police interviewed me for five hours when Sara-Jane and Abby were taken? As if I would have anything to do with the abduction of my only grandkid and her friend.'

I know. Crazy. Dale of all people. The police should've been using their resources more wisely.

'If the victim in the school chapel turns out to be my little girl, at least I'll be able to mourn her properly.' I look sharply at him, my eyes dark with determination. 'But I tell you this for nothing, Dale, after I lay my beautiful Sara-Jane to rest there won't be any rest for me. I won't stop until I find the evil brute who did this.'

With the back of his hand, Dale shifts his cup to the side and then stares at me. His gaze is like steel, not stern exactly, more like how a father would look at his child. 'Do you know why I gave you that money?' He's not looking for me to answer. 'So that your life doesn't become consumed by hate. You wake up eaten up by hate. You go to bed at night eaten up by hate. Whoever took Sara-Jane, I wasn't going to allow them to take you as well.'

I know what he's asking me to do. Forget it. Move on. How can I?

'Dale, I've got a hole right here.' My palm rests over my pounding heart. 'Success can't fill it. Money can't fill it. Love can't fill it. Only that bastard-devil who took Sara-Jane being put behind bars for life will make me whole again. I'm going to do everything in my power to see that happen. That's why I need to ask you something. That's why I've come to see you.'

'Anything.' He doesn't hesitate.

'Could you arrange for me to speak to Laura? I know that's probably a long shot since you don't have much of a relationship. Every time I've seen her, she blanks me, won't speak to me.'

His jaw clenches. He knocks back the dregs of his coffee. 'I'll contact her for you, Gem. I wouldn't do it for anyone else. I'm probably wasting my time, though. I can bet you a hundred quid she won't speak with me.'

At the front door I remind Dale, 'As soon as you make contact with Abby's mum, let me know. Even if she doesn't agree to see me, I need to know.'

He stands on the doorstep until I'm almost at the gate. With a wave, Dale closes the door behind him. Turning, something catches my side-eye. The door to the sizeable garage is half-closed but there's a vehicle visible. There's no sign of Dale at the windows, so I retrace my steps and peer into the garage. A black van is parked inside. It jogs a recent memory.

The black van near the school. But after seeing Charlie in a black van I'd assumed it was him. And Dale has just told me he was on the coast that day. Does the black van I saw at the school belong to Charlie or Dale?

I look closer at the van and realise that it's a dark navy blue.

My blood runs cold when I think about vans. Because that's what was used to kidnap the girls.

A black van.

Chapter 15

Fifteen Years Ago

15.875 mm

Sara-Jane is missing.

The words revolved to the frenzied rhythm of Gem's wheels as she pedalled like a woman possessed through the streets towards the school. She was numb to the burning sensation of her calf muscles about ready to rip through her legs, the pressure on her backbone as she hunched over her bike. She was in a state of crippling shock. A parent's worst nightmare.

Gem had been serving a customer in the café when she felt her phone vibrate inside her pocket. Employees' phones were a no-no on the shop floor. Gem disregarded that rule because being a mother, a single parent, meant she needed to be available twenty-four-seven concerning her child. Sara-Jane always came first. Placing the order quickly, she had gone into the cramped staff toilets. When she saw the number on the screen was the school, Gem had groaned, slumping back against the wall. The last thing she needed was another 'Your child tried to do this 'n' that to the lady of the manor's kid' meeting. Sara-Jane was under strict instructions to keep her head down and work hard.

And stay away from Abigail Prentice. Well away.

Oh hell, unless it was Charlie again? *Please, please, don't let it be anything to do with Sara-Jane's dad.*

'You need to come to the school. Now,' Beryl had informed her. The other woman's tone had sounded odd. The air inside Gem's chest had squeezed.

'What's happened?'

She could hear muffled, quick-talking voices in the background at the school. Then it was Miss Swan speaking to her on the phone. 'Sara-Jane has gone missing.'

Gem went cold all over. 'What do you mean? Missing? She can't be, I dropped her off myself this morning.' Her voice sounded as if it were under water.

Gem remembered the little tiff they'd had about the socks. She also recalled not having the luxury of spending a minute longer watching Sara-Jane walk deeper into the playground because she had to get to work. Sometimes she hated being a single parent who had to graft all hours to make ends meet.

Gem stammered, 'I don't understand.'

'Miss Casey, please come to the school. Right away.'

Her boss had been hacked off she had to go. Well, stuff him!

Gem was so locked in her thoughts she didn't see the car as she turned the corner. The bike wobbled as she swerved just in time.

The angry driver yelled, 'Bikes shouldn't be allowed on the road. Are you crazy, lady?'

No, she was not crazy. She was petrified. Scared to death by what awaited her at the school. Outside Princess Isabel School, the first thing she saw was the police car. She stumbled off her bike, leaving it to fall carelessly on the pavement. A noise banged inside her head. At the school, Beryl met her at the entrance. She wore an expression of cold fear.

'What happened? Where's Sara-Jane?' Gem asked the school office manager in quick succession.

The other woman nervously swallowed. 'Best to follow me, this way, please.'

They entered Beryl's office and hurried past the double photo frame on her desk, which had a lone daffodil in a small glass of water beside it today.

Gem froze on the threshold of the head teacher's office when she saw the police officers in the room. If the police were involved this was bad. Really bad. Clare Swan was present too, and someone else.

Laura Prentice.

Gem's heart sank with dismay. After the incident with Sara-Jane and Abby, Gem had made a point of staying out of her way. She didn't need any trouble and she sensed that Laura and her child were exactly that, trouble.

'What's happened?' She was paralyzed in the doorway. It was as if her legs wouldn't take her any further because Gem was so terrified by what they were going to tell her.

The head teacher got to her feet and, with the gentlest of care, drew her inside and got her sat down. The officers remained standing in the background.

Miss Swan looked grave. 'Sara-Jane and Abigail Prentice did not return to their lessons after lunch. We've searched the school grounds and can't find them.'

Abigail Prentice? Oh, Sara-Jane! I told you to stay well clear of that girl.

The banging in Gem's head got worse. 'I don't understand. Where could they be?'

One of the officers, who was female, sat next to her. 'We are looking for them right now. Can you think of anywhere that Sara-Jane might go?'

Gem's mind went round trying to think of places. 'My Sara-Jane knows better than to leave the school premises. She doesn't go anywhere on her own, I'm always with her.'

Laura Prentice interrupted, that cut-glass accent of hers resembling the screech of nails down a blackboard. Her red scarf, usually around her neck, was draped over her legs. 'They must be somewhere on *that place*, the estate you live on. Maybe she took Abby on an adventure to show her things she has never seen in her life. Like where the drug dealers peddle their trade and women of the night sell their flesh.'

Gem stretched her neck. She didn't care about anyone insulting her, she was a grown-up and could take it on the chin. But start on her Sara-Jane and the other person better be gloved-up ready for a fight. 'I don't know anything about any drug dealers. Or criminals. Or bogeymen.' How dare she! And at a time like this. Gem turned her full startled attention to Miss Swan. 'How did they manage to get out of the school?'

'They don't know.' It was Laura who supplied the answer. For the first time Gem registered how terrible she looked. All that professional armour couldn't hide the waxwork texture of her face, the intense redness in the bottom of her eyes. 'The school is still investigating that. I have every confidence that the police will find them.'

The officer asked, 'Is there any chance that Sara-Jane could have taken them to her father? We have a record of there being an incident with him outside the school. Didn't he try to take Sara-Jane?'

'He's long gone.' And he was. She'd got Charlie's blood money for him, leaving her once again up to her eyeballs in debt. He wouldn't show up for another couple of years. 'And I'm glad of it because he's a bad sort who's probably already found his allotted place in hell.'

Was that a scoff she heard from Abby's mother?

The static of the police officer's radio came on, so she excused herself and got up.

While she was gone Laura Prentice looked over at Gem. 'When your daughter and *the others* joined the school I considered taking Abby out of Princess Isabel and placing her in a private school.'

The others. Made the children from the Rosebridge sound like aliens from another galaxy. That really upset Gem. She'd had enough of this woman sticking needles in her open wound. 'My daughter and all the other girls and boys are just as clever as your child. I'll tell you what the difference is? You happen to have a load more cash in your pocket. Your money doesn't make your kid any better than mine. More intelligent than mine.'

Disdain pulled down the corner of the other woman's mouth. 'This isn't about money. It's about polish. That isn't something you find in the 99p shop, it's something that you're born with.'

Polish? More like poison.

Both mothers stared daggers at each other. Gem looked away first. And made a decision. When Sara-Jane was found she was taking her out of Princess Isabel and placing her in another school.

'Ladies, please.' Miss Swan's taut gaze shifted from one mother to the other, trying to calm the tension. 'The only thing that is important is finding Sara-Jane and Abigail.'

When the police officer came back, one look at the grimness of her features made Gem's nails dig into the arm of the chair.

The officer told them, 'Two girls matching Sara-Jane and Abigail's description were seen in the vicinity of the market. Screaming was heard. A few minutes after, a van was seen leaving the corner of Stroud Road and Glass Alley at speed.' She paused, before adding, 'It was a black van.'

Screaming.

A black van.

A black van.

Suffocating with bloodcurdling horror, Gem's world fell apart.

Chapter 16

It's late when I get back to the flat, although there's no sense of time in my head any more. I only know it's night because of the darkness outside and the dark is one thing that is revolving around my head all the time now. In an armchair, all my limbs are crushed and limp. Soon a half-sleep tugs me under and my eyelids droop. That blurry no-man's-land of the sleep world where you're not sure what's real or not.

When the letterbox rattles, it's not real. But the running feet out on the balcony, that's real. He's back. My tormentor. The man who took Sara-Jane. With something else that was my daughter's and he's put it through my letterbox and caught me cold.

In a righteous fury, I jump to my feet and hurry towards the front door, but I tumble over my bike parked in the hallway. What he's dumped through the letterbox this time lies on the bare ground. I ignore it. Make a decision.

I'm going after him.

I'm at a disadvantage because time has already marched on. I clamber over my fallen bike. Throw the front door back. Silence. The footsteps have already vanished.

Damn! Damn! Bloody damn! My fist thumps the door in raging frustration. And that's when I see it again.

My bike.

I don't think, just do. Lunge for it, scramble on board and pedal along the balcony in pursuit. The steep stairwell yawns before me. I don't hesitate. I ride and clatter right on down, every step jarring and bumping my backside and spine. My arm scrapes a wall as I turn, but my bike and I keep going. Even when I narrowly miss a man coming up the stairs who barks abuse after me, I keep going. Out through the arch on the ground floor and into the courtyard outside. I keep going.

Lucky for me the moon is bright tonight, so I see HIM. Running out on to the street. He's dressed in black baggy clothes with a hood, black gloves and a ski mask. Even his pumps are black. He's the picture of a demon risen from hell.

For a moment, a few seconds, he stops. Glances backwards.

Fatal error. Big mistake. I'm going to take you down.

'You're dead!' The cold wind buffers my bellow of revenge.

His body jerks with surprise. Ah, he wasn't expecting me to come after him. He stumbles sideways as if he's lost his rhythm. Now it's him at a disadvantage. I'm on a sleek new bicycle now and he isn't. My feet hit the pedals. He starts running. I swoop across the yard and out on to the street. Up ahead he runs and runs, searching for an escape route. I'm getting closer. Closer.

Abruptly, he changes tack and ducks and weaves between cars. He's using a route that he thinks my bike can't follow. I keep motoring forward. He doubles back. So do I. We're not going anywhere, us two. We've got time. Soon we are parallel to each other, a row of parked cars between us.

Voice breathless, I demand, 'Who are you?'

Silence. I know the animal can hear me.

'What did you do with Sara-Jane?'

Silence again.

'Where is Sara-Jane?'

Nothing.

'Did you fucking murder my daughter?'

I scream the words I've never allowed myself to say aloud. That have been buried somewhere deep and forbidden inside me. For fifteen years. Fifteen years I've tortured myself with the unthinkable. That Sara-Jane's dead. Dead.

My anger is ferocious now. 'I'm going to fucking rip you apart.'

He makes a break for it in a full sprint. But there's nowhere for him to go. Either side are blocks of flats fronted by patches of grass. The street is lined with cars that he can't hide behind because I'm too close. He's trapped like the filthy rat he is.

He keeps going.

So do I.

Wish I had one of my electric bikes.

I motor up the boot of an abandoned Volkswagen Beetle. On to the roof. Glide and skid down the front. Hit ground level. Pedal like a person possessed.

I'm gaining on him.

Gaining.

I place one foot on the saddle, leave my other dangling behind and lean forward on the handlebars like a ballet dancer. 'Did you bury Sara-Jane in the school?'

I use all my leg power to accelerate up a plank leaning on the ground out of a rubbish skip. I leap over to the other side. For a moment I'm suspended. In the air. High up. Untouchable. Finally, I'm going to catch the monster who took Sara-Jane.

I land on the other side of the skip. Hard. My backside and poor bike jar and rattle badly. I don't care. Pain no longer matters.

He's running like a hunted animal, head darting from one side to the other in a hopeless attempt to find a way of escape. I jump the kerb and ride alongside him. He about turns. Zigzagging between the cars again. Slamming on my back brakes, I reverse in one smooth move. Belt after him down the street. His whole body vibrates with fear.

Now he's scared.

Knows what it's like to have someone bigger and tougher chasing him down.

Knows what Sara-Jane felt when he snatched her.

I pull up behind him and pull a wheelie, close enough to push him on the back with my front wheel. 'You had enough yet? Why don't you stop running?'

Up ahead, the road gives way to a patch of waste ground, covered in litter, overturned bins and a fly-tipped fridge and cooker. Beyond that is a railway embankment. That's OK, he'll have my hands around his neck before he reaches that. But only at the last moment when he throws himself against a wire fence and tries to climb it, only then does it strike me in a moment of horror that he might escape.

Furiously, I mount the pavement and fly over the waste ground. The railway embankment looms large up ahead, bathed in foggy, blurred light. The mouth of its Victorian arch resembles the ghostly opening to a haunted house. If he gets over the other side of the fence, he's gone. I can't let that happen.

Sara-Jane, I won't let you down again.

My body balloons with a massive, deep breath. I open the gears. Steer my very soul into my legs and hurtle towards him.

Nearly there.

Nearly there.

I'm so close I can almost smell him. We collide as he's halfway up the fence. The crash throws me over the handlebars, spinning into the air. Bang! I hit the ground on my back. He tumbles over and over like an acrobat before coming to rest on his side.

Get up. You need to get up.

But I can't move. I watch him struggle to his feet.

No! No! No!

He throws himself on to the fence again and slogs his way up it and falls over the other side, struggling up the embankment, falling backwards, righting himself and then grappling his way to the top. Finally, I move. Get up. Follow, but my sore leg muscles won't play ball.

He's getting away. I had him and he's getting away.

No amount of pain will stop me climbing that fence. No amount of pain, and it's terrible. At the top of the embankment, there's no sign of the black-clad devil. In either direction are the rail tracks but he won't have gone down there unless he wants to be electrocuted or hit by a train. Anyway, it's lit up and I could see him. When I turn back, I've got a good view of the road that leads back to the Rosebridge. And that's when I see him, he's doubled back, gone over the fence again and taken his place at a bus stop, waiting for a bus, which is just pulling in. As bold as brass he gets on the bus. The bus pulls out on to the street and drives off.

I had him.

I had him.

And he got away.

Chapter 17

'Gem?'

The alarmed, slightly uncertain voice belongs to William, Traci's reformed son. The bike chase has left me winded. The damp night sticks to my body. My legs were throbbing so much there was no chance of my riding the short distance home. Leaning on the saddle, I've stumbled and scooted my way back to the estate in the night. I don't want him to see me like this. Defeated. A mother who can't protect her child. I try to hide my face – and burning shame – in the shadows.

Take the hint and leave me alone. Of course William doesn't.

'What's going on?' His alert gaze runs over exhausted me and my bike, trying to work out the answer to his question.

'Will you take my bike and get it upstairs for me?'

I'm in a muddle, my head's a mess and the last thing I want to do is talk. Plus I need to work stuff out. Work out who might be doing this to me. At least I know it's not William because he couldn't get on a bus and be here at the same time. Once we reach my flat, he can't help but notice that the door is open.

I take my bike from him and head inside. 'Thanks.'

He stares at me, desire written on his handsome face. I stare right back. Any other night I'd invite him in and see what happens.

Close my eyes and maybe allow his lovemaking to take the pain away. For a time at least.

William steps away from my door. 'I'm next door with Mum tonight. If you need anything you know where to find me.'

I close the door and slump back on it. Once my composure's back I rest the bike against the wall. And then I look down. At what that bastard dropped through my door. It's a pair of small glasses. They're Sara-Jane's. There's a length of decaying plaster around one of the arms. The plaster is distinctive because it has a picture of Wonder Woman on it. I mended the glasses with that plaster because I couldn't afford to get them professionally fixed.

I sit in the main room and place my daughter's glasses in my lap. Why would anyone want to torment me like this? Wasn't stealing my kid enough? Who knows I'm in this flat?

Again I run through names of the people who know I'm here:

William? I dismiss him. Unless he's a modern-day Houdini, there's no way he could've both been on a bus and helping me just now.

Traci? Stop being ridiculous. Then again, I recall what she said to me: '*You should not have come back.*' Is she trying to merely look out for me or is she warning me? But warning me about what? No . . . No! If Traci had information that could help, she would tell me. She was the one true friend I had back then.

Dale? I didn't tell him I was back living here, but he would know. Dale knows everything that's going on. My mind flashes back to the naked adoration written all over his face as he stared lovingly at his granddaughter's picture. Plus, Dale might be fit and healthy for his age, but no way does he have the vigour of the person I chased.

What about that bastard Charlie? His black van is like the one that took the girls. Is he only back here for money, like he says he is? Or is there another reason for his unwanted presence? Why was he so chummy with Abby's dad all those years ago? Or was that my imagination seeing things that were not really there?

Laura Prentice? Abby's mother. OK, she still hates my guts and won't tell me where her daughter is. Still, she would remember what it felt like to be a grieving mother, so she must have some sympathy for me, however tiny that might be.

Clare Swan and Beryl Spencer? Both are devoted to Princess Isabel School. Miss Swan remains devastated about what happened.

I scrub my hand over my face with frustration. Then I pick up Sara-Jane's glasses, my lust for revenge back with a vengeance as I stare at them. Unbearable sorrow shatters my heart. You see, they look different to the last time I saw her wearing them.

One of the lenses is cracked.

The next morning I hover outside the police station. Sara-Jane's cracked glasses are in my hand. Last night, I tossed and turned about whether to come here to show Wallace what has been shoved through my door this time. But let's face it, he didn't lift a finger to help me before. So what the hell am I doing back here? *You're here because this is right for Sara-Jane. Anything for Sara-Jane. Remember.*

There might be DNA on the glasses.

'We've got a backlog of evidence that needs testing from other cases. We can't justify testing these socks with our limited resources.' That had been the detective's response to me about DNA the last time. And when I pressed him, what did he do? He rubbed my past mistakes and trauma in my grieving face.

I'm wasting my time.

As I'm about to mount my bike my phone rings. Heather.

She tells me, 'Abby is apparently away at college or uni or something. Anyway, she's studying.'

'Where's she studying?'

'That I can't seem to pin down.'

I frown. Hard. 'Shouldn't that be relatively easy for you to find out as a journalist? You must have all kinds of contacts and access to databases. The internet.'

Heather sighs, short and annoyed. 'I never claimed to be a magician. Abracadabra is not my middle name.'

Oops! I've pissed her royally off. The last thing I want to do is alienate the one ally I have.

So, I probe, with tiptoeing care, 'Did you ask around locally about Abby?'

'People clam up when I mention her name. Probably too scared of her mother.' Her tone shifts and changes. 'Give me the headlines about what Dale Prentice told you.'

'I gave you a heads-up last night.'

'Double-checking in case you remember something else. We need to dig around more about Abby.'

Heather's right. It's time to stop waiting and push forward. 'I'm going to drop in on Laura.'

'Unannounced?' She's surprised.

'We won't know if I don't try.'

I end the call and swing on to my bike.

Chapter 18

Raised voices. Two of them pitted against each other. An argument. That's what I hear coming from inside Laura Prentice's house as I ride up to her driveway. It disturbs the peace of the South Side. It's usually so still. So quiet. A place where birds come to sing. It's the other side of the school, where all the families worth gazillions live. The South Side isn't its real name. It's the tongue-in-cheek nickname residents of the Rosebridge have gleefully given it because so often 'South Side' means the bad part of a town.

Where Abby's mother lives is known as Croydon Hill and it has breathtaking views. Back in the day, I'd come up here on my bike to ride the hill. The houses here are not just tall and wide. Carve one of these up and four families from the estate could easily live here with space to spare. They curve together in a half-moon shape. Sniff hard enough and you can almost smell the stench of money in the air. Inside those houses they're all probably doing yoga before proceeding to afternoon tea while the rest of us are grafting, trying to earn a crust. Although, admittedly, I could retire tomorrow if I wanted. Still, I can't help remembering what it was like being a working mum pinching pennies, bone weary after working every hour I could find. Despite all the money I've earned I've never splashed out on anything big. My London three-bedroom is good enough for me, a guest who comes to stay and a room for Sara-Jane when she comes home.

Laura Prentice has the most prominent house at the end. Detached. Five storeys of white brick, twin black-railed balconies and an attic window that juts out on the roof. There's a floor below street level with black railings as if hiding what happens down there.

The voices get louder as I move down the driveway shadowed by enormous trees. I notice a man about my age clearing something along the side of the house. His face is familiar. I've seen him recently . . . Ah, yes, he silently greeted William in the pub, The Hangman's Retreat. Of course. It's Jaswinder Bedi. Everyone called him Jas. Back in the day he created merry hell with William in his Billy-Bob days on the Rosebridge.

Jas stands straights and stares at me. I give him a tentative wave. He doesn't wave back. How odd. Well, each to their own.

I turn my attention back to the front of the house. I'm surprised by the person I see with Abby's mother through the large front window. Miss Swan. Even from here I see how tense her body is, straining against her buttoned-up style. They look like Punch and Judy, on their feet, facing each other, arms moving to emphasise their words. The glass stops me hearing most of their argument, but I catch snatches of words.

'No . . . Can't . . . Police . . . Don't . . . Calm . . .'

I must've made a noise then, because both women turn my way and see me outside. I stand there, hands tense against my bike, feeling like a guilty child who's been caught with her very naughty hand in the cookie jar. They react in different ways to my presence. Miss Swan turns away and Laura Prentice stares hard at me. From her expression I know she's not going to let me in.

Straightening my back, I strengthen my resolve. This time I won't be put off. Even if she slams the door in my face I won't go until she speaks to me. And if that means me creating drama and putting on a show for her 'I'm way better than you' neighbours, then so be it.

But she blindsides me when she opens the door with a one-hundred-watt smile. That's not what I was expecting. Her body language screams open and friendly. 'Gem? I'm so glad that you came to see me. Please do come in.'

The door widens for me to come through. I hesitate like I'm about to step on a booby trap. Why is she being so nice? Maybe Dale spoke to her after all? Whatever the reason, it's a good thing that she's stopped playing hardball. Brushing off any lingering misgivings, I step in to a circular reception that captures the afternoon light streaming through the cleanest glass windows I've ever seen in my life and a polished marble floor. There are four open doors off the reception and she guides me through into a room that she probably calls a morning room. It's gorgeous, and I can't help sweeping my captivated gaze around every last bit of it. Pale blue dominates – the wallpaper over the grand fireplace, the sofas, the large rug over the hardwood floor. Don't they say that pale blue makes a room chilly? Well, this room is filled with warmth. So much so I could curl up by the fire and fall asleep.

My gaze halts abruptly on Miss Swan. She should fit right in here, but she looks out of place and uncomfortable. Although she nods at me, her gaze can barely meet mine. I want to ask her straight what they were arguing about. Do they know something about what happened to Sara-Jane which they are keeping from me?

With a nervous clearing of her throat – Miss Swan doesn't usually do nervous – she tells me, 'You must have seen my display of bad manners while you were outside. I'm sorry about that.' Her gaze flicks to Abby's mum. 'We were having an intense discussion about whether the school should approach the police with a view to reopening.'

'Which I am completely against.' Laura sweeps into the centre of the room. 'As a prominent member of the PTA, parents have told me that they do not want to send their children to a school that's an ongoing crime scene.' Prominent member? By all accounts, Laura still ran the association with an iron fist. Hadn't Traci told me that even the parent who was the director always seemed to defer to her?

Miss Swan answers, 'Nevertheless, the decision will be that of the governing body guided by my opinion. I do have a say in this.'

My gaze darts from one to the other. Something strange is going on here. What are these two women *really* crossing swords about?

Miss Swan picks up her bag. 'I need to get back to the school.' She gives me a warm smile. 'The invitation for you to come to my retirement celebration is still open.'

Then I'm alone with Abby's mum. After we're seated she crosses her long legs, showcasing her Gucci leather sandal heels. 'Would you like some tea?'

'No. Thank you.' The only thing I want is to get closer to the truth. 'I would like to speak to Abigail.'

'That won't be possible.'

Urgency or desperation pushes me to lean forward. 'Abby is the only one who can give me answers.'

'You don't understand.' She sounds flustered for the first time. Unlocks her legs. 'She can't help you, the police or anyone else, because she still doesn't remember what happened that day.'

'Nothing?' Naked despair.

'I took her to see a hypnotist who deals in so-called memory recovery. I know so much of that type of work has been discredited, but back then I was willing to cling to anything, *anything*, even if it had thorns in it, that would help Abby remember. Do you know what happened?' Pain criss-crosses her face. 'She started screaming and screaming. You should have heard it, it was like she was losing her mind. I had to get our family doctor, who sedated her.'

'I'm so sorry.' And I am. 'That must have been an awful thing for you, as a mother, to witness.'

'The medical advice I was given was to leave Abby alone. Under no circumstance should I force her to recall something she wants to forget.'

'But what about me? What about Sara-Jane?' I cut in. 'I can't forget. I wake up some nights screaming too.' My fingers twist together. 'My intention is not to bring Abby further pain. All I want to do is speak to her.'

'The truth is Abby is away at medical school. I won't tell you where. She's managed to grab back as normal a life as she can. Seeing you might turn her back into that terrified girl again.'

'Help me.'

She stands up. 'I can't take that chance.'

The heaviness of disappointment pins me to the seat for a time, making it impossible for me to get to my feet. Abby is the only witness to what happened and if I can't get access to her . . . Frustration makes me rise. Almost pushes me in her face.

'I understand what you're telling me, but at least Abby came back. SHE CAME BACK.' I've wanted to say that for so long, but I haven't, because it sounds so unfair, so mean. I take a breath. And another. But still I feel my body rocking and thrumming inside with out-of-control emotion.

'That day the school told us that the girls were missing, do you know what I did after? I didn't go back to work. I got on my bike and went to all Sara-Jane's favourite haunts to see if she was there. The playground on the estate. The big slide and swings in Isabel Park. The activity centre where she loved ice-skating and ten-pin bowling. She wasn't at any of them.'

I plead one final time. 'Sara-Jane is my world. She. Never. Came. Back.'

A muscle in Laura's cheek ticks. Then she steps back. 'I'm sorry.'

I leave, because Abby's mother doesn't realise that she's given me a clue. She claims that her daughter is studying medicine. So it shouldn't take me and Heather long, putting our heads together to check out all the educational establishments that offer medical courses. Add to that that the Prentices have money, so Abby's mother will probably have shelled out a fortune to get her into one of the more distinguished schools.

Outside, there's no sign of the man I saw here, Jas.

Laura's voice makes me turn. She's standing inside the door, the strain on her face ten times worse than it was before. 'The reason I'm telling you that you can't see my daughter is that I don't know where she is.'

'I don't understand.'

Her tongue darts out to wet her bottom lip. 'Abby was studying medicine at the Harriet Clisby College. It's a very prestigious institution.'

Was? Why did Laura use the word, was?

'Three weeks ago, Abby disappeared.'

Chapter 19

'What did Abby's mum tell you?'

It's Heather on the phone. Breathless and excited. I've barely made it to my bike outside Laura Prentice's house.

'How did you know that I've just left the house?'

'Coincidence.'

Coincidence? Really? I don't believe in it. All at once I have a suspicion, a hunch about what's going on here. So I keep talking as I wheel my bike away from the house further down the road. I catch the flash of someone ducking down in the front seat of a car. Quickly, I turn my gaze away and keep moving casually down the street as if I've seen nothing. I reach the car. Look through the driver's window at the hunched figure and, with an irritated cluck of my tongue, briskly knock on the window. The person sheepishly glances up.

Heather.

'What are doing here? Are you spying one me?' I confront her once she's rolled the window down.

With a heavy sigh she answers, 'I came in case things turned nasty with Abby's mother. Truthfully, I thought she was going to slam the door in your face.' Her voice thickens. 'I was worried that you might be upset. Need a shoulder to lean on.'

I'm flummoxed by the genuine emotion she displays. Her sincere desire to look out for me. That type of kindness towards another human being is not what I've come to expect from a journalist.

Her care kind of chokes me up, so I refocus our discussion back on our search for the truth. 'Abby Prentice has disappeared.'

'Vanished? Again?' The weight of the unexpected news pushes Heather back into her seat. 'Abby hasn't been taken—?'

'No! Thank goodness. Her mother said that she received a call from Abby stating she was safe but she wanted space to be alone. No contact. She wouldn't say where she was.' I shake my head sadly. 'It must be hell on earth for her mother not knowing where her child is.'

'But she's not a child, is she? She's an adult.'

'Spoken like someone who's never been a mother.'

She cocks her head at me. 'Does motherhood change your outlook on life?'

Heather takes me by surprise. I don't think anyone's ever asked me what it's like to be a mother. I gnaw on my lip, thinking. Then, 'It taught me that I wasn't the only person at the centre of my world. What true love is.' I swallow back the unexpected tears. 'The problem is that when that unique, special love is snatched from you, your heart, your soul, your very world crumbles and falls apart.'

Beneath all those heavy layers of privilege and manners, I suspect that's what Laura Prentice is experiencing, her world tumbling down around her.

I shake off the gloom. 'Open the boot of the car.'

'Err . . .? Why?'

My sudden arched brows tell her to do it, and when she does I push the back seats forward so I can store my bike in the back. I slide into the passenger seat.

'Are you going to fill me in on where we're going?' Heather asks.

Determination stiffens my spine. 'We're going in hunt of Abigail Prentice.'

◆ ◆ ◆

Heather slows the car outside Harriet Clisby College where Abby was, until very recently, studying. This stately Victorian building of red bricks and clock towers has exclusive with a sniffy capital E written all over it. The car is filled with Heather's annoyance and the perfume she loves so much. She's miffed that we're coming here, her theory being that we're wasting our time because Abby isn't here. No Abby means zero info in her books.

Switching off the engine, Heather's still got a beef with me. 'So, explain again what you expect to find here? *With no Abigail Prentice around.*' Ouch! She's tetchy.

'I'm going to hit the student bar and see if anyone remembers anything about Abby. Yeah, you're probably right that it's a wild goose chase, but I've got to try.'

Another lengthy sigh from Heather, this one bristling with reluctant resignation. 'I'll wait for you here. It will give me time to catch up with some promising sources, in particular one who remembers Abby when she was in hospital.'

Inside the building, I easily locate the sign for the bar, which takes me down a single flight into a world of low music, drink and young people. I was expecting something like a pub but the atmosphere here isn't as heavy. It's lighter, although a few wear the serious expressions of people who think they're going to change the world. Most are sitting at tables while a small group play pool in a corner. I'm not sure how I'm going to do this, but here goes.

With confidence I move in and start asking around if anyone remembers Abby. Most people aren't able to help; then I come across a table of four, where their initial openness turns into guarded caution on hearing my questions. An oppressive atmosphere descends, all avoiding my eyes. And it doesn't matter how much I press them, they shrug accompanied by, 'Dunno.'

What has caused their reaction? Are they friends of Abby's who swore to keep secret where she has gone?

So I say, 'If you know where she is, her mother is ever so worried about her.'

One of them, a young woman with a pink fringe, flips her face up, brimming with such icy disdain it makes me step back. 'Know where she is? Are you having a laugh?' Then she clams up and looks back down at her drink.

'What do you mean?'

No answer. Not from her or any of them. That girl sounded like she hated Abby. Goodness, what could have happened? Disappointed that I can't get any more answers, I exit the bar.

'Wait,' a voice calls out behind me as I step back outside. It's the student who spoke to me. It's obvious she's very uncomfortable, barely able to meet my eyes. 'Look, I don't know what really went down—'

'So, something did happen,' I challenge.

She nods briskly. 'I have the room next door to the one that Abby shared with another student.' Her hands push deep into her black jeans. 'One night there was a load of drama. Screaming.'

Screaming? I have to hold back my natural instinct to interrupt. 'Her roomie moved out that following morning. I don't know what went on, all I can tell you is that her roomie looked like she'd been through hell.'

'What's the name of the girl who shared with Abby? Can I speak to her?'

'No can do. She packed her stuff and went home the same day. And never came back.' Her voice turns angry. 'We all liked her roomie. Whatever Abby did to her must've been bad. Really bad.'

'And you don't know what that was? Picked up on any rumours?'

'Her roomie looked shit-scared.'

She glances over my shoulder and stumbles away from me. I suspect in the cold light of day, here outside, she feels vulnerable and has got cold feet again.

'No wonder Abby disappeared,' I muse.

The student looks at me strangely. 'Disappeared?' Her voice is low and tight. 'She didn't disappear. Abby was asked to leave.'

With one last furtive stare past me, she's gone.

My phone buzzing with a text draws me away from the student's hurried departure.

I read the text: I need to see you. Now.

My heartbeat quickens because it's from the last person I expect to contact me.

Abby's mother. Laura Prentice.

Chapter 20

FIFTEEN YEARS AGO

'You're only torturing yourself, doing this. Coming here.'

That was Traci's terse warning to Gem outside the door into the main building of Princess Isabel School. When the dreadful news of the abduction had reached Dale Prentice yesterday, he'd gone into action and, working with the police, put out the call for volunteers to help search for the girls to attend this evening's meeting in the school hall.

Gem existed in a nightmare, a floating I'm-not-really-here fog. She hadn't slept last night. How could she sleep with her darling baby out there? Convinced that Sara-Jane would somehow make her way back home, Gem had stayed up, tense and alert, watching on her bedroom balcony for her daughter's return. For the sight of Sara-Jane's figure appearing in the distance. Traci had remained by her side all night long. Bless her neighbour. Traci had become her rock. Gem had turned down the police's offer of a family liaison officer staying with her, mainly because the word on the Rosebridge was that they were usually plants for the cops to snoop on the family. And the last thing Gem needed was that because it might expose the other doomed cloud she lived under.

No one could find out about that. No one.

'Let me take you home,' Traci coaxed. 'You need to rest.'

Rest? How could anyone think that would make this real-life horror story go away? Gut-wrenching pain go away? Would bring her Sara-Jane back?

Gem defiantly shook her head. 'I need to know about everything that is being done to help find my Sara-Jane.'

Sighing heavily, Traci accompanied her into the school and into the hall where the meeting was being held.

The response for volunteers had been overwhelming, the hall packed, mostly with parents, and interestingly, they came from both the north and south side of the school. The kidnapping of the girls was not a time for difference but a time to pull together.

Abby's mother, Laura, was sitting among the supportive members of the PTA. Despite appearing straight-backed and composed, the tightening of her jaw and the flexing of her fingers in her lap were dead giveaways of her unimaginable suffering.

Conscious of the eyes that followed her, Gem kept her head slightly bowed as she made her way with Traci to sit by the far wall. She hated being the centre of attention.

Dale took to the stage. 'I want to thank you all for coming here this evening. For being willing to give up your precious time to search for our girls.' His grave words washed over the gathering. 'Our task is to search for two girls who are loved by their families. Loved in this community. One is called Sara-Jane Casey. The other Abigail Prentice, who everyone calls Abby.'

Dale swallowed hard, momentarily robbed of words. Everyone's heart went out to him. There was not a person here who did not know how much he loved and cherished his granddaughter with his whole heart and more. It couldn't have been easy for him to get up on that stage and talk. The community was reeling and dazed in shock. You heard of such evil happening in the world but never expected it to occur on your own doorstep. How could two girls have gone to school and not come home? A school was meant to be a place of safety. A place where the Big Bad World only exists in storybooks.

And the person in charge of the school was Clare Swan. No one outright pointed the finger at the head teacher; nevertheless, truth was truth. The girls had disappeared on her watch. She stood erect by the stage with her trusted right hand, Beryl, the strain and exhaustion visible on her face.

'Beryl has flyers of both girls for you to distribute.'

It was very brave of Beryl to be part of this considering the disappearance of her own husband a year before. Although people had their own lurid stories about why Teddy Spencer had vanished, that didn't make any of this easier for the wife left behind.

Dale paused to stress the importance of their task ahead. 'If you find anything, *anything*, make it your business to inform one of the police officers . . .'

His voice faded away, his stare fixed on a newcomer who had slipped virtually unnoticed into the room. It was Dale's son, Abby's father, Henry Prentice. It was common knowledge that he and Laura Prentice had ended their marriage almost a year ago now. What started the whispers behind people's hands was not how ill he looked; it was what he was wearing. His pyjamas, open dressing gown and slippers. His hair appeared uncombed and he hadn't shaved for some time.

'Henry!' His son's name tore out of an alarmed Dale.

Laura calmly eased to her feet, more adept at hiding her appalled reaction than Dale. She moved quickly to her ex-husband and took his arm. And then turned to her former father-in-law. 'Maybe one of the good officers can assist.'

Dale didn't need to even ask because two police officers were already on their way to her and Henry. While she whispered to them Dale explained to the crowd, 'Please excuse my son. He's taken his daughter's abduction very hard. Imagine yourself in his shoes.'

Imagine yourself in his shoes. That's what stopped most of the gawking. And respect towards Dale. Still, turning up in your nightclothes was very odd. The police escorted a silent Henry out, while Laura retook her seat. A silent message passed between her and Dale.

Dale gestured to Beryl and the flyers. 'Help us bring our Sara-Jane and our Abby home.'

A voice called out, 'Do the police know how the children got out of school? This is the best school in the district, so what happened to the security?'

Finally it was out in the open – what had been playing on the minds of many.

Miss Swan addressed the gathering. 'Thanks to Dale's generosity, the school has had new security cameras for more than two years now, which work. A thorough check of the premises was carried out and we think the girls got out via the chapel. As you all know, the chapel is old and these old buildings do have their secrets. One of those secrets is a panel with a tunnel that leads out into the street. We think that's how they sneaked out of school.'

'Sneaked out of school?' an outraged Laura Prentice repeated.

Losing her composure, she jumped to her feet. Her face had lost so much colour the red of her lipstick looked like blood smeared across her face. 'It was *that girl*. She led my Abby astray. Sneak out of school? My Abby wouldn't dream of doing such a thing. In all of her years at Princess Isabel my daughter has been the model of exemplary behaviour.' She twisted, her distraught and accusing gaze on Gem. 'Wasn't it enough that your daughter tried to choke Abigail? Put her wicked hands around her throat, trying to snuff out her life?'

A horrified gasp erupted. Stare after stare swung to Gem, hot, hurting, intensifying the pain she was already in. If someone had told her that this nightmare could get worse, she wouldn't have believed them.

Gem stumbled to her feet, rocking back slightly. She could barely speak. 'My Sara-Jane is a good girl. She's always been good. I don't know what happened, but it was a mistake—'

'Mistake?' Laura sliced over with derision. Fumbling in her bag, she yanked out her mobile phone and displayed a photo for all to see. 'This is what her daughter did to mine.'

The volunteers who could see it looked grim and uncomfortable. A fog of disquiet descended over the room.

'She did this to my Abby, so what is she doing to her now? The children from that housing estate should never have been allowed in this school.'

'Now, Laura,' Dale cautioned.

She ignored him. 'What if there's no third party involved? What if the monster is her daughter?'

Gem felt herself being pushed backwards by the waves of open hostility. She stood her ground. Sara-Jane wasn't a monster. It wasn't true. Wasn't true. WASN'T FUCKING TRUE.

No one spoke. Silence, uncomfortable and thick. Then it was shattered by the swing doors smashing against the wall. A small figure staggered into the hall. She was dirty, with blood running down the side of her head. She swayed into the centre of the hall.

A dazed-looking man rushed in right behind her. 'I saw her while I was driving my bus. I—'

'Help me,' the small figure cried out. 'Please help me.'

Urine began running down the inside of her thighs, soaking her socks, the inside of her shoes. Pooling on the floor below her.

She wobbled and her legs went from under her.

Abby crumpled like a paper doll to the floor.

Chapter 21

I recoil in jaw-dropping astonishment at the sight of Laura in her front doorway. After her text message I headed right here from the medical college. Dark tracks of mascara ruin Laura's usually flawless make-up. Her cheekbones appear stark. Has she been crying? Her lips fold and unfold in a nervous pattern of anxiety. Something bad has seriously shaken her up. Badly scared her.

I rush forward. 'What's going on? Shall I call the police?'

I get no answer. Instead she grabs my hand, stunning me. Laura touching another human being? I never thought I would witness that. She's always given off a *don't touch me* vibe that screams 'keep your distance'. Especially against me of all people, the hated mother of Sara-Jane. Her flesh against mine is warm but clammy. She draws me inside the house and shuts the door.

She looks even more terrible in the bright heavy light streaming in to the large hallway.

Urgently, I say, 'Tell me what has happened.'

Swallowing convulsively, the veins in her neck strain against her skin. 'Please, follow me.'

She takes me to the lounge where there's someone else waiting. It's Jas Bedi, the man I saw doing work on the side of her house when I came here earlier.

Laura hurriedly introduces him. 'This is Jas. He does odd jobs for me.'

Does she know that he was William's bad-boy partner in crime back in his Billy-Bob tearaway days?

I tell him, 'I lived on the Rosebridge when you did. Good seeing you again.'

He nods and glances nervously between us, his eyes on me filled with curiosity, his stare on Laura filled with deference and respect.

Laura instructs him, 'Tell her. Tell her what you told me.'

He begins. 'It was fifteen years ago. When the girls were taken. About a month after Abby came back.' Nervously he wets his lips. 'What you've got to understand is I was doing a lot of gear back then. Especially ecstasy. The so-called party drug.' He scoffs, his expression suggesting the last thing he'd felt was happy. 'All that shit . . .' He looks sharply at Laura. 'Oops! Sorry.'

'Don't worry about anything,' Laura encourages, 'except telling Gem what you saw that evening.'

Jas's tense gaze jumps over to me. 'That's why I'm telling you about the drugs. They left my mind muddled. So it might be my fried brain back then got it wrong. Heard wrong. I was licking my wounds one night in The Hangman's Retreat. I'd borrowed money off the wrong people. Three nights before they jumped me and battered the living crap out of me.'

That's the Jas I remember, always being on the wrong side of trouble. And seeming so sad. He'd roamed around the Rosebridge with William looking lost and lonely.

He carries on. 'I went outside to smoke a bit of weed. Hid in a corner so no one could see me. That's when I heard Charlie Fraser.'

My backbone stiffens. Anything concerning Charlie won't be good.

123

'No disrespect,' Jas quickly adds, 'but Charlie wasn't a man I liked. A loudmouth. A nasty piece of work, some called him, while others a proper gent. A man with those types of reputations were the worst because you never really knew where you stood with them. The friendly snake.'

That sums up Charlie. Charming and deadly. I ask, 'What was he doing outside?'

'He was arguing with someone. He was fucked off. Y'know, angry. Whoever he was rowing with, I couldn't see them at first. It was dark out there. Charlie was insisting that they had an agreement and that he was owed money. For a job.'

'What type of agreement?' I cut over him.

'Charlie said that he kept up his side of the bargain and now wanted paying. The other guy said that he wasn't paying up because Charlie had messed things up big time. That Charlie and him had agreed to a mutually beneficial deal. Charlie said if he didn't get his money there was going to be major league payback. Trouble.'

I'm still not getting this. 'I don't understand.'

Jas draws in a shaky breath. 'I think – think – that Charlie was discussing the kidnapping of the girls.'

A frightening cold seizes my body. 'No way. Even Charlie wouldn't do that.'

Jas's words are coming rapid-fire now. 'It might have been the drugs messing with my head. But Abby escaped, didn't she? That wasn't meant to happen. I think that's what Charlie fucked up.'

Laura gently coaxes him again. 'Tell Gem the rest.'

Quietly, Jas does. 'The other man came out of the shadows. It was Henry Prentice.'

Abby's father.

Did the two dads organise the girls' abduction together?

I don't want to believe it. It's unthinkable. Monstrous. Grotesque. Can't be. Just can't. I'm finding it hard to take this in.

It's hard to feed air into my lungs. I'm being sucked down, down, down. Into the deepest darkest nightmare. It leaves me shaken and sickened.

Two fathers kidnap their own children? *No! No! No!* They would never do that.

Would they?

Subject their own flesh and blood to a campaign of hell? Snatch their children – *their own kids* – kicking and screaming for their life off the street? There's evil in this world but this brand of vile evil is in a league of its own.

My mind flashes back to Charlie holding Sara-Jane for the first time after she was born. Looking down at her with wonder. Gently holding her in his arms like she was the most precious person on this earth. Wearing the pitch-perfect glow of a new dad. Could he really switch so easily from the pride and love of fatherhood to an animal who would snatch his own flesh and blood?

Then I think back to my suspicions. The black van outside the school. His greediness for more and more money.

Then again, it's those closest to us who damage us the most. If Sara-Jane's dad did this to her, how can I trust anyone again?

My vision starts blurring, changing. I'm no longer in Laura's lounge. I'm on the street. Stroud Road and Glass Alley. I'm on the corner. Shivering. Invisible. A ghost no one can see. But I see them. See Sara-Jane and Abby. Skipping and laughing. Holding hands. So happy.

The black van's coming up behind them.

'Look out!' The girls don't hear my anguished roar.

The van is silent. Creeps closer. Closer. A moving terror in the strong daylight. The driver's door flies up.

'Run, girls! Run!' They don't hear me.

A man leaps from the van. No mask covering his evil face. It's Charlie. The face switches, changes to Henry Prentice. It changes again. Charlie. Henry. Charlie. Changing and changing . . .

A harrowing noise drags me out of the terrors of my mind. Back to Laura's lounge. It's the heartbreaking sound of uncontrollable weeping. Head hanging low, shoulders shaking, Laura cries. I've often wondered if she was capable of an open display of emotion. She's always been so poised, so stand-offish. Her head slowly rises and she stares at me. She looks so vulnerable. So fragile.

The mother in me responds to her distress. In a flash, I'm beside her, arms around her. She's all hard bones and pointy angles. Stiff. This woman doesn't allow herself to be comforted very often.

But here we are. Two mothers. Were the fathers of our children the demons behind this heinous crime?

Jas is standing there looking helpless, so I gesture with my eyes for him to leave us alone. He can't seem to get out of the room fast enough.

Laura says, 'When Jas told me what he saw and heard all those years ago I couldn't believe it.' A deep breath vibrates through her. 'I know Henry and I didn't part on the best of terms, but to do this to his own daughter.'

There's no way to verify her ex-husband's story. He's dead. He passed a few years after the kidnapping. I don't know what the circumstances of his death were.

She continues, 'He left us. Said he didn't want to be a family man any more.' She shudders. 'One day he turned up and demanded I get Abby. I refused, and he swore blind that he would take her. Any way he could.'

I gasp in stunned disbelief. Gently, I move Laura out of my arms. 'Did you contact the police?'

'Of course I did.' Delicately with a finger Laura smooths the tears from beneath her eyes. 'But Dale has got a lot of contacts, including the police.'

'Are you talking about police corruption?'

She waves her palm. 'It's more like you scratch my back and I'll scratch yours.'

What she is telling me is huge. Then Laura bursts my bubble of hope. 'I'm not stating that that's what actually happened. It might have, it might not. You need to be aware that Henry's dad was well connected.'

In other words, this could all be bile she's spilling against her ex-husband. And he doesn't get a right to reply. Because he's dead.

'Do you think they, Charlie and Henry, knew each other? Were in this together?'

Which reminds me of the incident outside the school fifteen years back with Charlie doing his hateful routine, showing me up in front of the other parents. And Henry Prentice. They were talking in an easy manner. Like they knew each other.

Standing up, she moves to stare at the pretty garden through the wide bay windows. She locks her arms about her no-doubt churning stomach. 'I really don't know. Henry was . . .' She holds her words back.

I get to my feet and move to stand next to her. 'What?' I coax.

'A complex man. I don't think growing up with his father was easy. He always measured himself against his father's achievements.' Bitterness coats her next words. 'How can anyone live up to the great Dale Prentice?'

This is a whole other take on the story that Dale gave me about why there's bad blood between him and his former daughter-in-law.

Out front, I spot Jas trimming a hedge. It prompts me to find out one more thing from Laura. 'How did Jas end up working for you? From what I remember about his young days, there weren't many who would've given him a job.'

Her brows go up. 'Years back, I found him passed out in my garden shed. How he got there I will never know.'

How weird. 'Did you call the cops?'

Her head slowly shakes. 'I know, that's not my usual style. God, he was in a terrible state. Stank to high heaven. He reminded me of Abby when she came back. In such pain and hurting so badly. I got a doctor for him.'

I've had Laura wrong all this time. She does have a beating heart after all.

She continues, 'I felt an obligation to help him because he'd grown up on this street—'

'What?'

Her brows go up 'His family were well-to-do members of the community with a house on this street. How Jas ended up the way he did, I don't know.'

Because I'd seen him hanging out with Billy-Bob on the Rosebridge I'd assumed Jas must have lived there. I'm starting to realise that I can't make assumptions about anyone in my search for the truth.

All at once, Laura's expression changes, the shade of her face becoming bloodless again. 'Something has come back to me. I think Henry did know Charlie.'

'What do you mean?' I'm rattled by her revelation.

'You asked me before if our exes knew each other. I thought they didn't, but . . .' Her voice becomes urgent. 'Henry needed a decorator. That's right. I think Dale found him one.'

'Dale?'

Her tone is back to highbrow and crisp. 'It was Dale who put Henry in touch with him. The decorator was Sara-Jane's father.'

Chapter 22

'She said WHAT?'

Dale's bellow bounces off the four corners of his traditional rustic kitchen, rattling a set of hanging cups. I've come here straight from Laura's. Although the first suspect on my list was Charlie, the problem is I don't have any contact details for him. Which is typical of him. He likes to be in control. Plus, he doesn't want too many people to know which seedy rock he's currently living under.

I've told Dale plain and straight what Laura confided in me. That he was the link between Sara-Jane and Abby's fathers.

'I'm going to swing for that woman one day.' His teeth are clenched so tight it's a wonder they don't shatter.

'So Henry didn't meet Charlie through you?' I decline Dale's offer to sit down, instead preferring to stand a touch inside the doorway.

Dale clams up, lips rubbing together, his fingers tapping against the top of the large table. If it wasn't for the tick-tock of the wall clock I'm sure I could hear him think. Finally, he answers. 'Look, I may have introduced them.' He waves his hand airily in front of his face, obscuring his expression.

'*What?*' The power of my response drives me further into the room.

He folds his arms, giving me one of those legendary Dale stares that's designed to put me in my place. 'Don't jump out of your pram. Look, part of my business is introducing and connecting people. Setting up partnerships, sometimes to my advantage and sometimes not.'

To his advantage? 'How would a relationship between your son and Charlie have been to your advantage?'

He stands, looking thoroughly irritated. 'You're twisting my words, girl. I don't like that.'

'And I don't like being called "girl".'

Silence. We size each other up. He's the first to speak. 'I meant no offence. It's just what they said around here at one time. Boy. Girl. Young 'un. My mum – rest her kind-hearted soul – always called me boy. Even when I was in my forties.'

I notice something about Dale I should've seen before. He always tells stories from the good ole days. What is clear to me now is how he's very careful about when he chooses to tell them. Often it's when he's in a corner. When he wants to avoid discussing something. He uses the stories as a distraction.

Well, that won't work with me. Not today. 'Dale, did you or did you not connect Henry with Charlie?'

'Did you know what happened to Henry. How he died?' His expression looks like someone has walked over his grave.

His words alarm me. Make me tense. I shake my head.

'He drank himself to death.' Dale cups his work-roughened palm over his mouth. But it's not quick enough to cover the terrible sound that grunts out of him. The sound of pure sorrow.

He slumps back on the stool, the portrait of a defeated man. A defeated parent. 'When he married *that woman* things went from bad to worse. Then little Abby was born.' His gaze brightens. 'I thought Henry would be all right, that things would work out. But they just went downhill. She kicked him out of the house. A house I bloody bought for them.'

I remain silent, allowing him to tell me about Abby's father. 'If I'm honest, Henry was a drinker before his doomed marriage. Being a husband only made him hit the bottle more. He was a devoted father, though. He'd have laid down his life for his baby girl. After he got divorced he was like a man cast adrift. So I tried to pick him up. Get him involved in the business.' His world-weary eyes stare right into me. 'I introduced him to so many people. One of them may have been Charlie Fraser. I doubt it though. No disrespect, but he wasn't known as a man you could put your trust in.'

I believe what he's telling me. 'Thanks for your time, Dale. I'm sorry to have brought this upset to your door.'

Then I remember. 'You've got a dark van.'

Lately, I've been thinking that maybe the van I saw wasn't black. What if it was dark blue? It's easy to mix that kind of blue with black.

'I've got a white one too.'

'You said you were out of town on the day I came back. I'm sure I saw a dark van near the school.'

Scowling heavily, he thinks. 'Must've been some of the lads who work for me. Out doing deliveries.'

He gets to his feet, signalling our time is over. 'Gem, my door is always open to you.' I remind myself that this is the man who helped me set up my business.

Before I turn to go he has one last thing to say. 'Remember when Henry turned up for the volunteers' meeting to search for the girls?' I nod. 'He was in his pyjamas and slippers. Me and Laura explained it away that he'd taken Abby's disappearance hard and had been resting up.' He pauses. 'That wasn't true. Well, not all of it.'

'What do you mean?'

131

'He hadn't come from home.'

I still don't get it. Dale continues, 'He had his nightclothes on because he was in hospital.'

'Was he sick?'

'I know what you've been thinking. That Henry had something to do with his daughter's abduction.'

'Did he?'

'He could not have. He'd been in hospital. For months.'

Dale pulls in a distressed punch of air. And tells me the rest.

'My son was in a psychiatric hospital.'

Chapter 23

Piercing bright headlights temporarily blind me when I walk on to the Rosebridge. It disturbs the falling darkness of the evening. Oh hell, not more drama. That's the last thing I need. I'm dead on my feet, completely exhausted. However, my head's buzzing.

If Henry was in a psychiatric hospital, how could what Jas told me be true?

Then again. Jas did say his head was mashed by the drugs, so maybe he got the dates mixed up when he heard Charlie and Henry arguing?

Is Jas lying?

Dale lying?

Before returning to the Rosebridge, I checked in The Hangman's Retreat. No one had seen hide nor hair of Charlie.

A relaxing bath and bed, that's what I need. But clearly someone else has other ideas because the blinding headlights are soon joined by the jarring honk of a horn.

The lights snap off. For a moment my vision is filled with colourful dots, so I shake my head until my vision returns to normal. In the darkness, not far up ahead, I see a van. A black van.

My heart jumps. I go still. My eyes widen with disbelief. Is this for fucking real? Is someone playing a filthy trick on me? Mind games? With determination I march over to the driver's side, about ready to let rip.

It's Heather.

'What are you doing with *this*?' I flick my fingers disdainfully towards the van.

Heather picks up on my discomfort. 'Bloody hell, I didn't think this through. I should've realised . . . I'll go.' She reaches for the ignition key.

'No! Don't.'

Her hand hovers over the key, her eyes wide with indecision.

'Just tell me why you've brought a black van here.' I join her in the front cab, pensive and tense in the passenger seat.

Heather explains, 'When I trained as a journalist, I learned about this technique that's got a fancy technical name. Us students simply called it the "get in their head" method.'

More students. Do I really need this?

I don't express my inner turmoil, Heather carries on. 'You try to get inside a victim's head to see if you can find out more information about what might have happened. It's like walking in a victim's shoes. Often it works better if you use some objects that were part of the crime. In this case, a black van. And . . .'

She leans down and picks something up. Shows it to me. A crowbar. 'One of my sources found information that suggests there may have been a crowbar in the back of the van that took the girls. Something that Abby said after she escaped.'

A crowbar? Abby told them this? This is all news to me. I'm about to ask her who her source is, then stop. There's no point. I'll only be wasting my breath because Heather will never tell me. I suppose she feels I'm treading on her journalistic integrity. *Journalistic integrity?* Now, that's a phrase I never thought I'd use.

My uneasy gaze settles on the crowbar. It's made of metal and looks hefty. Heavy. In my mind it slashes through the air. Crashes down through flesh to bone. Blood everywhere.

My gaze snaps up to Heather. 'Do you think they used it on . . . ?' The words jam in my throat. I can't say them.

'I don't know.' Heather's honest with me. 'But it may help us find out more.'

'OK.' Although the last thing I feel is OK. I'm still confused by what she's telling me. 'So, it's a bit like hypnosis?'

'It's nothing like that.' *Is that impatience making her lips twist?* 'Just let me do it. But there are rules. It works better if we go to the crime scene.'

The colour leaves my face. 'You can't mean—'

'We need to go to the place where the girls were taken.'

Don't go there.

I've never been to the place where Sara-Jane was snatched off the street. Where she vanished. Fifteen years back, I tried to come here one day, did my best to let my feet propel me forward. I never made it. I threw up in the gutter and ran back home. I didn't sleep a wink that night, my mind consumed with images of some bastard grabbing her and taking her away.

But this is different. I'm different. I'm no longer the scaredy-cat Gem from before.

Something touches my leg. It's Heather's reassuring hand. 'This is no easy thing for you to do, I know that. You're a strong woman. One I admire. I'll be with you every step of the way.'

If this brings me a step closer to my Sara-Jane . . .

'What are you waiting for?' I say.

135

I'm tense the whole journey. We reach the corner of Stroud Road and Glass Alley. The place where the girls' screams were heard. Where a black van was seen. It looks so innocent, like any other street. Normal. But there's nothing normal about the thud of my pulse, the squeeze of air in my chest, the oily film of sweat slicked against my forehead. Rubbish, empty boxes and floating paper are leftovers from the nearby market. There's a greasy sheen to the ground that's probably squashed fruits but puts me in mind of blood.

The jarring sound of my phone ringing in my pocket startles me, making me shuffle back. I let it ring and ring until it stops. Everything else will have to wait.

Heather turns to me and I'm shocked by her appearance. Her face is strained. Her fingers contorted in her lap.

'Has something upset you?'

'No, of course not.' *Why have I never noticed how sunken her cheeks appear?* 'Well, maybe. I've only done this once before. Let's get out and I'll tell you how it works.'

Outside I want her to keep on talking about anything. Anything rather than hear the silence of this street seeping into my flesh. My daughter disappeared into the darkness here. The pavement beneath my shoes feels warm from Sara-Jane's footsteps. The sound of her laughter echoes off the walls of the buildings, disturbing the air. Then the air abruptly changes with the sound of the breeze in the scraggy trees.

Did Sara-Jane hear the same noise before her laughter was cruelly cut as evil came after her?

Heather, crowbar in hand, guides me to the back of the van. And explains, 'What I'm attempting to do is figure out how Abby escaped. She doesn't remember, so I'm going to try to remember for her.'

My face scrunches up. This all feels strange to me, but, hey, if this is what they teach them at journalism school, who am I to say any different? Plus, Heather is convinced this will help. I've got nothing to lose. And everything to gain.

I continue to listen to Heather outline her plan. 'Once inside the van I'm going to try to get a feel of what Abby went through. This crowbar should help me. While I'm doing that, I want you to drive the van to the place where the bus driver found Abby. I've set up the GPS for you.'

Heather opens the van doors. She hesitates. There's an audible hitch in her breathing. She climbs in and, with a final shaky smile, closes the doors.

I tend not to drive, bikes being my thing, so I find the van heavy and awkward to drive. The partition between me and the rear means it's impossible to see what Heather is doing. The darkness swallows the van as I head towards the place where Abby was found.

A muffled mumbling comes from the back. Is Heather speaking to someone on the phone? If she is, it sounds really weird. The mumbling goes on and on. The darkness around becomes denser. Thicker. I turn on to a more secluded road.

An ear-piercing scream from the back of the van shatters the quiet. Then another. In a state of utter panic, my fumbling hands on the steering wheel, I swiftly pull over. Scramble out into the frigid night. Heart beating like it's about to crash out of my chest, I cautiously approach the back of the van. The screaming's turned to an unnerving silence.

Cautiously and slowly I turn the handle. Pull open the door. Heather's crouched on the metal floor, wheezing and gasping for air. She looks like something straight out of a horror movie. The little hair she has leaves her head looking like a skull. A skeleton-head. Face stark. Colourless. Cheeks hollow. And eyes . . . Good God, her eyes. They bulge in their sockets with tears and terrors.

I rush inside and take her hand. It's frozen and trembling. 'Heather? Speak to me.'

She snatches her hand back. And through gritted teeth insists, 'It's working. This is what it must have been like for Abby. Hiding in a corner. Terrified.'

I don't like any of this any more.

She springs closer to me. Her breath fierce and hot in my face. And those eyes of hers . . . 'I need you to drive. Please! For Sara-Jane! For Abby!'

I'm back in the driver's seat with no idea what to do. This is when I wish I did have some kind of chemical dependency. I'm not talking an illegal Class A substance but something like a swift whisky or a punch of nicotine. There's a hammering on the partition, a warning for me to get moving. I pull out the same time as my phone rings again. I'm too shaken up to take the call.

I try closing my ears to the horrifying noises coming from the back of the van. Hisses like a witch casting a spell. Unearthly shouts. Groaning and struggling. Rapid-fire whispers. Then comes the hammering. Against the van's bodywork. Steady at first. Then faster and faster . . .

I can't take this any more.

I jam on the breaks. Tyres squeal and skid to a screaming stop in an area that borders a wood. The sounds in the back stop. It's the most ghostly and penetrating silence I've ever heard.

Above the noise of the engine, I shout, 'Heather? What's happening?'

I tumble out of the driver's side, fear eating away inside me as I try to open the back doors. They won't budge. They're locked from the inside. Panic-stricken, I run back to the cab and start violently kicking the partition. I don't stop until it finally gives.

I see inside.

Dear God! No!

Heather's lying sideways on the floor, clutching the crowbar. Her face is distorted. Misshapen. Her body still. Too still. Is she . . . ?

Frantically, I crawl inside, tearing my clothes as they catch on the jagged hole in the partition. I feel for Heather's pulse . . . Wait . . . Relief when I feel the flow of blood. It's not weak, it's racing. Her eyelids flicker. Slowly open.

'Heather! Talk to me. Please.'

She doesn't answer, instead sits up. She looks like she's been to hell and back. Finally she speaks to me, her voice tight and barely above a whisper. 'I think the girls fought to get out of the van with the crowbar.'

Her face crumbles. Voice chokes as if she's gagging. 'It was horrible. So horrible.'

Then her shoulders shake with a silent outpouring of tears, so I take her in my arms and hold her tight. Make her feel safe again. 'Everything is going to work out fine. You'll see.'

Abruptly, Heather jerks away from me and scrambles towards the door. Her eyes dart around like an animal scenting danger. Before I can react, she jumps outside. And runs.

'Heather!' The night air swallows my desperate shout.

She ignores me, weaving and bending like a fragile branch in the wind through the traffic on to the other side of the road.

'Heather!'

I jump behind the wheel and drive after her. But she's on the other side of the road. I make an illegal turn. Drive. And drive. But Heather's gone.

Like Sara-Jane in the black van in my nightmare.

Into the evil darkness.

Chapter 24

It's the next morning. There's someone banging at the front door. Well, at least I think that's the door. I'm still in bed, half-asleep, half-waking up. Truth is, my brain's a pile of mush owing to how much time I spent desperately searching for Heather during the night and early hours. When I couldn't find her in the van I came back here and headed out again on my bike. I couldn't find her anywhere. I don't know where Heather lives, so she may very well have gone home. However, my gut's telling me that isn't the case.

It's left me feeling destroyed. That another young person may have gone missing in my search for the truth.

Seeing her swallowed up by the night . . .

The banging's back. Definitely someone at the door. Reluctantly, my eyes open and I shift out of bed. And groan. The muscles in my legs are murder, probably from all the walking and pedalling I did trying to find Heather.

'Gem!' That's William's insistent shout on the other side of the door. What does he want at this time . . . ? I check my mobile on the bedside table . . . 10:15.

'Where have you been?' he almost snaps when I open the door. 'I've been looking for you since last night.'

I tense up. 'What's happened?'

I let him in and shut the door. We remain standing in the cold hallway. Up close I can see how agitated he is. 'Detective Wallace paid you a visit yesterday evening.'

My heartbeat starts pounding against my ribs. 'What did he want?'

'He wouldn't say. He did say that he'd called you a number of times yesterday evening.'

My mind hurtles back to being in the van. My phone ringing. Me ignoring it. Coming back to the present, I rush back to the bedroom to locate my mobile. William hovers uneasily just outside the room. Suddenly, I get why that is. Coming into my bedroom is stepping over a line of intimacy.

'For heaven's sakes,' I mutter impatiently under my breath, followed by a beckoning motion of my hand, waving him inside.

We check over my phone together.

Three missed calls. Three voice messages. All from Wallace. Damn! Damn! Damn!

First message: 'Gem, please contact me on this number. I need to urgently speak with you.'

Second message: 'If you get this message early enough tomorrow, please come to the police station.'

Third message: 'It concerns Sara-Jane.'

My heart drops. Desperately, I look up into William's worried face. 'I've got to get to the police station.'

Anxiety levels hitting the roof, I start madly hunting around the room for clothes. Shoes. Hot tears sting with the power of acid behind my eyes. The sensation of William's comforting, reassuring hand on my shoulder stops me in my tracks. With care, he turns me and stares tensely into my eyes.

'You won't find Wallace at the station. Not now. That's why he said only go there if you get his call early this morning. He'll be either on his way or at the school by now.'

The school? 'Why would he be going to Princess Isabel?'

William's hand drops to his side. 'He's organised a small community meeting there. A couple of minutes ago he left a message on my voicemail telling me that if I saw you, I was to bring you as well.'

◆ ◆ ◆

My head lolls listlessly against the passenger door window of William's car. I feel numb. Can't believe how unprepared I am for this. Finding out if my daughter was the one murdered and buried in the school's chapel was the reason I've remained here. A place that has such bad memories. And now the moment is here . . . I just want to pedal with the speed of lightning in the opposite direction. I thought I was ready for this. Ready to be told that my baby is truly dead. But that means finally letting go.

Letting go of Sara-Jane.

In a voice so broken it doesn't sound like me, I tell William, 'I don't know if I can do this. I've hoped and prayed for years. How am I going to go on?' I stare forlornly at the traffic going the other way. 'Sara-Jane's dead, isn't she? She's gone. For good this time.'

He pauses, flicking me a momentary sideways glance. 'Wait and see what the police have got to say.'

There's still hope. That's what most people would tell me. Not William. That's not his way. He doesn't play fast and loose with the truth. I've come to respect him so much.

I choke up. Raging too. 'How the hell am I going to bury my precious baby girl? How does a parent watch their child being lowered into the ground? Dirt thrown over them. No one should have to bury their own child.'

I feel the heat of his concerned gaze. 'Do you want me to stop?'

'For fifteen years I've stopped. It's only going to put off the inevitable.'

We reach the school. The sun's strong this morning, almost blinding, its rays catching the windows and brickwork and the roof terrace. It should look pretty. It doesn't. It looks foreboding. As we get out of the car the sun disappears, leaving the school building sinking into a gloom of something terrible to come.

Inside the school a uniformed officer escorts us into the head teacher's office. There's no sign of either Beryl or Miss Swan. Wallace stands behind the desk, the sunlight from outside now back and glinting off the grey in his hair. His features are grim and grave.

I'm glad when Wallace invites us to sit down because my limbs are shaking so badly.

The detective starts in a sympathetic tone. 'I'm sorry that I haven't been able to do this in the privacy of the station. Unfortunately, due to the timing of the meeting I've organised here, I had no alternative. I don't want you finding out from anyone else.'

'Tell me,' I rasp quietly, voice trembling.

After hesitating he answers. 'The human remains that were found are *not* your daughter. *Not* Sara-Jane.'

Not Sara-Jane.

Not Sara-Jane.

'Are you sure?' Hope burns back, bright and alive. My baby girl may still be alive. Out there. Somewhere.

Nodding, Wallace confirms, 'The bones are the remains of an adult—'

'Hang on a bloody minute,' William erupts in righteous fury. 'Surely, the police would have recognised that they were adult remains and not those of a child from the beginning.'

'Is that true?' Wallace doesn't need to answer my damning question; the expression on his face says it all. Shooting to my feet, my outrage rises. 'When we talked in the playground, the first day

I got here, you knew all along it wasn't Sara-Jane. At the police station when I showed you her socks. Do you know what agony I've been through? Thinking what's left of my beautiful daughter was in a grave in that chapel? How could you be so cruel?'

The detective gets to his feet too. 'I wanted to tell you. But was under strict orders from the top brass not to reveal details about the investigation.' Sympathy lines his face. 'I did ask permission to tell you but was told under no circumstances could I do this.'

'Why?' William asks, slowly standing.

Wallace considers his answer. 'Any criminal investigation connected to children is sensitive. Throw into the mix a school, the most academically outstanding school in the area, and it becomes even more of a minefield, needing delicate handling.' His expression shifts to that of a cop. 'It was the right decision, though. We took time to carry out all the correct tests to ensure we made an identification.'

I ask, 'Whose body was in that grave?'

Wallace looks even bleaker than before. 'The reason I've called a meeting is to tell relevant members of the community who the victim is.'

◆ ◆ ◆

A hush falls in the school hall when we enter. All eyes are on me, no doubt trying to desperately tell from my expression whether the body is that of Sara-Jane. Moving with William to stand at the back wall, I notice both Laura and Dale are in attendance. They're sitting at opposite ends of the front row of seats. I notice something else. No Miss Swan or Beryl Spencer.

When Wallace mounts the stage, Dale demands, 'What the sweet loving heaven is going on here?'

Wallace never gets a chance to answer because the twin doors suddenly fly forward. A figure staggers into the room. I'm shocked.

'Heather?' I cry with disbelief.

Oh God, she looks appalling. Even worse than when I saw her last night. At least she's all right. No longer missing.

A cop is hot on her heels. 'You're not permitted in here.'

She's sobbing, on the point of collapse. 'Sara-Jane's dead, isn't she? They've found her, haven't they? Not Sara-Jane! Not Sara-Jane!'

Laura staggers to her feet, her usually controlled expression one of incredulity. 'Abigail?'

Abigail? Abby? Why is Laura addressing Heather by her daughter's name? Heather's not Abby Prentice.

It's only when Dale rushes over to Heather that the truth becomes glaringly clear. 'Good God, Abby, what's happened to you?' He hugs his granddaughter close to his chest, kissing the top of her head.

Heather is Abby Prentice. There's a buzzing in my head. What the living hell is going on here?

Suddenly, it's not this older Abby I see, but the eight-year-old who burst into this very hall, fifteen years ago. Bloodied and dirty, shocking everyone with her reappearance.

Laura swiftly joins Dale and her *daughter*, tugging Abby away from her grandfather. 'Where have you been? Good Lord, what have you done to your hair?'

Over her mother's head, Heather . . . Abby makes nervous eye contact with me across the room. I'm seething. And so hurt. Heather-Abby has been playing me like a naive fiddle from the off. Why did I come back to this community of liars?

'This family reunion will have to wait.' Wallace's firm voice gets everyone's attention. 'We've identified who was murdered and buried in the school.' A deathly silence falls. 'The first thing to say is the body is not that of Sara-Jane Casey.'

Abby's choking sobs of relief fill the room.

'Who was found?' I ask.

Detective Wallace tells us, 'Someone who disappeared sixteen years ago. The school manager's husband.'

Dale weakly says loud for all of us to hear, 'Teddy Spencer.'

Chapter 25

FIFTEEN YEARS AGO

'I'm here to see Abigail Prentice.' Gem's voice shook as she spoke to the woman behind the entrance desk in the reception area in the hospital.

Gem felt so out of place here because it wasn't the local hospital but a private one a few miles outside the city. It was all silver chrome, mauve and white and the shiniest floor she had ever seen. And clean. Gleaming. Gem hadn't wanted to come here, but what choice did she have? She needed to speak to the last person to see Sara-Jane alive.

It had been two days since Abby had burst into the meeting at the school. Two very long days. Abby's reappearance had shaken the community to the core and left them reeling. Gem's mind flew back to the shocking scene in the school hall. When the little girl had collapsed, everyone had rushed over to her. The only one who hadn't was Gem. She'd rushed up to the bus driver who had found Abby and brought her back.

Tears streaking her face, Gem had pleaded with him, 'But where's the other girl? My daughter. She must have been with her.'

With sadness and pity he shook his head. 'She was alone.'

'I don't believe you,' Gem spat in his face. 'Where is she? What have you done with her?'

Gem hadn't thought twice about what to do next – she'd punched him and tackled him to the floor.

He'd tried to get her off him, but Gem had held him tight. She hadn't known she possessed such strength. It must be that special power that a mother summons up to protect her child.

One of the police officers had managed to drag her off and was about to place the man under arrest when the man insisted, 'You've got it wrong, mate. I'm a bus driver. I found her walking by the side of the road.'

'I know him,' someone shouted. 'He's telling the truth. Look at his work uniform.'

His ID soon verified who he was. Originally, he'd wanted to take Abby to the police station, but the child insisted she had to come to the school because she knew her mother would be at the PTA meeting. The child had begged him. So he had brought her here. Besides, his heart told him that the girl being reunited with her mother was a priority. The most natural place for a child to be was in the arms of her mother.

Gem wouldn't believe it and had run out of the school, frantically searching the roads nearby in a frenzy. Sara-Jane had to be here. Just had to be. Traci had found her, an exhausted mess, slumped against a wall. Her turmoil was made worse because she was sleep-deprived. Every night Gem huddled on her bedroom balcony in a blanket, waiting for Sara-Jane to make her way home. She wasn't eating much. She lived in this foggy existence racked by panic and fear. And, God help her, she couldn't stop thinking of the terrors that her child might be facing.

Gem sobbed in Traci's arms, 'I don't understand. Why hasn't my Sara-Jane come home? Why?'

But at least one of the girls was safe, back in the embrace of her loving family. Gem was over the moon for Abby's family. Their little girl had come home. But deep inside, the truth was she was experiencing this grudging envy that it hadn't been Sara-Jane who had burst through those doors. But now at least Abby could tell Gem what had happened. Who had taken them. Where Sara-Jane was.

And that's when the trouble had started. Abby had been bundled away in an ambulance by the time Gem and Traci had returned to the school hall. Then, when Gem had called at Laura's house, the family's police liaison officer had coolly informed her that she wasn't able to see the girl. That Abby was traumatised and under medical supervision in hospital. When she asked for the name of the hospital, Gem was told that was confidential information.

Gem had felt powerless. And in such deep pain. Her darling daughter was out there somewhere and Abby had the answers. All she wanted was to speak to Sara-Jane's best friend. That wasn't asking too much, was it? What almost ripped her heart out was thinking about what some evil monster was doing to her child. Were they hurting Sara-Jane even more in revenge for Abby having run away? That night, as usual, Gem had sat on the bedroom balcony with its view of the estate, waiting for her child to come home.

Traci had been appalled, spitting nails at the way Gem, a traumatised mother, was being treated, so she had asked around and discovered what hospital Abby was in.

The receptionist gave Gem a tight smile. 'What's your name, please?'

'Gem. Gem Casey.'

The other woman checked out her computer screen. When she stared back at Gem the smile was no longer on her face. 'Your name's not on the list of official visitors.' Her features turned hostile. 'You should be ashamed of yourself, hounding that poor child after what has happened to her.'

Gem was shocked by this unexpected attack. 'I haven't done anything to be ashamed of. I'm the mother of the other girl who was abducted.'

The receptionist's mouth formed an 'O' of surprise. She spluttered, 'I'm so sorry. I thought you were a journalist. We've had two of them so far trying to worm their way in here. You must be going through hell. As much as I sympathise with you, I won't be able to let you see Abigail Prentice. Only certain hospital staff, her mother and grandfather are able to see her.' She looked embarrassed, her eyes filled with an emotion that Gem was growing tired of. Pity. *Poor Gem, don't you feel sorry for her?* She didn't want people's compassion – that could come later. What she needed now was all the help in the world to find her daughter. And her best chance of achieving that at present was to speak with Abby.

Gem thanked the other woman for her time and marched out of the hospital. She wanted to smash her fist into something. Anything. Why was life so unfair? Why hadn't her girl come home too?

'Did you get to see her?' Traci was waiting for her outside. She had insisted on accompanying her to the hospital.

Dejected, Gem stared at the floor. 'They wouldn't let me. A few journalists tried to see her, so she's being closely guarded.'

'Poor kid,' Traci muttered beneath her breath. Then she clamped her jaw so tight her teeth must have hurt. 'You haven't come all this way not to see her.'

Gem raised her head, suddenly feeling like the weight of the world was on her shoulders. 'There's no way I can get to see her.'

Traci squared her shoulders and lengthened her neck, her jaw set with determination. 'I've got a plan. This is what we're going to do . . .'

◆　◆　◆

'Help! Help!' a voice screamed near the hospital entrance. 'He's nicked my purse. Hurry, someone help me. I've been robbed.'

The receptionist left her station and flew out the door, closely followed by the security guard standing near the entrance. Gem watched it all from the corner on the other side of the ground floor. While Traci carried on playing her part in their plan, collapsing in front of the guard, Gem managed to sneak into the reception area. While speaking to the receptionist she had noticed how the other woman's eyes would stare every now and again at the automatic doors behind her, which led to the ground floor ward. Gem might be wrong, but she was sure that was where Abby's room was.

The automatic doors silently opened and Gem walked into the ground floor ward. How was she going to find out which room it was?

'Can I help you?'

Gem nearly jumped at the authoritative voice behind her. *Remain calm. Cool.* Small smile attached to her lips, she turned to find a nurse behind her. 'I'm here to give Abigail—'

'Abigail Prentice?' Her austere features lit up into a smile. 'Her grandfather said he was sending over a gift for her.'

'Yes, Dale asked me to bring it. He would've done it himself, but he's having to attend a meeting.'

'Room six.' She pointed down the corridor. Her face turned serious again. 'Leave the gift and go. She needs to rest.'

Gem quietly entered room six. It looked so large compared to the small girl sitting up in bed. Gem's heart went out to her because Abby looked dreadful. Her eyes were big and sunken in her tiny face, her cheekbones so sharp the bone looked about ready to cut through her cheek. Usually her hair was neatly tied back in a bow but today it was loose, a thick mane around her tired face.

Poor, poor child.

'Who are you?'

Gentle smile in place, Gem approached the bed. 'Don't you remember me?'

Abby's big eyes got bigger as she checked Gem out. Then she shook her head.

Gem asked, 'Is it OK if I sit down on the bed?'

The little girl hesitated and then nodded. Still smiling, Gem sat down. 'I met you at the school and you might remember me from the school gate—'

'You're Sara-Jane's mummy.' The girl's eyes came alive. 'You ride a bike. It looks old. How do you stop the wheels falling off?'

Gem laughed. 'I mend bikes. Lots of people bring their bikes to me so I can fix them.'

'They sound sick, like me. I wish I was a bike and you could make me better.' Her little body quivered.

Gem placed a calming palm on Abby's leg. But the girl's shivers only got worse. 'It's OK now. You're back home. But Sara-Jane isn't. Can you tell me what happened to her?'

Abby's breathing became ragged, a heavy and harsh sound in the room. 'I don't remember.'

'I want you to take your time. There's no rush. But I need you to think—'

'I don't remember. Don't remember.' Suddenly Abby started knocking her knuckles to the side of her head. Rocking back and forth. 'Don't remember. Sara-Jane.'

Eyes wild, her neck flipped back with a piercing scream. It was one of the most terrifying sounds that Gem had ever heard. Abby leapt out of the bed and slumped down into a corner of the room. Her knees raised to her chin. With sightless eyes she rocked back and forth again and again.

Then she wouldn't stop screaming Gem's daughter's name.

'Sara-Jane! Sara-Jane!'

The door flew open. A shocked Laura Prentice, a nurse behind her, stood in the doorway. 'Get away from my daughter!'

The nurse rushed across the room to attend to the hysterical child.

Shaken, Gem walked over to Abby's mother. 'All I want to know is what happened to my Sara-Jane. I want her to come home just like Abby has.'

Laura got into Gem's space. 'If you come *anywhere* near my daughter *again*, I'll have the full force of the law come down on you.'

Chapter 26

'You are a liar,' I tell Abby flat out in my coldest voice.

She's standing there on my doorstep, anxious, hands wringing in that nervous tic of hers while my fingers bite into the door, resisting the urge to slam it in her face. *Lying face.* I can barely look at her. No wonder she knew about Sara-Jane having to have stitches after falling off her skateboard, she was her bloody friend. What hurts, really hurts, is that I genuinely thought Heather-Abby-Whatever-her name-is was on my side. That, finally, I had someone to lean on. That I wasn't going to have to do this tragic journey on my own. It turns out she's a liar too. Yet another person to add to my list of people who have done all in their power to stop me finding out the truth.

But, at least, there was an important truth I found out. The body in the makeshift grave at the school isn't Sara-Jane. Relief. Heartbreak. I feel both at the same time. On the one hand, I can breathe easier knowing that the human remains found are not my beloved daughter. There's still hope Sara-Jane is alive.

Suddenly the weight of everything presses down on me. Despite my hold on the door, my legs start going from under me.

'Gem!'

Abby's cry of alarm is a buzz in my ears. Rushing forward, she saves me from hitting the floor. Somehow, she guides me back into the main room, getting me sat down on the sofa. My chest heaves heavy with a lack of oxygen and too much emotion.

Her gaze darts around. 'Have you got anything strong around here?'

'I don't drink.' Closing my eyes briefly, my head shakes, trying to remove the mental muddle. My eyes snap open to find Abby hovering, her fingers flexing, not sure what to do. I look her over and something occurs to me. 'Abby was so small, but you're tall.'

'Are you OK?' When I nod she sits on the ground at my feet and folds her long legs. How could I have been so stupid to think that this troubled, frail young woman was really a journo trying to uncover the truth about the kidnapping of my daughter?

'One night, when I was thirteen,' she informs me, 'I went to bed a little itty-bitty thing and woke up the next morning as tall as a beanstalk.' Her voice lowers. 'I suppose I take after my mother in more ways than one.'

'She's so worried about you,' I say softly. 'You just upped and disappeared from medical college. Why? I don't understand.'

Sorrow floods her face. And the pain in her eyes . . . it hurts me so much to look into them.

'You have no idea what it was like. I was the "girl who was abducted". That's how everyone around here saw – sees – me. Poor little Abby who managed to get away. Even after all this time I still feel their pity. Hear their whispers.' She draws in a shaky breath. 'It kept bringing up the guilt that consumes me about being the one that got away. That I left Sara-Jane behind. That's why I decided to go off to study medicine. I couldn't take it any more.'

I don't interrupt. How can I when someone is in that much agony? 'Once there I thought things would magically sort themselves out. But they didn't.' Her face clouds. 'I'm a twenty-three-year-old woman. All I want to do is remember.' Her fist slams into her thigh. 'Remember! Remember!'

'Hey! Hey.' She looks so torn up that I settle down on the floor facing her. 'Take it easy. I'm not going to pretend I'm not as angry as hell with you, but the last thing I want to do is make you think that I don't care. Then again, that's why I'm so bloody furious with you. You made me start to care.' *To love you.*

'I care about you too.' Her whisper shakes. 'It was like my mother didn't want me to remember. I think she was afraid that if the memories came back I'd have a breakdown or something. End up like Dad in a psychiatric hospital. Each time I asked her to get me help to hopefully trigger the past she flat-out refused. Mum just wanted to wrap me up in cotton wool. She thought she was helping me but all she was doing was making it worse.'

I put myself in her mother's shoes. Sara-Jane has come home and can't remember a thing. Do I help her recover her memory? Or do I deliberately do everything in my power to stop those terrible memories from coming back? And they will be terrifying, there's no doubt about that. What mother wants her child to live with an everlasting horror?

'But it's my life. I'm an adult.' Abby must be reading my mind because that's exactly what I was about to utter next. 'So I decided to do something about it. I waited for the right opportunity to arise, and it came when the body was discovered at the school. I suspected that you would be coming back—'

'So you faked an identity, that of a journalist. A journo of all things.' The bitterness is back in my words. 'Do you know something? You'd have made a great journalist. Most are a bunch of liars too.'

Abby doesn't answer, sitting there quiet and mousey. In my head, my conscience says, '*Enough. Leave the poor girl alone.*' But I'm not listening.

'So you drop a significant piece of information in my lap, that Abby thought one of her abductors was familiar. You made it up too, to hook me.'

She looks shame-faced and nods once. 'I had to get you to believe that I had sources and contacts who could provide some of the answers we need.'

'And, of course,' I start, 'you used me to get information from your mum and granddad. And it had to be me, not you, because you couldn't take the chance of them recognising you even with the short haircut.'

She touches her head. 'It does make me look different, so most wouldn't recognise me as Abby. Mind you, Mum would. She'd suss it was me even with a bald head. Still, I took great pleasure in cutting off Little Abby's hair.'

'So you manipulated me?'

Her mouth opens, then closes as if rethinking what she's about to say. She admits, 'Yes, I did. In a sort of way. I'd never do anything to hurt you, Sara-Jane's mum. *Never*. But I needed answers and you were the only person who I could see would help. I wanted to help you, help Sara-Jane and help myself. If that's manipulation, then, yes, I'm guilty.'

I'm not ready to let her off the hook quite yet. 'As for that stunt in the van? Practise that in front of the mirror, did you? I was scared out of my wits.'

Her eyes flash with outraged indignation. She's raging. 'Practise? You were scared out of your wits? You weren't the one slung in the back of a van fifteen years ago. You weren't the one who thought she was going to be dead before the end of the day. You weren't eight years old. Too young to even grasp what the fuck was happening. Eight years old! Can you even begin to imagine what that was like?'

The silence heaves with her ragged breathing. Her fingertips brush her lips as if she's said too much.

Then it hits me what she's actually admitted. 'So you *do* recall being in a van? So you do remember what happened.'

'The crowbar was real.' Her trembling fingers fall from her lips. 'See, I've been having these flashbacks.' A sheen forms over her eyes. 'Sometimes I see a man . . . Men . . . I don't know. Crowbar . . . Other times a van. Black. Big. Inside a bottomless cave, dragging me in.'

Her hand whips out. Grips my arm like a chain around the bone of my wrist. Its imaginary cold metal sends a chill creeping through my bloodstream. She's talking so quickly I can barely keep up. 'I thought: what if I got a van and travelled to where we were . . .' Her voice falters. '. . . where we were abducted. And then drive to the place where the bus driver found me. I might remember. And if you were with me, I'd feel safe.'

It comes back to me, the whimpers and scary noises she made in the van. The washed-out colour of her face. The lifeless eyes. It's then that it really hits me.

This is Abby.

Abigail Prentice.

The girl who was my daughter's best friend. The child who was abducted with her all those years ago.

The one who got away.

I gently ease my hand away from her grip. 'Did being in the van jog your memory?' *Please let her say yes.*

'Some of it. I see the flash of a crowbar in the back of the van—'

'So the information about the crowbar really came from your recovering memory.'

She nods. 'Maybe the crowbar was how I managed to escape. I can't be sure.'

'You should go to the cops. Tell them everything.'

Abby pulls her knees to her chest. 'They won't believe me.'

'But you're the only witness. They won't have any option but to listen to you.'

Her eyes become glassy, a little frightening, as if they're blanking out secrets. 'I went off the rails when I was younger. Got into all sorts of trouble. Mum was always having to bail me out with the police.' Her expression becomes intense. 'If I had remembered, the police wouldn't have believed me. Just another tale that mad Abby Prentice is telling. And, yes, before you ask, I've had my mental health issues.'

She looks so broken. So very broken. My heart goes out to her. I want to embrace her and hold her tight. Tell her that it will all get better. Be like a mother to her. But, see, that's the problem – I'm not sure I have it in me to be like a mum. To anyone. It all withered and died the day that Sara-Jane was taken.

Something occurs to me. 'When we went to the medical college, the student who I was speaking with outside looked over my shoulder and practically ran for it after that. Was it because she spotted you in the car?' Abby doesn't need to answer for me to know the truth.

'What happened in the room you shared with your roommate?'

She takes a breath, but breaks eye contact from me, my guess is because she's embarrassed about what she's about to disclose. 'I had a nightmare. A terrible one. I started shrieking. It freaked her out. The medical college asked me to leave.' She ends with a shrug.

Don't they offer mental health services? It doesn't make sense that they wouldn't support someone with Abby's history.

'We can find the truth,' she pleads. 'Together. Me and you. Like we were doing before.'

Alarm suddenly clouds her face. Shakily, she stands up. 'You're leaving, aren't you?'

'Sara-Jane wasn't in that grave. There's nothing more for me here.'

Abby tears up. 'I can't do this without you.'

Abby looks so lost. Exhausted. Like she's been swimming out at sea for years with no sign of the shore in sight. And I'm her only lifeline. But I can't. No more. I have to save all my strength for me. For the hope I still have for Sara-Jane.

I get to my feet. 'Goodbye, Abigail.'

Abigail. That's the first time I've said her name to her.

She takes out her notepad and writes in it, tears off a sheet and leaves it on the side table. 'I'm staying in rented accommodation. That's the address.'

I take her in my arms and hold her tight. 'Abby. Abby. Abby,' I whisper her name over and over in her ear. This girl is going to need all the love she can get.

Finally, I step back.

Break our bond.

Abby says one last thing before she leaves. Something that puts me on edge again.

'I don't know how. Not yet. But Teddy Spencer's murder is connected to the truth about me and Sara-Jane.'

Chapter 27

It's over.

I can't go on like this.

There's tons of advice out there for people in my position. The people who've lost someone but never get any answers. The people who haven't had the one who was lost returned to them, laid to rest, somewhere you can go and weep. Even someone you can hate for what they did. Advice that tells you to keep looking, keep believing and keep hoping. Never give up. That's what I've done and look where's it got me. A police service that thinks grief has driven me mad. Years of false leads and false hopes, ending up with a dead body in the school chapel that I think must be my girl and turns out to be someone else entirely. Not to mention bringing me back to this flat and the Rosebridge that hates me.

There'll be other false leads and false hopes, but I won't be following or believing them.

It's over this time.

I'm leaving here. For good.

I check my phone. I've been doing this a lot since I asked Abby to leave. Part of me thinks she'll get back in touch. Plus, I'm wracked with guilt. That silly trick she played wasn't meant with any harmful intent and now I've chucked her overboard. Just like so many other people have been turning their backs on her trauma for years. I make a note to let Dale have Abby's address so he can make contact with her. That girl needs looking after.

But not by me. There's nothing more I can do for her.

Then there's a knock at the door. My heart jumps slightly. Perhaps it's Abby come back?

But it's only Traci. Only now do I recall how I'd left William after the remains were identified, fleeing back here to find my bike. Then riding and riding, pedalling on a road to nowhere.

She lets herself in. 'Can you believe that the body was Teddy Spencer? At least it wasn't Sara-Jane, which means there's still hope.'

Hope. She's so right. Hope still remains a bright light in my life. And where there's hope there's Sara-Jane.

'Did you know Teddy at all?' Traci's gossipy voice brings me out of my thoughts.

'No.' I'm not in the mood for small talk. I just want out.

'Poor Beryl. She thought the sun shone out of his backside. When he disappeared, word on the school grapevine was that he'd done a runner with another woman.'

'Why would people think that?' I go through the motions for Traci's sake.

'No disrespect to Beryl, but her husband was a nice man and probably got bored to death with her. Or the sight of those awful clothes of hers.' Traci makes a face as she follows me into the bedroom. 'Don't get me wrong, I'm not one of those who calls her Batty Beryl – you know me, if I've got something to say it will be to your face. But maybe he got tired and wanted a change.'

Her words dribble away and her eyes grow wide when she spots my open rucksack on the bed. 'You're not leaving, are you?' Her tone is a mixture of disappointment and hurt.

I turn my face from her. This woman was my lifeline when I needed someone fifteen years ago. Out of everyone, she never let me down. She was my protector when others wanted to cut me down to size.

Softly but firmly I reply, 'There's nothing left for me here. The last thing Sara-Jane would've wanted is for her mummy to be sad.'

'You're not coming back, are you?'

My jaw works, trying to find the words, but she already knows what the answer is. There are too many memories here and I need a fresh start. But Traci deserves more than the back of my head. I twist back around and our gazes catch and hold. Which one of us rushes forward first I will never know, but suddenly we're in each other's arms. Her smaller, stouter body presses against mine, giving me a cushion of security.

Into my ear she murmurs, 'You look after yourself. By rights, you should've found a good man and had a bunch of young ones years ago.' There's a catch in her voice. 'Gem Casey, you were made to be a mother.'

She leaves me speechless. Overcome with sorrow. I did meet someone once, but each time we broached the subject of kids I'd feel swamped as if I was drowning. How could I bring more children into this world when I wasn't able to protect the one I was given?

With a sniff, Traci breaks our embrace. Then smiles. 'Don't be a stranger. You're welcome back here anytime.' Suddenly her brows dip together. 'What about William? He's gone home. He'll be upset that he never got a chance to say goodbye.'

I'm sad too that I won't see him; nevertheless, even the sexual pull between us can't make me stay. 'You tell him how proud I am that he made something of his life. And give him the biggest hug for me.'

'I'll leave you to it.' At the door she slaps her forehead and rolls her eyes. 'Nearly forgot. Something came in the post for you while

163

you were out. It was too big to go through the letterbox. You'll want it before you set off.'

She returns with an A4 brown envelope. Once I'm alone, I take it to the kitchen table and open it. Inside is a sheet of paper with a drawing scrawled on it. It's a pencil drawing of an angel. Its wings are spread. It's carrying a harp in one hand and has a golden crown over its head. It has a face. But no features. No mouth. No eyes. No nose. Nothing. It looks like the angel in the stained-glass window of the chapel that Sara-Jane was scared of. I ease down into a chair. My mind hurtles back in time.

'I hate computer studies, I just hate it,' Sara-Jane moaned.

She was sitting on the ground next to me in the hallway while I repaired a bike.

'But why? Computers are fun.'

There was a pause before she admitted, 'I don't like going in there.'

I held my hand out and she knew to pass me a small screwdriver. 'Where's there?'

'The chapel.'

I stopped working and gave her a penetrating stare. 'The chapel at school?' Now I understood – that's where the computer suite was. 'What's wrong with the chapel?' I began working again, tightening a screw.

'The angel in the window.'

The terror in her voice made me stop working, to give my daughter my full attention. I slowly explained, 'Many years ago people thought angels would protect you. And in some religions, they have them on windows—'

Impatiently, she interrupted. 'I know all that stuff, Mum. It's just this angel hasn't got a face. What I mean is, it has got a face but it's empty.'

'Empty?'

Sara-Jane had reared on to her knees beside me and the bike. 'No eyes. No nose. Or mouth. Empty.'

I had tried to picture it, this faceless angel. If I was honest, I found all types of religious imagery weird, and that included angels. Some of that stuff is downright scary.

I put down the screwdriver and took her little face between my palms. 'Do you want me to have a word with your teacher?'

Her response was a vigorous shake of her head. 'She'll think I'm a baby or something. I'm OK, Mum.'

But she wasn't. That night, Sara-Jane screamed the house down during a nightmare. Eyes wild, she'd clung to me, her small body heaving, fighting to find air.

'He's here! He's here!'

'Who's here?'

'The angel! The angel with no face!'

Perhaps I'd read somewhere that the way to help a child overcome their fears is to encourage them to confront them. So, I suggested that instead of being afraid of the angel with no face, she should draw it instead. To my surprise this worked, except that she didn't stop drawing it, she kept on doing it. In the end, during parent-teacher time, her teacher told me that whatever subject Sara-Jane was given to draw or paint – Mummy and Daddy, birds in the trees or a steam train on a railway track – there was sure to be the angel with no face somewhere in the background.

I run my fingers across the drawing, slightly smudging its edges. Sara-Jane's killer has struck again. However, this time they've been careful. His last visit resulted in me chasing him down and nearly catching him. I've obviously spooked him, but not enough. Now he's using the mail to torment me. The envelope gives nothing away, my address typed on a generic label no doubt from a generic printer. The envelope may have DNA evidence, so maybe I should pay Detective Wallace another visit? I suspect the cop has got his hands full with the Teddy Spencer murder investigation.

I thought I was the only one who knew Sara-Jane was both frightened of and obsessed by that angel. Someone else obviously knows too. How did the person doing this know about the angel? Did she tell him? Why would she do that? Or did she tell someone else about the angel before she was taken? Someone like . . . My mind spins with names, people, with . . . Of course. Her bestie.

Abby.

What if she told Abby as well? Good grief, although I'm convinced it was a man, what if it's been Abby all this time putting my daughter's belongings and memories of her through my door? What if the dark and confusion were playing funny tricks on me, making me assume it was a guy? When I previously confronted her about this, Abby swore blind it wasn't her.

Unless . . . Something unbelievable strikes me. I sit ramrod straight in the chair. It's too horrible. No way. Yeah, but what if . . . ? I can't think it. No . . . I have to.

I say it aloud. 'Unless eight-year-old Abby was Sara-Jane's killer.'

That's crazy. Madness. Isn't it?

When Abby reappeared after the abduction, she had blood on her head. What if it was Sara-Jane's blood? What if all that stuff about her not being able to remember is make-believe? A cover-up for her to conceal the truth of what she did as a child? I mean, you hear the awful stories about some children becoming murderers. Maybe this explains why, as a child, I always found her a strange little girl.

Has a faceless angel led me to the identity of my child's killer?

God, has Sara-Jane's killer been with me all this time? Inside the sanctuary of the home I shared with my daughter? It leaves me feeling sick and raging. Boiling hot with anger.

I'm going nowhere.

I'll never be at peace until I get the answers I want. With steely determination, I empty my rucksack. Find the paper Abby wrote her address on.

Then I leave and go gunning for Abby.

Chapter 28

Fifteen Years Ago

My Agony

Sara-Jane's Dad

Exclusive Interview

Gem almost missed the newspaper headline on the rack at the local store. Perhaps it was because of the chilly reception the guy behind the counter gave her when she came in. Which was strange because this man had always been so friendly and supportive since Sara-Jane had been taken. He'd refused to allow Gem to pay for anything, offered to help with any search. And placed two 'missing' flyers of Sara-Jane in the store window. But today he was avoiding Gem's eyes.

A whole week. That's how long it had been since Sara-Jane was gone. Taken. Snatched. Ripped out of her mother's life. Gem wasn't sure how much more of this she could take.

She called the police at least four times a day: 'Have you found her?'

The answer was always the same: 'There have been no sightings of Sara-Jane.'

Every night Gem sat on her bedroom balcony waiting for Sara-Jane to appear. Waiting for Sara-Jane to come home. Abby's family continued to keep her well out of Gem's reach. Why couldn't they understand that all she wanted to do was find out where her beloved daughter was? Although the lead detective on the case had delivered the bad news that Abby still hadn't recovered her memory and they weren't sure whether she ever would.

Gem set her shopping basket on the counter.

Over her shoulder, the store owner glanced pointedly at the newspaper display. 'I'm sure it's all made up.'

Gem didn't answer him. For the first time since Sara-Jane was gone he took money from her.

Approaching the newsstand, Gem's fury grew.

Charlie.

The bloody gall of that lowlife. Not once had he contacted her since Sara-Jane had vanished. Not bloody once. Not a phone call, a visit to the flat. Nothing. She wondered what diseased hole some seedy journalist had found Sara-Jane's father in. She didn't need to read the grubby article to know it would basically be Charlie dragging her name through the gutter. Of course, he'd have missed out the part where a bleeding Gem had grabbed her shrieking child and run for their lives after he'd belted her in the mouth, loosening two of her teeth. Gem hadn't got on with her mother, but there was one piece of valuable advice she had given her: *'If a bloke raises his hand to you, don't stick around to give him a chance to do it twice.'* Gem had heeded those wise words and never gone back.

Let the deceitful bastard milk his fifteen minutes of worthless fame and damn him to hell.

Despite her better judgement, Gem picked up the newspaper. It shook with the motion of her trembling hand. Her eye was immediately drawn to the photo accompanying the story. It was a large photo of her. Gem was flanked by two police officers outside the police

169

station. She looked emotionless. Gem looked at it with dismay. It made it appear like she was being arrested. For kidnapping her own child.

Put it down. Put it down. Don't read this poison.

But, unable to resist, Gem read. Her head started spinning out of control. The paper seemed to turn to ash between her fingers as she read Charlie's account of his *agony.* Each crafty lie began with the catchphrase: 'I'm not blaming anyone.'

> 'A child needs a father. I'm not saying if I'd been there, this wouldn't have happened but it's a question I torment myself with every hour of every day since my little princess went missing.'

> 'Her mother did her best, no one's saying she didn't. But she couldn't cope, you know? Perhaps that's why she turned on me in the way she did. You know how people always have to find someone else to blame for their own mistakes.'

> 'The incident outside at the school? Where she attacked me? I don't want to get into that, you'll have to speak to the police about it, they were involved. But whatever happened, there's never any excuse for violence.'

> "It's usually someone in the victim's family who did it. That's definitely what happened. In my opinion anyway. Although I'm not suggesting these two mums were involved, that would be stupid. Why would they kidnap their own kids?'

> 'You can't imagine the agony I'm going through.'

Gem felt like she'd been run over. And over. Again and again. How could Charlie say that rubbish about her? Even she didn't think that Charlie could get this down 'n' dirty. Whatever else, she still deserved the respect of being the mother of his child. Lost child. Oh God, when's Sara-Jane coming home?

Gem stood isolated and alone in a long shuddering silence.

'If you read it, you have to buy it,' the store owner's rough voice intruded.

'I'll take care of that.' It was Traci who had just entered the store. She marched over to the man behind the counter and practically chucked the coins at him. In a harsh whisper she continued, 'You wanna be ashamed of yourself. Your dear departed wife will be turning in her grave at your treatment of a poor, grief-stricken young mother.'

'Traci, I didn't mean anything by it—'

She shoved her palm in his face. 'Speak to the hand because this pretty face ain't listening.'

And, with a smart turn, she headed to Gem. And took her for a pick-you-up drink inside The Hangman's Retreat. Gem's phone rang as soon as they sat down.

'Hi, Gem. I'm a researcher on *Drivetime Hour*. We'd really love to have you on for an interview. You know, to put your side of the story. To correct the lies Sara-Jane's father is telling. I mean, they are lies? Gem? Are you there?'

Seeing the distressed expression eating away at her neighbour's face, Traci snatched the phone. In her best menacing voice she growled, 'Piss. Off.'

Gently, Traci tugged the newspaper still clutched in Gem's hand, which was now furrowed and limp from being gripped so tightly. Traci scoffed nosily after she'd finished reading.

'That idiot was bound to raise his snake head. It's all rubbish, Gem. No one's going to believe it.' Then she added hopefully, 'Sue the bastard. That's libel what he's said there.'

'Sue him? What with? Buttons?'

Traci's forehead furrowed. 'What does he mean by the incident at the school? He says you attacked him.'

Two men who lived on the Rosebridge came into the pub. They were laughing and joking and then they spotted Gem. One nudged the other and whispered something. Both stole glances at Gem as they headed towards a table. Gem felt like a caged animal in a zoo.

Gem shot to her feet. 'I just want to go home.'

She never noticed Traci's eyes burning into her back. Wondering why Gem had never answered her question about Sara-Jane's dad accusing her of hitting him outside the school.

At home, Gem headed straight for the bedroom balcony. Waiting. Watching.

For Sara-Jane to come home.

Chapter 29

Abby lives in a building that looks more like a homeless hostel than a home for an ambitious young journalist. But then again, she was never really a journalist. It's a three-story tenement with a takeaway fried chicken shop on the ground floor, a charity shop next door on one side and a pawnbroker on the other. There's a strong door to the side of the takeaway that leads up to the rooms above. I check out the handwritten names near the intercom system. They show there are eight rooms in the tenement. The names suggest that this is one of those 'here today, gone tomorrow' places, a refuge for people who don't want to be found. Steve H, Jimbo, Old Sparky and at number 8, Heather. It's the last room to be listed so I assume it's located at the top. And I betcha there's no lift.

I ring *Heather's* room number but get no answer, so I try one of the other numbers instead.

A bad-tempered woman answers. 'Who is it?'

'I'm looking for Abigail . . . I mean, Heather.'

'Why don't you ring her number then?'

It's important to play nice when you want access to a building like this. 'She's not answering. She's been unwell. Could you let me in to check on her?'

After some muttered swearing, the deadlock drops, allowing entry. A lone and unsteady light shines in the hallway. Room 8 is up a musty staircase with a carpet that's frayed and pockmarked with cigarette burns. The place reeks of mildew and damp. The stairs creak as I go up. When I pass Room 2 on the first floor, the door is open. According to the intercom downstairs, this room is occupied by Steve H. I tap on the door and a young guy with long unkempt hair, thin and unshaven with tats breeding all over his neck and arms appears. I catch a glimpse of a guitar propped against the wall behind him and a strong whiff of marijuana.

'I'm going in the right direction for Heather, right?'

At first, he's blank and then he beams, literally from ear to ear. 'Heather's at the top along with the sky and the moon and the stars.'

Obviously, he's been puffing merrily away on weed for maybe too long, so I move along before he can pick up the guitar and play a piss-poor version of something like 'What The World Needs Now Is Love'.

He's not finished with me though. 'She said if anyone comes looking for her, tell them she's moved.' His bloodshot gaze narrows in suspicion, guarded. 'You're not the cops, are you?'

'Why would the cops be looking for Heather?'

'Why do the cops look for anyone?' He studies my face to see if he's getting a cop-like vibe off it. When he's satisfied that he isn't, he goes on, 'She's probably not answering because she's upset. Heard her crying.'

I'm alarmed. 'Upset? What about?'

He's suspicious again. 'Why don't you ask her? Top floor, room on your right.'

Number 8 is an attic room with a door that some would call retro while others would chuck out with the trash. There's a light shining out from under Abigail's door. I knock. No answer. I wait a few seconds and then knock again. No answer again.

I press my ear against the door and there's no sign of activity inside.

'Abby?' An invisible hand seizes my belly because something feels off.

The lock looks fragile, so I turn the handle and try to force the door, but it falls open because no key has been turned. This room is as grim as the staircase that leads up to it. Everything is tinged with a smoke-stained brown. The walls and ceiling are cracked. Furniture mismatched and tatty. I'm grimly reminded of the first few places I stayed in after fleeing the Rosebridge. The first bedsit I stayed in was worse than this, reeking of something far worse than mildew and damp – unhappy lives. The smell of lemons is strong in here. In fact it reeks of her perfume of choice. Maybe her perfume doubles up as air freshener.

A solitary lamp glows on a bedside table. Next to it is a half-finished bottle of vodka with an empty glass. But where's Abby? My pulse kicks up as I slowly move around the unmade bed. Stop. There's a body lying on the floor. Its limbs are twisted, its face turned away.

'Abby!' I scream and rush over.

I'm on my knees beside her in an instant. Seeing her this vulnerable I know there's no way she can have killed Sara-Jane. I feel the pulse in her neck. It's there, but barely; it's thready and weak. That's when I notice several pill bottles on the ground not far from her, one turned on its side with some of the contents spilled out.

Urgently, I roughly shake her. 'Abby, wake up.'

No movement. I do it again. The same happens.

'Not Abby as well,' I plead. 'Not another girl gone. I won't lose Sara-Jane's best friend as well.'

Her colour is that worn by the dead.

I'm in the hospital, holding my head in my hands, riddled with guilt. I've felt terrible guilt about Sara-Jane for so many years and now the death of her best friend may be on my conscience too. After I'd called the emergency services, the paramedics hadn't been able to revive her at the scene, so they'd gotten her quickly to the hospital with me right by her side. But Abby had remained unresponsive.

'What has she taken?' a nurse had brusquely asked on arrival as a medical team got Abby on a gurney.

'What?' I was dazed, not understanding what he wanted from me. Then the penny dropped. Hell, I didn't read the label on the pill bottle. *Stupid! Stupid!* Then he fired a barrage of quickfire questions, none I'd been able to answer:

What tablets did she take?
Did she mix them with anything?
Does she do drugs?
Take any medications?

Stunned and shaken, I'd rushed behind them as they wheeled her urgently to a large room. Through the glass window I'd helplessly watched Abby fixed up to a machine and tubes and lines being attached to her. I'd been hypnotised by all the coloured lines on the machine monitoring her vital organs. Wiggly-worm lines moving up and down, up and down. That was good, was it? That's what you see on the medical dramas on the telly. It's when the lines go flat accompanied by a terrible momentous droning sound that there are problems. That you know the person is dead.

A nurse spotted me and guided me away.

Please God, I'm begging with all my heart, please don't let that be the last time I see Abby alive.

I slumped into the chair. I was catapulted back to the bleakness and terror of the nights I'd sat forlornly on the balcony waiting for Sara-Jane to come home. She never did. And now would the same happen to Abby? Are they still fighting for her life or is she dead? Abby cried out for help and what did I do? Turned her away. Put my own shit above her needs. It now feels as if I have two daughters to rescue and this one is the more urgent.

Let her live. Please God, let her live.

A voice penetrates the fog in my mind. 'You're the woman who brought Abby Prentice in?'

There's a nurse standing in front of me, a different nurse this time. She's older, looks like she knows how to deliver bad news. Shakily I get up, my breathing leaving my body in erratic spurts.

'She'll be OK. Physically at least.' *Thank you! Thank you!* 'She hasn't taken enough of anything to do herself any real harm. Everything's in working order, but she won't be feeling too good for a couple of days.' She pauses, her expert eye levelling me with a penetrating stare. 'Are you a relative?'

'Her aunt.' I have to lie or they won't allow me to see her otherwise. 'Can I speak with her?'

'For a few minutes, only.' Then the nurse is gone, obviously rushed off her feet.

Only then do I see the name of the ward on the wall:

Dale Prentice Ward

That doesn't surprise me. Not only is Abby's grandfather an important figure on the governing board at Princess Isabel School, he's also a prominent contributor to many organisations, obviously including this hospital. That his granddaughter should end up in a ward dedicated to him feels very sad.

My heart clenches with dismay when I look down at Abby. She lies there listless against the blue sheets, her chest rising, desperately seeking air. Her fluttering eyes look at me. Her fragile hand reaches for mine and squeezes. Gently and with the care of a mother, I wipe the damp off her forehead. She smiles at me like a little girl who's woken from a bad dream. She looks so innocent.

'Sorry,' she rasps, her eyes bruised with pain.

'I'm the one who should be apologising. I should have realised that things were bad.' Another squeeze of her hand. 'What happened?'

She shrugs. 'I don't know. Just had a drink and some pills to help me sleep. It must have got out of hand.'

Callous though it may seem with her lying in the hospital bed, I have to ask. 'Did Sara-Jane ever talk to you about an angel in the stained-glass window in the chapel?'

'The one with no features on its face?'

It's my turn to tense. So I wasn't the only one who knew that my daughter was scared of the angel.

I feel so hurt knowing what Abby has done. 'It's been you all along, hasn't it?'

Abby stammers, 'I don't understand.'

'Someone sent me a picture of an angel with no face. Sara-Jane told me. It turns out she also told you. No one else knew—'

'Hang on a minute—' Abby loudly protests, hastily attempting to sit up, but weakly flopping back again.

I refuse to allow her to have her say. 'It was you who sent me her socks and glasses. I asked you straight out before and you denied it.'

'It wasn't me.' Her cry of denial is so weak. 'I only know that she didn't like the angel because every time we went to computer class she would look up at it and shiver. I asked her if she was scared of it, but of course she said she wasn't. But I knew she wasn't telling me the truth.'

'Did you murder Sara-Jane? Maybe it was an accident. Or something.'

'How can you even ask that of me?' She's furious, eyes flashing. 'I loved Sara-Jane with all my heart. She was the only true friend I had.' She's gulping, having difficulty getting the words out. 'We were kidnapped off the street by two men. In a black van. Since you came back, I'm remembering more.'

Abby's gaze becomes bleak. 'If Sara-Jane's mother doesn't believe me, what is the point of me going on?'

'Don't say that. Life is precious.'

'I'm on the edge.' Her voice wobbles. 'I'm tired. I don't have enough strength on my own to stop from falling off.'

It sucker-punches my gut that I'm her last chance of helping her remember what happened. 'I believe you,' I say. 'I had to ask. I have to find the truth.'

'I thought you were leaving.'

'I was. Then the angel arrived.' I also ask, 'What did you mean about Teddy Spencer being connected to—?'

A furious voice from the door brutally cuts me short. 'Get away from my daughter!'

Chapter 30

'Get away from my daughter!'

It's a re-run of the past. The same vindictive words Laura used to warn me off Abby fifteen years ago when her small daughter was in another hospital room. Abby's raging mother bears down on me. I stand my ground. I'm not scared of this woman.

Bring. It. On.

'How long has *this* – you and her – been going on?' She talks over my shoulder to her daughter as if I'm not there.

Shifting ever so slightly, I block her view of her daughter. 'I discovered Abigail ill at home. I accompanied her to the hospital so she wasn't alone. In these situations it's always best to have another person with you.'

Laura uses being taller than me to look down her nose. That expression of distaste tells me I'm beneath a worm in the food chain in her eyes. 'And why would you be visiting Abigail? What business is she of yours?'

She doesn't express any level of thanks for me finding and rescuing her only child. What mother behaves like that? Then again, Laura Prentice has always blamed my Sara-Jane for what happened to her daughter. Her accusation of my girl trying to strangle hers still rings in my ears to this day.

Laura's pretty mouth is flecked with spittle. 'Have you been conversing with Abby behind my back?'

'Mum,' her daughter urges, clearly nearly at her wits' end, 'I don't need your permission to talk to other people. I'm not eight years old any more.'

I hastily add, 'Abby and I met by accident outside the school when Teddy Spencer's body was discovered, and we got chatting. We've stayed in touch because obviously we have something in common. When I called her and got no answer, I was worried, so paid her a visit to check she was OK and . . .'

This seems to be the final straw. Laura's face is inches away from mine. Up close I see the layers of make-up she wears, which can't quite disguise the darker circles beneath her eyes. The grooves dug deep either side of her mouth.

'You've got her address! A stranger has my daughter's address and I don't!'

Two porters wheeling a patient past us into a cubicle at the far side of the ward look at us with open concern. Laura finally realises the spectacle she's making of herself. In public. She always maintains an icy performance in front of others. She's no doubt got an etiquette book that has a rule that goes something like: *Never behave like a woman from the Rosebridge Estate in public.*

Her neck reels back, a muscle flexing in her jaw, struggling for control. Her voice drops, cool and collected. 'My daughter's a very vulnerable young woman. You should be aware of that. We don't need outsiders, like you, interfering.'

Abby, poor girl, seems to shrink at the implication of her mum's words.

I think it's best that I leave. Tomorrow will be soon enough to talk to Abby about Teddy Spencer's murder. 'I'll see you—'

Abby cuts over me. 'Gem! Please! Don't go yet. Wait outside. Please.'

Under the open disapproval of her mum, I do what she asks. But I don't go far. I listen to them speak.

'How could you do this?' Laura accuses her daughter.

'Not now, Mummy.'

'I've got to hold my head up in this community. You'll be the talk of town within the hour.'

'Is that all you care about? Other people? That fucking school?'

I quietly gasp, waiting for Laura's reaction. I've always suspected that she's the kind of woman that if you press the wrong button she'd backhand you right back in your place.

'I hear you might have tried to kill yourself.' Her voice is so soft, sounds so caring that I start to revise my opinion of her . . . 'Well, the next time you try, come to me. I've got the lot. Antidepressants, tranquillisers, heavy-duty painkillers. Plenty to go around.'

I can't have heard right, can I? Abby's own mother encouraging her to kill herself? My heart thunders.

Laura continues. 'You may call me wicked for what I've just said. But ask yourself this question: what is the point of your existence, Abigail? What good are you contributing to the world? All you had to do was be Little Laura and you'd be living the same wonderful life as me now.'

How can she do that to Abby? It makes my skin crawl. I suppress my natural instinct to storm in there and protect Abby from her mother's poison.

Aching with sadness, I walk away and wait. After five minutes, Laura leaves her daughter and joins me outside. She's changed tack. Laura just manages to squeeze out the words. 'Look, I'm sorry, Gem. I shouldn't have spoken to you like that. Obviously, I'm upset.'

But she can't quite bring herself to thank me for most probably saving her daughter's life.

'All that matters is that Abby is going to be fine. You're a mother. You understand how it is? You want to protect your child.'

But my child never came back. Yours did. You're still a mother. And I'm . . . I don't know what I am any more.

Instead I say, 'It would upset me too if you thought I was going behind your back by talking to Abby.'

Laura chooses her words carefully. 'Abigail is a very troubled young woman. It's inevitable given what happened to her. In the same way that she can't remember anything about the abduction, she imagines she remembers things that didn't happen, but which she's convinced did.'

That had never occurred to me. What if her memory of the crowbar wasn't real? Her other flashes of the past really false memories?

Her mum has my full attention as she carries on. 'As you'll understand, that made her growing up difficult and put a tremendous strain on my relationship with her. I've done my best to shield her from future trauma. It's not healthy for her to be obsessing about the past. When she recently disappeared . . .' Her mouth wobbles.

'That must have been terrible for you.'

'It was one of the worst periods of my life. I thought I had lost her again.' She considers me. 'You do what you need to, but please leave my daughter out of it. You'll understand if I overreact a little when it looks as if someone is raking over the past. It's not good for Abigail.'

A door at the end of the corridor flies open and a man in a suit and highly polished shoes rushes through the corridor. He's holding a glass of red wine and wouldn't look out of a place at a raffish cocktail party. Perhaps that's why it's a few moments before I realise who it is. Dale.

He ignores his former daughter-in-law and snaps at me, 'What on earth is going on? I'm attending a charity benefit upstairs and then get word that my own granddaughter is on a ward after a drink and drugs overdose?'

Laura glares and gasps. Dale doesn't wait for a reply, handing me his glass of red wine and marching into the ward. The heels of his smart shoes click-click along the floor. A clearly stunned Laura takes a few moments to recover from his appearance before she follows him, calling to his back, 'Where do you think you're going? Stay away from my daughter!'

I sink what's left of Dale's wine. My first taste of alcohol in years. After placing the glass on a chair I hurriedly follow them. They've stationed themselves on either side of Abby's bed.

'Right, young lady,' Dale starts, 'you're coming home with me.'

'I'm warning you, Dale,' Laura threatens, baring her perfectly polished teeth. 'My daughter stays in *my house*.'

He explodes with anger. 'You've always been vindictive and spiteful.'

'I think you're forgetting something.' Her voice is sinister and low with triumph.

The colour drains from his face. He says not another word, but still looks like he wants to hurdle the bed and shake the living daylights out of her.

During the whole exchange Abby lies stiff and unmoving, ignoring both her mother and grandfather, her gaze focused on the ceiling.

A nurse comes in to intervene. She looks determined to throw the pair of them out, but she wilts a little when she realises the man is Dale Prentice. However, she holds firm. 'I'm sorry, I've called hospital security. If you don't leave immediately, you will be escorted from the building.'

Dale is unimpressed. 'You remember me, nurse? You should do, you were here when the renaming ceremony for the ward was held. No doubt you're aware that I have friends at a senior level in this hospital. Now, perhaps help me collect Abby's things, she's being discharged.'

'That's out of the question. Now, please leave.'

Tenderly, Dale takes his granddaughter's hand. 'Don't worry, my sweet flower. I'll be back in the morning with a senior member of the hospital management team and we'll go back to my house. You'll be more comfortable there.' He nods respectfully to me. 'Gem. Have a good night.'

His son's former wife receives a deathly glare.

When Dale has stalked off, Laura gives Abby a quick peck on the cheek. 'I'll be back in the morning, my darling.'

I turn to Abby, who's no longer still, but visibly trembling. Then I realise she's silently weeping.

The nurse insists, 'You'll have to leave too.'

'No.' Abby pulls herself into a sitting position, tears rolling down her face. 'I'm leaving.'

The nurse warns her, 'I don't advise that.'

Abby ignores her and turns to me. 'I want to come home with you. Your home. Sara-Jane's home.'

Chapter 31

'I haven't told you everything,' Abby tells me once we step inside the flat.

Annoyance tightens my lips. 'No more lies, Abby. The number one rule, if you stay, is you treat me with respect.'

Her hands flutter in the air. Abby looks so thin and weak. 'You misunderstand me.'

'Then enlighten me.'

Abby draws in a deep breath, then another. 'When I said I can't remember what happened, it's not just the day we were taken. There are days, sometimes weeks that came before the kidnapping where I can't recall a thing.'

That shakes me up. I hadn't realised the extent of her amnesia. It must be so debilitating for her to go through life with part of her memory just gone. Thank God, she's starting to remember more and more.

Shivering, her arms wrap around her middle. 'I've seen untold therapists to try to unravel the past. But I can't remember most of what happened.'

I decide to leave it alone. Abby has been through the depths of hell tonight. The last thing she needs is having to revisit more trauma. Tomorrow will be soon enough for us to talk about the past. About Sara-Jane again.

But there is one thing I can't leave. I speak to her as a mother would: 'Sara-Jane was a lover of life. When she woke up she would do the same thing every morning – she'd open her mouth as wide as she could, suck in as much air as she could and fill up her lungs. It was like she was trying to capture and keep as much of life as possible.' I take my own deep breath. 'It's not my business, Abby, but I'm making it my business. Whatever happened back at your flat, please don't do it again. If you ever need to talk, I'm just a telephone number away.'

'Even if the memories come back with monsters I can't fight?'

'You won't be fighting on your own, this time. I'll be gloved up right alongside you.'

I don't know how she knows – sixth sense maybe – but she automatically gravitates to Sara-Jane's bedroom. It leaves me as jittery as hell. I hover behind Abby as she stands in the doorway. She takes in the functional, ordinary furniture.

Abby's hands ball by her side. 'Me and Sara-Jane would talk about having sleepovers at each other's homes. We'd play all types of games, put on our favourite music.' Her voice dips. 'Of course we knew that was never going to happen. My mum would have walked through the fires of hell before allowing her daughter to stay on the Rosebridge Estate.'

My head cocks to the side, giving me a better angle to assess Abby. 'Do you remember many things from back then?'

'Sara-Jane told me she had a really big poster of Beyoncé on the wall.' Abby turns to me. 'I'd like to sleep here, if that's OK with you. I feel close to her here.'

I want to cry, you know, bawl my eyes out. I stopped crying about this long ago, but today . . . Today, the pain of it all squeezes and won't let go.

A knock at the front door interrupts us. I pull away and allow Abby to get settled in.

'Hey, stranger.' William's all smiles at the front door. I need his ray of sunshine.

Instead of inviting him in, I step out, quietly closing the door behind me. We lean on the balcony and take in the view. There's the laughter of small kids in the background, having a good time in the playground. Thank goodness the council has refurbished it, it was like a death trap before, all concrete and jutting rusty nails. I was so nervous about Sara-Jane playing there, expecting at any moment to get a call that she'd had an accident.

William asks, 'How's Abby doing?'

Scowling, I look at him sideways. 'How do you know what happened?'

'I'm a man with my ear to the ground.'

'Oh yeah,' I tease. 'Been gazing in your crystal ball, Mystic William.'

Our elbows touch. Our heads shoot up at the same time. Our gazes catch. Then, by mutual consent our mouths meet. I close my eyes to savour the taste and sensation of his lips. Hold my breath as the stress drains out of my body. He doesn't use pressure to maul my mouth like so many guys do. What William does is gently explore, take his time as if we have all the time in the world. The heat of his large hand cups the back of my head. I raise my hands with the intention of drawing him inside. Then I remember.

Abby.

Snapping my eyes open, me and my throbbing lips step away from him. God, my face is burning.

With a nervous laugh I tell him, 'This is where I'm meant to say, that should've never happened. But you know what, I'm glad it did. You, William Waddell, are a very sexy man.' Traci's son makes me feel mellow and leaves me with that *the living is easy* vibe. Back in the day I was so shy about talking about sex, even with Charlie,

Sara-Jane's dad. What success has taught me is you speak up for what you want and you go after it. And I want William.'

His gorgeous eyes crinkle as he laughs back. 'I hear you. Mum's at home, so best to cut it short or she'll have us both married by morning.'

We giggle. Then I get serious when I remember my search for the truth. 'What can you tell me about Teddy Spencer?'

He leans his folded arms back against the balcony's edge again. 'His connection with the school was long before my time working there.'

'I remember that the talk was he disappeared just before us Rosebridge families brought our kids to the school. Your mum's convinced that he left Beryl. That Beryl was too embarrassed to admit it, so made up this story about him disappearing.'

'Poor Beryl was right all along.' He pauses before adding, 'That's probably why the police took their time announcing who the body belonged to. What I've heard is that when she went to them to report her husband missing they investigated, but as soon as they heard the rumours that Teddy was probably playing away from home and had run off with his lover they pulled the plug.'

With a shake of his head, he carries on, 'They're probably scared shitless that Beryl's going to take legal action against them. No doubt the police have used the time to cover their tracks. I mean, considering who Teddy was they should have done a thorough investigation.'

I frown. 'What do you mean? Who he was?'

'He was the school's moderator.'

'What's that?'

'The children in the final year of the juniors, Year 6, have to take a range of tests.' I nod, because as a parent I knew all about the SATs. 'Someone outside the school marks them. After that they are passed to a moderator who goes through all the papers to ensure that the correct grades are given.'

'Gotcha. So Teddy Spencer got the final say on what the results were.'

'He was the moderator for most of the primary schools in the area.' He pauses and looks at me. 'Does that help?'

'Not really.' I let out a very long sigh. 'His job sounds like a heck of a lot of boring paperwork. And, no disrespect to the dead, Teddy sounds really boring too. Why would someone kill him?'

Silence. We both look out across to the playground again. This time it's empty. One of the swings tips and shifts in the breeze.

'Can you do me a favour?'

William switches back into professional mode. 'I can't break rules concerning confidentiality.'

'I'm not asking you to,' is my swift response. 'Can you ask around – discreetly – about Teddy Spencer? See if there was any dirt on him. A man as boring as that had to be getting his kicks from somewhere.'

◆ ◆ ◆

Inside, Abby's fast asleep on the bed in Sara-Jane's room. She's the picture of peace, curled up on her side, knees tucked into her tummy. Her small rucksack is still on the bed, so I take it and, with it still in my hand, sit on the chair. Folding my arms around it, I hold it tight to my middle. And watch Abby. She's under my care and protection now. I'm scared I won't be able to protect her, just like I didn't protect Sara-Jane. The guilt's back, biting chunks out of me. I'm not fit to be a mother. Anyone's mother. Nevertheless, I can't leave Abby on her own, she's so vulnerable.

I must've fallen asleep, because the next thing I know I'm slowly opening my eyes. There's a strange noise coming from somewhere.

Whimpering. Moaning. The sound an animal makes when caught in a trap. Eyes fully open, I'm not sure where I am. Why am I in a chair? There's a bag at my feet. There's something in the corner of the room. Moving. Alive.

Abby. She's in the corner, her knees under her chin and rocking, just like that time I visited her in the hospital when she was eight years old. Her face looks scary. I rush over to her.

'What's going on?'

Her eyes are wide. Haunted. 'I remember how I escaped.'

Chapter 32

Fifteen Years Ago

The Girls

Sara-Jane slowly regained consciousness in the back of the van. Pain screamed in her head. She hurt so much. Trying to open her eyes only made the pain worse. Her breathing was ragged. Uncontrollable. The sound thick in her ears. Her chest trembled as it rose and fell, rose and fell. Something was wrong. Why was she lying down? What had happened? Her chest trembled with fright, she was so scared. She knew she had to open her eyes no matter how much it hurt. Her eyelids twitched and slowly opened. Above her was a metal ceiling covered in peeling black paint, dotted with orange-brown rust. Wherever she was, *it* was moving. Her features scrunched up in confusion.

Why am I lying down? Where am I? What happened? Suddenly her mind flashed with a storm of images.

Van.

Man.

Men.

Screaming.

Screaming.

Abby.

Oh my God! Abbeeeee!

Sara-Jane sucked in a shattering punch of air as it all came back to her. Men grabbing and dragging them into the back of a van. Her hands moving in a frantic motion to support her, Sara-Jane managed to sit up. A hot, piercing pain in her ankle made her struggle to breathe. She gasped, sucking long and hard to fill her lungs with air. The pain was so bad. So bad. Her ankle had been injured while trying to break free from her kidnapper.

'Abby?' she urgently called.

Some of her other senses kicked in. Whimpers. Like a wounded animal.

Abbeeeee!

Her best friend was huddled in a corner, her knees locked under her chin. Back and forth Abby rocked, whimpering and sobbing, tears staining her small face. Her eyes were wild and lost. Her face a mask of terror. Seeing her friend in such a terrible state was almost too much for Sara-Jane. She nearly burst out crying.

That time she fell off her bike in the playground on the estate came rushing back to her. She had fallen and cut her knee. It had not been the pain that made her cry but the sight of the blood. As she cried that day on the estate, someone hunched down next to her. Billy-Bob from next door. He might have stunk of drink, but she liked him. Liked his sideways smile. Liked his nickname for her, Sara-Jay. She would never forget what he had told her, looking her straight in the eye: *'Sara-Jay, in life, you can't always cry when you're in pain. Sometimes the best way to deal with pain is to get up and do something about it.'*

She had dried her tears and done something about it, then he'd helped clean her knee.

Gingerly, swallowing back pain and tears, Sara-Jane crawled over to her friend. The girls stared at each other and then threw themselves into each other's arms. And wouldn't let go. Sara-Jane said nothing, rocking her friend, caressing her hair. She felt every harsh breath coming from Abby's terrified small body.

Abby sobbed, her body leaning heavily into Sara-Jane's. 'I want to go home.'

The girls stayed like that for some time, holding on to each other for safety and strength. Nevertheless, Sara-Jane knew that they needed to somehow get away. They had to '*do something about it*'.

Gently, she tried to disentangle Abby from her arms, but the other girl wouldn't allow her. She sobbed harder, clinging to Sara-Jane for dear life. With as much tender but firm care as possible, she managed to free herself from Abby's embrace.

Sara-Jane dropped her tone to a whisper, her gaze furtively checking the divider behind which their captors were driving. 'We need to talk quietly because we don't want *them* to hear.' Abby nodded. 'Do you know who those men are?'

Violently, Abby shook her head. Sara-Jane was scared too, because whoever these men were they were bad people.

Sara-Jane squeezed the other girl's trembling hand and then began moving away. The pain in her ankle throbbed with a vengeance. Abby fell forward, frantically trying to grab Sara-Jane back. 'Don't leave me. Don't leave me. Pleeeeze!'

Sara-Jane pressed a finger urgently to her lips. Abby needed to be quiet. 'We need to get out of here. Now.'

Her gaze scanned around for something, anything. Anything to help get them out of here. It wasn't going to be easy, because the van was moving. Where it was taking them, she didn't know, but she wasn't going to hang around to find out. She had noticed that the van had a motion of going fast, slowing down and sometimes coming to a stop. Sara-Jane was a clever girl. She would bet her life that the stopping was caused by the van having to stop at traffic lights. She searched the van, under the tarpaulin she had been lying on. Nothing. She looked and searched. Nothing. Nothing. Then she spotted a steel crowbar. Sara-Jane was comfortable with all sorts of tools because her mum used different ones to fix bikes.

Before starting their bid for freedom, Sara-Jane looked over to check on Abby. The smaller girl was no longer sobbing, but her poor body was shaking so badly. Sara-Jane focused her whole attention on the twin doors. She used as much pressure as she could muster on the crowbar against the lock. Too much pressure, because the crowbar slipped from her hands and clattered to the floor. Both girls froze in fright, breath catching in their throats. Their terrified gazes swung towards the driver's cabin. They waited in dread. For the van to slow down. For someone to get out. For the thud of menacingly loud footsteps coming towards the door. For the doors to be flung open.

The van kept moving.

Sara-Jane got back on with her plan of escape, more careful with the grip around the crowbar this time. Face filled with determination, she twisted and turned. Turned and twisted. Click. The lock was released. Quietly, she pushed the door slightly with her fingertips so she could see outside. It looked like the countryside with trees and lots of green grass. It was a long road with no other cars in sight. Sara-Jane didn't know where they were.

She turned to Abby. 'When the van stops at the next traffic light you have to get out.'

Abby gasped, 'Aren't you coming?'

'My ankle is hurting really bad. You have to get out and get help. Read the number plate and then find someone to call the police.'

Abby's eyes widened. 'I'm not going on my own.'

For the first time ever Sara-Jane was getting annoyed with her friend. She didn't have time for this. And she was scared. So frightened. 'Come over here.'

After a moment's hesitation, Abby reluctantly crawled across the van to sit beside Sara-Jane. They held hands as they waited. The van slowed down. Came to a halt. Sara-Jane wanted to throw her arms around her friend and never let go, but there was no time for that. She pushed the doors back and helped Abby get down into the road.

'Get help,' she mouthed.

Abby looked at the van's number plate. Then she looked back at her friend. And mouthed her name like a silent scream: 'Sara-Jane! Sara-Jane!'

Twisted around, Abby bolted off into the trees.

With care, Sara-Jane quietly closed the doors. Held her breath until finally the van began its journey again. Slumping with relief against the van walls she let out noisy, jagged punches of air. Sara-Jane had another plan. She wriggled and hid herself under the tarpaulin, hoping when her captors came, they'd think that the van was empty and that both girls had got away. When the time was right, she'd escape from the van and run for her life.

The van finally finished its journey. Sara-Jane heard voices outside. She lay still. The van doors opened. The beat of her heart boomed in her ear.

She heard voices.

Silence.

The van shifted with the weight of someone climbing in.

Sara-Jane felt the heat of their body almost suffocating her. She stopped breathing. Footsteps moved around. Stopped. Suddenly the tarpaulin was snatched back off her.

'Do something about it.' That's what Billy-Bob told her she should do.

Sara-Jane sprang up. And attacked.

Chapter 33

'I need to get some air.' Once Abby's finished telling me the truth it's my turn to escape. I have to get out of there.

Really, I should stay with her, make sure she's all good, because recovering such a traumatic memory must be tearing her up inside. I'm breaking apart too. I go into my bedroom, open the French doors and step out on to the balcony. Suck in as much fresh air as my body can handle.

All I can think about is my brave Sara-Jane. My brave, brave girl. To help Abby escape like that. I see her struggling with the crowbar and not giving up until she's busted the lock of the door. I'm so proud of her. Sara-Jane, always standing up for the underdog.

'I love you, Sara-Jane.' My whisper of love floats away on the wind.

Abby's arm circles my waist. I didn't hear her join me. I say, 'The past is coming back to you. But first and foremost, we have to make sure it doesn't destroy you. The return of memories can be a very powerful thing.'

I think back to Abby as Heather in the black van. Crowbar clutched in hand, desperately trying to recover the memory of what happened. That took true courage to do that. True grit. But it nearly destroyed her. Is all this worth putting her well-being in jeopardy?

'One of the kidnappers said something strange,' Abby abruptly reveals. 'I'm sure that he called Sara-Jane by her name.'

'What?' My brain clicks into gear. 'Did he know her?'

Abby looks at me straight on, her face a mixed bag of emotions. 'You might think I've lost the plot, but I know this has got something to do with Teddy Spencer's murder.'

She'd told me that earlier. 'What makes you think that?'

She taps her temple. 'The memories locked up in here.' Excitement glints in her eyes. 'Everything leads back to the same thing. It's in the middle every time. One place.'

We say it together: 'The school.'

Abby and I lean on the balcony. She says, 'Somehow we need to get inside the school.'

Punching off the balcony wall, I grimly smile. 'I know the exact person who may be able to help us with that.'

◆ ◆ ◆

'Are you sure they're going to show up?' Abby asks the following night, shivering against the late evening cold.

'They'll be here.' Although the truth is I'm starting to doubt they will too. The person we're meeting should've been here ten minutes ago.

Here is inside the grounds of Princess Isabel School. We're tucked behind a brick shelter where the school's large metal bins are stored. The school premises that once seemed so innocent now looms over us like a house of horrors, hiding all kinds of morbid secrets. But it's the chapel that holds my reluctant attention. Although it's dark, and despite the street lighting shrouding an unnerving hazy light around it, its rose-coloured glass and pottery front almost sparkle. The stained-glass windows are multicoloured and so alive. And filled with angels. The angel with no face, I swear, is looking down at me with no eyes. I'm hypnotised. Can't look away. Abby curls her arms around her body as she shivers and eyes the chapel too.

A noise in the undergrowth nearby rips my attention away from the chapel. A black shape appears by a brick wall that looks like a small child crawling on its hands and knees. Only when it draws closer do we see the outline of a fox that has come hunting for food among the bins.

'How long are we giving this?' Abby's impatience shows.

The sight of a shadowy and hooded figure appears by the iron fence that separates the school from the street. They expertly monkey-climb up the railings and down into the playground. The person walks towards us, emerging out of the darkness. The street light strikes half of their face.

Rosa. The lovely young woman staying with Dale for the summer while she gets work experience at the school.

It was a long shot to ask her if she would let us into the school so we could search the head teacher's office, but she was my only hope. I remember how kindly she spoke to me, telling me how sorry she was to hear about what happened to Sara-Jane and welcomed me into Dale's home. I was banking on Beryl Spencer having given Rosa the keys to the school building. I was right.

Rosa bites her lip, looking so uncomfortable. 'I still not sure about this.' Her Italian accent is much thicker when she's stressed. 'I feel that I betray Miss Beryl and Miss Clare.'

'You won't get into trouble,' I reassure her, as I did when I saw her earlier. 'We're trying to find out why Beryl's husband was murdered.'

Rosa makes a hasty sign of the cross. 'Miss Beryl so upset. My heart break for her.' Her expression changes. 'Shouldn't you leave the *polizia* to find the killer?'

'Of course, but us helping won't hurt.'

Rosa considers what I've told her, before informing us, 'Things are bad here. Miss Clare receive a letter from inspectors of schools that they want to inspect school in the new term. She's scared they will lose their out-up status.'

Out-up? Ahh, she means outstanding. I'm not surprised to hear that the inspectors will soon be coming through the school gate. It's not just any dead body that was found. Teddy Spencer was also the school's SATs moderator. Sixteen years he's been buried in the chapel.

Rosa's voice is low, thickened with urgency. 'Don't take hoods off. Whatever you do, don't switch on any of the main lights. Let's go.'

Following Rosa's lead, we crouch low and hug the wall towards the entrance of the school building. With a jangling of keys Rosa opens the locks. As soon as we're inside, a burglar alarm begins to flash on the wall, warning that it's about to go off if the security code isn't punched in. Rosa uses the light on her phone to light up the keypad. She taps in the code.

The alarm continues to flash. We've got a problem.

'What's wrong?' My whisper is urgent and breathless.

'I don't know. If they've changed the number without telling me, we run like crazy. It's directly linked to the *polizia*. They'll be here within minutes.'

She takes a deep breath and tries again. I hear my heartbeat in my ears. We wait. The alarm falls silent. I have the urge to sag heavily against the wall in relief, but we don't have time for that. We follow her down a corridor to the school manager's office, where she works. Once she's opened up, she leads us through Beryl's office towards Clare Swan's.

The twin photos in the double picture frame still sit on Beryl's desk. The black and white one of Beryl and her husband as a very young couple. They look young, teens really. She's staring at him

200

adoringly while he looks longingly into the distance. It's the other photo that draws my attention more. I've never really studied Teddy Spencer before. He's in a formal grey suit, holding a glass of champagne to the camera lens. He's not smiling. I imagine that Beryl fell hook, line and sinker for his homely face. The expression in his eyes is calculating – or is that my mind working overtime and making it up?

Rosa's speaking again. 'I don't feel good about this. Dale has found me a good summer job and I feel wrong.'

I don't have time for her guilt. I hold my hand out for the key. 'You stay in here while we open up.'

Rosa ignores my instruction and opens the head teacher's door instead. She tells us to wait while she checks the blinds are down, before switching on a desk lamp. The room fills with shadows.

'Ten minutes only, that's what we agreed.' Then Rosa leaves and waits inside Beryl Spencer's office.

Me and Abby stare at each other. She says, 'Ten minutes isn't long enough.'

'It's going to have to be.'

'What exactly are we looking for?'

'I'm not sure. But we're agreed that at the centre of everything that's happened is this school.' I do a three-sixty turn, taking in the measure of the room. 'You do the bookcases and tall filing cabinets. I'll check the smaller units and Miss Swan's desk. And don't forget, put everything back exactly as it was.'

We hit the room like burglars. I begin with the small cabinets on the side wall. They're not locked. They're stuffed full of old, yellowed children's records. And letters. And report books. Basically nothing.

'Anything?' I call out to Abby as I head towards the head teacher's desk.

'Nothing.'

'Keep going.' If those don't yield anything then we search for loose floorboards.

In my experience, people are not very inventive when it comes to hiding physical things.

There's a folded letter on the desk. I pick it up. Hell! It's a notification from the local inspectors that they will be visiting the school in two weeks' time, which is when the children will be back. So Rosa was right, the school and Miss Swan are under tremendous pressure. I refold the letter and place it back.

Guilt starts gnawing away at me, which is ironic since I swiftly batted Rosa's concerns aside not that long ago. If we find something incriminating tonight, it will bring more trouble to Miss Swan's door.

Sara-Jane. Finding Sara-Jane is all that matters.

This reminder gets me looking through the first three drawers of Miss Swan's desk. The bottom drawer won't open. It's locked. That's the other problem with people and their secrets, they think a mere lock and key will keep it hidden. Not from the likes of me who knows all about picking locks. Mending bikes has taught me lots about the ins and outs of the mechanical workings of things.

Inside is a single item. A pale yellow A4 envelope.

'Abby.' I can't keep the excitement from my voice.

'What if it's something really personal?' Abby says over my shoulder, conscience obviously pricked.

The only conscience I have concerns the truth about my missing daughter. I peel the envelope open. Inside are a set of papers. Scanning them, nothing jumps out at me; they seem innocent enough. However, why keep them under lock and key in a drawer?

It's Abby who figures out what we're looking at. 'They are the individual SATs test results for children in . . .' She carefully reads. 'In English and maths. The date on them is from seventeen and sixteen years ago.'

Two and one year before Sara-Jane and the other children from the Rosebridge started attending the school. Sixteen years ago was when Teddy Spencer disappeared and was obviously murdered.

'But,' Abby continues, sounding puzzled, 'there's another set of test results from the same years.'

'Two sets. That's weird, isn't it?'

Rosa rushes into the room. 'We must go.'

I put the drawer back. Grab the envelope. As we flee, I knock over the photo frame on Beryl's desk. The frame smashes to the floor. Shit! I lift it up and the black and white picture of Beryl and Teddy flutters to the ground.

'We must leave. Now.' Rosa sounds desperate. 'I will fix Teddy picture.'

Panicking, I shove the black and white photo inside my jacket along with the envelope containing the two different sets of SATs results.

Chapter 34

Someone's waiting at my front door when we get back. I smell trouble in the air. I'm bang on right, because when we get closer, I see who it is.

Laura Prentice.

Trouble is wearing clothes that are classic-chic, topped off with a lightweight jersey coat and sky-high ankle boots. And, of course, a scarf. This scarf's lilac with a poppy flower pattern. She looks totally out of place here. The irony of her, of all people, being here, on the Rosebridge, isn't lost on me. I never thought I'd see the day. The wrinkle in her nose like she's going to catch some deadly disease is the dead giveaway she's not comfortable one bit here. Then she sees her daughter and her expression changes in a heartbeat. There's such longing in her face, such open suffering, I actually feel sorry for her. How can I not respond to a mother wanting desperately to see her child?

However, Abby has got other ideas. She's in front of me and starts backing away, feverishly mumbling, 'No. No. I won't do it.'

Her mother looks so hurt. 'Darling, I only want to speak with you.'

Consciously I move my body in such a way as to block Abby escaping along the balcony. Maybe I'm wrong. Laura did spew all that crap at her daughter in the hospital. But I feel rotten seeing a mother's pain. Somehow, mother and daughter will have to mend bridges.

I cut through the tension. 'Let's take this inside. A nice cuppa should start us off on the right foot.'

I lead the way, Abby behind, then her mum. Except Laura Prentice hovers on the threshold of my home. Her expression of disdain is back. Her hand rubs down her side as if she's forgotten to wear her gloves. I'm back to being hacked off with her again. Huffing, I start walking. I wish Abby's mum and her 'my shit don't stink' attitude would get lost, so me and her daughter can figure out the significance of what we discovered at the school. And I know exactly the person who might be able to help us do that.

A while later I arrive with tea in the main room to find mother sitting gingerly on the single sofa and daughter in a corner almost trying to disappear through the wall.

After laying the tea down I say, 'I can leave you both alone if you want.'

'Yes.' That's Laura.

'No.' That's Abby.

Right. I sit down and stay. And something occurs to me. I ask Laura, 'Why would a school have two sets of SATs test results? Two for English and two for maths? There should only be one set for each of those subjects. I only ask because you've been part of the PTA for a long time. You'd have access to that type of information.'

'When I was the director of the PTA, you're right, I did have access to many things. Not test results though. Because they concern individual children's results, they are confidential.'

So she proves to be a non-starter.

Laura stirs her tea. And it's not the delicate stirring that comes with years of practice of having afternoon tea, it's the loud sound of cement being stirred before being poured over my dead body. After sipping her tea, her attention quickly fixes on her daughter.

Her features soften. 'I didn't know where you were. I couldn't sleep at night because I was so worried.'

Avoiding her mum's piercing gaze, Abby quickly looks at the floor. 'I had stuff I needed to work out. I wanted to find out what happened that day.'

That day. We all know what day she's referring to.

'And did you recall anything?' Her mother knocks back her tea in one strong swallow.

My breath catches. The last thing I need is Abby sharing that we've broken into the school. And why I'm asking about SATs results.

'A few things. This and that.'

Good girl. Her gaze rises and she catches my expression of approval.

The other woman gets to her feet. And starts walking towards her daughter. Abby's palms flatten against the wall. Her mother stands in front of her. I notice that they are a similar height, such a contrast to how small Abby was as a girl.

'You need to come home.' Laura caresses her daughter's cheek. 'Your old room is all ready for you.' She leans in and whispers something in her daughter's ear. Abby remains rigid against the wall.

Then, wearing a satisfied smile, Laura tells me, 'I think it's best that I go now.'

I accompany her to the door. Before she goes, she asks me a question. 'What is the most important thing about a school?'

It sounds like a trick question. 'The education it gives children.'

'Wrong. The answer is three things. Reputation! Reputation! Reputation! If a school loses that, it's nothing.'

'That's a bit cynical, isn't it?'

'Too many people think that schools are still about children running around doing tree rubbings with crayons and growing cress in soggy cotton wool. Those days are long gone. Schools are businesses that need money. That money comes from funding. They thrive on the excellence of their reputation because that's how they get more money.'

Continuing, her gaze intensifies. 'The problem for Princess Isabel is it now has the revolting stench of death about it. Murder. Murder and outstanding don't go together. That's why I was at the Town Hall earlier today, having a meeting with education inspectors who are very worried about the school. If you keep sticking your nose in, asking questions, you will ruin the school's reputation once and for all.'

◆ ◆ ◆

'Can you tell us what all this means?'

We're sitting on the floor in my main room. Me and Abby have spread out all the SATs test results for the one person who might be able to help us.

William.

Scrutinising them without picking them up he answers our question with a question. 'Why are there two lots of results for each year? Why do many of the child have two different marks for English and maths?'

I reply, 'That's what we're hoping you can tell us.'

He sends me a suspicious stare. 'Where exactly did you find these results? Children's individual marks should be confidential.'

Me and Abby share a knowing glance. I say, 'We both think that whatever the reason for most of the children having two different sets of SATs marks will be the answer to why Teddy Spencer was murdered.'

'But his death hasn't got anything to do with Sara-Jay's disappearance.' He looks baffled, adding, 'Has it?'

It's Abby that fills him in. 'Every which way we turn, the school is in the centre like a spider's web catching its prey.'

William observes Abby closely. 'I'm not accusing you of anything, but the way I hear it, it was your idea to sneak out of school that day, not Sara-Jay's.'

'But only she knew that I'd been leaving school,' Abby threw forcefully back. 'What if someone in the school sussed out I was doing this? I did it the first Wednesday of every month. What if they figured out this pattern? All they had to do was wait for me to do it again. And pounce.'

Mulling over what she's told him, William crosses his long legs. Without responding, he looks back at the papers, this time picking one up. And scrutinising it closely.

He addresses us, slowly and carefully, making sure we understand what he's telling us. 'Each school in the country is sent a set of maths and English tests for their top junior class. The test papers are exactly the same. When the children have completed their tests the head teacher keeps them under lock and key somewhere secure. Miss Swan kept Princess Isabel's tests in her safe. Then they are sent to an external examiner to be marked. Are you with me so far?'

After our nods, he resumes. 'Then they are passed on to a moderator to make sure that the results given are fair. And consistent.'

He picks up the other piece of paper. 'These look like the moderator's assessment of the results. The moderator has made significant changes. The big problem being that the moderator's altered results are much better than the actual results.'

I say, 'And it's the results of the moderator which are the final ones.'

William quickly looks through the results for the following year. 'It's the same pattern as the year before.'

We all glance at each other with the same unspoken question. Who was the school's moderator? And collectively announce: 'Teddy Spencer.'

William curses under his breath. 'It looks like Teddy was cooking the test results for the school. Beefing them up so they looked better than they actually were. Why would he do that?'

Abby tentatively asks, 'Do you think that's why he was murdered?'

I shove in, 'That doesn't make any sense. They're only exam results.' *Reputation! Reputation! Reputation!* Laura's earlier words come back to me. 'Unless,' I hesitantly add, 'this had something to do with maintaining the standing and stature of the school.'

William looks angry. 'If you're going where I think you're going, you're wrong. So wrong. Clare Swan would never be involved in this.'

There's something about William's face . . . He's holding something back.

'What aren't you telling me?' I demand.

His lips screw up. Ah, I'm right. With a resigned sign, he admits, 'Clare and Teddy were in the same class at primary school. They both went to Princess Isabel.' His voice turns harsh. 'Which doesn't mean anything. Not really.'

Abby simply points out, 'Once again, that school is at the heart of it.'

He grabs the remainder of the papers, the test results for the following years, after Teddy Spencer's disappearance. 'These all show that fifteen years ago, the results and the moderated results more or less matched. Miss Swan definitely had nothing to do with it.'

I add, 'That was the year the Rosebridge children started coming. It shows that when the kids from the estate came the results got better. There was no need to cook the books any more. Do you know how many people insisted that our kids were going to drag the results of the school into the gutter?' I can't help the triumphant smirk that spreads on my face. 'Looks like my Sara-Jane and the other kids from the Rosebridge Estate saved that bloody school.'

My mind scrolls back to the parent protest outside the school on the first day the families from the Rosebridge turned up. All those banners about how the school needed to remain outstanding. All the time it was a lie.

Abby hikes her knees up and leans her chin on them. 'We can't ask Miss Swan because she may be involved.' She ignores William swearing again. 'We need someone who knows the school well. Knows it inside out.'

I jump to my feet and look down at them. 'I know the *perfect* person.'

Chapter 35

Fifteen Years Ago

Gem's hand trembled as she read the letter. She read it three times before dropping back into the chair in the main room. No one could find out about this. No one. Gem folded the letter and placed it on the table.

There was a knock at the door. It was probably Traci, who continued to be a great comfort. And a protector, because word had got around about what Sara-Jane had done to Abby at school. And of course, people were only too willing to believe Abby's mother's 'choking' version of events. It was not that people were hostile to her; they still greeted her and wished her luck, showed their sympathy for her plight, but there was now a wariness, a knowing in their eyes that had not been there before. The only person who stayed true was Traci.

And, of course, Sara-Jane's father's newspaper interview had only made matters worse.

Thinking it was her neighbour, she opened the door. It was not.

'What do you want?' Although Gem did not recognise the woman standing in front of her, there was something familiar about her.

'I'm a friend.'

Her daughter's abduction had made her a lot of *friends*, like the psychic who turned up a few days ago insisting that she could 'feel' Sara-Jane's presence. Despite thinking that type of stuff was a load of hocus-pocus, Gem's hope had blossomed in a way it hadn't for so long. What mother wouldn't try anything to get her daughter safely back home? Of course, she should have known better. It turned out that the psychic could feel Sara-Jane's presence more strongly . . . for a flat fee of five hundred pounds plus VAT. Gem's hope had withered and died. How could people be so cruel?

Gem knew she should simply tell this woman to get lost, but instead all her frustrations boiled over. 'And which friend are you? Harry with the ghost dog tracker? Muriel who communes with the stars?'

'Kate Palmer. I'm a journalist from *The Herald*.'

That's why this woman looked so familiar – she was the journalist who had interviewed Laura Prentice during the protest outside the school on Sara-Jane's first day at Princess Isabel. Gem tensed up. The media wouldn't let up contacting her, wanting to know the ins and outs of her and Sara-Jane's life. The last thing she needed was someone digging into her background.

Her mind strayed to the letter on the table.

Gem started to close the door. 'I'm sorry—'

'Sara-Jane's dad has had his say. Painted you as a bad mother.' Gem froze, her hand tightening on the door. The other woman leaned in. 'He's going to keep dishing the dirt on you. Abby Prentice's family have the money to make sure she's shielded from publicity. But what about you, Gem? You're a mum, on your own. I bet having to save every penny you work your tail off for.'

She didn't want this journalist to be right, but Gem knew she was. Charlie was a man with a mouth who knew how to use it.

He was going to use any and every chance he got against her. The Prentice family wouldn't let her anywhere near Abby.

'Sara-Jane's not here,' the journalist continued, passion visible in her tone now. 'We need to be her voice. Let me tell *her* story. *Your* story. Don't let the father who never looked after her spread his lies.'

Gem hesitated. What if this was the only opportunity she got to let the world know what a special and unique child Sara-Jane was? Gem pulled the door back, letting the journalist into her and Sara-Jane's lives.

The other woman noted the two broken bikes against the hall wall. 'I hear you mend bikes.'

Gem answered, 'A mum's got to do what she needs to for that extra bit of change to feed her kids.' Gem liked that this made her sound like a mum who would do anything for her child.

Then why didn't you keep Sara-Jane safe?

Pushing the agonising question aside, Gem escorted Kate into the main room. The letter on the table immediately caught her eye. Nervously she grabbed it, walked briskly across the room and stuffed it in a drawer.

'Any chance of a coffee?'

The sound of the other woman's voice almost made her start. She twisted around, her fingers flexing as if the feel of the letter was still in her hand. 'Of course.'

When she came back, Kate put on her recorder. Gem swallowed. That made her nervous. She coughed, getting her voice ready.

The journalist smiled softly. 'Just be yourself. Our readers want to read about an ordinary working mum whose life has been torn apart.'

Gem took a big gulp of tea and then spent an hour or so laying bare her life. It felt so good to be able to tell the world about her little girl. To talk about how the toughness of life hadn't stood in her way in ensuring her kid got the best education.

At the end, Kate asked, 'What would you like to say to the person who has abducted your daughter?'

Shivering, the blood draining from her face, Gem answered. 'All I ask is that you take Sara-Jane to a place of safety and leave her there. Somewhere busy where people will see her. I miss my daughter so much. Please let Sara-Jane come home.'

Hot tears streaming down her cheeks, Gem stared at Kate as if she were the only person who could save her. Kate understood this, saying, 'I'm going to do my bloody best to bring your child home to you.'

Ten days. The odds on Sara-Jane being found alive grew slimmer every day. *God, please let the story that Kate Palmer will print change all of that. Please leave my girl in a place of safety.*

◆ ◆ ◆

Gem knew something was up the following morning. Walking her old bike across the Rosebridge, people kept casting her odd looks. There was the nasty sound of whispering behind her back. Confused, Gem scowled. What was going on?

She bumped into the one person she could do without speaking to. Billy-Bob. Traci's troublesome son. He was lurking on a stairwell. Her nose wrinkled. She could smell the drink from here.

Wearing a sly expression, he waved his beer can at her. 'Well, well, well, who's been a naughty girl, then.'

Gem cut her eyes at him. 'I don't know what you mean. Then again, you're always talking bollocks.' Despite sounding flippant and shoving him off, her heartbeat kicked up. Something was going on here.

Billy-Bob insolently drank from the can and then wiped his mouth with the back of his hand. His bloodshot stare became deadly serious. The slur in his voice vanished. 'They'll never let you forget. It doesn't matter what you do to try to be good. They'll never let you forget.'

He was frightening her. Her stomach muscles twisted so hard that a punch of pain was forced out of her. Gem clambered on to her bike and rode to work. When she walked into her work place, the café, she was met with stony stares from some of the customers and her fellow workers.

Her boss gestured at her. 'In the office. Now.'

Once inside he thrust a newspaper at her. It was the article Kate Palmer had written about her. Gem's heart dropped when she read the headline:

SARA-JANE'S MUM CONVICTED ROBBER

With dismay, Gem read the article. Read it again. The third time only snatches of it remained with her.

> The magistrate was tired of hearing feeble excuses from thieves for their criminality in his court. On sentencing the offender for robbery, he described her as a typical example of the kind of arrogant anti-social criminal who believes they can flout the law. Insult the public with pathetic bleating about poverty.

One word stood out.

Robbery.

Kate Palmer had done a hatchet job on her. *I'm going to do my bloody best to bring your child home to you.'* What a bitch. What an absolute bitch. She had conned Gem good and proper. *What a dupe I've been. A first-rate fool.*

How had Kate Palmer found out about her conviction? Suddenly she knew.

The letter.

With her crafty journalist gaze she must have noted how Gem had hastily picked up the letter and hidden it in the drawer. All that talk of wanting a coffee was a ruse to give her enough time to get to the drawer and read it. Probably took a photo of it too. The journalist had only been interested in digging up as much dirt on her as possible. Kate Palmer gave new meaning to the term *the gutter press*.

'It's not true,' Gem desperately told her boss. 'I'm not a robber.'

'So you haven't got a criminal record?'

'Yes, but . . .'

'So you lied on your application. Just like you kept your poor kid away from her dad.'

That article, the so-called exclusive interview Charlie had given, wouldn't stop haunting her.

Gem pleaded, 'You've got it all wrong.'

'We don't employ jailbirds here.' He pulled out a cashbox and counted out some money. He slapped it on the table with contempt. 'That's what's owed to you. Now sod off.'

Working, doing something, had kept her mind off Sara-Jane's abduction. Cut off from her work Gem thought she would go mad. Plus, what was she going to do for money now? She needed this job. How was she going to take care of her daughter when she came home? Sick churning inside her, Gem rode swiftly back home.

She didn't even close the front door, instead rushed to the drawer with the letter. It was still there. The letter detailed Gem's

216

suspended sentence and confirmed that her probation period was now complete.

'Did you do it?' a voice inside the hallway confronted her.

Gem turned to find Traci holding a copy of the newspaper. Her neighbour's face was flushed with anger. 'Is this true?'

Stepping into the hallway, Gem answered. 'I've got a criminal record, that's true. But I'm no robber.'

Gem knew how terrible this must be for Traci. Two years ago, when her husband was a security guard, he was so badly injured in a robbery that he had not been able to work since.

Traci waved the paper. Open anguish twisted her features. 'Then why are they calling you *that*?'

Gem hung her head, knowing it was time. Time to tell a shaming truth she'd hoped no one would ever discover.

'When I got the news that Sara-Jane had got a place in Princess Isabel School I was over the moon. My little girl going to the best school in the area was a gift from heaven. But she needed a school uniform.' Gem looked at the floor, her voice quieting. 'The problem was I didn't have the money. Long story short, I went to the shop, found a skirt and blouse for my girl and put them in my bag. And got caught.'

Gem raised her head, wearing a fighting spirit expression. 'I did wrong, I know that. I got convicted of shoplifting, not robbery. That journalist found out about my record and turned it into something that it's not. "Robber" will sell more papers than "shoplifter".'

Traci looked resentful and hurt. 'Why didn't you tell me?'

'Because I'm ashamed. I didn't know where to get help. Who's going to help me pay for a school uniform? I was already in debt up to my eyes, owing the council rent, I still owed money on the fridge and TV. And Charlie . . .' Her voice broke. 'All I tried to do was the best for my little girl.'

Traci covered the distance and took the younger woman in her arms. And rocked her. Gem sagged against her, desperate for the unconditional love her neighbour was always prepared to give. Maybe she was imagining it, but she was sure there was a stiffness in Traci's body. Like her best friend was on the verge of pushing her away.

Chapter 36

'Gem Casey? Abigail?' Beryl's eyes widen with surprise at finding me and Abby on the doorstep of her grand Victorian house on the corner of Isabel Park.

If anyone knows about what was happening with the SATs results in the school it will be Beryl Spencer. I'm conscious of what a terrible time this is for her.

Hell, that's what Beryl looks like. Undiluted hell. Her face is a study in agonising grief. Skin loose and folded in haggard waves, eyes lost in a sea of bloodshot-red. There're no clashing colours in her clothing today, she's wearing only one colour. Black. The discovery of her husband's remains and his murder have clearly devastated her. Always so filled with vigour and life, and now . . . now she's a ghost of her former self, barely clinging on to life.

A moment of heavy regret falls on me because Beryl is an innocent in all of it. We're only here to see if she can fill in the blanks about her husband's relationship with Clare Swan and the school. The last thing I want to do is bring Beryl more pain. More sorrow.

'I know this is a bad time to call,' I start. 'But we wanted to extend our condolences about your husband.'

'We won't keep you long,' Abby adds, accompanied by a soothing, caring smile.

Beryl beckons us inside. She looks dazed. If I'm honest she resembles someone on a wagonload of medication. Her doctor has probably dosed her up on some strong stuff to help her cope with the shocking turn of events.

I'd always assumed that her home would be a reflection of the eccentric style of her clothing, bordering on trashy. You know, gilt pretending to be gold, mock-marble floors and all the colours of the rainbow. But her home is none of that. The hallway is under-stated with a simple polished wooden floor and calm green wallpa-per. And a spicy scent that would go pitch-perfect with a cocktail. Comfy and cosy, obviously well cared for with tons of love.

Beryl clutches Abby's hand, startling the younger woman. 'What a beauty you've turned into. And as tall as the Eiffel Tower. Who would've thought that little itty-bitty Abigail Prentice would grow up to be such a glorious gazelle. You, my girl, are your grand-dad's pride and joy. I hope you're going to stay here with us for longer this time.'

Surprising me, Abby presses a gentle kiss to Beryl's cheek, which the older woman sinks into, her eyes crinkling with delight.

Abby discreetly asks, 'Where's the bathroom?'

After Abby has gone upstairs, Beryl guides me into the sizable lounge, which is filled with delicate, fussy knick-knacks, plump puffed-up cushions and a bay window with a commanding view of the park. And there's something else that catches my attention. Something I was not expecting to see.

'Oh, look at me with no manners.' Beryl's hands flutter ner-vously in the air. 'Can I offer you a cup of tea? Coffee?'

'Coffee, please.'

Once she's gone, I cautiously move across the room. To the makeshift shrine Beryl has created to her husband. There's a side-board against the wall filled with a collection of small silver-framed photos of him. In between the photos are three lit tealight candles, which explains the spicy smell I encountered in the hallway. On the wall above are more photos arranged in the shape of a heart. Inside this is a large photo of Teddy. He's standing, suited and booted, his fingers tightly gripping a black leather briefcase. Chin slightly raised, he stares seriously deep into the camera lens. I don't know why the whole set-up freaks me out but it does. Goosebumps plump up high along my arms.

'He always loved that suit.' Beryl's voice has me twisting around. She's holding a tray with a coffeepot and delicate-looking cups. 'He wore it the day he never came home.'

'I was so sorry to hear about your husband. I didn't know him but I was so sad to hear of his passing.' I offer my condolences as soon as we've sat down and Beryl has had a chance to pour us both a cup of coffee.

'Passing?' Her voice takes on strength. 'My Teddy was murdered. When he disappeared I told the police that something was wrong but they chose to believe those that were putting it about that he had another woman tucked away somewhere. He loved me with all his heart and his tender soul.' Her voice crashes into an agonising croak at the end.

I don't fill the awful silence by telling her how sorry I am again. Most people would do that, but not me. I know what it feels like to lose someone. *Sorry*, that's what people would say to me over and over. *Sorry*, as if Sara-Jane was already dead.

Beryl looks so bewildered, her eyes glinting with unshed tears. 'Why would someone murder my Teddy? And bury him in the chapel to cover up their evil deed?'

'Can you think of anyone who might have held a grudge against him?'

Her small fingers grip her cup. 'Everyone loved Teddy. Larger than life, he was. Always a good word to say about everyone.'

The heat of the coffee stings my lips. Carefully, I put the cup down. 'I didn't realise that your husband went to Princess Isabel when he was a boy at the same time as Miss Swan.'

'They were in the same class. Not that he had much to do with her, you understand. Teddy was too busy with his books. Teddy didn't come from a privileged background like she did. He had to put his head down and work hard. Getting a cracking education was his way of getting on in the world.'

'I didn't realise that your husband was connected to the school through his job?' I tentatively continue.

Beryl's face lights up. 'He took care of the SATs. My Teddy had a very important job.' Her chest puffs out in pride. 'He checked every exam paper individually to make sure that the marking was done correctly. Any mistakes – *any* – he immediately contacted the marker to make sure it was sorted out.'

Is that what we'd found? Exam results that had been changed by the marker after Teddy had inspected them? But so many of the exam results had been changed. And not for just one year, but two. If everything was above board, then why did Miss Swan have them under lock and key in her desk drawer?

I ask, 'Were Teddy and Miss Swan close?'

Beryl frowns and puts down her cup. Her head tilts to the side as she looks at me. 'Close? What do you mean, close?'

Oh hell, I hadn't meant it to sound like *that*. 'He must have come to the school to meet with her, just as Teddy will no doubt have met with other head teachers in the area.' Seeing her reassurance, I plough on. 'Did he ever talk to you about his work?' Inwardly I wince at how clumsy I sound talking about this stuff, exams, test scores. Who'd have thought that Gem Casey, who didn't even stick around to take her school exams, would be trying to talk about them as if she's an expert?

A haunted expression grips her features again. 'Sometimes I think he worked too hard at that job. Especially when it came to the Princess Isabel.'

'What do you mean?'

'I think because he went there as a boy he always double-checked the exams from the school.'

I waltz into the opening Beryl has nicely created for me. 'Would there be any reason why Teddy would ever change most of the SATs results of a school?'

Beryl grapples to answer. 'I don't understand what you mean?' Her face twists with hurt. 'Are you suggesting that—?'

'I'm suggesting absolutely nothing.'

I can't bear the pain in her eyes that accuses me. I feel disgusted with myself. This woman always went out of her way to make me and my child feel not just comfortable but accepted at Princess Isabel School. And how am I showing my gratitude? Interrogating her about her murdered husband. Poor Beryl must be in the depths of such despair.

Beryl points to the shrine on the opposite side of the room. 'Teddy was my life. We did everything together. I know what some folks call me. Batty Beryl.' I grimace. 'Cowards, he called them, because they weren't brave enough to say it to my face.'

I tell her, 'I never called you that. Neither did my Sara-Jane.'

'Thank you. My parents died when I was young and I ended up living with my grandmother. She was a very bitter and unhappy woman. Why that was I don't know. She believed that bright colours made the angels weep, so I was only permitted to wear blacks and greys. Teddy was the one that encouraged me to dress how the hell I liked. Wear what colours I liked. And whoever didn't like it, well, frankly, stuff them.'

She stares at me with such fire. 'Some days I might look like a blancmange with sprinkles on top. But at least I'm a very, very happy blancmange.'

The life abruptly drains out of her eyes. 'I thought he was coming back. That's why Teddy's office upstairs is exactly the way he left it. He didn't like anyone touching his desk. Very organised. Every Saturday, at midday, I give it a spit and polish.' Grief sparkles in her gaze. 'But he's not coming back, is he? No need to clean it any more.'

A solid frown wrinkles her forehead. 'Abby's been gone a long time. I hope she's OK.'

Using the arm of the sofa to lever herself, Beryl stands just as Abby makes an appearance in the doorway. She's huffing as if she's been running. 'I got lost. Beryl, this is such a beautiful house.' Abby sends me a meaningful glance. 'I got a call . . . Um . . . So sorry, Beryl, we're going to have to go.'

Beryl shows us to the door and before we leave she tells us, 'Thank you for coming to pay your respects to Teddy. I wish you had had the chance to meet him. Teddy was such a good man.'

Over her shoulder I glance back at Teddy in his suit in his shrine.

'What did you find?' I ask Abby when we're far enough away from the house.

Our plan had been simple. I try to find out as much from Beryl as possible while Abby uses the pretext of going to the loo to snoop around the house.

'I'm not sure this is anything,' she answers. 'It could all be innocent.'

She pulls three items out of her rucksack. Three DVDs.

'What are they?'

'I don't know. I found them in an office.' *Teddy's office upstairs is exactly the way he left it.* That's what Beryl told me, so I suspect it's the same room that Abby found herself in.

In a rush she carries on. 'But look what's written on them.'

One word. Block letters. Thick black pen:

CLARE

Chapter 37

'Hold your galloping horses,' comes her loud response after I bang on Traci's door.

She opens up, surprise striking her face when she sees it's me and Abby.

'Is William around?'

Traci narrows her gaze, assessing with a sly undertone, 'You and my William have been hanging around together quite a bit lately. Should I expect the arrival of another grandkid in nine months' time?' She bursts into peels of uproarious laughter, eyes twinkling, body shaking.

I don't join in. Seeing my serious expression her laughter dies. She looks angry now. 'My William hasn't really gone and got you in the family way?'

Her long-suffering son peeps from behind her. 'Mum, are you creating trouble again?'

With solemn eyes, Traci glances at me. 'I was only having a little tickle, a bit of fun. I didn't mean any offence by it.'

She makes way for me and Abby to follow William into the front room. But before I do, I give Traci an almighty hug. I don't want any bad feelings between us.

Instead of letting me go, she murmurs in my ear, 'I don't want things to change. I want them to stay as they are.'

Baffled, I pull back and look deep into her eyes. 'What do you mean?'

'Oh, nothing.' She giggles, bubbling away again. 'Silly me. It's that old brain of mine. I'm going back to the chicken biriyani I'm cooking in the kitchen.'

I watch her go until she disappears. And stay rooted to the spot for a time. Why was Traci so upset? We have such a bond that it wounds me deep inside to think of her being hurt and unhappy.

'Gem.' William's call breaks my spell and I join him and Abby in the main room.

'Abby has already filled me in,' he tells me. 'You need a DVD player. Well, you've come to the right place. Mum's still got one. And a video machine. She's probably got a gramophone stashed under her bed somewhere.'

William connects the DVD player to the telly. He puts in one of the DVDs marked 'Clare'. We all watch. It's scratchy and grainy at first. Then the image changes. My mouth sags open. My head shakes with disbelief. I can't be seeing what I think I'm seeing. Abby gasps. William swears.

'Billy-Bob, you're not still looking at porn.' Traci unexpectedly strolls into the room, eyeing her son with displeasure. 'I thought you knocked that on the head when you were . . .'

Her voice dribbles to a horrified nothing when she realises what we're all looking at. Who we're all looking at.

Miss Swan. The head teacher of Princess Isabel School. In kinky bondage clothes, bare-breasted inside the chapel in the school.

'Right! That's enough of that.' Traci surges towards the television like an avenging angel and ejects the DVD. She holds it threateningly between her hands as if she's about to snap it in two.

'No!' we shout in unison.

She's fizzing with fury. 'In my eyes this is *filth*. I know it's all modern to have all manner of sexual relations. But think! This is

227

Miss Swan. The best head teacher I've ever known. In the whole area. A heart made of the purest gold. If this gets out, she'll be crucified.'

'It isn't going to get out,' I promise, slowly standing. 'On that DVD might be the biggest clue yet to what happened to Sara-Jane. Teddy Spencer. If you destroy it, I'll probably never know what happened to my baby girl.'

Traci's horrified gaze catches mine. She whispers, 'But it isn't decent. Miss Swan would die of shame if she knew you had this.' Her brows snap together. 'And by the way, where did you get it?'

I don't answer. Instead I extend my hand. The battle for what she should do openly rages in the changing expressions of Traci's face. Then, lips compressed, she walks over and slaps it in my palm. 'If there's nothing on here that helps you, promise me you'll destroy it.'

I nod. Traci leaves, closing the door with a controlled quiet behind her.

William puts the DVD back in the machine. He hesitates. Presses play.

We're back in the chapel. The chapel where Sara-Jane and Abby sneaked out of school. The chapel where Teddy Spencer's remains were found. The chapel where I can't believe Miss Swan, head teacher of Princess Isabel School, appears to be leading a double life.

This Clare Swan is sexy, provocative, appearing like she wears bondage gear with cut-outs to display her bare breasts every day of the week. Standing beneath the stained-glass window with the face-less angel that scared Sara-Jane, her hips sway and she smiles coyly into the camera. And that's when I see it. She might be smiling, but those eyes of hers are terrified. Crying out for help.

William beats me to it. 'She doesn't want to be there. Someone is forcing her to do this.'

Abby adds, 'And that someone is the bastard holding the camera.'

We keep watching, hoping for a clue about who is behind the camera. We can hear their excited, ragged, heavy breathing. It leaves me feeling dirty as if it's against the skin of my neck.

A man's voice growls, 'Now bend over, you slut.'

'Do you recognise the voice?'

William and Abby both shake their heads. Damn.

I listen as the faceless man talks nasty and filthy to Miss Swan, making her pose in the most humiliating positions. Sexually, this isn't my thing. However, I'm no prude. If Miss Swan was enjoying this, good luck to her. But she isn't. It's not only the expression in her eyes that's a dead giveaway, it's the nervous pop of veins in her neck, the stiffness in her fingers. Miss Swan gets down on her knees, arches her back and over her shoulder she displays a very timid come-hither look. The man's breathing becomes harsh, so loud . . .

We turn it off and put in another DVD – more of the sickening same.

While we cringingly watch the final one, Abby firmly calls out, 'Stop! Right there! Stop it!'

William pauses the DVD. Abby scrambles to her knees in front of the TV and taps the screen. 'Here! Look! I think there's a reflection of his face in one of the computer screens in the chapel.'

Me and William gather around her and peer hard. There's definitely a face there, but it's so blurred and meshed with the background it's hard to make out.

'Move back,' William instructs us. And when we do he uses his phone to take a picture of the frozen scene on the TV. 'There's an app on my phone that should enlarge it and make it clearer.'

A few minutes later he's finished. As he looks at what's on his phone, he sucks in air with disbelief. 'No bloody way.'

'Who is it?'

He turns and holds his phone so we can see.

I see the face. Whisper, 'Teddy Spencer.'

◆ ◆ ◆

'Was Miss Swan having an affair with Teddy Spencer?' My question lands like a hand grenade between us.

We three are around my kitchen table. The DVDs lie in the middle of it. We decided to come back to my flat because we needed to be able to talk confidentially without Traci being there.

William shakes his head. 'Miss Swan is a very distinguished-looking woman and Teddy Spencer – no disrespect to the dead – was not in her class. Plus she wouldn't have had an affair with Beryl's husband behind her back.'

I nod in agreement. 'We're missing something.'

Abby has been strangely silent. Through my hooded side-eye I notice that her arms are wrapped tight about her middle.

So I ask, 'What's going on, Abby?'

At first, she stays in her silence, her head dipping down. Then she's on her feet, filling a glass of water from the tap at the sink. Frowning, I get to my feet too. I'm worried about her.

'Abby, what's got you so upset?'

'I don't know.' She places the glass down on the draining board and turns to me. 'It's his face—'

'Teddy Spencer?'

Hesitantly, she nods. 'I've seen him before. It must've been when I was with Mum at the school. I don't know.'

She's trembling. Badly spooked. An odd reaction to seeing a face briefly in an office when she was a child. Unless, of course, it's much more than that.

I hear William's voice behind me. 'I think that maybe my mum was right and we should stop. Leave this alone.'

He's on his feet too, with his hands awkwardly jammed in the front pockets of his jeans. He's tense and avoids my gaze. I move over to him, just close enough not to crowd his space. 'Remember who we're doing this for. Not you, not me. We're doing this for Sara-Jane.'

We all sit back down, my brain zooming at a mile a minute through the information we have:

The altered exam results.

Teddy Spencer was the school's SATs moderator.

Teddy and Miss Swan attended Princess Isabel School when they were children.

Miss Swan decked in bondage gear looking like she wanted to die.

Then I understand. 'We're all agreed that Miss Swan wouldn't have touched her trusted office manager's husband with a barge-pole. We all saw her on the DVD. She looked about ready to chuck up. The only way Teddy Spencer got her to do those things was by force.'

The sickening forced sexual scenes from the chapel flick through my mind. 'I suspect he was blackmailing her. He knew full well that the reputation and status of the school would go down the drain if the real SATs marks were revealed. What if he came to her with a proposition: he would change the results if she had sex with him? But it was more than just sex. He wanted to humiliate her, make her his property.' *Bastard.* 'The school is Miss Swan's life's work. She couldn't let the outside world know that the school wasn't as outstanding as she pretended. So she allowed herself to become his sex toy.'

'What if she didn't want to do it any more. She'd had enough.' Abby takes up the story with a strange faraway, glazed expression. 'But he wouldn't listen. So she murdered her tormentor.'

231

A dreadful silence falls over us. Is that how Teddy Spencer's body ended up in the chapel? Miss Swan had had enough and took her revenge?

'Miss Swan a murderer?' William's on his feet again. His fingers rake through his hair. 'No! No way! She would've gone to the police—'

'And let the parents who trusted her know that Princess Isabel wasn't the brilliant educational institution that they all thought it was? I don't think so.' I'm back on my feet too. 'She would've done anything, *anything*, to protect the school.'

William comes over and places his hand on my arm. I feel his plea in the pressure of his flesh on mine. 'Go see her. Give her a chance to explain what happened. That woman is no killer.'

William leaves and Abby goes to Sara-Jane's room. I'm eternally grateful that they give me time to think. I sink on to a chair at the kitchen table and think back.

Fifteen years back, to the time when Miss Swan was one of the only people at the school who welcomed the working families from the Rosebridge Estate.

I see her a few days ago, giving me Sara-Jane's academic report book with such compassion.

I see her behind bars because I put her there.

I'm stuck between a rock and a hard place – and it hurts. So badly. I genuinely don't know what to do.

Go to the school?

Call Detective Wallace?

I look at the DVDs on the table. Then I make my decision.

Chapter 38

'Miss Swan? It's Gem. Gem Casey, Sara-Jane's mum,' I say to Clare Swan on the phone.

I sound so rattled. So nervous. The reason I've decided not to contact the police – yet – is there's still a seed of doubt in me that worries I might have got this all wrong. What if the evidence against Miss Swan means nothing at all?

I know from bitter experience how so-called evidence can be used to demonise you. How easy it is to take what looks incriminating and turn it into something explosive. Something that has the power to destroy a life.

And what about the letter from the inspectors I found on the head teacher's table? How Rosa said everyone at the school is on edge? If I go to the cops first and it turns out I've got this wrong that won't stop a shitshow from coming down on Miss Swan's head. And when it comes out how I obtained this information, I'll be in the firing line too. Whatever happens, Rosa and Abby's names won't be mentioned. I don't care about my name any more.

'Gem. This is unexpected.' She sounds pleased to hear from me, which leaves me feeling even more crap about what I'm about to do.

'Miss Swan, I wanted to speak with you first before I go to the police.'

'Please do call me Clare.'

Clare. The name chimes in my head. It feels wrong. This woman will always be Sara-Jane's head teacher.

'*Miss Swan*, it's only fair to warn you that certain information has come into my hands.'

'Did you find something out about Sara-Jane? Can I help in some way?'

She's using that patient, professional tone that reminds me of the time, fifteen years ago, in her office when she explained how my daughter tried to strangle Abby Prentice.

'The information concerns you.'

'Information that's about me? You're not making sense.'

'It concerns the SATs results a few years before Sara-Jane attended the school. And your other connection to Teddy Spencer.'

The images of them together flash through my mind. Repulsive. Loathsome.

Clare Swan doesn't say anything at all for a few seconds. Then, voice still cool and even, 'Before you do anything rash, why don't you speak with me first.'

'That's exactly what I'm doing now.'

'I mean come to the school and we can talk.'

'What good would that do?'

Silence again for a few seconds. 'It's always best to discuss such things face to face.' Her tone has changed. It's sharp and strained now. 'There are things I want you to hear before the police get involved.'

My heart skips a beat. And another. 'Is this connected to my daughter being abducted?'

I hear a sound on the phone. Is that her door opening? Someone coming inside her room?

Suddenly her voice lowers to a quiet rush. 'We can't speak properly on the telephone, Gem. Everything is connected to every-thing else in this school. That includes Sara-Jane.'

Her words rock me. What does she mean?

I hear Miss Swan's voice again, but she's not speaking to me. It's like she's talking to someone in the background. Is it the person who just entered her room?

Miss Swan comes back on the phone, her voice all businesslike. 'Thank you for calling about the playground equipment.' *What?* Then I realise whoever is with her, she doesn't want them to know it's me she's talking with on the phone. Or the incendiary information we're discussing. 'This evening. At six. At the school. I'll see you then.'

The disconnected dial tone drones in my ear.

Who is in the room with Miss Swan?

What does she know about the disappearance of Sara-Jane?

The school is shrouded in a half-darkness that leaves me jittery. It's a different dark to the one that was here last night when me and Abby broke in. Tonight there's no moon. The street light is foggy. In the daylight and brightness the sounds of children talking, laughing, shouting turn this large Victorian building into the happiest place on earth. Now, in this half-light, it doesn't look like a school at all. Its jagged peaks vanish into the deep dark of the sky, making the school appear never-ending. My heart rate kicks up.

I reach over to press the entry phone so that Miss Swan can let me in. However, before I can, the lock on the gate clangs as it unbolts. The gate swings open. Is Miss Swan watching me through the camera? How does she know that I'm already here? I stare at the inky-black space the gate has opened up for me to go through. And hold back. Some sixth sense warns me not to go forward. My hands tighten against my bike. Then I remember Sara-Jane standing here with me, alive, on the last day I ever saw her, wearing her Princess For A Day socks.

Filling my lungs with a long, deep suck of air I walk my bike past the gate. Inside, I make the mistake of glancing over at the chapel. Maybe it's the vibrant rose-coloured front that catches my eye. Or the stained-glass windows. The faceless angel is watching me. Turning away quickly I park my bike and head for the main door. The door's already open. That's weird. Beryl Spencer is shit-hot about the school's security. Then I remember: Beryl isn't here any more, she's not been back since her husband's remains were discovered at the school.

There's no lighting in the corridor that leads to the reception area and Clare Swan's office. I've never noticed how long it is before. Long and with lots of doors off it. I know some of the rooms are open because the shadow of their doors are against the floor. I hug the wall and make my way down, my pace slow and careful. The corridor appears to go on for ever in front of me as if in a dream. A funny sensation runs down my spine.

Twisting, I search behind me. Is someone watching me? Hiding away in a dark, silent place, watching me? There's someone here. I know there is. It's probably just Miss Swan.

'Miss Swan! Are you there?'

My voice travels down the empty corridor towards the reception area, rebounds around the empty classrooms and boomerangs back to echo in my ears. I reach the reception area and open the door into Beryl's office. No one's there, so I head straight for the head teacher's office.

I knock on her door. 'Miss Swan?'

No answer.

I knock again and get the same response. My hand lingers above the handle. Circles it. It's cold in my palm. I start to turn the handle. Push. Click. The door opens. I push the door and call her name one more time.

'Miss Swan?'

Shoving the door wider, I step inside. The light's on. Her desk lamp. My gaze scans around because I can't see Miss Swan anywhere. Her chair's empty. The room looks different than it did yesterday. There's a package of throwaway cups and plates, a bag of balloons, all evidence of Clare Swan preparing for her retirement party.

Cautiously, I move further in and see that there are splashes of something on the walls. Whatever it is, it covers some of the children's mounted artwork. Miss Swan loves showing off the children's work. My shoe sticks to the floor. So firmly that it takes some tugging to dislodge it. I look down and gasp. A sticky, reddish resin-like substance trails from under the desk. Lifting my foot into the light shows it's a darkish purple like claret wine.

It's when I look over the desk to see where it's come from that Clare finally appears. Her body has slid off her chair and is now splayed on the floor. The lamplight turns her twisted limbs into huge and grotesque shadows on the wall. Her head is at an odd angle to her body because her throat has been slashed, a long gash oozing blood. There's a slash across her chest and her stomach. Whoever has done this has cut her to ribbons. There's blood everywhere. The stiffening features on her face show fear and horror in the shadowy yellow light. Her jaw is slack, leaving her mouth partially gaping.

'Clare?' I know she's dead, but I'm in shock. Strange that the first time I address her by her first name is when she's dead. Murdered.

I retreat backwards towards the switch for the main light. Flick it on and make a high-pitched noise of distress. The splashes I saw on the wall are her blood, even on the children's drawings. Clinging and thick. And . . . I want to retch. Gulp back the acid bile rising inside me. It's a scene of utter carnage. Cautiously, I creep back to Miss Swan and that's when I see it. Something stumpy, long and pink on her bloodied chest. It looks like a large dead slug from here. I know I shouldn't but I can't help it – I inch closer and closer. I'm above her body and look down. Past her gaping mouth to . . . I'm puzzled, what could it be? I stare back at her mouth, at the way it's half-opened, at the congealed, sticky blood around it. Look back down. Oh God! Oh God! It can't be . . .

Clare Swan's tongue.

Someone has cut out her tongue. There is no jagged pattern at its edges, which I'd expect from a knife – it's been severed with a clean, straight line. What tool could do that? I know – a pair of scissors. The horror of it all rises up, suffocating me. In my terror of rushing back my feet become entangled. Wobble. I begin to fall. Fall. Forward instead of back. *No! No!* My arms flap sideways in the air trying to stop my fall. Too late. I topple on to the dead body.

It's still warm. The horrible heat seeps into me. Then so does Miss Swan's blood. It sinks and spreads into my clothes. I freeze with stomach-churning revulsion because I'm a hair's breadth away from the dismembered tongue. Is it my imagination or is it starting to turn dry and black already? A dreadful terror creeps over me. Urgently, my palms press into the blood, gooey and treacle-like against my flesh, to help me back on to my feet. My clothes and hands are covered in blood.

A large shadow flickers against the doorway. Petrified and pan-icked, I spin around.

'Who's there?'

No answer. Did I see the shadow or was that my shattered mind playing tricks on me?

I hear a noise, a sound. A sort of shuffle. Footsteps against the floor? This time I don't call out. I run. Out of the office. Shove my palm urgently against the office manager's door. It flies open. I skid into the corridor, arms raised ready to fight whoever's there for my life. No one's there. I run. Run.

Someone's out there. Chasing me. I can feel them. Or have fifteen years of grief and pain, and now death, finally driven me over the edge?

There's a crashing noise behind me. Good grief, is that them getting closer to me? *Don't look around. Don't look around.* I do. The noise was the sound of the door slamming.

Run! Run!

My breathing is noisy, ragged, buzzing loudly in my ears. Or is that the breathing of the person chasing me? Getting closer to me. The angel with no face? I burst through the main door. The cold air punches me like a swimmer coming up for air. I grab my bike . . . A hand clamps over my arm. They've caught me. I'm not going down without a fight. I pull back my fist and turn at the same time.

A voice rings out, 'If you want to add assaulting an officer of the law to the pile of trouble you're already in, go right ahead.'

It's a young police officer who has clamped his steel-like fingers around my arm. Out of the dark walks Detective Wallace.

They both stare at my sticky, bloody clothes.

The police officer cuffs me. I desperately plead, 'You've got this all wrong.'

I should never have come here. I should've known better.

Chapter 39

I'm surprised when Wallace instructs one of the uniformed officers to take the cuffs off me about an hour later. I'm in an interview room at the station with the grim-faced detective facing me. I've been searched and my bloody clothes replaced with a bog-standard T-shirt and trackie bottoms. Despite my protestations, Wallace had dragged me back to the murder scene inside the school. Back to the head teacher's office. I'm still in a state of crippling shock. All I can see is Clare Swan lying there, her limbs twisted, her throat. God, her tongue . . . A tremor runs through me from my head to my numb toes.

'So you believe me now, do you?' I ask him.

He makes a sour twist of his lips. 'CCTV near the school suggests that your arrival at the school doesn't fit with the timing of Clare Swan's murder.'

'And the school's security cameras? Did they manage to record who the murderer is?'

'The cameras were not on.'

Leaning forward, I emphatically tell him, 'Which suggests whoever murdered her knew exactly where the security cameras are kept. They know the school well.'

'No shit, Sherlock,' he tartly answers. He's peeved, obviously thinking I'm trying to do his job for him. Too right I am! I'm tired of the cops playing it safe. 'So, you say you had a meeting with Clare Swan.'

It's my turn to be annoyed. 'You've asked me that once before and my answer hasn't changed. I had a meeting with her—'

He tilts his head so he can have a good look at me. 'That's a strange time to have a meeting.'

My gaze snaps away from his. I've been holding out on him. I genuinely don't know whether to tell him the truth. To voice my suspicions and give him all the evidence that me and Abby found at the school.

My dilemma must be as plain as day on my face because he says, 'I could give you a lecture about the penalties for withholding evidence . . . But I won't.' There's a sympathetic gleam to his expression. 'A leading member of our community has been murdered. Some scumbag took her life. Both my son and daughter went to Princess Isabel Primary School, and Clare Swan was the best head teacher my children could have had.' I look at him with surprise. 'She was a woman who touched and changed many lives.'

And that's what my dilemma is all about: that she changed so many lives, that she was so well respected, that she gave her life for the school. In reality, is that what has happened? Has Clare Swan given her actual life for her beloved school?

He continues, 'Are you going to let whoever carried out this evil and heinous act get away with it?'

I confess a truth to him. 'If I tell you all of what I know – *suspect* – it may stop me finding out the truth about what happened to my daughter. Who took her.' My folded hands shake. The words still have the power to create images so bad in my head I want to stand in this room and scream.

He stiffens, his brows flip together. 'You think Clare Swan's murder is connected to the girls' abduction?'

I take a breath and reply, 'Don't you think it's odd that so much is connected to the school? The chapel? Sara-Jane and Abby sneak out of the school from there. Teddy Spencer's murdered remains are found there. And . . .' I clam up.

'Do you mean this?' Wallace opens the brown envelope on the table. He pulls out the one DVD I had taken to my meeting with Miss Swan. When I was brought here the sergeant at the desk in reception took it from me. 'What is this and where did you get it?'

Another dilemma. If I tell him the truth it's going to be me royally in the shit again. 'Let's just say it came into my possession.'

'Then again, I don't need to hear it from your mouth. All I need to do to find answers is to play it.' Wallace looks like he's got me by the short and curlies. I don't warn him about what he's about to see.

Five minutes later the pictures and sounds of the sordid tape in the chapel play in the room. I suspect that Detective Wallace is one of those cops who's seen some nasty things in his life, leaving him immune to being shocked by anything. But his jaw is slack with disbelief at what he's seeing.

He turns it off, mercifully before it reaches places where I'd have to insist on leaving the room.

He takes a lengthy drink of water, the manic bobbing of his Adam's apple showing how stunned he is about what he's just watched. 'Who is the unseen man in the video? He's bound to be our killer.'

'It can't be.'

He huffs with impatience. 'You're not covering up for someone. Again.'

'It's Teddy Spencer.'

'Mother Mary.' Wallace is not the kind of cop who does astonishment. He's always level-headed and composed. Not this time though. This one has knocked him for six.

'I think he was blackmailing her.' I keep talking, telling him the whole story. Well, as I see it. I finish with, 'She may have been the one to murder him.'

By now Detective Wallace has a nasty film of sweat coating his forehead. 'This is going to create one almighty stink.' He sinks back. 'Do you have proof of this?'

Reluctantly my head moves in a short, frustrated shake. 'I wish I did because whoever it is knows about what happened to my Sara-Jane. Someone rang you to tell you that I was at the school, right?'

'How do you figure that?' He's being cagey.

'The killer was there when I was. They must've contacted you to set me up.'

There's a knock at the door before he can answer. It's opened by a junior detective who also attended the murder scene at the school. Wallace joins him. Heads together, the other officer whispers something to Wallace. Whatever it is makes him stiffen.

When he comes back to the table his expression is grave. 'They still need to do tests on her body, but preliminary reports suggest that Clare Swan was knocked out. Then strangled before her throat was cut.'

I gasp. The horror of her neck, broken and bent, slashed, returns. What an awful death. How could someone do that? Take their hands, or some other type of implement, and squeeze.

Then I remember something I saw on the television many years ago. 'Choking someone with your hands is considered personal, isn't that right?'

He nods. 'Which may indicate that her murderer knew her. But we don't know if it was manual strangulation or some other type of weapon was used.'

With that sombre piece of information, he allows me to leave. But before I go, he informs me, 'Teddy's skull was cracked, which suggests he suffered blunt force trauma. Probably hit with a heavy object. But there was something else.' He pauses before continuing. 'Forensics can't be sure after all this time but they suspect that Teddy Spencer was also strangled.'

◆ ◆ ◆

William's waiting for me outside. He's shuffling his feet and rubbing his hands trying to keep warm.

'Is it true? Clare's dead?' His eyes are wide with disbelief; anger stains his face. And grief. He looks so sad. I don't need to answer because the truth is written all over my face. I throw myself in his arms and hug him so tight. His heartbeat trembles through my body.

We stay like that in the street, in front of the police station, taking comfort from each other, giving and receiving strength. Finally we draw apart. He looks so haggard and ravaged.

'God.' My voice trembles with the weight of all that I've been through. I still can't get the image of Clare Swan's mutilated body out of my head.

I grab my bike. 'I'll give you a lift back to the Rosebridge.' I want to get away from here as quickly as possible. Hell, if I could fly I would.

He mounts the seat and arranges his legs in a side-saddle style. I lurch up on to the pedals and off we go. Away from the horror of the murder of Clare Swan. The blast of the wind in our faces feels so fresh. I will the rain to join us, but it doesn't come. At first, my riding partner hangs on to me for dear life. But eventually I sense William relaxing.

We dismount on the Rosebridge and walk silently upstairs.

I say, 'I'd invite you in for—'

'Yeah, I know,' he cuts in. 'It's been a terrible, sad day.'

The door to his mum's flat opens and Traci appears in the doorway. Her eyes are red. She's been crying. 'How could anyone kill Clare? She was beautiful inside and out.'

William turns to me. 'We'll leave you to sleep.'

Traci holds out something towards me. 'I think you dropped this when you were here earlier.'

It's the black and white photo of young Beryl and Teddy. It fell out of the photo frame on Beryl's desk after I'd knocked it over in my haste to get out of the school with Abby and Rosa.

She asks, 'What are you doing with a picture of Teddy and Beryl? And Clare?'

My brows jump. 'Clare Swan? She's not in the picture.'

'Yeah, she is. Look.'

Traci pulls back part of the photo revealing that one end of it had been folded over. It now turns from a photo of two people into three. A teenage Clare Swan now joins the other couple. While Beryl looks adoringly at the man who would become her husband, Teddy stares longingly at . . . Clare Swan.

I say, 'I knew that Clare and Teddy went to school together. It's a total surprise to me that Beryl and Clare knew each other when they were young as well.'

'Of course they did,' Traci informs us. 'It wasn't just Clare and Teddy who went to Princess Isabel School. Beryl went to school with them too. They were in the same class. Teddy, Beryl and Clare.'

Me and William look at each other. At my bike. Despite the late hour we head again off into the night.

Chapter 40

'You murdered Clare Swan, didn't you?'

I spit the damning accusation at Beryl. She stands in her doorway staring at me with eyes that don't seem to see anything.

'Wh . . . What? What are you doing here at this time of night?' Startled, she rocks back in shock. Her fragile fingers grab the door edge to steady herself. She looks terrified, like a bird that's about to have its wings pulled. And I'm the villain about to do the pulling.

William stands by my side, the rasping of his breath showing how uneasy he is about what I'm doing. Quietly, in a kind, reassuring voice, he asks her, 'You did know that Clare Swan was murdered today?'

Lips quivering, Beryl appears totally fazed by his question. A glassy glaze coats her eyes, evidence that she's been crying. When it finally sinks in, she answers, voice scratchy and small, 'Yes. Clare's gone. How can she be gone?'

'I think it's best if we take this inside,' William advises, no doubt conscious of the potential for Beryl's neighbours hearing.

Beryl mumbles shakily about where have her good manners gone as she stumbles back, allowing us to follow her in. The lounge door is closed, leaving me feeling like we're marooned in the hallway. The area is lit by a solitary wall light which bathes the hallway in an uncomfortable half-light. Beryl's shadow appears so small against the tall and looming ones of mine and William's, making us look like bullies ganging up on someone tiny and defenceless.

'The police contacted me,' Beryl fills us in, her chest rising as she takes huge lugs of air. 'I can't believe it.'

'Can't you?' My voice is harsh.

'Take it easy,' William cuts in, his warning aimed at me.

No! I'm not prepared to do that. This isn't going to be one of his 'listen and learn from our mistakes' mentoring sessions he does with the children. This is about finding the truth, which is a journey that can feel as brutal as walking barefoot across jagged glass. The path to the truth doesn't often end with lots of hugging and learning.

So I plough on. 'When I phoned Miss Swan earlier it became clear that there was someone else in the room. Someone who she was obviously familiar with. I heard her talking to them.'

Beryl's lips flap like a swimmer coming up for air. 'And you think that was me?'

'Was it?' William interjects, still treading very carefully.

'No! No!' Her defence is both strident and indignant. The expression she wears is as if I've put a dagger through her heart. 'How can you accuse me of such a monstrous thing? I can't believe that anyone would murder her. First Teddy, now Clare.' Her agonised gaze pierces into me with the power of an ice pick. 'And Sara-Jane.'

Sara-Jane. My heart squeezes.

'Why didn't you tell me that you attended Princess Isabel School with Clare Swan and your husband?'

'I don't understand.' She looks so bewildered and sends William a quick glance as if pleading with him for help. Although he remains silent, a muscle in his jaw flexes with barely held back displeasure. He's not comfortable at all.

I ignore his festering disapproval and carry on. 'When we spoke about Teddy being at school with Clare you never once mentioned that you were in their class too.'

Beryl makes a small helpless noise before turning her puzzled stare back on me. 'But you came here to talk about Teddy, not me. I didn't think that my history with Clare meant anything.' As if a spell has been put on her, Beryl's features brighten with a dreamy faraway expression. '1969. That's when we started school together. Five years old. It feels like only yesterday. Of course, at first Teddy didn't want to be seen hanging around with two girls, but when he realised how much fun we were he was stuck to us like royal icing on a cake.'

William jumps in again, 'We're sorry to have disturbed you—'

'Did you know that Teddy was abusing Miss Swan?' I ask her with force.

'Jeezus-Christ,' William cracks out in disbelief.

Shell-shocked, Beryl whimpers. 'Abusing her? Do you mean Clare? My Teddy?'

My flaming eyes warn William not to step in again. If he wants to go the door is right behind him.

'He was forcing her to have sex with him.' I shut out her horrified cry. 'In his role as moderator he discovered that the school's SATs results were on the slide. He blackmailed her. If she let him have sex with her he would put everything right.' I pull in a harsh, deep breath. 'In my book that's called rape.'

Beryl rocks slightly, hunching over, appearing on the point of collapse. 'It's a wicked thing to make an accusation against a man who can't defend himself because he's dead.'

'Beryl, I'm sorry, but this is all true.'

'What proof have you got? What evidence?'

William gently responds, taking a small step closer to her. 'You've known me for years. I respect you, Beryl. I always have. And you know I would always tell you the truth. I've seen the altered SATs results. And there's a DVD—'

'Get. Out.' Beryl straightens her backbone and pulls her shoulders back. 'I want you to take your nasty lies and leave.'

Leave? No bloody way. I smell the truth in the air around us and it has a stench that belongs to the ripeness of a decaying body.

I'm about to speak when I hear a noise coming from the lounge where the door is closed. There it goes again. A groan? Moan? Whatever it is it sounds completely out of place in this cosy house.

I ask Beryl, 'What's that noise?'

The blood leaves her cheeks. 'What noise?'

Without another word I march over to the lounge.

'You have no right,' Beryl shrieks behind me.

I reach for the handle of the door and thrust it open. And stagger back. There on the TV screen are Teddy and Clare Swan. This time he's got her tied up, hanging from a beam in the chapel on a rope with an elaborate pattern of knots. Clare's body sways, her gaze wide with fear. Intense disgust, that's what rolls inside me at how any person could derive pleasure from subjugating someone to this level of terror. And compassion for Miss Swan finding herself in the hands of this sadist.

I swing to face Beryl and in shocked disbelief say, 'You knew?'

Trying to be more rational than me, William carefully adds, 'Did you discover the DVDs recently? Is that why you're playing this?'

Then something alarming on the DVD happens that answers his question. It's a voice. Excited. Coming through harsh breaths. *'Go on, Teddy. Please. I can't wait any more. You know what to do.'*

Beryl.

I'm stunned. Can't speak. I never saw this coming. Not in a million years.

While I still grapple to get my mind sorted out, William calmly finds the TV remote and switches the nauseating DVD off. With a superhuman calmness he ejects it and slowly turns to Beryl. There's nothing calm about his words, though.

'You watched that vile husband of yours abuse Clare. You would film her degradation so you could watch it together. Is that how you got your rocks off? Sexually turned on watching Teddy assault her with you egging him on?' Revulsion stains his face. 'Is that what you've been doing for the last fifteen years? Watching the DVDs on your own?'

'I feel close to Teddy when I watch them. It's like he's alive again.' Her tearful Little Bo Beep act disappears before our eyes.

Her words push the bile high in my mouth. She sickens me. 'It was double blackmail, wasn't it? Teddy got sex and you got to keep your job.'

It's coming back to me, the rumours at the time that the head teacher was going to get rid of her office manager due to Beryl's incompetence, part of the reason the parents called her Batty Beryl behind her back. And when it didn't happen how surprised many were. Now it's clear why that was.

Beryl rears forward, the grieving widow no longer in existence. 'Clare was going to fire me. Me!' Her finger stabs into her chest to emphasise how she believes she has been wronged. 'Boot me out like worthless trash. After all I did for her.' A malicious smile clings to her twisted mouth. 'Then Teddy told me how shocked he was to see how low the school's test scores were—'

William savagely interrupts. 'And you allowed your husband to blackmail her. Repeatedly rape her.'

Her eyes are solid ice, leaving my blood running frozen cold. She snarls, 'Rape? Stop being so dramatic. She was a bitch. Even when we were in the infants, Clare always wanted to have her way. She'd been panting after Teddy since we were at school.'

I won't let her carry on with these lies. 'It was the other way around, wasn't it?' I shouldn't be, but somehow I feel more in control. 'Teddy was the one who wanted it. This all started at school. This was never just about the SATs scores. Your husband used it as an opportunity to get his filthy hands on something he had wanted for years – Clare Swan.'

Her cheeks blaze. 'He loved her more than he loved me.'

'Loved?' Was this woman crazy? Outrage makes me shout. 'That's not love. What you and that rotten reptile you married felt for her was twisted. Sick. If Clare had wanted to do this, that was her choice. But you both never gave her a choice. You forced her to do sexual things she did not want to do.'

Suddenly, I feel dirty. I don't want to be in this house any more. However, there's one last thing I have to do before I leave here.

'You are going to show us where all those DVDs are and I want every last one of them. Every. Last. One.'

The cupboard in Teddy's neatly cleaned office upstairs is stuffed full of DVDs. The length of time that these two animals must have abused and tormented Miss Swan leaves me raging. William joins us, holding a black bin liner from the kitchen, and with a shake of his head he begins to dump the films inside it.

Stomach churning, I accuse, 'Is that what you do, Beryl? Watch one before you go to bed at night?'

Her lips curl. 'You wouldn't understand.'

That's when I see it so plain in front of me. 'Of course, you never murdered Clare. Humiliating her and bringing her down – that was what you were really after. It was the only thing you had going in your pathetic life, so there was no way you were going to get rid of it.'

Suddenly I remember the day that Miss Swan called me to the school to give me Sara-Jane's report and when I left how they stood in front of her window watching me go. But how the power dynamics had been reversed. Miss Swan standing behind Beryl. Because it was Beryl who had held the true power.

'Jealous. That's what you were and are. You've been jealous of your so-called friend, Clare, since you were at school. Jealous that the man you loved wanted her. Clare. Not you. Since you were children you've envied her. All these years you've watched these DVDs not to be close to Teddy, but to watch what he did to her. How he hurt her. Humiliated her. Inflicted pain. You've hated Clare Swan since you were at school and these disgusting films are your revenge on her.'

Her face is a cold mask of contempt. 'You have no idea what you're talking about.'

'The only reason I won't go to the cops is because Miss Swan's reputation will be trashed for good.'

I pull out the photo of her, Teddy and Clare.

'Where did you get that?' she demands, voice rising. 'That's the only photo of me and Teddy when we were young. Give it back.'

She tries to snatch it. But she knows she's no match for me. Angry me.

I shove it in her face. 'Look at Teddy's face. He's not gazing longingly at you. He only has eyes for Clare.' I step closer. 'Did he ask her out? And she turned him down?'

Beryl snarls, 'She always thought she was too good for us. He could never see that. But when she turned him down I was there. To comfort him. To give him the love he needed.'

'Love?' I scoff. 'You and that filthy man you married wouldn't know the first thing about love.' My finger stabs the photo. 'This is how you will always be, no matter how much you tried to humiliate her. You behind her. Inferior. Insignificant. Always in Clare Swan's shadow.'

I chuck the photo on the floor and storm out. Away from this twisted love triangle.

Chapter 41

Fifteen Years Ago

Sara-Jane Abused By Mum

Gem staggered back after reading the headline in the packed local store. What did they mean? Abused Sara-Jane? Abuse her own daughter? Gem desperately tried to stop her face from crumbling as she read.

It was Charlie.

Rearing his despicable, lying head again after his exclusive interview – 'My Agony'. And after she was falsely labelled a robber by the media. Now Charlie was back, sticking the knife in again, this time claiming that social services had threatened to take Sara-Jane away because Gem had hit her.

Hit her Sara-Jane? No! That wasn't true. It had been Charlie who had hit her. That one time. It was Gem who had called social services. All the journalist needed to have done was check with social services. Why were they taking Charlie's word for it?

But that was the problem, it wasn't only Sara-Jane's dad this time. Some of her former neighbours had been interviewed:

You could hear that poor kid crying most nights.

I heard her hitting that sweet little girl more than once.

Always rows going on inside that flat.

The police were called more than once. Child endangerment I heard.

None of it was true. Well, only the part about her and Charlie having arguments. Why would people make up such vicious lies about her? Gem's stomach knotted with agonising panic. What she spotted next to the front-page story made her want to be sick:

Reader's Vote:

Should hanging be brought back?

There was a macabre noose at the end.

Acid rose in her throat. *Why do they hate me so much?*

Gem lifted her head. Everyone was staring at her. Her paranoia grew. *They'll all be after me now. Wasn't taking my Sara-Jane enough? My reputation, my very self, or what's left of it, is being kidnapped by liars.*

Every day there seemed to be a new headline about her life – even about her mother's prison sentence for passing bad cheques, so Gem had ended up living with an aunt for eight months when she was ten years old. The old neighbour who claimed that Gem's childhood home had been a hotbed of booze, drugs and criminality.

Angrily, Gem shook the newspaper in the air. 'Why are they wasting time on these fake stories? Why aren't they writing about Sara-Jane any more? They should be helping to search for her.'

That's what hurt Gem the most. The media didn't appear to be interested in finding Sara-Jane. All they wanted were salacious stories about Gem.

Just then, a police siren ripped through the air and seconds later a police car came to an abrupt stop outside the store. Two officers walked in and strode directly to Gem.

The newspaper tumbled from her quaking hands. Sweat leaked down the middle of her back. Her pulse jumped wildly in her neck and wrist.

'Are you Gemma Casey?'

Her reply was full of fear. 'It's Gem.'

Someone on the Rosebridge must've told them she was here shopping because they would've looked for her at her flat first.

'You're under arrest.'

'What?' Gem tried to catch her breath. Arrest? What were they talking about?

They weren't listening to her as they frogmarched her out. For some reason they decided to handcuff her outside the shop, in public where all the other shoppers could view her humiliation. A camera clicked. The growing crowd whispered, their features openly accusing. Gem felt like they were vultures picking her bones at her public execution.

The room Gem was escorted into inside the police station had a table with four chairs, two on each side, and was painted an ugly blue. No window. Airless and suffocating. Her handcuffs were removed. Absently rubbing her fingers around her wrist Gem cautiously sat down. Two detectives, a man and a woman, sat facing her. They introduced themselves. But she didn't remember their names. What worried her was the file lying on the table. It had her name on it. What was going on here?

Shouldn't they ask me if I need a lawyer? She'd had one for the shoplifting charge. Then again, they hadn't charged her with anything yet, so maybe she didn't need one. Still, maybe she should establish what her rights were. But she didn't want to upset them, so she kept her uncertainties to herself.

It was the woman officer who started. 'There's been an accusation made against you.'

Shock slammed into Gem. An accusation? All her composure disappeared. Her heart started racing. The muscles in her tummy flip-flopped and tightened. The ragged noise of her breathing thundered inside her head.

Her jaw moved, grappling to find the words. 'What do you mean? I don't understand. What accusation?'

The officer opened the file in front of her. The file with her name on it. 'You were convicted of shoplifting not that long ago.'

Shame burned a nasty path across Gem's face. 'I took those clothes so Sara-Jane had a school uniform.'

'Do you always blame your daughter for your criminal activities?' The male officer spoke for the first time. Gem found the hardness of his face intimidating, especially his eyes, which were a bottomless blue.

'I never blamed my daughter for anything,' Gem cried. 'She is my life.'

'There's a social services case file that says you hit your child.' Back to the female officer again.

'Another lie. That was Charlie. Her dad.'

Gem felt such shame, such guilt to admit her daughter had a violent father. As Sara-Jane's mum she should have protected her.

The woman flicked through the file. 'What social services concluded was there were plenty of fights going on when you lived with Sara-Jane's father. Is that what happened? During one of these fights you hit her?'

Gem's hackles were raised. She bared her teeth. 'You accuse me of hitting my kid one more time and I'm going to—'

'Hit me?' The male cop smoothly jumped in.

Gem slumped back, knowing full well she'd displayed the behaviour she'd denied using on her child. *Idiot! Idiot!*

Leaning forward, Gem's fighting spirit returned, more in control now. 'You said an accusation has been made against me. I'm not prepared to say another word until you tell me what it is.'

The female officer referred to her notes. 'Yesterday an accusation was made that it was you who told your daughter to take Abigail Prentice and to leave the premises of their school.'

'What?' There was a buzzing in Gem's ears. She must have heard wrong. 'I'm the one who told the girls to sneak out of school?'

'Are you admitting it?'

Gem was trembling, a thin, cold film of sweat coated her forehead. Her fingers twitched. She didn't know what to do with her hands.

The police started almost barking at her this time. 'Gem Casey, did you instruct your daughter, Sara-Jane Casey, to take her friend, Abigail Prentice, and abscond from school?'

'Did you meet them?' said the other officer. 'Take them away? But Abby managed to escape. Where have your hidden your daughter?'

Something suddenly occurred to Gem. 'You're not just trying to pin this on me, you're trying to pin this on my girl too.' *How dare they.* She spat, 'I know what you're trying to do. Make it out to look like me and my Sara-Jane took Abby.' Gem flung her arms wide. 'Sara-Jane is out there missing and what are you lot doing? Sitting on your arses, giving me the third degree when you should be searching the face of the earth for her.'

'Why would you tell Sara-Jane to leave school?'

Gem stubbornly folded her arms. 'Who's made this accusation against me?'

'That information is confidential.'

'Let me guess. Abigail Prentice. She's made the accusation, hasn't she?' Gem could have smacked her forehead – she should have figured this out earlier. 'She's the only one in a position to point the finger. I told Sara-Jane to stay away from that girl. That she was trouble.'

They wouldn't stop hammering away at her. Over and over. By the end, Gem was a defeated wreck with her head on the table. When it was clear she was too exhausted to answer more questions, the interview was stopped.

A uniformed officer escorted her out of the room. When she realised that she was not being taken out of the building, she called out, 'Where are you taking me?'

No answer. She was led down a series of corridors that left her dizzy and disorientated. Where were they taking her? She soon found out.

A cell.

It was stiflingly hot. The metal door clanged behind her. Only as the time went on did Gem understand. She was being kept in the cell overnight. *No.* She had to get home. She had to be there. Frantic desperation pushed her to pound her fists against the cell door.

'If Sara-Jane comes back tonight I won't be there. I need to be there to help her. How's she going to get in? Who's going to hold her tight?'

Sobbing, a crushed Gem slid to the floor.

◆ ◆ ◆

The following morning they came for her again. Gem had no idea how she was walking. She was listless and dead on her feet. Inside the interview room the barrage of questions started up again.

One hour. Two hours. A suffocating cloud descended over her until Gem wasn't even sure she knew what her own name was any more.

Her fingers tangled in her hair as she sobbed, 'I never did any of it. Let me go home. Please! Please!'

All at once, in the corridor there was a commotion accompanied by a furious argument. A light tap sounded on the door. The tape recorder was punched off before one of the detectives left the room. The door was suddenly pushed back to reveal Dale Prentice and a man in a suit. Dale looked furious.

Gently, he asked Gem, 'Did they advise you that you could have a solicitor?'

Gem didn't answer, wondering if any of this was real. Maybe she was back in the cell dreaming that Dale was here. No . . . He really was here. She shook her head.

'Right.' He turned to a police officer whose distinguished uniform and brass singled him out as a top cop. 'First off, you know that's bang out of order. My solicitor here will represent Gem, if need be. But I don't think there's a need for her to be here any more. Am I right?'

The other man briskly nodded and Gem was escorted to the door. Dale took her gently by the arm. Before he left, he rounded back on the police. 'You should be ashamed of yourselves. The lot of you. Her daughter's gone missing and you decide to lock her up. It will be Gem's decision of course, but my solicitor will be advising her to make an official complaint.'

Chapter 42

'What if Miss Swan didn't kill Teddy Spencer on her own?'

Abby's talking and following me around the flat when I get back. It's so late, it must be coming up to midnight. She's as jittery as a cat that's had its tail trodden on. When I informed her about her former head teacher's murder, emotion bent her forward and she dissolved into floods of noisy tears. She was much closer to Clare Swan than I expected. So I embraced and comforted her as best I could. Once she dried her eyes, that's when the talking started.

Maybe, this is her way of working through her grief. Which is fine for her, but I'm holding everything together by an incredibly thin thread.

'What if it's the same person you heard in the room with her when she was on the phone? The one you think was still in the school when you found her body? Set you up with the cops?'

Give me a break.

She follows me into the kitchen, barely able to catch her breath. Yak! Yak! Yak! My head's pounding. I want her to shut up. I don't have the headspace for more theories, regardless of whether they make sense. Not tonight. Not after seeing Miss Swan repeatedly stabbed, choked, brutalised, bloody, her tongue . . .

But Abby's locked in her own little world and keeps going. She looks manic, her face streaked with the dirty tracks of her earlier tears. 'What if she had an accomplice back then? You know, to kill Teddy. Maybe someone . . .'

Her hands stretch out, her fingers claw, scratching the air. 'Maybe?' Her voice catches in her throat. 'Maybe . . . ?'

For the first time I observe her properly. Abby's leaning so far forward she looks about ready to fall down. And she's shaking. Hell, I'm not sure she's even breathing.

Firmly, I touch her arm and instantly the tremors in her reverberate through me. 'Abby, tell me what's going on.'

She doesn't answer, instead stares at her hands. But the look on her face suggests that it's not her hands she's seeing, but something that's awful and terrible that she doesn't want attached to her body. I remind myself that she was in the hospital not that long ago. Maybe tried to harm herself. My mind goes back to her apartment, the discarded pill bottles on the floor. Is she having another episode?

The girl's still traumatised and what did you do? You made her sleep in the room of her best friend who she was abducted with. If that doesn't send her over the edge I don't know what will. What the hell were you thinking?

I get her sat down in the front room. Her fingers flex and twitch in her lap. She appears lost in another world. I'm not even sure she can hear me.

'I'm going to call your grandfather.' Looking back, I should have made her stay with him after leaving the hospital.

Her hand clamps on my knee, so strong I feel its grip right down to my bone. 'Please. Don't.' The air's harsh in her chest. 'He'll baby me, stop me from trying to think about the past. He hates seeing me in pain. Doesn't want me to remember the past.' She wrings her hands. 'I have to remember! Remember!'

'It's not worth your mental health.' I tell her the truth as I see it. 'I get why Dale wants to wrap you in cotton wool. He wants you to be happy—'

'Do I look fucking happy to you?' She jerks away from me. 'I want to be happy. Be normal. But that's never going to happen until the past comes back to me.'

In a soft tone I say, 'Get a good night's sleep. Tomorrow will be here soon enough for us to plan our next move.'

A weak smile, for an instant, lights up her face. 'There is one place I am happy. In Sara-Jane's room.'

A few minutes before I hit the sack too, I check on Abby. The tight expression on her face suggests that even sleep doesn't offer her the refuge of peace. I lean down and kiss her on the cheek, hoping that will lessen her turmoil. The scent of lemon is strong, but strangely it's not against her neck, which is where I'd expect her to dab perfume. Where's the smell coming from? I sniff and find where it is.

Her hands.

Not a dab on her wrist. It's all over her hands.

Why does she put lemon perfume on her hands? Or is it even lemon?

Feeling I've invaded her privacy I turn and leave.

The scent of lemon remains with me.

There's something heavy on my chest. Crushing me. It feels like my ribs are about to cave in. I can't breathe. Can't find any air. Am I awake? Asleep? I'm not sure. After Abby went to sleep in Sara-Jane's room I stayed up for a good twenty minutes, thinking everything over, including Abby's suggestion that Miss Swan was not working alone. Then I went to bed. Surprisingly, almost instantly, I fell into a deep sleep. Now, I'm not sure what's happening.

Is this a nightmare? Or real? I wonder if I'm having a heart attack. Isn't that what they say happens, you feel a tightness in your chest and find it difficult to breathe? It's not just my chest, I figure out, it's my neck as well. What's your neck got to do with having a heart attack? Nothing.

My eyes slam open. There's a shadow, a silhouette kneeling on my chest. My reasoning comes back. This is no phantom, it's a person. Somebody. And, God help me, the pressure on my throat is because they have something wrapped around my neck. And they are pulling it tight.

I freeze, paralysed with shock. Petrified of what's happening to me. Someone is trying to choke the very life from me. I feel the material around my throat, pressing into my skin. My windpipe. The dark presses down, disorientating me.

Fight! Fight!

Somehow, a thread of air whizzes past my lips and down to my chest. It balloons inside me. Grows. Gives me the energy to fight back. I shake my head madly from side to side, trying to break their hold on my neck. It has the reverse effect because their hands pull whatever is wrapped around my neck. Tighter. Tighter.

Air. Need air. Oxygen. Please.

My chest arches unnaturally seeking air. It finds none.

I'm going to die. Going to die.

My narrowed side-eye sees Sara-Jane's socks and glasses and the faceless angel picture pinned to the wall.

Sara-Jane.

Her name gives me the strength I need more than air. With all the power in me I buck my legs. Rock my body one way, then the other. Keep rocking and bucking. Move my body any way I can to get this murdering maniac off me. The person on me, their legs slip from my chest, but their tightness on the thing they have wrapped around my neck holds. However, their grip loosens.

I kick their stomach. Once. Twice.

With a cry of pain they roll over, off the bed and land harshly on the floor near the side table. Coughing violently, I grab the material from my neck and fling it on the bed. It's a towel. One of my own from the bathroom.

Lunging sideways, I find the lamp and jerk it on. Swivel its head to shine on the bastard on the floor. The bastard who I know must be Miss Swan's killer. From the bedside drawer I take out a penknife. I jump down. Carefully crouch over my attacker. My fingers dig into their shoulder and roughly shove them over so I can see their face. Gasping in disbelief I lurch back.

Abby.

Chapter 43

'I'm not like other girls.'

That's what Abby tells me, her voice flat, devoid of life.

The shocking horror of the situation has me cringing against the wall. Both as a way to protect myself from my attacker. And . . . And . . . I cannot believe this.

Abby?

My grip is solid around the penknife. She was choking me. Didn't Detective Wallace say that's how Teddy Spencer had died? Miss Swan had been choked too? Strangled. Good grief, did Abby kill them both?

But she was a small child, my inner voice reasons. *How could she do that to a grown man?* And she was such a small mite then, she wouldn't have had the strength to hurt a fly. Would she? If she murdered him what would stop her from murdering . . . No! No way! Stop! She would never do anything like that.

Kill Sara-Jane? Murder her own best friend?

Kids killing kids.

What if she had murdered Sara-Jane. And her mum and grand-dad knew. And all of this has been a set-up. They planted the stories about the black van near Stroud Road and Glass Alley? The kidnappers? What if it was one of them who called the police and pretended to have been someone nearby who heard screams on the street? What if the girls never sneaked out of school? What if . . . ?

Have I been in a hall of smoke and mirrors all this time?

My shattered gaze assesses Abby. The lamplight is doing awful things to the colour of her skin. She's back to resembling the skeleton-head that she was in the back of the black van. A ghoul. Someone who's lost control of themself. *Lost control . . .*

I make a run for it. Knife still in hand. Bolt out of the room. Enter the jet-dark hallway.

'Gem!' I feel the blast of her voice against my back.

Pulse banging, heart thudding, I reach the door. Grab the lock. Sweat makes my fingers slip and slide, eventually slide off.

'Gem! Please!'

The heat of her is behind me. I twist around and jam my back against the door. I'm trapped. Don't know what to do. I point the knife at her. My hand shakes badly.

Abby stares at me, breathing erratic. Hard. An awful noise hisses from the back of her throat. She looks like the one who is being hunted down.

'Please! Let me explain.'

'That you tried to kill me?' My free hand desperately searches behind me for the lock.

'I know what you're thinking,' she pleads. 'I didn't kill – murder – anyone.' Abby takes a single step towards me.

'Stay there,' I harshly command.

She sniffs back her tears. That's when I notice how she's continuously rubbing her hands up and down the side of her naked legs. 'Let me explain. I know what you're thinking. But I couldn't have murdered Miss Swan because I spent the evening with Traci, next door. Ask her.'

I don't need to. I bumped into Traci earlier, on my way back, on the communal balcony. Playing Mother Hen, Traci had made it her business that Abby got a decent meal down her. I bite nervously into my lip. I don't know what to make of this. She has an alibi for this evening and was too small as a child to be able to strangle anybody.

It's my turn to plead, 'Abby, what's going on here?'

'I'm not going to hurt you. I'd never do that. Not on purpose. Can we talk in the lounge?'

I don't move. Mull it over. Hell, what if I'm placing myself in danger? I feel the sensation of the towel around my neck.

I nod. 'But you stay on one side of the room while I stay near the door.'

'No problem.' She lets out a tiny shaky smile. 'I need to get my bag first.'

This is your chance to get away. Open the door. Alert Traci.

I do none of that. Instead I wait until she has returned and entered the main room with her bag. What her bag's got to do with this I don't know. I suppose I'm about to find out. With a pinch of hesitation I slowly pull off the door and warily move towards the room. But I don't go inside, instead remain on the threshold. Abby hovers behind the two-seater sofa, creating enough distance for me to feel, not quite at ease, but safe enough. The strap of her satchel is on her shoulder.

She starts, strangely calm, her every word clear. 'Do you recall the incident when Miss Swan asked you to come to the school because Sara-Jane had tried to strangle me?' No mother will ever forget an event like that. 'It wasn't Sara-Jane. It was me. I tried to strangle myself.'

My shocked gasp tears through the air. 'What? All these years I thought—'

'I know. And I'm sorry for that. Sara-Jane was only trying to cover for me. That's how we became friends.' She looks so beaten down. 'Sara-Jane found me in the toilet with the handle of my bag wrapped around a window frame and the other around my neck.'

'Oh, Abby.' Horror doesn't do justice to what I feel for her.

'Don't interrupt. Please.' Anxiety pushes her voice higher. 'If you do, I'm not sure I'll be able to find the words to continue. This is the first time I've ever told anyone.'

My soft nod is my way of communicating that I understand. So I listen.

'Sara-Jane stopped me. She was so gentle when she unwound it from my neck. I don't know why I was doing it. But I knew Mum would go ape-shit if she found out. But of course she saw the marks on my neck and made me tell her who did it. Sara-Jane's name just came out of my mouth.'

She pulls the strap of her bag closer to the twisting muscles in her neck. 'Sara-Jane played along and took the blame for me.'

That's my Sara-Jane. Always got enough kindness in her for the whole world.

I ask, 'Had you tried to harm yourself before?'

She makes a dismissive noise. 'See, it's not self-harming. I don't just want to choke myself. I want to strangle other people.'

With a tentative step, I enter the room. 'When was the first time you did it to anyone else?'

'It wasn't a person. When I was about seven, a year before me and Sara-Jane were taken, I started strangling my dolls. Having mock hangings.'

Jesus Christ! I'm paralysed with shock. Panic. Distress. I've never heard of anything like this before. This is *way* out of my comfort zone. I've seen and heard some freaky stuff in my time. But this . . . ?

Then something occurs to me. 'Is that why your roommate at medical college left? Did you try to strangle her?'

Her eyes widen. 'It's like tonight, I don't remember getting up. Doing it.' Her eyes shine. 'I used a belt on her. I only came to when she managed to throw me off and started screaming.'

'Why didn't the college authorities call the police?'

'They didn't want any trouble. For whatever reason, they didn't want the cops snooping around. And my roomie obviously didn't tell anyone. But she never came back. I hope I didn't ruin her chances of becoming a doctor.'

I move closer as my brain tries to sort through and make sense of what she's told me. 'Why would you, a little girl, start behaving like this? Aged seven? Did something happen to you then?'

In a weak, barely there voice, she answers. 'That's the thing, it's part of the time that I don't remember.' Her hand stretches out to me. 'Look at them. My hands. They keep doing this. I'm not normal, am I?'

Abby urgently reaches for something in her bag. A small transparent bottle filled with yellow liquid. She squirts some on her hands. Lemon. Not perfume, but real lemon juice. With frenzied motion, she rubs and rubs the lemon over her hands.

'My hands are unclean. They make me do dirty things. No matter how I try to cleanse them they're still filthy.' Her body heaves with sobs. 'They won't make the stain of my past go away.'

She starts hitting her fist against her head. Back to being the traumatised Abby crouched in a corner in a hospital room. Degraded. Bewildered. Drained. That's how Abby looks. I can't watch her go through this agony any more. The knife slips from my fist as I rush over and take her in my arms.

Through her trembling tears she whispers, 'When you told me Miss Swan was strangled I think it triggered something. I kept seeing my hands. I think I was remembering something. It kept fleeting across my mind, but before I could make it out, it had gone. My head's a blank.'

An unspeakable possibility grips me. 'Did you witness one of those monsters trying to choke Sara-Jane in the van? Is that what this is?'

'No! I remember us in the van. She helped me escape. And this started before we were taken. Sometimes I don't want to remember. I think whatever it is was so horrible – I don't want to go back there—'

Abby's body stiffens. 'What's that? I heard something outside the door.'

I listen carefully. She's right, there's a noise in the hallway. The baby hairs on the back of my neck stand up. There's something in the air.

'What's that smell?' Abby's nose twitches.

I know what it is. We both rush into the hallway in time to see a gloved hand push through the letterbox. It holds a lighter. Beneath is a pool of liquid.

Petrol.

No!

It's too late. The lighter flicks on. A flame ignites. It drops on to the petrol-soaked floor. Fire rapidly climbs up the front door.

Chapter 44

Abby's mouth's moving, but I don't hear her because I'm paralysed in chilling horror by the fire sweeping the hallway. I might not be able to hear her, but the noise of the flames overwhelms my mind. Crackling. Hissing. Spitting. Fiery orange and yellow coiled snakes trying to get us.

Something shoves and shakes me hard. It's Abby pulling me out of my grisly trance.

She's terrified. 'How are we going to get out of here?'

'I . . . I . . . I don't know,' I stammer back.

Poisonous smoke starts snaking towards us.

Think! Think! Think!

Suddenly there's a brutal banging against the door. Someone's trying to kick the door in.

'Stand back!' It's William outside trying to rescue us.

His mum yells, 'We'll get you out. We've called the fire brigade.'

He tries again and again, but the door won't give. No wonder, I locked the door securely tonight using both bolts at the top and bottom. I can't wait around, there's no time to lose. I rush into my bedroom and come back out holding the towel Abby tried to strangle me with. The heat is intense. I head into the bathroom and drag another towel off the rail. Soak them both with water.

Back in the main room I chuck one at Abby. 'Tie it over your mouth. The smoke is more deadly than the fire.'

I do the same with the other towel. Now what?

Think! Think! Think!

Abby bends double, spewing her guts out, coughing. Come on, there must be an escape route out of here. William is still hammering at the door. In despair, I begin to turn around and that's when I see it peeping through the curtains. The balcony. The bedroom balcony where I would once wait all night for Sara-Jane to come home.

I rush back into the hallway. The flames are fierce here, they'll be licking at the bedroom soon. I shout at the door, 'William, go out to your mum's balcony at the back!'

'What? I can't hear you!'

It's my turn to double over and cough. The smoke is nasty and thick in my throat and tongue. 'Your mum's balcony!' I scream it this time, leaving my voice hoarse and rough. 'Get to the back.'

I don't have more time to tell him. If he hasn't heard me, we'll have to do this on our own. Back in my bedroom I snap the curtains back. Abby and I go out on to the balcony. I kick shut the French door. Mentally, I estimate the distance of Traci's balcony from mine. A five-foot gap, a drop of four floors to the ground below. It doesn't occur to me think about the danger, it's a matter of survival now.

Abby bravely tells me, 'I can do this. Don't worry about me. You need to go first.'

'No.' I smile ruefully. 'Beauty before age.'

Traci's balcony door swings open and William appears. He looks so upset and frightened.

But he also wears an expression of pure determination. He knows what to do. Abby gives me one last, apprehensive glance before climbing on to the iron railings at the side. I hold on to her as she leans across, then stretches over. Finally her hands grasp the top of Traci's balcony.

'Easy does it,' William says as he pulls her in.

Finally, she's in his arms. Only then do I catch view of a fretful Traci waiting with a blanket, which she wraps around Abby. 'You poor love.'

Sirens tear up the air outside. More lights in the block facing us come on. I can hear the chatter of people somewhere downstairs. People will have been roused from their beds because it's the early hours of the dawning morning. The Rosebridge must be in uproar.

'Your turn.' William coaxes me with a tender smile.

I see the flames at the bedroom doorway. I don't think, just do. I climb, lean over and stretch. I'm not as tall as Abby, so my hands don't quite reach the balcony. Damn! With a grunt, I try again and this time I grab the end of the balcony. I feel William's safe hands around my arms. He begins to pull me over . . . And I freeze.

'What's happening?' William looks even more scared.

'I've got to go back.' I start pulling away from him.

He won't let go of me. Looks incredulous. 'What? Are you crazy?'

In fact he starts pulling me back. I resist. He doesn't understand. I have to go back. Have to.

'Socks and glasses. Sara-Jane's report. The angel.'

His face creases in confusion. 'I don't know what you're going on about, but I know this much, I'm not letting you go back.'

Unwittingly, his hands have relaxed. I manage to snatch one of my arms back.

'Let. Me. Go.'

He has no alternative, because if he doesn't, I might fall. Swearing, he pushes me back to ensure my safety. I drop back. I take off the towel, so I can inhale lots of fresh air. I refuse to look at William, because if I do, I may not be able to do this. I have to get those last memories of my daughter. I open the French doors. A gust of wind blows me backwards while the smoke billowing out takes me the other way. It's an inferno. I cover my face and head with the towel and plunge in.

The acrid smoke covers my face and worms into my throat. The fire's growling and gushing. I start wheezing with the horrible pressure on my lungs. Crawling along the floor I see Sara-Jane's socks, report book and glasses on the table where I keep them. My heart twists and falls because I'm too late. They're already becoming unrecognisable anyway. The glasses are melted and the socks and report book are embers. It's like watching my child burn in front of me. I'm crushed. I wonder if I should just lie here and be swept away by the fire. Perhaps Sara-Jane will be waiting for me on the other side. I'm so tired of searching for her.

The fire's orange glow casts strange shapes, moving shadows over a sheet of paper that is pinned to the wall. The drawing of the angel with no face. It energises me and I come back to life and snatch it off the wall.

I'm back on the balcony. William is there. The expression he wears is one that shows I've put him through hell. I'm so, so sorry. I do the same actions as before to reach the balcony next door, but this time I misjudge the distance.

'Nooo!' William roars as my leg flops over, dragging my weight with it. I'm falling. I snatch at the railings and I'm hanging there by one arm. The fire seems to have taken all the oxygen in my bones and body. The world sways. Blurs. How fitting that I should fall and die from the same balcony where I once sat all night, convinced that I'd see Sara-Jane coming home.

Suddenly there's an arm around my waist. I look down to find a fireman on a ladder below me. I can't speak. I feel Sara-Jane's faceless angel in my pocket.

When I get downstairs the paramedics check me over alongside Abby.

It's been a day for murder. First Clare Swan. Now someone tried to murder Abby. Murder me.

Chapter 45

'This looks like a classic hate crime,' Detective Wallace announces to us all. He glances my way. 'We suspect that it's an individual from the Rosebridge Estate, someone from the past who wanted you gone.'

We've all gathered in Dale's comfortable main room in his house the following day. Me, Abby, Dale and two detectives. Mercifully, Dale provided shelter for both me and Abby last night. Rosa's hovering in the background, bringing us all much-needed mugs of strong coffee. A triple brandy, that's what Dale tried to get down me for the shock. Even if I was a drinking woman I would've refused. I need to keep a clear head. The cop is spot-on right, this is a hate crime; however, it's not the type that he means. Someone hates me and Abby enough to try to murder us.

Who would do that? Whoever it is they must be spooked, which means we must be getting nearer to the truth.

My hooded gaze shifts to Dale, who paces furiously from one end of the room to the next. His movements are jerky, his stride long, he looks about ready to explode. After the paramedics had checked us out at the scene I'd wanted to go straight to the police station, but Abby wouldn't have it, insisting on calling her grandfather. When Dale arrived and saw the state of his granddaughter and was told what had happened, I thought he was going to collapse.

No one could dispute the love they have for each other. There was no way that the person who tried to burn us alive could be Dale.

Tried to burn us alive.

I shiver. The taste of acrid, nasty smoke remains in the back of my throat, the stench coating the inside of my nose. But do you know what the worse thing is, the absolute worst? Sara-Jane's home is gone. Up in flames. I know it's irrational; however, a part of me still thinks of her making her way home one day. What will she do if her home isn't there? Where will she go? I knock back my coffee, its taste as fiery as brandy.

'Gem?'

Someone's calling me. I snap out of myself, come back to now. It's Abby. She looks at me closely and says, 'Detective Wallace would like to know if we want to add anything else to our statements.'

Oh yeah, I want to add something all right. The cop gets my undivided attention. 'Maybe if Detective Wallace had believed me, instead of treating me like a crackpot when I first went to the police station and showed him my daughter's socks that someone had posted through my letterbox, none of this would have happened.'

Dale swings to face me. 'What? Sara-Jane's socks? But how would someone get . . . ?' His voice trails off as his brain makes all the connections like a game of dot-to-dot. 'Gem, I never knew.' He turns his full fury on the cop. 'And you did nothing about this?'

'That's not quite accurate,' Wallace splutters.

Dale doesn't give him a chance to finish. He lengthens his neck. 'I've got a meeting with Commander Stacy coming up next week, and I think I'm going to add a new item to the agenda.'

My hand comes up. The last thing I want is more tension. I've had a bellyful of it. 'Someone doesn't want me to find out about what happened to my precious girl. Someone doesn't want Abby to remember what happened.'

And with that I leave the room, thread through the back of the house until I'm outside in the beautiful gardens that lead to the stable. With an urgency, like my life depends on it, I gulp sharp, cold air into my lungs. God, I need this. The sensation of life flowing back into me.

'It is a good thing that his granddaughter is here now.'

Rosa. She's standing behind me. Instead of turning, my gaze remains on the brooding sky.

'When me and Sara-Jane came to live here we didn't know anyone,' I quietly confide to her. 'It was our first week here and we were coming back from the shops. This huge Range Rover comes up alongside us and this man in the front peers at us and then smiles. He says, "If you ever need anything, you ask for Dale," and he was gone. I have no idea how he knew we were new to the area.'

I hear the scuff of her feet against the kitchen's stone floor. 'Dale has been lonely without her.'

I don't hear Rosa go, but I feel it. It's a type of emptiness I've come to know since Sara-Jane disappeared.

My phone rings. It's William. 'Where are you?' When I tell him where I am, do I imagine the tension in his reply? 'Why are you at Dale's?' When he adds, 'You should be at the hospital,' I get where his anxiety is coming from.

'The paramedics checked us over. Dale has been a lifesaver because I can't go back to the flat. I'm OK. Well, as OK as someone can be after someone has tried to murder them.'

'Fancy coming over to mine?'

'Your mum's?'

'No.' He strings the word out. 'I mean *mine*. My place. My pad. My cave. My des res.'

He does make me laugh. It's one of the things I like about him. And laughter is what I need at present. To make me feel alive. 'Your des res. Well, put like that . . . Give me a couple of hours.'

◆ ◆ ◆

William's desirable residence is a duplex flat overlooking the canal in a building that was a derelict factory when I lived here fifteen years ago. It's all bare bricks, shiny metal and chrome fittings and a spiral staircase that leads to a smaller floor above.

'You in that fire scared me to death.' Those are his first words to me when I step into his spacious open living space.

I sense he wants to do more than speak so I lean in ever so slightly, giving him permission. He doesn't kiss me, like I expect; instead he runs the pad of his finger gently down my cheek. Lavishes teeny-tiny kisses on the bruises on my neck.

It's me who makes the first move by cupping my hands around his face and kissing him. Long and deep. We stagger up the spiral stairs in a tangle, our clothes chucked off at some point. Then we're sinking into the lush mattress of a double bed. I close my eyes now, all I want to do is feel. The roughness of his hands against my skin. The heat of his lips against my mouth. His tongue doing wicked, wicked tricks all over. I wrap my legs around his. He fits so perfect against me.

My back arches as my neck stretches and tips back. 'Now, William. Please.'

I go into free fall. Let go. Let go in a way I haven't done for years. Since Sara-Jane I've had one proper relationship. All the rest have been sex that's been about letting off steam. You know, doing it because that natural itch needs scratching. Nothing wrong with that. But this now, this with William, it's all about utter pleasure. Delicious decadence, pure passion. At the end we come together and cling. Then we roll on our sides and face each other. I expect to feel some embarrassment – this is Traci's son after all – but I don't.

He's grinning at me, his eyes shining. 'Thanks for that. I needed it.' He surprises me again. Most guys are all about, 'Was that good for you?', 'I hope you enjoyed it as much as I did.'

'I never thanked you.' I tentatively tell him. 'That time . . . on the Rosebridge . . .' He knows what I'm talking about. 'Thank you.'

'What they did was plain wrong. They had no right.'

What happened flashes through my mind. I don't want to go back there.

'Who do you think is trying to kill me?' Yeah, I know, total passion-killer.

Releasing a loud punch of air, he rolls on to his back. My fingers drop away as he relaxes his arm above his head. 'If I knew who it was, I wouldn't hesitate to contact the police. Normally, I'd go get them, but this person is dangerous.' Abruptly he rolls back to face me. 'Swear to me that if you find out who it is, you'll go to the cops. Gem, they are vicious. I know you. Back in the day I'd watch you fly around the estate on that broken-down bike of yours. You looked like you could take on the world. You're brave and bursting with courage. But the problem with bravery is it can blind you, make you feel invincible. And that's when your enemy comes out of nowhere and strikes.'

The weight of his wise words pushes me on to my back. The ceiling is as bland white as the walls. 'Who would hate Abby and me enough to kill us?'

'With this fire the cops can't ignore you now,' William insists. 'They'll have to carry out a proper investigation and that's going to include looking again into the disappearance of Sara-Jay.'

Hope rises again. 'Do you think they will?'

He doesn't answer. There's a sadness around his eyes that I'm about to ask about . . . But I never do because he gathers me close and we make love again. I fall asleep in his arms.

In the evening we order in a Vietnamese. Then we make love some more. We can't get enough of each other.

I awake the following morning wondering where I am. Then I recall. William. The fire. He bounces into the room half-dressed, buttoning his shirt. He's still glistening from a recent shower, his hair spiky-wet. 'Want a coffee?'

'I probably need to go,' I say, although my body's got other ideas, snuggling back into the softness of the bed.

He slots the final button into place. 'I've got to get to the school. I'm doing some planting in the roof garden for a group of my kids, ready for the new term. Plus, there's a million and one things I need to do.'

'William?' He stops, recognising the seriousness of my tone. 'When all this is done, maybe we can still see each other?'

He considers me before looking sharply away. 'Let's talk when all this is over.'

My phone rings before I can respond. I find it among the tangle of my clothes on the floor.

It's Abby.

Her voice sounds weird. 'Meet me. Now.'

Chapter 46

I still feel all lovely-fuzzy and warm from being with William. Still have the security and comfort of his body wrapped around mine when I arrive back at Dale's house. An anxious Abby is waiting for me in the kitchen. She's pacing, and from the looks of things has been doing so for quite some time.

She sees me and rushes over. 'It all came back to me this morning—'

'Slow down. Take it easy.' I manage to get her sat at the table. 'What do you remember?'

'If you recall, when I told you about Sara-Jane and me in the van, I was sure that one of the kidnappers called her by her name. But he . . . he didn't.'

'That doesn't make any sense to me.'

She loops her thin fingers together on top of the table. 'I hear him saying her name. Sara-Jane.' Abby makes direct eye contact with me. 'Because that's what it sounds like he called her. But, in reality, he didn't. He called her something else.'

'You've totally lost me now.'

'He didn't call her Sara-Jane. He called her Sara-*Jay*.'

◆ ◆ ◆

I find William, his back to me, pottering around the raised flow-erbeds. He must have heard me because he declares straight away, 'You've found out, haven't you?'

That catches me off guard. This isn't what I expect him to tell me. To confess even before I've confronted him. Knowing what I know about him now makes me feel sick to my stomach. I stare at his hands in the earth. Hands I allowed to caress me all over my body. Hands that must've grabbed and subdued Sara-Jane. Thrown her bodily into the back of a van like she was a bag of trash.

We're on the top of the school building. It's a roof garden, brimming with a dazzling array of colours and so much perfection, its vegetables and flowers reaching for the sky. How can we now bring such horror to this place of exquisite beauty?

He's on his haunches down beside a gorgeous spray of flowers that are a mix of purples and orange petals. His back remains to me. 'I was going to tell you—'

'That you kidnapped my daughter?' The rage inside me burns harsher than the fire that was set in the flat. 'That you snatched her from me and my mother's love? Did you set the fire? It would've been so easy for you. You were next door, at your mum's. All you had to do was creep one door down and do your wickedness and then go back to your mum's and close the door.'

He stands and twists to face me. Inwardly, I gasp at his appear-ance. Hollow-cheeked and colourless. His hand clenches and unclenches by his side. Good! I want him to look like shit. I want him to look as grim as if his world's about to end. And, by God, if I have my way, I hope it does.

'Guilt is a powerful emotion. Dangerous. The things we do in the past have the power to destroy us in the present.' When he said those words to me in the pub, I thought he was talking about me. Now I see he was also including himself.

Unsure of himself, he stumbles with what to tell me. 'You know I would never do that—'

'Like I thought I knew you would never take my precious baby. Is that why you slept with me? To make me think you could never be involved in this?' The betrayal of him making love to me hurts so much.

His stare is unnerving. 'I haven't slept with anyone since my wife packed her bags and left me a year and a half ago. I know you won't believe me, but there's something about you, Gem, that's always called to me.'

'Did you kill Sara-Jane?' The words scrape with the power of steel wool against my soul.

His whole body changes. Stiffens. If it's possible he loses even more colour in his face. He cries, 'I didn't know. Didn't know it was going to happen!'

I scream out, 'Are you telling me she's dead?'

Oh God! Help me! Someone help me! My baby is gone. All these years of hope. Of staying strong. Of keeping a room ready for her in my real home in London. My legs start to give way . . . Startled, William rushes towards me . . . I bellow at him, 'Stay the fuck away from me! Don't touch me!'

Crouched like someone forsaken, my hands grip my hair. Oxygen turns to the texture of sandpaper in my chest. *Someone help me!*

Sara-Jane is dead.

My head snaps up. My eyes feel dead in their sockets. 'Tell me where I can find her body.'

He looks ravaged. 'I don't know.'

Rage rears me up to my feet. 'What do you mean, you don't know? You killed her and put her somewhere—'

'I never killed Sara-Jane. Never touched a hair on her head.'

I stare at him. There's something in his face. 'Don't you fucking well hold back on me now. What aren't you telling me?'

His eyes flash in denial. 'I would never murder Sara-Jay.' He inhales deeply. 'I know how you found out. I made a mistake that day. I called Sara-Jane "Sara-Jay".' A husky quality enters his tone. 'I called her Jay because she reminded me of this jay bird I saw one day. It sat there, not frightened of anyone, head high, at peace. That's what your girl was like, just like her mother.'

Unbelievable agony tears through me. 'I don't get it. Why have you been helping me all this time? Was this all a mind-fuck?'

'No! I'd never—'

Brutally, I cut over him. 'But you asked the people in the pub to come to you if they had any information about Sara-Jane.' I'm spitting rage. 'Or were you planning to withhold any information anyone told you so you could cover your arse?'

His hands hopelessly lift in the air. 'I don't know what I planned. Maybe I was looking for redemption.'

If William didn't kill Sara-Jane, then . . . 'Did someone pay you to kidnap the girls?'

'I never took any money. I wouldn't do that.' His voice is just below a snarl. 'Neither did Jas— Shit!'

Too late, I catch his mistake. 'So you abducted the girls with Jas. Jaswinder Bedi.' The same Jas who told such a convincing story at Laura's house implicating Sara-Jane and Abby's fathers as the men who did this. 'You said you never took any money. You and Jas were doing the job for someone else.' His strongly drawn breath is the dead giveaway that I'm right. 'Who was it? Tell. Me.'

'We knew that the girls sneaked out of school—'

'How? Who told you?'

'Getting the van was taken care of.' He skates over my questions. 'All we had to do was wait near the alley on the quiet road near the market.' He's avoiding telling me who was behind it all.

'It was meant to be easy. Grab and go. It wasn't meant to end the way it did.'

I take a despairing step closer to him. He compresses his lips. This close up I see the murky shine of unshed tears in his eyes.

'The police will be here soon.' By rights, I should've gone to them and let them deal with it. But I need to understand what's going on here. Instead I called Detective Wallace just before I entered the school.

'I know,' William answers simply. He looks around the garden. 'Each of these plants and vegetables belongs to one of the children I work with. I impress on them that it's a living thing so they need to water and care for it. It doesn't take long for them to see their plant or vegetable as themselves. When it starts growing healthy and strong, they start becoming healthy and strong. I know because I was one of them once.'

His voice chokes up. 'I won't be able to face them after this.'

Then he starts moving backwards.

A dread comes over me. I rush forward. 'William! Don't do this!'

He stops near the edge. Way too close. 'You don't understand. It's all over for me now. I'm ruined. Everything I did here. It's over.'

I'm shaking while he appears so calm. It never occurred to me that he might consider throwing himself off the roof. 'Nothing is worth your life.'

He talks as if the wind's grabbed my words before they can reach him. 'But this is my life. Was my life. When the truth comes out I'll lose my job. The work I do here is everything to me. I'll lose the respect of the children. The parents. Go to prison.'

'You can get that all back. Just come away from the edge.'

'How will I be able to look the kids I work with in the eye?'

Screeching sirens sound below, signalling the arrival of the police.

The wind picks up strength. I step closer. 'I hate you at the moment, William. But I'm not letting you die. There's going to be no more deaths. No more.'

I leap forward and grab the front of his shirt. It's wringing wet with sweat. He wobbles. I manage to bring his weight slightly forward.

A sad smile crinkles the skin at the corner of his faraway eyes. 'Don't blame Mum. She didn't know what she was doing.'

'Traci?' *Please God, don't let the one person who was my protector during those dark days have anything to do with this.*

'Sara-Jay was never meant to be there.'

What? Astonishment makes me almost lose my grip on his shirt.

'Gem, it's over for me.' The air expands in his chest.

He pulls away from me. My hand falls from his shirt.

'Noooo!'

William tips back into nothingness. I drop to my knees. Then he's gone. A wail splits the air. That terrible sound is coming from me.

Chapter 47

Fifteen Years Ago

'Thank you. You're a good man,' Gem sweetly said to Dale.

Not too long ago they had left the police station after he'd rescued her and given the police a proper dressing down. Sometimes she felt that Dale and Traci were the only friends she had left.

'Will you be alright?' he asked her, bringing his car to stop on the edge of the Rosebridge.

'I won't be normal until Sara-Jane comes home.' Before she left Gem asked him, 'Why would Abby accuse me of telling Sara-Jane to make them both sneak out of school?'

Dale sighed heavily. 'Abby is having a hard time. Poor kid. She's working with a therapist who is trying to help her remember what happened.' Emotion clogged his throat. 'Seeing her is breaking my heart. She's a shadow of the child she was before.'

Gem's heart went out to Dale. Seeing the twisted, open emotions on his face was a reminder for her that she wasn't the only one affected by Sara-Jane being taken. Wasn't the only one crippled with pain.

After she left him, Gem stepped cautiously in the spitting rain on to the Rosebridge. Her paranoia was back, crippling and scary. Stiffening, she felt eyes watching her everywhere. Hostile eyes. Head down, Gem didn't go home; instead she headed for The Hangman's Retreat. Usually Traci could be found there playing a game of bingo with a few friends. Gem used the entrance around the side, which had originally been created for women to discreetly enter the part of the pub called the snug.

'I think it's my round, gentlemen! Again!'

Charlie.

She'd know that big-mouthed voice anywhere. Loud and arrogant rising above the hubbub of noise in the bar. He was holding court with some of his cronies at a table in the corner. Showing off, waving money around, performing as he always did when he had a win. And just in case his friends didn't know what his latest win was, he explained it to them.

'That's right, the journalist sent a car to pick me up. A fucking Merc. Bought me lunch. And then paid for my info in cash so I don't have to worry about the taxman.'

'You never did worry about the taxman, Charlie!'

'Can't argue with that!'

The provoked a round of uproarious laughter.

Bastard.

Gem couldn't believe he was in here, bragging about the money he'd made from telling stories and lies about her. And his own daughter. She hadn't seen any money out of him for years to support Sara-Jane's upkeep and look at him now – splashing the cash on bigging himself up.

She took a few steps forward but noticed she was already attracting glances from strangers. The stares were hostile, leaving her frightened.

Gem quickly backed towards the door.

◆ ◆ ◆

Something was off on the Rosebridge. There was always some type of noise coming from somewhere, shouts, laughter, arguments, singing. Today it was quiet. Deathly quiet. And there was no movement. Where was everyone? In fact, there was no one around. Immediately Gem was on her guard. She put her head down, picked up the pace and headed towards her block and then up the stairs. Along the balcony. In front of her door.

Gem staggered back as if someone had gut-shot her. Someone had painted two words on her door. Vicious words. Huge letters. In blood-red paint.

CHILD KILLER

Nervously she looked around, as if sensing others watching her. No one was there. She wasn't a child killer. She'd never touched a hair on Sara-Jane's head. Never. Why were people doing this to her?

Urgently needing moral support, she banged on Traci's door. Her friend would make everything right again. Traci always knew what to do. Maybe Traci had even seen who had painted this shit on her door. No one answered. Strange, that, because Gem was sure she could hear someone inside. Twice more she knocked but still no one came.

Gem rushed indoors. And leaned against the front door. She didn't feel safe here any more. Gem didn't even think. She stuffed as much as she could into a large rucksack, including all the albums containing the photos of Sara-Jane growing up. Grief-stricken, she gazed around this place that had been the home she had made for her child.

A bang at the front door made her jump.

Gem marched into the hallway. Whoever was on the other side of that door she sensed was no friend. 'Go away.'

A loud voice said, 'You're not welcome here any more.'

'Leave me alone.'

'One hour. That's all you've got left to pack your shit and get out of—'

Gem swung the door open to confront her accusers. She was shocked by how many there were. A long line that stretched all the way back to the stairs. What hurt her most was so many of them looked scared of her. Why? She didn't understand what was going on. What had she ever done to any of them?

Her shock deepened when she saw that their appointed spokes-woman was another mum with a child at Princess Isabel. They sometimes walked their children to school together.

She told Gem, 'People around here aren't comfortable with the likes of you being within a metre of our kids.'

Gem was stunned. 'I'd never harm any of your children. Never.'

It was then she noticed that the mob were not alone. Many of the other residents of the estate were watching events unfold from their doorways, windows and balconies. Gem realised she needed to get out of there. She grabbed her bike and shoved through the crowd, deliberately bumping them with her bulky bag on her back. They bellowed:

Child abuser!

People like her shouldn't be allowed to have kids!

Bang her up and chuck away the key!

They screamed and hissed. Downstairs, Gem swung on to her bike and ran into a smaller mob in the courtyard. More insults and cursing hurled her way. All of a sudden, a missile thrown at the group smashed in their midst. They scattered. Another one came. Eggs. Gem looked up. It was Billy-Bob taking careful aim at the group. He looked upset, his expression so serious. Their gazes met and held. He nodded; he didn't need to speak for her to understand.

She mouthed, 'Thank you.'

Gem bolted away on her bike. She didn't look back. When she was sure she was out of danger she cried. Tears streamed down, her gut clenching uncontrollably. As she pedalled away, with no idea where she was going, one thing tortured her over and over again.

If Sara-Jane comes back home, I won't be there. I won't be able to protect her. Again.

Chapter 48

'*Don't blame Mum. She didn't know what she was doing.*'

That's what William told me before he . . . He's falling. And falling. It never ends. Keeps falling. I squeeze my eyes tight to make it go away. *Go away.* I slump back into the wall outside his mother's flat on the communal balcony. The smoke and debris from the fire still lingers in the air. Inside my flaring nostrils.

My home with Sara-Jane is gutted. Damaged. Broken.

Broken. Broken.

A guttural groan escapes me. My hand slaps over my mouth to muffle my anguish. My head hangs low. My shoulders shake with silent tears. Sara-Jane's gone. Gone. Never coming home. She's lost to me.

Forever.

I told Detective Wallace that William had confessed to being involved in her abduction. That Jas Bedi was his accomplice. The police should have him in custody by now. And I pray that he tells them who was the vile puppet master who organised for them to kidnap the girls.

'Gem?' I hear Traci's trembling voice beside me. Blindly, I turn to find her standing in her doorway. She whispers, her heartbreak open, 'Did my Billy-Bob really do what they're saying? Oh God, my son. My boy is dead. Dead. May the angels love and protect him in eternal peace.' *And Sara-Jane too. May they cocoon her in peace too.*

By the looks of things Traci doesn't know that Sara-Jane is dead and, therefore, that William will have played a role in it, although he denied it. I'll leave that for the police to tell her. My job isn't finished. I'm going to find out who ordered the kidnapping and killed Sara-Jane with the last breath in my avenging body.

Her face is ashen, a mask fixed into place where only the lips and the eyes occasionally move. Grief has shrunken her. I guide and support her inside her home. I'm shocked to see that the carpet in the main room is littered with cuttings and clippings of the old news reports with stories about me from fifteen years ago. Traci must have kept them all these years. I don't ask what they're doing on the floor. Now isn't the right time.

I make tea for both of us while she sits in the main room staring at a family photo that includes William.

Traci looks at me, a piercing stare. 'Billy-Bob wasn't my husband's kid. Biologically, blood, you know.' She reveals her secret so quietly I wonder if she's spoken at all. The cup of tea I made her lies untouched. I'm not even sure that she knows I'm really here.

She continues, 'When I was younger I had my head turned by a married man. It shouldn't have happened. Then I'm expecting my Billy-Bob.' Her lashes flutter. 'It was Dale.' Her stare becomes strong. 'Dale Prentice.'

I conceal my shock quickly. *Oh hell! I never saw this coming.* 'Did William know about Dale?'

'No. Dale never turned his back on him though.' She's fierce in defence of her former lover. 'Of course, he couldn't acknowledge him. People couldn't know. But he did what he could, always put his hands in his pockets. I met Roger through Dale. They were friends.'

My mouth twists with outrage on Traci's behalf. Dale no doubt pushed Roger forward to be her husband, absolving him from all responsibility of openly acknowledging William as his son. While he goes on his merry way, Traci, left literally carrying the baby, is grateful for any help he can give. Anything to protect her child. That's what we mothers do.

'Did William know he wasn't Roger's son?'

Some of the old fight comes back into her. 'We told him a week before he started secondary school. I sometimes wonder if that was when all the trouble started.' Her face falls, the fight draining away as she slumps back into her seat. She looks so fragile, like she's about to break apart.

'Did you know that William was one of the men who abducted Sara-Jane?'

Traci looks so horrified she can't get any words out. Then, 'Are you sure he was involved? Maybe he got mixed up—'

'He carried out the kidnapping with his friend Jas.'

Traci sits up straight. 'But he loved Sara-Jane. He had his own pet name for her – Sara-Jay.' She doesn't see me wince at the name that trapped her son in his own lie. 'Why would he do something like that? He worked so hard to change. Everyone around here looks up to him. He's done such great things for the kids in the school. He's gone cap in hand to so many organisations to get money so the children could have special things, like all those new computers.'

She sobs, 'What are people going to say when they find out?' Her hand claws across her mouth.

Mother to mother, my heart calls out to her. However, I can't let that get in my way. Only the truth matters. 'William said that he didn't take any money for abducting the girls. Why would he do that?'

Traci glances listlessly at her hands curled in her lap. 'People got my Billy-Bob wrong, thinking all he ever wanted to do back then was make a quick buck. He had a good heart. He helped people in his little way when he could. Don't get me wrong, I know he was no saint, but he wasn't evil.'

'Then why did he do something so evil as take the girls?'

'Once he started working for Dale, that's when he started turning his life around. Grew into the man he was meant to be. I don't understand any of this. It doesn't make any sense.'

'Do you recall seeing him speaking to anyone you didn't know? Or maybe someone he did know but he was in their company for longer than usual?'

Traci's expression is lost in the William in that family photo. I don't know if she's even heard me.

I carry on. 'William told me to forgive you. That you didn't mean to do it. Were you involved in Sara-Jane's abduction?'

Rearing forward, her eyes flash with fury. 'Never! Never!' Her head shakes with such force I don't know how it stays on her shoulders. 'I didn't know . . . I would never do that. I loved Sara-Jane like she was my own flesh and blood.'

'Then what did William mean? Traci, what did you do?'

Determination pushes me to lean closer. I know she's grieving, but she needs to understand I've been grieving for the last fifteen years and REFUSE to stop until I get the truth.

Traci averts her gaze, the muscles in her jaw working. When she looks back, I sense she's ready to tell me the truth.

Chapter 49

FIFTEEN YEARS AGO

Traci Waddell, unofficial matriarch of the Rosebridge Estate, kept her head down as she scurried away from the pawnshop. The last thing she wanted was anyone to spot her. That was the problem with folk around here, they couldn't stop sticking their nose where it wasn't wanted. Of course, they were not so obliging when it was their own secrets revealed in public for all to see like dirty washing. Traci had just pawned her silver engagement ring for money. She had kept what she was planning to do from her husband, Roger, because he would be so upset if he knew. He would know in an instant what she needed the money for – to pay Billy-Bob's latest court fine.

Drunk and disorderly for the umpteenth time. Roger said she shouldn't pay up this time and let their boy face the consequences. But she couldn't see her boy put in prison. She was a mother. That's what mothers did, they kept their children safe. Besides, this fine was from before Billy-Bob started working for Dale. Paying it off was like drawing a line under Billy-Bob's past. Now he had a chance to go only one way – straight.

Traci turned on to the shopping parade and immediately saw that a crowd were milling and talking outside the local store. It was clear that something had happened. Traci held back. Maybe she should mind her business. Then a few of those gathered spotted her. So did others. Suddenly everyone stopped speaking, their gazes fixed squarely on her. This could mean only one thing. Billy-Bob had gone and done something stupid, again.

Her heart sank. People on the Rosebridge didn't like him and his illegal antics and she couldn't blame them. She suspected they didn't blow the whistle to the cops about his *activities* most of the time out of respect for her.

Knowing there was no way out of this, Traci pushed her shoulders back and marched forward. 'What's got your feathers all in a flap?' She waited for the dreaded answer.

Someone scoffed, 'I told you she was involved. I knew it in my bones.'

'The cops have got her now.'

She. Whoever had them all in a lather was not her son. Traci's restraining finger in the air stopped the talk. 'Who are you talking about?'

People shuffled their feet, some not making eye contact. Janice Adeyemi, an older woman who Traci trusted, pulled her to the side. The woman wasn't alone; she had her three-year-old granddaughter with her. She guided the child with a safety strap. This wasn't an unusual sight now. Since the girls' abduction, parents had started taking more security measures to keep their children safe.

'The police were here a minute or two ago. They arrested Gem Casey.'

Traci went deathly still. 'Are you sure?'

'They came in all sirens blazing. Put her in handcuffs, they did. It's always the ones you least expect. She looked guilty as hell.'

Unconsciously Traci's head moved in denial. 'I don't understand. Why would they do that?'

Headlines flashed in her mind:

My Agony Sara-Jane's Dad

Sara-Jane's Mum Convicted Robber

Traci tried to shove them out of her mind. Shove the growing doubts away.

'I heard it with my own ears,' Janice continued. 'They said they were taking her because she killed her own daughter.'

Traci gasped. 'I don't believe that. Touch a hair on her daughter's head? Gem would never do that in a million years.'

However, there was a lingering doubt in the corner of Traci's mind.

'She abused that poor girl for years. Read it for yourself.' Janice slapped a newspaper in her hand.

The headline leaped out with sickening effect:

SARA-JANE ABUSED BY MUM

Traci rocked with stunned shock. This couldn't be true. Could it? Social services had been involved, which in Traci's eyes damned Gem even further. And Traci knew from experience that social services never got involved unless things were seriously bad.

Traci's head was buzzing, barely able to hear the rest of what the woman was saying. 'To think the killer was right here on the estate all this time.'

Traci couldn't answer, lost in a fog. All she saw was the headline: *Sara-Jane Abused By Mum*.

Janice leaned in close. 'People don't want a child killer on the Rosebridge. We want her gone. We don't want her anywhere near our kids.'

Dazed, Traci staggered away, moving quickly to get home. Usually, she would be down the police station in a heartbeat demanding to see Gem. Not this time. The police must know something, must have found some new evidence that pointed to Gem as the killer. Traci's doubts and suspicions overwhelmed her. Back home, Traci first checked on Roger in his chair in the front room. He was so grey now, quite a bit older than her.

Roger's wise gaze scanned her face. 'You look a bit peaky, love. Something on your mind?'

'I'm all good.' She gave him an overbright smile and kissed his forehead. 'I feel dead on my feet though.'

After she left him, Traci went into their bedroom and opened a drawer. She took out a pile of newspaper clippings she'd been keeping about the girls' disappearance. About Gem. She laid them flat on the bed and scanned each headline. And added the new newspaper story. She stared at Gem's face in the photographs and began to feel angry then. Could she really have murdered her own child?

If she had, Traci knew how she would answer the newspaper's poll about bringing back hanging.

Sara-Jane's dad had been right; Traci had asked around. Gem had got violent with him in front of the school. And she'd attacked the bus driver after he'd brought poor Abby back. From what he said in the paper she hit poor Sara-Jane as well. Gem was a convicted criminal. Robber! Robbers were the reason that Roger couldn't work any more. They had battered him one breath away from death. He had to use a stick to walk and even that was proving more difficult these days.

Gem had sworn blind that she had only shoplifted, but every new story in the papers made Traci question whether she was telling the truth. Could she trust a word Gem said? She felt so stupid, making friends with her. And now she had been arrested for murder. Gem had pulled the wool over her eyes. She was a good actress, she'd give her that. Traci felt the rage rising inside her.

She thought about her own children. All this time had they been living next door to a murderer? Traci's tummy twisted at the thought of it. Her adored children so close to danger. Gem had been making a fool of her all along. Laughing behind her back. Pretending butter wouldn't melt. It's always the ones you least expect. Isn't that what they say? And cosying up to Traci, using her position as a trusted member of the estate to conceal her wicked crime.

It was a reminder of her responsible role that made her calm down. What she needed to do was to give the young mum an opportunity to account for herself – again. So Traci stayed up until the early morning waiting for Gem to come home. But there was no sign of her, which clearly meant that the cops had kept her overnight. For hours Traci stewed in her chair in the front room. If Gem was innocent, why didn't the police just let her go? Because she's guilty, came the answer. The police don't arrest you unless they have cause to. They will have built up a case, brought together all the evidence, and arrested Gem.

The dreadful truth dawned on Traci. Sara-Jane could never come back because she was dead. Her mum had killed her. No wonder Abby couldn't remember anything. Her child's mind couldn't deal with the horror of what she'd seen. The murder of her best friend by her own mother.

The rage was back now, stronger than ever. Blinded by fury, not in her right mind, Traci stormed into the kitchen. In a cupboard she found what she needed. Outside it was dark. Quiet. Making sure no one was there to witness what she was about to do, Traci headed for Gem's front door. It took less than a minute. She stepped back to admire her handiwork. What she had painted. In huge writing. Blood red. On Gem's door.

CHILD KILLER

Chapter 50

There's a terrible silence after Traci finishes revealing her secret. What surprises me is that I don't feel angry. What I feel is sad. A stark sorrow that leaves me feeling hollow inside as if I'm missing something vital. This woman I trusted above everyone else. My friend, my protector. The one who spoke up for me when I was young. I finally realise what I'm feeling – betrayed.

'I knew I'd done wrong. Got it wrong,' Traci explains. 'Not long afterwards the police let you go. I shouldn't have got so worked up. Believed all those lies that people told about you. I was so ashamed.'

You should not have come back.' I recall what Traci told me that first night back in the old flat. 'Is that why you suggested I leave this all alone?'

She can't look at me. 'I never wanted you to find out it was me. When I convinced myself you'd done that to your daughter I just lost control.'

There is one saving grace here: at least this proves that Traci wasn't involved in Sara-Jane's abduction. I need to go now because I know that I'm close to finding out the truth.

Traci finally looks up at me with bleak, bloodshot eyes. 'Gem, tell me how to do it.'

'Do what?'

'As a mother, how do I cope with the death of my child?'

◆ ◆ ◆

Before I leave I bend down and clear away the newspaper clippings scattered on the floor. Just as I'm ordering them something in Charlie's interview, about his so-called *agony*, grabs my attention.

> 'It's usually someone in the victim's family who did it. That's definitely what happened. In my opinion anyway. Although I'm not suggesting these two mums were involved, that would be stupid. Why would they kidnap their own kids?'

Charlie is so sure it's not the two mothers – me and Laura. What he says is that it's someone in either Sara-Jane or Abby's family. Well, he knows I don't have any family. Which leaves someone in Abby's family.

'*Sara-Jay wasn't meant to be there.*' What did William mean by those words? There's a clue in there somewhere.

Sara-Jay wasn't meant to be there.

Sara-Jay wasn't meant to be there.

So if she wasn't meant to be there, who does that leave?

Abigail Prentice.

Whoever organised the kidnapping wanted Abby.

So it must have been someone who knew that Abby sneaked out of school the first Wednesday of every month and expected her to be there on her own. Was she kidnapped for money? No, because William said he didn't take money for kidnapping her.

Who would he work for free for? Who would he trust and believe? Someone in Abby's family.

That was around the time that his mum got him work with someone influential enough to give him opportunities to change his life.

I freeze. My mind rewinds. To a name. Someone who connects all the dots William left me.

Abby's grandfather.

Dale Prentice.

There's one person who can confirm my horrifying suspicion. The last person on this earth I want to speak to.

I jump on my bike and ride hard. Like I'm trying to outrun death.

◆ ◆ ◆

'You knew who kidnapped Sara-Jane and Abby all along. Didn't you?'

I confront Charlie. He's sitting at a table in a drinking club frequented by lowlifes like him. Although few of them are as low as him. I finally figured out where he was. He's a creature of habit who's barely changed his routines in the last fifteen years. Same places, same people, even the same women. He doesn't appear in the least surprised to see me butt into his drinking session with his cronies. Nor is he fazed to hear my accusation or the volume it's made in.

He looks at his friends and sighs. 'I'm sorry about this, boys. The mother of my missing child seems to be having some kind of nervous breakdown. Let me take her outside and call an ambulance. This won't take a minute.'

He stands tall, although the drink is already kicking in, grabs me by the arm and frogmarches me out on to the street. 'You've got the nerve of the devil trying to show me up in front of my mates.'

I was steely and calm when the cab picked me up, but now I'm close to clenching my fists. 'You knew full well Dale was behind the kidnapping of our daughter but you never said a word.'

He looks hurt. There's no denying that he's very good at denial. 'I don't know what you're talking about. Who told you this? Why on earth would you believe something like that?'

I pull the newspaper out of my bag and read him the damning lines. '*"It's usually someone in the victim's family who did it. That's definitely what happened. In my opinion anyway. Although I'm not suggesting these two mums were involved, that would be stupid. Why would they kidnap their own kids?"* I look up at him and push the newspaper in his face. 'That's what you told a reporter fifteen years ago. How did you know that's definitely what happened?'

He shrugs. 'It's just a turn of phrase. The journo probably made it up anyway. That's what they do, that's not on me, that's on them.'

'You might not tell the truth very often but when you do, you choose your words carefully. Someone in Abby's family leaves only two people.' I round on him. 'Dale Prentice. Or Henry, his son. Which was it?'

He pulls a face while a sarcastic smile plays on his lips. 'I might have heard something. Then again, I might not.'

I'm burning up with rage. 'Henry was too sick. It was Dale.' I cry out, 'You knew Dale took our daughter and you said nothing!'

'I'm not saying that at all. And anyway, what I heard was only hearsay. Talk to a lawyer, hearsay's not evidence, everyone knows that.'

The anger makes my voice go quiet and metallic as if it's someone else speaking. 'I could have got my daughter back if you'd said something.' The heartbreak of it is killing me.

'OK, this is it,' Charlie tells me. 'I did a bit of painting and decorating for Henry. One day I found him upset in his house. He was out of his head with worry about his kid, Abby, living with his ex-wife. Told me the woman was deranged. He was trying to get the kid out but he couldn't. Every legal route to him getting his daughter turned out to be a dead end. He thought his father hinted at doing something to get the girl. When his child and our kid were lifted, I put two and two together. You'd think the cops would have worked it out. Maybe Dale was too smart for them, I don't know. Anyway, that's it.'

I'm so upset. And in a fury. 'You should've told the police! They could've saved Sara-Jane!'

He leans into my face. 'I'm not a snitch.'

'No, you're worse than that. You kept your mouth shut to keep the money rolling in. If they'd found Sara-Jane that would've cut off the supply of cash from all those bogus media stories and appearances you did. Well, I hope all those pay cheques dripping in our daughter's blood were worth it.'

Of all the pure evil that I've found on this terrible journey to the truth, Charlie has to be there at the top. A father willing to sacrifice his child for money . . . Human corruption doesn't get worse than that.

He tries to rub even more stinging salt into my wounds. 'I think Sara-Jane getting lifted by Dale was the best bit of luck that girl ever had. There was no way Dale was going to do her any harm—'

'He murdered Sara-Jane.'

Charlie loses a little of his colour. 'You're joking.'

'William and Jas Bedi kidnapped the girls for Dale. But it was meant to be Abby alone. Abby escaped and he killed our daughter.'

'Well, she's gone now. Rest her soul.' He's back to his selfish ways. 'It's lucky for me I've got another little girl and boy with a couple of other ladies . . .'

I walk away. Never look back.

And go after Sara-Jane's killer.

Dale Prentice.

Chapter 51

I've come to confront Dale on my own. With my trusted bike for company. I should be a raving emotional mess, thinking of what he did. But instead, I'm ice-cold. Ready to find out the whole truth. And if this is true, God help Dale because I'm going to take him down with everything I've got.

I find him in his stables. I stand back and look at him for a time. Isn't he the picture of the kindly grandfather, everyone's friend, the man at the centre of the community?

He senses my presence and turns. 'Gem. Lovely to see you as ever.'

'William is dead.'

He stares at me, the colour leaching from his skin, leaving it waxy. 'That can't be true—'

I won't let him continue and step closer to him. 'He told me that he kidnapped the girls. That he was a gun for hire. He didn't say who it was, but I figured it out.' The emotion I don't want to show momentarily chokes me. 'The wicked monster was you. All along it was you, Dale.'

The blood beneath his skin deepens. 'Now, look, he—'

'Don't deny it. William said that Sara-Jane wasn't meant to be there—'

'She wasn't,' he slams out before he can catch himself.

I stagger back at his admission.

Finally! Out in the open.

I have to hold myself back from attacking him. If I do that I might not get the truth. And I need the truth now. Every last tormented, crucifying detail. I've got to. For Sara-Jane.

'You've been playing me like a fiddle all along. All those years ago turning up as my avenging angel while the cops had me banged up behind bars and getting me out and threatening to sue them. Giving me blood money to start my bike business.'

It's all so appallingly clear now. It's like I've got window wipers on my memory that are finally doing their job properly and clearing my vision.

'You don't understand, I had to get Abby away from her mother.'

'That has got nothing to do with me and my daughter.'

He gets into my space. 'You don't understand. Something bad was happening.'

'What happened to Sara-Jane?'

There's an arrogance to Dale I should have always seen. He tells me, in a matter-of-fact tone, 'In life, sometimes you have to do something wrong to make something right.'

He takes me back to the terrible past . . .

Chapter 52

FIFTEEN YEARS AGO

Snatched:
Day One

Finally. Dale heard the engine of the van coming down the driveway. He knocked back his second glass of whisky. Drinking during the day wasn't his usual style, but today was like no other day. It wasn't every day that he kidnapped a child. Although to his mind kidnapped was too strong a word. He was doing what needed to be done. Finally, he was going to get Abby away from the pernicious influence of her mother. His beautiful granddaughter had been behaving strangely since last year. He knew who was to blame – that crazy mother of hers. And then when he found Abby in a trance-like state choking the crap out of her dolls with a black ribbon, that had sealed his decision about what he was going to do. He had to steal his granddaughter away. Dale was a man used to getting his way.

Walking with the purposeful stride of someone who believed right was on their side, Dale eagerly headed towards the van. To the men who he had paid to snatch his granddaughter. Billy-Bob Waddell and Jas Bedi.

'William?' Dale called out.

Dale had told the lad that if he wanted to mend his ways, best leave Billy-Bob behind and rise up to use his given name, William. Traci had asked Dale to find her son work and of course, considering their connection, he'd done it. She'd go mad, rip his head off if she knew what he'd involved her boy in. Dale knew he should feel more guilt. But he didn't. In business the thing that matters is securing what you've got your eye on, even if that involves manipulation. And he'd needed to secure Abby.

Almost instantly, Dale noted how nervous William looked. The young man told him, 'Everything went well. Except . . . There was a problem.'

'Problem?' And he didn't believe in problems. There was always a solution somewhere.

'Her friend was with her. Sara-Jay . . . I mean Sara-Jane.'

Dale let loose with a string of curses that would make the devil blush. 'You should've left her behind.'

Jas joined in for the first time. 'We couldn't. She wouldn't stop fighting. Dale, we didn't have a choice.'

Dale eyed him with extreme displeasure. He hadn't wanted another person involved, particularly someone he didn't know. But William had insisted that he couldn't do the kidnapping alone. The way he heard it, Jas was too fond of booze. A man too fond of his drink was also one too fond of his mouth. And that's what worried Dale, that Jas would talk. But William had vouched for him, so he'd left it alone.

Dale stomped over to the back of the black van. 'Get it opened.'

When they did there was no one inside. He rounded on William. 'You said there were two of them, not that there were none.' He grabbed William by the front of his T-shirt and slammed him into the van. 'If you've double-crossed me and—'

'I swear, I haven't.' William didn't move. 'They were both in there.'

'They were, Mr Prentice.' Jas backed him up.

Abruptly, William pressed his finger against his lips, calling for quiet, his eagle-eyed stare resting inside the van. He jumped inside and approached a large piece of tarpaulin at the back. With speed, he bent and yanked it back. A small girl sprang at him, fighting and kicking and trying to bite him. He managed to subdue her with his arms around her middle.

If there is a God, this has to be Abby, Dale prayed. William turned, displaying who he held.

Sara-Jane.

Defiantly, she spat at him, 'You're in so much trouble when my mum and the police find you. You're dead!'

In a fury Dale tore into William. 'Where's my bloody granddaughter?'

Snatched:
Day Two

The plate of food came hurling towards Dale a split second before he managed to rush out of the room and slam shut the door. And lock it.

'I want to go HOME!' Sara-Jane bellowed with all her might at him on the other side of the door.

Dale was keeping her in the room he'd prepared for Abby. The guest room was pretty, pink and plush, filled with lots of girly toys. Sara-Jane had thrown the toys at him and refused to eat. Not once had she cried for her mum. Dale liked her spirit. She was a tough nut, reminding him of his own feisty attitude when he was young. He recognised there was going to be a battle of wills. And there could only be one winner.

Him.

He'd come in the night to clean and dress her wounded ankle.

Thank God Abby had turned up at the school hall today after she'd managed to escape yesterday. Seeing her stagger in, bloody and dirty and half on her knees, had nearly crucified him. And he wanted to scream because the kidnapping was all a waste of time. Abby was back with her mother. Where she wasn't safe. And now he was lumbered with a child he wasn't meant to have.

Bollocks! What a right royal fucking mess!

Dale needed to make a decision in the coming days, weeks; there was no avoiding it. He was acquainted with Gem, Sara-Jane's mum. Actually knew her quite well, and not only did he like her, he'd spread the word that anyone needing their bike fixing should pay her a visit on the Rosebridge.

Witnessing Gem's grief over her missing child was gut-wrenching for him to see. But Dale had learned a thing or two on his road to success, one being to beware the things that bring you to the brink of tears. Too often they are the same things that can bring you down. Stamp on them. Crush them beneath your heel. That's how Dale rationalised dealing with Sara-Jane's mum.

That night was a long one. Dale deliberately kept the TV off; it was filled with coverage of the missing schoolgirl, Sara-Jane Casey. He had to figure a way out of this. He drank and paced until the early hours of the morning.

Snatched:
Day Three

Sara-Jane was gone. Shit! Not believing his eyes, Dale swore. He'd unlocked the guest room to find it empty. The window wide open. Rushing across, he checked. The girl was nowhere in sight. Crap! Crap! Dale was about to round up William, who was on the grounds working, to help search, when Dale stopped to think. Really think. Sara-Jane was a smart girl. Where would a smart child go in this instance?

Flee outside and keep running and hope someone would see them? The problem with that was you might never see anyone because this might be the middle of nowhere.

Or – find a way to communicate with her mum or the authorities.

Dale gambled on the latter, especially as Sara-Jane couldn't have got far on her wounded ankle. He checked the house and found her on the old-fashioned landline phone in the annexe next to the large kitchen.

'Hello! Hello!' Sara-Jane spoke desperately down the line.

'That won't help,' Dale informed her, quietly walking into the room.

Jumping in fright, the receiver slipped from her hand and dangled towards the floor. She twisted to face him, her small face both mutinous and terrified.

He continued, 'That telephone doesn't work. All the phone lines have been changed.' He also told her, 'The two men who took you and Abby are truant officers. Do you know what a truant officer is? It's their job to catch naughty children who sneak out of school. When they saw you both on the street, they were only trying to put you in the van and take you back to the school.'

She stared stony-faced at him, flattening her lips even tighter together. 'Why did they bring me here then and not take me back to school?'

'They saw Abby had escaped and they hoped I'd help find her.'

Sara-Jane snarled, 'Don't make things up, I'm not stupid. And why was Billy-Bob here? Why did they hurt me?'

Dale sighed. Just as he'd thought. He couldn't let the child go free. She would tell on him. A child like Sara-Jane wouldn't lie to her mum.

Snatched:
Days Four & Five

She threw her dinner at him. Tried the window again but it didn't budge this time; William had made sure of that, both inside and out.

Snatched:
Day Six

Dale was in a foul mood. That bitch Laura had found out that he was behind the kidnapping and barred him from seeing Abby. If he came one step near her house she'd have the police on to him before he could turn around. He suspected – he couldn't be totally sure – that bloody Jas had opened his trap to her and given the game away. Dale had turned up at Laura's house yesterday only to be barred at the door by her. And the truth of what he'd done spat in his face. There was no point him denying it because the truth was indeed written all over him. He'd begged and pleaded with her. Laura had actually laughed at him before slamming the door.

Now, he had no choice. He had to make a decision about Sara-Jane. A final one.

Snatched:
Day Seven

Dale had spent yesterday evening and this morning getting his preparations in place.

'Her mum is losing her mind. You have to take Sara-Jay back to her.' Alarmed and panicked, William did his best to reason with his boss. 'Please don't do this, Dale. I'm begging you.'

'Look, if Sara-Jane tells her mum I took her they'll put me in prison. You in prison. That idiot-fool, Jas. And throw away the bloody key.' Dale looked at William intently, so that he could watch the truth of what he was saying sink in. 'You know and I know that we can't take her back to her mum.'

The colour drained from William's skin, leaving him ashen and shaking. Dale patted him on the back. 'You go on home, lad. To your mother. Leave this to me.'

When a dejected William shuffled away, Dale called out to him, 'Remember what we talked about. You have to wipe this from your mind. It never happened. The biggest pretence is to keep telling yourself it never happened. That way you'll never be living a lie.'

Dale waited until the night was quiet. Took something from the kitchen and, gripping it tight in his hand, unlocked the guest room door. Then went inside.

Chapter 53

'Murderer!' I shriek at him. 'You killed my baby!'

I lunge at Dale and start beating him with my fists, slaps, anything I have in me to wreak revenge on him. How could he do this to my diamond girl? My Sara-Jane. She was my life. All I held dear in this unfair and unforgiving world. This man ripped my whole world apart. He tries to capture my arms and control me. Control me. I go mad, raking my nails into his face with such razor-sharp accuracy that he screeches in pain. I won't stop.

'Murderer! Murderer! Murderer!'

Hot, angry tears scald my skin and I keep hitting and hitting. That's what Sara-Jane did, she fought for her life. I kick and punch and scratch . . . His palm flashes through the air and pushes against my chest. Almost losing my footing I stumble into the wall. I try to move but my daughter's killer is too quick for me. He crowds into me, laying his palm firmly against my chest to keep me still. With all my might I fight to get away. Keep fighting. And fighting. Until I have nothing left.

I rasp out, 'You better get off me. Let me go.'

We're both panting horrifically, the noise slashing through the air.

Dale's mouth twists with frustration. 'Do you think I wanted any of this to happen? That this is what I planned?'

'You murdered the best part of me. My beautiful girl didn't do a thing to you. She really liked you. How could you do this to an innocent child?'

He springs back, walking away and turning his back. I bend forward like I've been kicked in the stomach. It gives me time to think. I could attack him again; however, what would I gain by doing that? I owe it to my dead daughter to find out why this happened. Straightening up I raise my face to his back and ask the cruellest question.

'Why did you kill her?'

The muscles in his back bunch, tensing together. Finally, he faces me again. Red lines of blood run along his cheek where my nails damaged his skin. Good. I wish I could rip his heart out.

After a heavy sigh, he tells me, 'I had to get Abby away from her mother. Something was not right in that house.'

My mind reels back. To all those years ago at the school where I heard Laura reminding her daughter that she was a mini-Laura. How strange it all was.

He continues, 'One night when Abby was staying with me, I woke up to find her strangling one of her dolls. She had a ribbon wrapped around its neck and was pulling.' He shivers. 'God, you should've seen her eyes. They were vacant. Emotionless. So cold. Another time she forgot one of her dolls here. I found it hanging from a noose in the bathroom.'

I see Abby above me. The tension of the towel cutting into my neck. The agonising pressure of air trapped in my body.

Dale's voice drags me back to the present. 'Where does an eight-year-old child learn to do that? I don't know what she'd seen. When it was clear that Henry, her father, wasn't up to the task, it was down to me to rescue Abby from her mother. The only way I could do that was to kidnap her. I was going to take Laura to court to get custody. But she was threatening to not let me see Abby.' His gaze fires up. 'You can see that I had no choice. What else could I do?'

Dale looks at me with an expression that pleads with me to understand and legitimise his actions. 'Laura kept Abby as close to her as a glove on a hand so there didn't seem to be an opportunity for me to spirit Abby away—'

'Spirit Abby away?' I scoff, openly mocking his choice of words. 'Don't use genteel phrases to excuse what you did. You. Abducted. Your. Grandchild.'

It's as if I haven't spoken because he ploughs on, 'I had to think of a time when her mother wasn't near her. That's when I figured out that the only time was when Abby was at school.' Dale's finger-tips roughly swipe against the blood on his face. 'But I couldn't just go in there and take her away. Then her father told me something. That Abby had confessed to him that she sneaked out of school the first Wednesday of every month during lunch time. At first I thought it was Henry's addled mind making stuff up. But what if he wasn't? What if it was true? So I watched the school, positioned myself near the market the first Wednesday of the next month. And saw Abby emerge from Glass Alley. I observed again the following month. The same thing happened.'

Frowning hard, I shoot back, 'But if you only saw Abby sneak out of school how did Sara-Jane become involved?' Trying to connect the dots, my temples start pounding.

'I made a mistake. Instead of liberating my granddaughter straight away I left it a few months. I should know from my business dealings that all it takes is a few weeks, much less months for things to change. What I hadn't reckoned with was Abby inviting her best friend to sneak out with her now as well. The day the job was to be done, Sara-Jane was there too.'

'So you got William and Jas to do your dirty work. Your own son!' I spit out at him. 'Traci told me. She asked you to guide him.

317

Keep him safe. The son you made together. How could you do that to your own child?'

Dale snaps back, 'Don't you think I know that?' Arrogance turns his features again. 'I left school when I was fifteen years old. Got my first job at that age too. Do you know what my first job was? Helping the caretaker sweep up after the well-fed and rich kids at Princess Isabel School.' His mouth becomes sour. 'Seeing them and their finery put a fire under me. A fire to be wealthy. Never to have to clean up the throwaway shit of other people. Now that school relies on me and the generosity of my money.'

'Well, you give Traci that pretty little pity-me speech the next time you see her. You explain to her why they had to scrape her son off the ground.'

He almost whispers, 'William kept insisting that I should take Sara-Jane back to you. It all got messed up when Abby escaped. It wasn't meant to play out that way.'

I have to restrain myself from going for him again. But I haven't finished with Dale yet. Not by a long shot. 'You're the one who's been terrorising me. Putting things that belong to Sara-Jane through my door.'

'What?' He wears an expression of complete confusion. 'What are you talking about? Sara-Jane's things?'

I rear closer to him. 'You heard me remind Detective Wallace how he refused to help me when I told him about someone putting Sara-Jane's socks through my door. So don't sit there lying to me. Her glasses. The picture of the angel. You put them through the letterbox of the flat. Who else could it be?'

'You've got this all wrong. I would never do that to you.'

He sounds so sincere. *Sincere? This is the vile beast who killed my daughter.* Although a part of my mind acknowledges that he doesn't match the description of the person I chased on my bike.

With fury, I rush on, 'Next you'll be claiming you didn't kill Miss Swan because she probably found out that you were behind the abduction of the girls?'

Dale stares incredulously at me. 'Murder Clare? Are you crazy? Of course I never killed her. Or Teddy Spencer, since we seem to be heading down that path. Or set fire to your flat. What do you take me for?'

'A man who goes around kidnapping and killing defenceless little girls.'

He looks me dead in the eye, his gaze cold and clear. 'I never admitted to murdering anyone.'

That leaves me reeling. Finding it difficult to catch my breath. 'You told me that when you went to the room that you'd locked Sara-Jane in you—'

His phone, lying on the kitchen table, rings, a violent rattling sound against the wooden table.

Finally, I do what I should have done earlier. Instead of coming here to confront this murdering bastard I should've gone straight to Detective Wallace. With determination I march to the door.

'You're breaking up . . .' That's Dale behind me, speaking into his phone. I keep going, ignoring his frantic tone. 'What? Abby?'

The mention of her name stops me in my tracks. Makes me turn back to her grandfather. His body is rigid, on high alert. 'Don't go there.' His breathing becomes shallow in distress. 'Abby? Abby?'

He clutches the phone in his hand, the connection obviously lost and stares at me, eyes wild. 'Abby. She's about to do something stupid.'

This family drama killed my daughter. I don't want to have anything else to do with these people. I pull my phone out. 'I'm calling the cops—'

Dale savagely interrupts. 'I'll tell you the truth. Every last thing you want to know. But first, please, help me with Abby. She's in danger.'

Abby. It hits me how much I've grown to love her. I can't leave her in a bad situation without trying to help.

'What makes you think she's in danger?'

'She's going to meet someone.'

'Who?'

'The line wasn't clear. I couldn't make out all that she was saying.'

'Where is she going to meet them?'

His features almost crumble. 'In the place where only bad things happen. The school chapel.'

The chapel seems to rear up in the playground. To my eyes, it appears much larger than it has ever been. Its rose-red glass-pottery front glints off the weak sunlight, creating a foreboding atmosphere. Outside there is no evidence that anyone else is here. No police cars either, despite Miss Swan's murder. In fact, the crime scene tape is no longer here. There's not a soul in sight.

'Are you sure about this?' I ask Dale in a rush.

He doesn't answer me, too anxious to get inside the chapel.

Rosa drove us here in Dale's SUV. Poor girl put on a good show of being composed, but her clenched hand around the steering wheel told its own anxious story. Dale wanted her to stay back at the house, but she insisted on helping in some way. She's in the car waiting for us.

'Abby?' Dale calls out his granddaughter's name as we near the chapel.

No answer. The chapel door is closed. I notice for the first time that it has long twin handles, both in the shape of an iron angel. It looks locked. But I'm wrong. When Dale reaches for the centuries-old door handles, they turn. The door creaks with heaviness and age as he pushes it back. The view of the chapel over his shoulder shows no sign of anyone.

'Abby?' He calls her name again as he steps inside.

I follow him in. I've never been in here before and my first impression is that I don't like it. The frigid cold sinks through my clothes into my flesh. And, of course, I make the mistake of looking up at the faceless angel. It looks so much bigger in here than it does outside. Shivering, I tear my gaze away.

Suddenly we hear a muffled sound coming from the direction of the office where the PTA hold their meetings. The office is at the back on the right-hand side. I reach it before Dale. The door is slightly open. The muffled sound I now realise is quiet sobbing. Cautiously, I push the door back with my fingertips.

It's the body I see first. On the floor. Bloody. The head at a strange angle. Dead. It's Jas, William's accomplice in the kidnapping. I press my palm to my mouth, sickened by this.

'I found him.'

The voice makes me start. I stumble back into the doorway. Abby emerges from behind the door. She's still sobbing, her face distraught.

'Darling!' Dale is in despair at the sight of his granddaughter. They embrace. But not for long. He pushes back from her. 'What happened here?'

Abby's gaze darts to me and then back to her grandfather. 'Jas's body was already here. He still feels warm.'

Which means he hasn't been dead for long.

I ask, 'Who murdered him?'

Abby answers. 'I don't know. Mummy was meant to be here.'

Her grandfather jumps in. 'Your mother? Was that who you planned to meet?'

Why would Abby ask her mum to come here? A violent shiver crawls across my skin. I want to get out of here. Urgently, I tell Abby, 'We need to leave. Now.'

But she shakes her head. 'I've got to wait for Mummy. It's got to be here. In the chapel.'

'Why?' her grandfather cries out.

With a decisive step back she answers, 'This is where it happened. Where it all started. Sixteen years ago. I wish I could blank it out. But I can't. I remember every terrible moment.'

Chapter 54

Sixteen Years Ago

The sound of frenzied sex echoed inside the chapel. The rough sounds of flesh slapping against flesh. Grunts and groans. Harsh breathing. His breathing fanned, moist and sour, against the side of Clare Swan's neck and face. She was on her knees at the altar. Teddy got his rocks off screwing her at the altar. He got his rocks off from humiliating her with the angels in the stained-glass window watching him. Perverted bastard. Currently, he was hunched over her, his hairy, sweaty body pounding into her from behind. His fingers clawed into her hips like talons. The feel of his repulsive flesh against her was hot and sticky. Clare felt filthy. She barely swallowed back the rising bile. But she didn't say a word, never complained. Instead, the head teacher of the most successful primary school in the area screwed her eyes tight and endured. Only one thing mattered.

The reputation of the school.

Clare cringed as Teddy's animalistic grunts twisted into rapid pants and strained wheezing noises. She knew what that meant, he was near completion. God, how she loathed Teddy. He was the most disgusting human being she knew. No, human was too good a word for him. He was a rutting animal. A beast.

Clare thought back to what an utter fool she had been to be taken in by Teddy Spencer. When they were at school together as children, she'd found him sly, always mooning after her behind Beryl's back. Those creepy longing looks she'd chosen to ignore. The way his hand would sometimes *accidentally* brush her skin. How she'd had to gently turn him down when he'd asked her out.

Beryl thought the world of her husband; she doted on him and couldn't stop talking about him, always keeping a photo of him on her desk.

Then, out of the blue, Teddy had contacted Clare one day. He needed to talk to her about the school's upcoming test results. Of course, when he'd shared with her how much they had dipped significantly from the previous year, her heart had dipped too. He'd been so sympathetic, so concerned and told her not to worry. He could sort it all out for her . . . Initially Clare was stunned because she knew exactly what he was implying. Change the SATs marks. In other words, cheat.

Cheat.

It twisted Clare's gut and moral compass. It went against everything that Clare Swan stood for. She couldn't possibly do this. How could she look her pupils in the eye? She taught every last one of them that the bedrock of life was kindness and care and honesty and integrity. Those were the foundations on which she'd built the outstanding reputation of the school. *And outstanding results*, her inner voice reminded her. The reputation of the school would be severely damaged if the current results were released. For most schools the results would be fine because they were good. But *good* wasn't good enough for her school.

If the school lost its outstanding status that would mean more education inspectors knocking at its door. With more frequency.

The school would be put under a blazing spotlight that would bring stress to her and her teachers and the children. They'd be subject to this target, that target. Targets! Targets! More damn targets!

Princess Isabel's results had to remain OUTSTANDING. There was no other way.

And Clare was fiercely loyal to Princess Isabel. As a former pupil it was such an honour to become its head teacher. The school was her life. She had never married, didn't have much of a social life, devoting her time and energy to the school and other people's children. Clare was determined to never see the school fail.

Clare had relaxed back in her seat, giving Teddy his answer. Then, as easy as you please, his hand had cupped her breast. Shocked, Clare had pushed him away. What the hell was he doing? That's when Teddy had explained there was a price for his help. A price to saving the school's standing and status. That was the deal from now on. Was she willing to make him a very happy man to uphold the reputation of the school?

Something else became very clear to Clare. Teddy had secretly carried the obsession he'd developed for her when they were at school with him all these years. Wanted her ever since they were in the same class at Princess Isabel.

This was unfinished business on Teddy's part. He'd now got his hands on what she'd denied him for years. Her.

Despite knowing that, she agreed to his deal. Only the school mattered. And she crossed another line into being exploited. What had shocked Clare to the core was Beryl's involvement in this. How had she misjudged the woman who had been her right hand running the school? What made Clare gag was that Beryl egged her husband on in his twisted games. Their twisted games. It was Beryl's idea to start filming these degrading scenes. It was clear she got a thrill from watching and filming while Teddy forced his sexual corruptions on her in the chapel, of all places. Tying her up was their favourite, with a huge gag bulging in her mouth. Some might lap up that type of stuff, but not her.

It wasn't the acts that were perverted, it was Teddy and Beryl.

After finishing, Teddy slapped her bottom and laughed heartily. He wriggled his spent body against her and leaned deeper into the side of her face. 'You love it really, don't you, you little tart.'

Degrading her. Calling her vile names. That's how Teddy liked his sex played. Usually Clare would meekly play along, knowing it was her assigned role in his sick sex games. However, for some reason today she was pissed off. Had had enough. Maybe it was the fact that Beryl wasn't present today, that there was no filming taking place. Or was it the foul feel of his flesh against hers? The stale odour pouring off him? Or maybe she had frankly had enough.

Had enough of letting Teddy and Beryl, who she'd been to school with, do this to her. With a mighty shove she moved him off her and he tumbled naked on the age-old floor.

She scrambled up and through gritted teeth told him, 'I refuse to do this for one more day.' Her lips curled. 'You. Disgust. Me. You know what I figured out, Teddy? If you tell the authorities about the test results, you'll be implicating yourself.' Clare was enjoying finally having the upper hand. 'My career will probably be over, but the tales of you raping me . . . You know what's going to happen. They. Will. Put. You. In. Prison.'

'You little bitch.' Teddy was on his feet so quickly that Clare didn't have time to defend herself. He grabbed her hair and smashed her against the floor. She cried out in pain. Her vision blurred, the room was spinning.

'Threaten me?' He stared down at her with pure venom. 'You always thought you were a cut above me at school. Too good to go out with me. I'm going to teach you a lesson you will never forget.'

Fear ran through Clare. He was going to do something awful to her. She tried to get up, but the chapel swayed sideways and she fell back to the cold floor. She felt his heat over her. He was back. Looking up, she cried out when she saw his belt in his hand. It snaked in the air. Her arm came up. Too late. It cracked with the burn of electricity across her skin. Clare jerked and screamed out in pain. He raised the belt up high again.

'What the hell is going on here?'

The outraged voice startled them. They turned to see Laura emerge in the doorway of the chapel. She wasn't alone. Her daughter Abigail was with her.

Breathing heavily, Teddy sprang back. He answered, obviously forgetting he was stark naked. 'We're having an affair. Don't tell Beryl.'

Laura smacked her lips together, considering him. 'An affair of the heart, you say?' Her gaze ran insolently over his nakedness. Her expression left nothing to the imagination: clearly she found him grotesque. 'Then why are you beating the living daylights out of Clare with a belt?'

It was the other woman who answered, as she gingerly straightened. 'He's been blackmailing me. Laura, I'm sorry but the test results for the last couple of years have been good, but not outstanding. They must be outstanding—'

The director of the school's PTA finished for her. 'And good ole Teddy here said he'd make sure everything was all good again in exchange for your body being available, twenty-four-seven.'

Teddy sneered at Laura. 'You think because you're Dale Prentice's daughter-in-law – oh, I forgot, *ex-daughter-in-law* – you can get the school out of this one? Well, you can't. You can't do a thing.'

'That's where you're wrong.' With purpose Laura smartly marched over to him and smashed his skull with something he hadn't noticed she'd picked up. A decorative candlestick.

He collapsed on the floor, moaning. Abby whimpered while Clare shoved her palm in disbelief over her mouth. Bending over him, Laura smashed the candlestick into his head again.

'No!' Clare cried out. 'What are you doing?'

Laura looked over at her. 'Clare, you would have never got rid of him. Leeches like Teddy Spencer never let go. For Chrissakes, he was blackmailing the school. We can't have that.' To underscore her point she hit him again.

And stood up. Inhaled deeply. In complete control, she stared over at the other woman. 'You know what we have to do?'

Clare frowned, not understanding what she meant, and when it finally sank in she backed away. 'I can't. Just can't.'

'We don't have a choice.' Laura glanced over at the incomplete work on the chapel floor for the installation of electrical wires for the computer suite. 'The soil's soft in here, so it shouldn't take too long to bury him deep enough. Then we let the workmen complete the job for us.' She turned back to Teddy's unconscious form. 'But first . . .'

Without another word, Laura swung her legs over him and dug her knees into his arms to keep him still. Then she unwound her trademark scarf, this one her favourite with the black cats stamped all over it. She wrapped and wrapped it tight around Teddy's neck and pulled with everything she had.

When his legs started to twitch, she told Clare, 'Fucking well help me, you stupid woman.'

Clare cowered away. And shuddered, shaking her head.

With cold, dead eyes, Laura turned towards her daughter. Abby was frozen, her face colourless, her eyes shining with horror. 'Abby! You must help Mummy. This is a very bad man. You saw him hitting Miss Swan. Good people don't hit each other. Come here.'

'Yes, Mummy.' That was Abby's usual robotic response to any request from her mother.

But today her lips froze, refusing to move. Abby's terrified gaze was hypnotised by what her mum was doing to Teddy's neck.

Clare finally intervened, crying out, 'She's a child. Your own daughter. You can't involve a child in the act of murder.'

Laura bit out, 'Then you come and do it.' Clare moved back, leaving Laura to sneer, 'Yes! I didn't think so.' Her murderous gaze twisted slowly back to her child. 'You don't want him hurting Miss Swan again, do you, Abby?'

Abby loved Miss Swan. She was so kind. When her dad had left, Miss Swan was one of the only people who had found time to make sure she was OK. Horrible men shouldn't be allowed to hurt her.

'Yes, Mummy,' Abby answered.

Trembling, Abby silently walked over. Her mother instructed, 'On your knees on the other side of his head. That's right, darling. Pick up the other end of the scarf. Yes, that's the way. Now, like a game, you pull your end while I'll pull mine. At the same time. Remember, pull with all your might. You can do it!'

Tears leaking from her eyes, seven-year-old Abby pulled on the scarf. And pulled. Pulled. As Teddy's face went purple.

'Good girl,' her mother praised, 'But harder. Harder!'

Then Teddy stopped struggling and Laura loosened her hold from the end of the scarf and used her bare hands. Choked him until she was sure he was dead.

Seven-year-old Abby stared down at her hands, her eyes as dead as she felt inside.

Chapter 55

We come out of the past back to the present. Recounting the horror she remembered happening in this chapel that day has clearly taken a heavy toll on Abby. She looks so fragile and about ready to drop.

But she hasn't finished. She looks down at her hands. 'I understand now. Understand why my hands never feel clean. I helped kill Teddy Spencer.'

I grab her shoulders firmly. 'You were a child. Made to do something by your mother. She's the murderer here, not you.'

The chapel door in the main part of the building bangs shut. Rushing out of the room where we found Jas's body and into the chapel, we all come to a dramatic halt when we see Laura. Wearing her scarf. She's standing in front of the main chapel door. There's a shovel in her hand.

Her cold eyes assess us. 'I should've realised that when Abby asked me to come here, she wouldn't come alone.'

I do some quick assessments of my own. 'You murdered Jas. He knew too much. Lying for you about seeing Charlie and Henry arguing in the pub and making it sound as if they were rowing about the botched kidnapping of the girls. You murdered him here. Then left to get a shovel to bury his body.'

She graces me with a small mean smile. 'Ten out of ten for being a bright spark, which isn't what you'd expect from the cretins who inhabit that slum Rosebridge estate.'

It will take more than murder to fluster Laura Prentice. She appears her usual elegant self. In total control.

Dale snarls, 'It's true, isn't it? You murdered Teddy. And now Jas.'

Laura jeers right back at him. 'Moral outrage from the man who goes around kidnapping little girls. He murdered your Sara-Jane.' That's delivered quickfire at me. 'Jas told me everything. He couldn't hold his drink or his tongue. It's a true story that I found him passed out in my shed. When he woke up, he was still slightly drunk and that tongue of his couldn't stop talking. Singing like a canary about how William had asked him to help snatch Abby off the street. And who had asked them to do it? Dale. Her own grandfather.'

A distressed noise leaves Abby. Only then does it dawn on me that she'll be hearing the truth for the first time. She asks Dale, 'Is this true?' She pushes closer to me. 'No! No! Granddad, tell me you didn't. Didn't murder Sara-Jane.'

He looks her dead in the eye. 'My priority was getting you away from this mad woman. Nothing else mattered.'

'Spoken like the ruthless businessman you are,' Laura contemptuously chucks at him. There's not much I agree with Laura on but this she has right. 'But what Jas told me allowed me to outsmart you. I told you what I'd found out and made you agree not to come near Abby. If you did, I'd go to the police and tell them all about who abducted Abby and her friend. I'm surprised you didn't try to kill me as well.'

He growls back, 'Don't think it didn't cross my mind.'

Laura cocks her head to consider him like he's a cockroach trapped under a glass. 'My parents loved their money more than they loved their children, so they would send us off to stay with our grandparents.' Her voice is emotionless. 'They had a huge house, an estate really, and a garden that went on as far as the eye could see. I loved the squirrels, but Granddad said they were a pest.'

She and the shovel take a slow step towards us. 'One day he caught one, filled a bucket with water, took it by the neck, shoved its whole body into the water. It choked and drowned. Its little body wriggled and squirmed. Then it was dead.'

Another step closer. I move nearer to Abby to protect her. 'Some people need to be put out of their misery. Teddy was a pest. Eventually he would've brought down the school.'

I call out, 'Did you murder Miss Swan?'

Laura dramatically rolls her eyes. Steps closer. 'The stupid woman was going to go to the police. She started bellyaching about feeling guilty. After all these years she couldn't live with herself.'

'It was *you*,' I accuse. 'You were the person with her when I called and she asked me to meet her at the school. You were there, watching me when I arrived. And tried to frame me to the cops.'

Laura doesn't answer. She doesn't need to because the truth rings silently clear in the chapel.

'You cut out her tongue. How could you do that?'

Her steely, evil gaze settles on me. 'A tongue is for talking and we know who she was planning to talk to.'

My mind rolls back to the time I went to Laura's house. 'Is that what you were arguing about at your house? Miss Swan was threatening to go to the cops?'

She scoffs, another step closer. 'She became a liability just like Teddy and Jas. And, as for you' – her eyes run over me with extreme disgust – 'you just couldn't take a hint. And fuck off. Keep that big nose of yours out of it. I burned down your flat and you're still here.'

I should have guessed. 'You tried to kill not just me but your own daughter in the fire.'

Laura's not far away from us now. 'Abby is my flesh and blood, but she's such a big disappointment. I had such high hopes for her. But look at her.' Poor Abby cringes, trying to disappear inside herself. 'She's weak, just like that idiot father of hers. Probably end up in a nut house like him too. Always blubbing and crying. And I knew' – her eyes widen with the first indication of how manic she really is – 'that she would never be able to keep our secret of what we did here. That traumatised brain of hers would eventually remember and confess.'

It hits me then. 'You didn't want Abby to remember. It was never about keeping her from remembering the kidnapping. What you couldn't afford for her to remember was you murdering Teddy here. You used her trauma about being abducted and loss of memory to your advantage. That's why you never wanted Abby to find a cure. As long as she never recalled what happened here, she was safe from you.'

Her hatred for her child crackles like lightning.

Dale growls, 'You're pure evil.'

'More evil than a child snatcher? Child killer?' She's back looking at him. 'You've got a fucking nerve. You tried to steal my daughter away from me—'

'You were sending her mad. I had no choice. You are a rotten mother.'

Suddenly, Laura lunges forward. Raises the shovel high in the air. And brings it down sideways, slicing straight and deep across Dale's chest. Blood splatters over me. Over Abby. Crying out in stunned, horrified pain, he collapses to the ground. Laura swiftly turns to her daughter.

'Run!' I scream at Abby.

I move to block her mother so that Abby can escape. Laura jumps me and takes me down. We tussle and roll on the floor. Then, there's a stinging pain in the side of my temple and I realise that she's used her fist to bash me in the head. My vision comes in and out. The chapel starts swaying. Above, Sara-Jane's faceless angel watches me. Then I'm free. Her weight no longer on me.

For a while I sputter and cringe at the pain in my skull. Blinking, I try to get my vision back to normal. When it does come back, I sit up. Look around. And gasp at the unimaginable scene playing out in front of me.

Abby has her mother on the floor. She's wrapped her mother's scarf around her neck. Both ends are in her hands and she's pulling with everything she has. Laura is making grotesque retching and gagging noises.

'Abby. No!' I stagger over to her. 'You've got to stop.'

She doesn't. Abby looks up at me. Oh God, she doesn't even look like she's there. Her eyes are dead. In a trance. She keeps tightening and tightening.

'No!' I won't allow her to become a murderer too. 'Stop it, Abby. Stop! Stop!'

Finally, my words penetrate the killing fog. She stops and topples over her mother. I crawl over and close my hands reassuringly over hers.

'Everyone stay where you are. Hands in the air!'

That's Detective Wallace's voice. Rosa must have contacted the police. She's kneeling beside Dale's still body. He looks dead because his chest isn't moving. In Italian, Rosa whispers a prayer over him. I damn him to hell. Although he told me he hadn't admitted to killing anyone, I don't believe him. He was the only person who could have told me where my Sara-Jane's remains are. Now he's gone.

Chapter 56

It's been a week since the chilling events at the chapel. I'm on my bike, rucksack on my back, ready to make the journey home to London. Before I do, I'm heading over to see Abby and Rosa to bid them goodbye. Rosa is going back to Italy today. It will mean me having to go to Dale Prentice's house, which I don't much look forward to doing. I told Detective Wallace the whole story. Left nothing out.

The bitterness of not knowing where Dale put Sara-Jane's remains is something I'll have to live with for the rest of my days. He should have been made to face justice, the full force of the law. That's what Laura will be facing. At least I know the truth about why my child was stolen from me. That she was never meant to be there. Dale had only ever wanted Abby, his granddaughter, and Sara-Jane ended up as collateral damage.

I round the bend and power-ride the driveway to the front of the house. Abby's in the main room. She looks like she's been to hell and back. It's going to take her a long while to forge a future pathway after what her mother and grandfather did.

She hugs me tight. There's a bond between us that I don't want to lose. I'm here for her. Anytime. We plan to see each other often.

'I'm going to sell this place,' she informs me. She looks so much older than her twenty-three years. In a good way. 'Probably use some of the money to travel for a while. Use it to have therapy to really sort my shit out. I talked with a support organisation on the phone and they think I've got a type of PTSD. So, I'm going to use some of the money for therapy. But Mum . . .'

I take her firmly by the shoulders. 'Your mum murdered people. Took away their lives. She forced you to do what you did that day in the chapel. Now she will have to face justice.'

Wallace had arrested Laura and she was now in prison awaiting trial.

Smiling, I ask, 'I want to say goodbye to Rosa. And thank her for all her help and for being so sweet. Where is she?'

'I think she's upstairs in her room. Shall I get her for you?'

'No. I'll go up.'

Which I do after Abby gives me directions. I call out Rosa's name. No response. The door to her room is partially open. I knock, which makes the door swing further back. I don't see her. Her packed suitcase is beside the bed.

'Rosa?' I hesitate before walking inside. I'm conscious that this is her private space and I haven't obtained permission to enter. There's another suitcase, smaller, that's open on the bed. I plan to leave, but something in the case catches my eye. I move closer and see that Rosa obviously enjoys drawing, because there are sketches neatly piled on top. I pick one up. It's a drawing of an angel. The angel has no face.

What? I don't get this. I look at another. The angel again, and this time it isn't faceless. Inside the blank space where the angel has no features there's the image of a woman's face. The face looks like it's been cut out of a magazine or newspaper. I look at another. The same woman's face, but it looks younger. My stomach twists and turns because this is feeling weirder the more I look.

Then I realise that the woman's face inside every angel is the same.

336

It's me. My face.

What's going on?

A voice from the door disturbs my confusion. 'I followed you for years.'

The voice confuses me because it's not one I've heard before. That's odd; Abby never mentioned anyone else, other than Rosa, being in the house.

Curious, I slowly turn. It's Rosa. But Rosa doesn't speak like that. 'Your voice—'

'I know, not very Italian. Of course, I speak Italian like a native now.'

Now.

What does she mean by that? The muscles in my temple start throbbing and pulsing. I look back at the pile of angels with my face on them. The one at the top that remains faceless.

Rosa moves further into the room where the sunlight coming in from the window captures her face.

I stagger back in numbing shock as I look at her. *Really* look at her.

My daughter.

Sara-Jane.

My legs go from under me and I tumble on the bed.

'I don't understand.' My voice is so weak. 'I thought you were dead.'

Am I going mad? Is this really happening? I place the heels of my palms against my forehead for a while, look down. And breathe. Breathe. In. Out. Trying to come to terms with this reality I never saw coming. I feel like I'm in a nightmare. Finding my daughter was meant to be a dream come true.

I hear movement. My hands drop as my head jolts up.

Rosa . . . Sara-Jane is walking towards me. Of course she looks different. My Sara-Jane was a little girl with braces and glasses.

337

Short hair. This Sara-Jane is a woman with long, dark bouncing curls. No glasses or braces. And the shape of her face is different – it's lost all of its baby fat.

I need her to explain what's going on. 'How is any of this possible?'

She stops moving to me. 'When Dale took me, he locked me in a room.'

'Bastard.' The curse rings savagely off my lips.

'Please, Gem. Let me tell you my story.'

Gem? I'm your mother. Call me Mum.

I allow her to carry on.

'Dale had a room all prepared for Abby. It was a proper girly room, all pink with lots of dolls and toys to make a little girl happy. Not Sara-Jane's kind of toys. I tried to escape, got to a phone—'

'That's my girl,' I say in triumph. I can't help it. I can't simply sit here and not acknowledge Sara-Jane's bravery.

'But the phone wasn't working,' she resumes. 'Dale told me he'd taken me by mistake. He was sorry, so sorry that he said I could write to you to come pick me up. He came into my room one day, a pen gripped in his hand. I wrote to you. I asked you to come and get me. But you never came.'

'I never got any letter. He was manipulating you. Why didn't he just bring you back to me?'

'I was eight years old. Scared. Confused. It seemed like he was trying to help me. And while I waited for you to come and get me he introduced me to one of his horses – Dexter.' Her face shines, to my dismay. 'I loved it. You know how much I adored playing outdoors. Riding Dexter was the ultimate trip.'

I have to speak. 'Dale was a master manipulator. He probably observed how you didn't like the dolls, which told him you maybe liked doing things outdoors. Dale played every last one of us.'

Rosa-Sara-Jane pauses and thinks. 'Maybe. But the thing is, I got to like him. He was like a dad to me. Way better than my biological father ever was.'

I see her praying and crying over Dale's dead body in the chapel. Her genuine grief.

'His original plans were to take Abby to his place in Italy and keep her there. When you didn't respond to the letter—' Seeing my angry outraged expression she concedes, 'OK, I know, he was playing me. Well, he took me to Italy instead. He has a massive villa and a business empire out there. Kept me under lock and key but always – *always* – permitted me to go out on the grounds of the house every day. He has horses there too – I'm a pretty good rider now.'

Her voice lightens with her memories. 'I was young enough to pick up Italian really quickly. In the end I wasn't under lock and key any more. I grew to like it there. I thought you didn't want me, so I decided to start a new life. I changed my name. Dale's housekeeper treated me with such kindness I decided to choose her name. Rosa. No more Sara-Jane. Dale had friends in Italy who were able to secure fake documents for me. Eventually, I was enrolled in an international school. The one Abby was supposed to have gone to. I did really well in my exams. Eventually I went to university.'

Pride swells inside me. At my daughter's achievements. I always knew she was such a clever girl.

'When you got old enough, why didn't you come home?' I demand.

'My home wasn't with you any more—'

'You're my daughter.' I stretch my arms out to her almost as if I'm beseeching her to come to me.

Her face twists. 'If I was your daughter, why didn't you recognise me that first time we met again at the school? At the school gate with Miss Swan and Beryl? When I watched you inside Dale's van?'

So it had been Dale's van near the school. Dark blue, not black, the colour of the van that had snatched two terrified schoolgirls. Her damning words are like stones being thrown at me and I don't know how to defend myself. She's right. How did I not recognise my own flesh and blood? I know she looks more like her father, though thank goodness she's not like him in any other way. She no longer has the glasses and braces, but I should know my Sara-Jane. She was mine for eight years. I should know my own daughter. Slowly, I close the distance between us. She's turned into a beautiful person, inside and out. My hand lifts and hovers over her face before it touches her cheek. She closes her eyes. Her skin is smooth, so warm. So alive.

Sara-Jane is alive.

The movement of my hand becomes feverish as it explores her features, all the nooks and crannies of her face.

'You should have come home,' I whisper.

I've said the wrong thing because her eyes snap open and she moves away from me. 'I liked living with Dale.' There's a stubborn edge to her voice that she's inherited from me. 'The horse riding, going out on boats. I had a good life in Italy. The whole outdoor lifestyle. Too much time had passed. Life was so much easier.'

I'm furious. 'You don't get the right to talk to me like that. I did double shifts, mended bikes, any bloody thing I could get my hands on to make sure you had clothes on your back, a little loose change for pocket money. Everything I did was for YOU.' I stare hard at her in bewilderment. Doesn't she understand? 'You were my whole life.'

Then it hits me. Rosa's about the right height and build.

'It was *you*. You put Sara-Jane's glasses through my door, her socks – your socks, that angel. Why would you torment me like that?'

'Because you didn't recognise me.' Her voice rises slightly. 'You keep saying that you never forgot me, so why didn't you know it was me when I was right in front of your eyes? I kept all the things I left England with in a small box. Memories of my past life as Sara-Jane.' Her mouth twists.

'You will never know how badly you hurt me. Each time you put something through the door it made me mourn for you harder.'

She makes a derisive noise with the front of her teeth. Taunts me. 'You didn't mourn me for long. You were too busy making a successful life. Businesswoman of the Year.' Now I see that the photos she cut out of me and stuck on the angels' faces were of me from different stages of my professional life. She's been following my progress for years. 'You soon had plenty of money, unlike when we lived together. Was I the problem all along? You didn't have money because of me?'

I hear the anguish in her. 'Never. We would've got there in the end, me and you. Do you know how I got my business started? With seed money from Dale. Blood money. He wasn't trying to help me, it was giving me a distraction to make me forget you. Stop wanting to find you.'

That shakes her up. I continue, 'Dale was a selfish man. Sure, I have no doubt he gave you the high and the good life rolled into one, but he only did that to cover himself. Letting you come home to me meant the truth would come out. The only person that was important to him was himself.'

'I know that now. But I just want to go back to my life. In Italy.'

I feel totally destroyed. I've spent years getting her room ready at home. I've kept the flat on in case Sara-Jane came back to the only place she'd known as a home. Home? All this time she had created a new home someplace else.

'I'm sorry.' Her voice is so small, so tremulous. 'Putting those things through your door was a wicked thing to do. I didn't mean to hurt you. But it's the truth. I'm Rosa now.'

I look at her. My mind's blowing up. God forgive me, but all I can think is that this isn't my Sara-Jane. My girl would never have long hair, she loved hair that didn't get in her way so she could enjoy her active life. The face looks like a grown-up version of my little girl's, but Sara-Jane's features were smaller, delicate, perfectly placed to create the most beautiful face. Where's her goofy braces? Her adorable glasses? She was meant to stay my little girl. Forever. And the voice . . . No, Sara-Jane's was sort of high and giggly.

Sara-Jane is eight years old and it hits me. Really hits me that I had expected the Sara-Jane who came home, even after all these years, to still be a child. Sara-Jane is forever eight years old. Sporty. Mischievous. Fun. Stubborn. Laugh-out-loud happy. Kind. Cheeky. Caring. Hates princesses. Boss Girl legend.

My girl.

My girl.

My girl.

This person in front of me is a stranger. My heart should be healing, but instead it's breaking apart all over again. My little girl was never going to come home to me, was she? When a child is stolen from you, even when they come back, can things ever really be the same?

The realisation of this awful truth has me stumbling back to the bed. My head falls into my hands. The mattress dips with her weight next to me. Her arm goes around me. We lean the sides of our heads together.

'Where do we go from here?' My question is so small, so defeated.

'I'm not sure.' She pauses. 'The other reason I didn't want to come back is that when I was thirteen I met the boy next door. Matteo. Matty.'

A boy. Of course. I should've guessed. *Matty*. I like the sound of his name.

'He's my fiancé.'

We hug even closer.

Then I remember someone else. Someone who has become a much-loved member of the family.

I take Sara-Jane's hand and gently pull her up as I stand. 'We need to tell Abby.'

We find her downstairs in the lounge. Initially she snaps a smile at us, but our intent and serious expressions must be a dead give-away because it soon slips from her face leaving her grim, tension visible in the stiffening of her body.

'What is it?' Her troubled gaze darts between us. 'What's wrong?'

It's Rosa who speaks after taking a big breath. 'I'm Sara-Jane.'

'Sara-Jane? What are you talking about? You can't be.'

'She is.' My voice is soft but firm with the authority I know Abby has come to expect from me. I explain the rest and at one stage she has to hold on to the back of the sofa for support. I'm glad in a way that I wasn't the only one fooled.

Silence. A silent signal crackles in the air between the two young women because they rush forward at the same time. Into each other's arms. Clinging to one another. Crying tears of loss and happiness. So tightly are they wound around each other I can't tell one from the other. It's as if they have become one.

I hear Abby whisper to Rosa-Sara-Jane, 'Thank you for being such a brave little girl and helping me escape.'

Then I join them. Put my arms around both these courageous young women who have been to hell and back. Have come out stronger. Braver. Walked forward in life with their heads lifted with pride. We embrace with all our hearts, a tight circle of three.

Tragic times like these either make a family or tear them apart.

We'll figure the future out.

Together.

Chapter 57

Five Months Later

The plane touches down in Rome. This is my first trip to Italy and I'm scared silly.

Abby sits next to me and squeezes my hand when the seatbelt sign turns off. She's wearing a wide smile, trying to be brave for the both of us.

'This is all going to work out fine. Rosa will show us the best time EVER in her home country.'

Rosa. That's what my daughter insists I call her now. That's so hard for me to do because she'll always be Sara-Jane to me. I won't lie, I'm still trying to get my head around all that's happened. But the last thing I want to do is disrupt Rosa's life. She has a great life here, with so many friends.

'Oh, I can't wait to see Italy. Can't wait.' That's Traci, all excited in the seat next to Abby. Her suitcase was packed to breaking point. She giggles. 'This champagne is gorgeous.'

Traci is lapping up flying business class. I didn't feel good about leaving our relationship where it ended up. She might have done a bad thing, I suspect crazed out of her mind, but she was the one who got the young, insecure me through most of it. Was the huge rock I needed to lean on back then. So, I've taken her under my wing and given her a job helping me with the online end of my bike business. Something to take her mind off William.

The murders at the school shocked the community to the core. Traci and Abby tell me it's still reeling. Princess Isabel was temporarily closed but is up and running again under the leadership of a new head teacher and leadership team. Minus Beryl. I heard that she's sold up. No one knows where she's gone.

A very respected journalist – there are still a few! – wrote a very thought-provoking piece about the school in a highly regarded newspaper. Not from a murder angle, but one about which parents get seen and not seen in school, which ones are heard and not heard.

I have no intention of going back to the Rosebridge. Or to Princess Isabel School.

Establishing a relationship with Rosa was a bit awkward at first, especially with me being so stiff and stilted in my chats with her. What made me loosen up was hearing that trademark cheekiness in her voice, that mischievous laughter. Pure Sara-Jane.

We've talked every week on the phone, which has gone well, because we now talk at least three times a week, including an hour we set aside for each other on Sunday. We email, share photos. Photographs have been so important. Seeing her grow from a girl into a woman has been so precious to me. There's a fly in the ointment of our bonding though – Dale. He is in some of the photos she sends me. She wants me to forgive him.

Never.

I can't do it. For his own ruthless and self-centred reasons he stole the life me and Sara-Jane would've had. Instead of him in those pictures with his arm round her it should've been me.

Rosa and Abby talk too. It really lifts my heart to see that these two women who share such a tragic past are able to recapture the

346

bond they once shared. I don't ask Abby if she visits her mother in prison; that's Abby's business. Whatever she decides to do, I wish her luck.

It takes us a while to get through immigration, which I'm grateful for because it gives me time to settle my nerves. Prepare myself and get my best smile ready. We see Sara-Jane – I mean Rosa – waiting for us in the terminal. She's waving and practically jumping in the air. Her gorgeous fiancé, Matty, stands proudly by her side. When I reach her, we fall into each other's arms. And hold on tight.

In my heart, I know, this time we will never let go.

ACKNOWLEDGEMENTS

Thank you, thank you, Sammia Hamer and Ian Pindar, for being the perfect editors in helping us shape this story. For helping us dig deep into characters and their motivations. And to Victoria Oundjian for kickstarting *Girl, Missing*, including that killer twist at the end. A huge cheers to our Amazon Team for the editorial, design, marketing and PR work. Bless you all!

ABOUT THE AUTHORS

Her Majesty, Queen Elizabeth II appointed Dreda an MBE in her New Year's Honours' List, 2020.

She scooped the CWA's John Creasey Dagger (New Blood) Award for best first-time crime novel in 2005, the first time a Black British author has received this honour.

Ryan and Dreda write across the crime and mystery genre – psychological thrillers, gritty gangland crime and fast-paced action books.

Spare Room, their first psychological thriller, was a #1 UK and US Amazon Bestseller. Dreda is a passionate campaigner and speaker on social issues and the arts. She has appeared on television, including *Celebrity Pointless*, *Celebrity Eggheads*, *Alan Carr's Adventures with Agatha Christie*, *BBC Breakfast*, *Sunday Morning Live*, *Newsnight*, *The Review Show* and *Front Row Late* on BBC2.

Ryan and Dreda performed a specially commissioned monologue for the ground-breaking Sky Arts' *Art 50* on Sky TV.

Dreda is one of twelve international bestselling women writers who have written a reimagined Miss Marple short story for the thrilling bestselling anthology, *Marple*. She talked about this on The Queen's Royal Reading Room.

Dreda has been a guest on many radio shows and presented BBC Radio 4's flagship books programme, *Open Book*. She has written in a number of leading newspapers including the *Guardian* and was thrilled to be named one of Britain's 50 Remarkable Women by Lady Geek in association with Nokia. She is a trustee of the Royal Literary Fund and an ambassador for The Reading Agency.

Some of their books are currently in development as TV and film adaptations.

Dreda's parents are from the beautiful Caribbean island of Grenada. Her name, Dreda, is Irish and pronounced with a long vowel ee sound in the middle.

Follow the Authors on Amazon

If you enjoyed this book, follow Dreda Say Mitchell and Ryan Carter on Amazon to be notified when the authors release a new book!

To do this, please follow these instructions:

Desktop:

1) Search for the authors' names on Amazon or in the Amazon App.
2) Click on the authors' names to arrive on their Amazon page.
3) Click the 'Follow' button.

Mobile and Tablet:

1) Search for the authors' names on Amazon or in the Amazon App.
2) Click on one of their books.
3) Click on the authors' names to arrive on their Amazon page.
4) Click the 'Follow' button.

Kindle eReader and Kindle App:

If you enjoyed this book on a Kindle eReader or in the Kindle App, you will find the authors' 'Follow' button after the last page.